THE GRAYWOLF SHORT FICTION SERIES

1986

Books by Laura Kalpakian

BEGGARS AND CHOOSERS

THESE LATTER DAYS

FAIR AUGUSTO AND OTHER STORIES

JERUSALEM ROAD *(forthcoming)*

FAIR AUGUSTO AND OTHER STORIES

Fair Augusto

AND OTHER STORIES

Laura Kalpakian

GRAYWOLF PRESS · SAINT PAUL

Grateful acknowledgment is due the editors of the following periodicals in which some of these stories were first published: *Ararat, Cosmopolitan, Good Housekeeping* (Britain), *The Hawaii Review,* and *Stand.*

Cover: Joan Ross Bloedel, "Twilight III," Monotype, 1986 (Centrum Press; Collection of Barbara Gemberling)
The type in this book is Galliard, designed by Matthew Carter
Book design by Tree Swenson

ISBN 0-915308-90-8
Library of Congress Catalog Card Number 86-81784

Graywolf Press gratefully acknowledges the Northwest Area Foundation for its support of this project. Graywolf Press is a member organization of United Arts.

Published by GRAYWOLF PRESS
Post Office Box 75006, Saint Paul, Minnesota 55175

TABLE OF CONTENTS

This book is for

VERITY MASON AND JULIET BURTON

many thanks

Veteran's Day

THIS IS A small town, or maybe it just seems small because I been living here nearly thirty years, the only thirty years I've lived at all. It's a beach town, but most our tourists are overnighters, people on their way somewheres else. Everyone in my high school always swore they was going somewheres else too, San Francisco or Los Angeles, but almost nobody went nowhere, except maybe to the Army or the pen. My brother went to both.

My brother Walter put Esperanza Point on the map. When Walter turned himself in we had TV cameras and reporters and lawmen crawling all over this town, snooping, sniffing like dogs at the grease can. They come into the DeLite Bakery to have a look at the mother of this criminal and certified loony and they hung out at Phil's Mobil where my dad works and they lined up at Lillian's Salon of Beauty to talk to me. They interviewed everyone who ever knew, or thought they knew, or might have known Walter Sutton. Yes, they just should have let school out in Esperanza Point the day Walter give himself up. It was a regular holiday.

I was sorry to see him give himself up. Walter's smart and he could have gone on a long time besting the sniffers and snoopers. They was all after Walter: police in a half dozen cities, sheriffs in four counties and the FBI besides. Walter stole more cars than they could count. He set off two small bombs in Orange County, one at the Bank of America and one at the courthouse and one small bomb in Los Angeles at a Bank of America there. The bombs didn't hurt no one, just blacked up the place and made a mess. Then he set fire to some oil storage tanks down the coast that belonged to one of them big oil companies. They caught him for the fires and then they figured out about the bombs. At first they said he was a political terrorist and then they said he was just a disturbed Vietnam veteran, but when Walter told them he was proud of setting them fires and bombs, they changed their minds and declared he was insane and committed him to the State Loony Bin. Walter didn't seem so insane to me. Those bombs wasn't meant to kill anyone and they didn't. The fires was real cleverly set too. The man that can do that is pretty smart if you ask me.

But when they drug Walter out of the courtroom, he looked crazy. He was kicking and screaming and cursing, calling the judge and jury pigs and sheep and sonsofbitches with a lot other stuff thrown in, mostly about how they was tools and stooges in the government's plan to make us all sick, destroy our brains, and when we was all reduced to tapioca pudding, the government and the oil companies and the banks would lead us all to destruction because there wouldn't be one thinking person left to stop them. Robots, meat-hooks and hot dogs, that's all that would be left of human beings. "They're killing you with Radio Carbons in the air you breathe!" Walter screamed while they drug him out of the courtroom, "They're killing you with Killer Enzymes in the food you eat!"

So maybe he did sound kind of crazy. But you'd be crazy too if you hadn't ate for days. And maybe he did look kind of crazy because he kept his gas mask on the whole trial. I don't think the jury liked looking at that mask with its goggles and long nozzle of a face. Anyway, they never would have caught him for setting fire to those tanks in the first place, but Walter already had a record and a man with a record is as good as deeded, stamped, and delivered up to the police. A man with a record can't go nowhere the computers don't snarl and snap at his heels.

About a year before the bombs and the oil tanks, Walter got caught child-stealing, but it was his own child, Tommy, that he stole and he didn't do Tommy no harm, just kept him out of school and tooting around the state for about three weeks. They got Walter for that and for speeding (which is how they happened to get him at all), speeding and evading an officer because Walter had to run out of gas before that cop could catch him. All that and Grand Theft Auto because Walter took Tommy around the state in stolen cars. Walter wouldn't steal a car that wouldn't do 90.

There never was a car Walter Sutton couldn't steal. In high school he used to brag he could start a car just by looking at it right, tuning his electric vibes to the car's. I never saw him do that, but I watched him steal a Mustang once to show off for Shelly Smith. The Mustang belonged to the math teacher. It took Walter about five minutes to have that Mustang unlocked and humming. Shelly Smith was so excited she was popping sweat all over. The girls just loved Walter. They always have. But Walter and the law's never gotten on too well. The judge sent him to the reformatory for the Mustang, and then again for stealing a Firebird, and on the third time the Judge sent him into the Army because he said that Walter was getting real close to being an adult and if he kept up the way he was going, he'd be in the pen before he was old enough to drink. Walter's social worker claimed he was just high spirited with a bit more mischief in him than most boys. The judge said even if that was so, the Army would still make a man of him.

My dad said the judge was right. My dad said the Army would shape Walter up and root him down. My dad's been rooted his whole life. He went to the same high school we did and he's worked at Phil's Mobil since before it was Phil's. My mom has worked in the DeLite Bakery for twenty years. I worked there myself when I was in high school, but I couldn't see living with my arms and hair and lungs caked with flour, so I went to beauty school, and I haven't done too bad. I've had a regular station at Lillian's Salon of Beauty for eight years and regular customers too and it's a good thing because my ex ain't any too regular with the child support. Me and my two kids though, we never once been hungry, but as I say, my mother works at the bakery.

I got two younger sisters too, Ginna and Val, but in our family, I always stuck with Walter because Walter was the smart one, and between them Ginna and Val don't have the sense of polliwogs. They was both pregnant when they got married. Ginna was showing. So me, I always sided with Walter because he's no dummy.

He proved it too. He escaped from the State Loony Bin about six months after that arson trial. The papers and the news only said that Walter escaped from two orderlies who was taking him from the Bin to Veterans' Hospital to be tested for Agent Orange. That's all they said, but Walter told me how it happened and I can just picture how he done it.

Walter's got real charm. He's tall and has thick sandy hair and clear blue eyes and skin that's smooth as cake paper except for the creases at his eyes and mouth. He's got a wide smile that no one can resist. When he's not smiling he looks a lot older than thirty-three, but when he smiles, why he's just a boy and no one can make you laugh the way Walter can. I can see him, smiling, joking with those orderlies on the drive down to Veterans' Hospital. Walter don't say a word about Killer Enzymes and Radio Carbons, just joked about the nurses' behinds probably.

When they're waiting in the hospital lobby, Walter asks the orderlies to unshackle him because how could a man pee with his hands in bracelets? "I gotta be able to hold my dick," Walter says, "or else I'll pee all over myself and people will think I'm crazy." The orderlies laugh and unlock the cuffs and Walter did go to the bathroom, but then he just walked out and stole the first car he saw.

Walter and me had a good laugh over that because one night about two months after his escape, Walter come up and visited me. He wasn't only smart, Walter was brave.

I knew it was Walter. I could tell from the sound of the car that pulled into the trailer park lot. No one around here drives a car like that, growling and rumbly, hungry for speed and the road. It was 9:30 at night, my kids was in bed, and I looked out and saw a low sleek gray car with a kind of muzzle over the front to keep it from biting you. "Hi Betty!" says Walter. "How you been?"

"You better get inside," I said. "Ray Stoddard's been by twice this week already." But that was all I said, didn't ooh and ahh and squeal. I knew Walter'd be by sooner or later, and Ray Stoddard knew it too. He's a cop here in Esperanza Point (we got ten, one for each Commandment). Ray and me dated pretty serious in high school. Now we're both divorced with kids, but Ray keeps up his support payments and my ex don't. Ray told me he would be watching for my brother. He said he was going to capture Walter Sutton and get his picture on the evening news.

I told Walter this while he ate. He hadn't ate in days, but still he wouldn't have anything but eggs or oranges or bananas or melons. He said he couldn't eat anything touched by human hands because the government was putting Killer Enzymes in our food to turn us into robots and hot dogs. Pretty soon they would be able to do anything they wanted to us and we'd all obey because by then our brains would be nothing but compost. But I did talk Walter into having some bread and cake from the DeLite. He wouldn't touch the margarine though.

Walter finishes eating and leans back. "Well Betty," he says, "Ray Stoddard could put you in jail too for harboring a fugitive."

"Is that what they call it nowadays when you give your own brother a bite to eat?" I picked up Walter's dishes and put them in the sink. "Ray Stoddard ain't putting me nowhere."

"Not even to bed these days?" Walter grins.

"How did you hear about that?" I feel the blush roll up my face.

"Bad news travels fast."

"I went out with Ray a few times, but you can't do nothing in this town. Next thing I know, my clients are coming up to me and asking if Ray and me are taking up where we left off in high school. I couldn't hack it."

"Mom wrote me about you and Ray while I was in the Bin. She was real happy you two were dating."

"She acted like I broke it off just to spite her."

"Mom takes things personally."

"You going to go by and see them?"

"No. Mom would just cry. I can't stand to watch her cry. It tears me up inside. And Dad, well, he don't want to see me anyway."

"Dad's strange."

"It's the Killer Enzymes and Radio Carbons. Wished I'd known about them when I was in high school. Dad and me might have gotten on better if I'd known it was the Killer Enzymes making him take the strap to me so often."

"Dad's strange," I said again, not knowing what else to say. Dad had taken the strap to me a few times too.

"Anyway, Betty, you tell Ray Stoddard it's going to take a lot more than him to catch Walter Sutton. Why, the FBI's sent their best men after me and I'm too smart for them. The government wants me real bad, Betty."

"They think you're crazy."

"No, that ain't it. They know I'm not crazy. They know I'm onto them. I been onto them since Nam. And they know they can't buy me off, so they got to shut me up. If they don't, I'll tell everyone what the government's doing to them. They know I know." He tapped his forehead and nodded. "That's why they sent me to the Bin."

"What was it like in the Bin, Walter?"

"That Bin is nothing but a meat grinder. They just force your flesh through the place and you come out in little strings. Even if you was sane when you went in, you'd be crazy when you got out. Those doctors are nothing but paid assassins. They don't give a shit about the crazies. It's the sane ones – the ones like me – they got to grind down and out."

"Well I'm glad you're out. I couldn't sleep nights while you was in the Bin."

Walter pats my hand. "We always was a team, Betty."

"That's right and you just tell me if you need any help from me. What are you going to do now?"

"I'm going to tell the whole country what the government's doing to them! I'm going to tell the whole world what I figured out in Vietnam." Walter leans over toward me and whispers. "It started over there, Betty. You don't think they cared about those little gooks or their little gook country, do you? Hell no. They got us into Vietnam so the banks could make more money and so folks at home would have something besides their own bad luck and hard times to think about. You notice how much worse everything's gotten since we been out of Vietnam, don't you? Well, things have always been bad, but while we had Vietnam to watch on the news and read about, we didn't notice what they was doing to us over here. But that ain't the worse of it." Walter quit whispering and his nice blue eyes lit like flints. "The worst of it is, they had the Vietnam War so's they could have a bunch of civilians trained to kill on command. To be like dogs. They turned us into dogs over there. 'Bark!'" He shouted so loud I thought he'd wake my kids. "'Bite!' 'Kill on command!' And we did. They did it to us with chemicals. How else could they take all those thousands of men and turn them into animals if it wasn't with Killer Enzymes and Radio Carbons? Chemicals, Betty. They got chemicals in the air and everything we eat and our water. They didn't get out of Vietnam till they was sure they could do to the whole United States what they done to the soldiers." Walter sounded sad. "They got what they wanted out of that war even if they lost it. Every veteran, Betty, every one of them is a walking bomb. Every soldier got his triggers primed in Nam, but they don't know it and they won't until the government sends out a radio signal that will activate their Killer Enzymes, and then those vets will take up their guns and shoot their neighbors and friends. They'll kill anyone who doesn't hear that radio signal. Anyone who hasn't breathed in enough Radio Carbons or eaten enough Killer Enzymes, they'll be shot by guys like Ray Stoddard and Jerry Burns."

Jerry Burns and Ray Stoddard was in Nam just a little after Walter. People said Jerry's brains was zapped in Nam, but he never was real smart to begin with. Now Jerry calls everyone "Hot Rod" because he can't remember names, even if he is our mailman. I could believe what Walter said about Jerry Burns and it made me scared, but I wasn't going to show it. Walter and me's always gotten on because we was never scared of anything. We're not like Ginna and Val who are scared of everything and always have been.

Walter sipped his tea. He'd drink the tea because I boiled the water ten minutes and the tea was from China. "Maybe I'll steal Ray Stoddard's car on my way out of town," Walter said.

"You wouldn't want it. He's still got that old Dodge."

"Not that car," says Walter, his eyes twinkling behind the tea-steam. "His police car. I bet that police car will do 150. Why Betty, that little 280Z I got out front will do 110 in a quarter mile. There's nothing that puts you in control like speed! I love speed. I love all that machinery packed around me, doing what I tell it to do. Cams and pistons and shafts turning and pushing and working and all that oil pumping and gas igniting! Speed is control, Betty. Control! It's the only control I've ever had in my whole life."

Walter's hands clenched at a make-believe wheel and he slouched down and pressed on the make-believe gas. His knuckles and face went white. "Speed and Control! Go!" He seemed to shoot right out of his chair, swerved and screeched like he could see the end of the world in front of him, and for a minute I was with him and I screamed too.

Walter laughed. "Gotcha, didn't I?" He got up and turned on the TV. "Let's watch the 11 o'clock news. I like to hear Tammy Takahara tell me to have a nice night and a good day tomorrow. She's real pretty, isn't she? Sort of reminds you of a little flower. Besides, maybe she'll have some news about me."

Me and Walter moved to the couch and settled in. "I'm like Paul Revere, Betty," he says to me at the commercial. "They got to catch me before I tell the whole country what they're doing to our brains with Killer Enzymes and Radio Carbons."

Walter fell asleep before the news was over, but I stayed up and listened to all of it. There was nothing about Walter. Tammy Takahara told me to have a nice night and a good day tomorrow and then I turned the TV off and covered Walter with a blanket and went to bed. I knew he wouldn't be there in the morning.

About a week later he calls me. His voice sounds scratchy and far away and the coins rattle as he puts them in the box. He wanted me to make Shelly let Tommy come over and play with my two kids on Saturday afternoon so he could see Tommy. Shelly and Walter got married on Walter's first leave from Vietnam, and they got divorced right after he come back. He never had too much time with Tommy, but he loved that boy. He was crazy about that boy.

I said I'd try. Shelly Smith and me was good friends in high school (mostly because she was in love with my brother, I think), and even after the divorce, I still did her hair once a week and our kids played together. Shelly and me got on all right as long as we didn't talk about Walter.

When Walter come on Saturday afternoon he was driving an old Chevy with bent fenders and a rusted-out paint job like you might have seen anywhere in this trailer park. He was wearing a disguise too, a wooly-looking wig and a hat and a pea jacket. But Tommy knew who it was the minute Walter walked into that trailer. Tommy flew into his arms. I nearly cried to see Walter on his knees with his arms around that little boy. I left and took my kids to the beach and I told them: the first one to open his yap about Uncle Walter gets a wallop in the chops. They knew I'd do it too.

When we come back from the beach, Walter had gone, but he left four gas masks, one for each of us. Tommy said his dad showed him how to use it and told Tommy to wear his whenever his mother wasn't looking.

Tommy said we could save ourselves from the Radio Carbons if we wore the gas masks enough.

The next I heard about Walter was from Tammy Takahara. On the news she says the Customs people caught a boatload of marijuana in a port just south of us and they said they were told that Walter Sutton was hiding on that boat. But they couldn't find him. I chuckled. Walter must have squeezed himself into a little ball of dust and blown right past them Customs men.

I read about Walter in the San Angelo County *Gazette* (Esperanza Point's too small to have its own paper) and in the big-city Sunday papers too. They said he'd been seen in San Francisco and Lake Tahoe and as far north as Oregon and as far south as San Diego. They said he was armed and dangerous, which was just a crock. Walter swore he'd never carry another gun after Vietnam, and he never has. So if he was armed, it was only with his brains; and if he was right about the government, then brains was probably the same thing as a gun. Maybe worse.

Me and Mom talk about Walter when my dad's not in the house. He won't have Walter's name spoke. He says he can't stand to be the father of a jailbird. Sometimes, though, it's hard to talk to Mom because she cries so much. Her whole face is puffed up like yeast dough. My two sisters say: That lunatic Walter has ruined us in this town – our husbands are so ashamed of the Suttons, they're sorry they even married us. I say: Your husbands didn't have no choice about marrying you, did they?

Sometimes my clients ask me about Walter and I say – Oh, Walter just stopped by last Saturday and took me and the kids out for ice cream and the movies. But it wasn't so funny after Shelly found the gas mask under Tommy's bed and shook out of him where he'd got it. Shelly stormed into Lillian's Salon of Beauty and threw the gas mask at me (nearly hit me too, right while I was in the middle of a henna) and she started screaming so the whole world could hear I was no better than my crazy, criminal brother and she'd kill me if I ever came close to Tommy again.

I began to think Walter was right about the Killer Enzymes and Radio Carbons because I'd never seen anyone froth about the mouth like Shelly did. I was lucky Lillian didn't sack me on the spot. I don't relish the thought of unemployment.

Ray Stoddard come by my trailer late one night not too long after this. (I figured Shelley screamed at him too. She was a real screamer, that girl, though you never would have guessed it in high school. In high school she was just a little flower.) Ray rapped at the door like he was using his boot instead of his knuckles. He said it was the police, but I knew it was only Ray. I said "Wait a minute" and I went in the bathroom and took the Nitey-Net off my hair and gave it a quick spray and put on a dab of lipstick and mascara.

"I got a message for your lunatic brother, Betty," Ray says when I come to the door. His black uniform was buttoned and badged with silver and his white helmet glowed in the night and he was resting his hands on a leather holster. He looked like a shiny beetle. "You tell Walter I'm watching this trailer like a hawk. You tell him if he sets foot in Esperanza Point again, I'm going to nail his balls to the station door."

"Tell him yourself, Ray. I'm no errand boy." I started to slam the door, but he stuck his boot in.

"Next time I come, I'll have a warrant."

"Next time you'll need it. Now bug off."

Ray bugged, but I was pretty shaken-up. I turned on the news, but I couldn't stand to hear Tammy Takahara tell me to have a nice night, so I switched it to the old re-runs of *Love American Style* instead and watched that till I fell asleep sitting up.

2

WHEN I was in high school, it seemed like every week one of my brother's friends was joining the Army or being drafted. A few of them went to San Angelo Community College down the coast and a couple, like Jerry Burns' older sister, went to colleges far away. I'd come home from school and watch the news and see college kids – kids I might have known – in San Francisco and Washington D.C. having what looked like peace picnics, protesting the war and singing "Give Peace a Chance" and calling for a halt to the senseless slaughter. I'd watch them being clubbed and gassed and lying limp while they was drug off to jail. Then there'd be a commercial for Anacin or Ex-Lax and then I'd see boys in Vietnam –

boys I might have known – getting gassed and shot at and scrambling up dirty hills and lying limp and dying in the mud.

People I'd known all my life suddenly stopped talking to each other. Ray Stoddard's mother, for instance, she quit talking to my mother and Jerry Burns' mother. Jerry Burns' mom would come into the De-Lite Bakery and she and my mom would go into the back room and have a cry together. Ray Stoddard's mom, she would come into the DeLite and have a look around to make sure everyone was watching and then she'd say in a loud voice: "My boy is over there protecting the free world from Communism. We only have to bomb the hell out of those little gooks to have the war over and done with and all the boys can come home."

Most of the boys came home. There was a few military funerals that left something like soot and ash over Esperanza Point for days and over whole families for years. Ernie Little's mother was never the same after they buried him. She wrote a note to Richard Nixon saying she was go-ing to kill him and the Secret Service came out and investigated the Lit-tles. Jerry Burns' older sister come back from college at Christmas and said she'd been gassed and in jail and she was proud of it.

"At least she ought to have the sense to keep her mouth shut about it," my dad said. We were sitting in the office at Phil's Mobil. The office al-ways smelled like Dad – oil and metal and disinfectant and carbon paper. "I wouldn't brag about going to jail."

"Well Dad, maybe they're right," I said, "maybe we shouldn't be over there fighting the gooks' war for them. Maybe our boys shouldn't be dy-ing over there for nothing. What if something happened to Walter? I wouldn't trade Walter for their whole gook country."

My dad threw down his cigarette and stomped it out. "That's what we have to do to Communism," he said, "Stomp it out. No matter what it takes."

It took plenty. Plenty out of the Suttons. Walter didn't come home when he was supposed to because he was in a military jail in Nam for going AWOL and then he was in a military hospital for hepatitis and then, before they'd send him home, they had to court-martial him. When the Army was all through with Walter Sutton, they gave him a dishonorable discharge and spit him back at us like he was a slug we'd tried to slip in the juke box.

But at least he came back. My mom took a few days off from the DeLite and did nothing but cook. Me and Ginna and Val stayed home to help with the cleaning and getting everything ready. Shelly (who'd been living with her folks all this time, her and baby Tommy), she moved into our house and started getting Walter's old room all ready for the two of them. My dad took some of Walter's old clothes and drove all the way down to Fort MacArthur to bring him back.

But when Walter walked in, no one moved and no one spoke. All we could hear was Mom's groan. She sounded like a beast.

Walter's old clothes hung all over him. Even his skin hung all over him. He was so baggy and gray and colorless, he looked like a toad. He didn't fit into nothing. Not his clothes. Not the house. Not the family. He wouldn't talk so we had to sit at dinner and chat about ourselves, just as if we was giving him a refresher course on the Suttons and Esperanza Point. It was terrible. Bad enough, Walter wouldn't talk, but he was clutching a sandal. He was clutching it when he come in the door and he clutched it all during dinner. We couldn't see it, but we knew it was there, in his lap and no one could bring themselves to ask. Finally Big-Mouth Ginna says, "Why won't you let go of that smelly old sandal, Walter?"

Walter's lips peeled back. His teeth and gums and tongue was yellow. "I killed the man who wore this sandal," he said, "I took it off him after I killed him. I made a promise when I killed him and I'm keeping this sandal so I won't forget even though I can't remember exactly what it was I promised."

Mom had to run to the bathroom to barf and I thought when she was done, I'd go too. Ginna and Val and Shelly, their faces looked like vacuum bags with eyes. Shelly left the table and took Tommy out of his highchair; he was goo-gooing the whole time. What did he care?

My dad put down his fork. My dad says: "You're lucky you weren't wounded, Walter. You came through without a scratch."

WHEN HE'D been home about a week, Walter put the sandal down and Mom rooted through his room till she found it. She put it in a bakery box and took it to the DeLite and put it in the dumpster there. She found other things in Walter's room she wouldn't talk about. She wrote the Pentagon a terrible nasty letter about Walter's rotten discharge, calling them a bunch of ungrateful sonsofbitches. I thought sure we'd have the Secret Service on our doorstep too, but they never came. The Pentagon never even wrote back.

So the sandal was gone, but then Walter went out and bought a gas mask. He wore it all the time except when he was playing with baby Tommy. He always was crazy about that child. But the gas mask was too much for Shelly and she moved home within the week and started to divorce him.

For the next few years Walter had about three dozen jobs. Sometimes he'd quit. Sometimes they fired him. Sometimes he lived at home and sometimes he lived with this woman or that woman and sometimes we didn't know where he lived. We'd just notice we hadn't seen him around town in a while. He never did stay away too long though because of Tommy. He never missed too many visitation days. He just loved to be with Tommy, push him in his stroller down to Esperanza Point Park and fly kites or feed the gulls from the top of the cliffs.

Walter said he was writing a book about Killer Enzymes and Radio Carbons and the last time he left town (he stole a car so he couldn't come back after that) he give me this book in a box tied up with rope. He said I was to keep it no matter what happened to him. I promised I would, but I couldn't keep my promise because later, when my husband and me was splitting up, we had some killer fights. We had one nearly every night of the week just before the end. One night I come home from the Beauty Salon and I see smoke pouring out the kitchen window. I ran in and got my kids who were huddling in their room and I yanked them out and sent them next door and then I went into the kitchen. My husband had started a bonfire in the sink, burning up Walter's book.

I guess I would have shot him if I could. Without bullets there was nothing I wanted to say. Anyway, I already called him every name there was to call and I'd hit him as much as I could. So I went next door and got my kids and got back in the car and spent the night at my mom and dad's. The very next day I rented this trailer and I been here ever since. I didn't bother to pack nothing when I left my husband. But I'm like

Walter, I'm no dummy. I took the checkbook and the first thing next morning I went down to the bank and cleaned that bastard out. I wrapped the money up and put it in the freezer and got me a smart lawyer and my old man never saw a penny of it.

3

JERRY BURNS brought me Walter's letter one Saturday morning. There was no return on it, but I knew Walter's writing and I was glad old Jerry didn't know tit from tat. I took Ray Stoddard at his word though – I mean about watching the trailer – so I took my letter into the bathroom and locked the door and sat on the can and read it.

It wasn't a crazy man's letter. Walter said at last he had a plan. He knew how he could let everyone know about Killer Enzymes and Radio Carbons. (For a minute I was afraid he was going to ask for his book back. I never could tell him what my husband done.) But Walter didn't mention the book. He had a new plan.

He wanted me to call up Tammy Takahara at the news and tell her Walter Sutton was willing to give himself up to her and no one else. Walter would turn himself in to Miss Takahara as long as there was cameras rolling and he could read his speech (which he said he was already writing) to the whole world. He said he wanted Tommy by his side when he read this speech on TV, but after that, they could do whatever they wanted with him, though he hoped they'd put him in the San Angelo County Jail and not the Los Angeles one. He said this plan was the only way, even though it was a sacrifice. He said if he didn't do it, no one would ever know about what the government was doing to them.

Well, Walter's letter sounded simple enough, but I had a devil of a time. When I called Tammy Takahara first I told the secretary I was Betty Lusky and it was personal. Two days go by. Then I called and I said I was Betty Sutton Lusky and it was personal. Three more days. Finally I called up and I told the secretary I was Betty Sutton Lusky, sister of Walter Sutton who wanted to give himself up to Tammy Takahara at 10 a.m. on Thursday, the 25th of May at Esperanza Point.

The girl said: Miss Takahara don't accept invitations over the phone.

"Take the gum out of your ears, spitwad! This isn't an invite! I'm talking about Walter Sutton – the man who bombed out the Bank of America! Walter Sutton wants to turn himself in! He wants Miss Takahara and the news crew there when he does it!" I slammed down the phone.

About half an hour later the phone rings. "Good evening, Mrs. Lusky. This is Tammy Takahara." She sounded just like she did on TV, but it's hard to talk to someone who seems like they've just glugged down a whole can of 30-weight.

It was easier to talk to her in person. She come up to Esperanza Point to see the letter from Walter and make sure all this was on the level. (She wanted me to mail it, but I said nothing doing.) She said they'd do everything Walter wanted and she would take care of contacting the police and the FBI. She said the news would like to interview me too and she'd like my kids beside me on the couch, but I drew the line and said no. Then she said, how about little Tommy? I said, ask Shelly. (I knew what Shelly'd say.) Then she wanted Mom and Dad, but I knew Mom was too weepy for television and Dad wouldn't have nothing to do with this. I told Miss Takahara: "It's me and me alone or no one." She said okay.

I cleaned up the trailer for them, but no one seemed to notice. Miss Takahara and her camera crew got dirt all over my rug, filled up my trailer with cameras and cords and nearly blinded me with the lights. I had to sit on the couch and chat, like they'd just popped in for a cup of tea and caught me in the middle of a manicure.

Miss Takahara explained to me what they'd do while the camera crew was getting ready. She was real pretty and little, but when I was talking to her, I felt like I was littler than her, even though two of her would fit in my clothes. She wore a cute navy blue suit with brass buttons and a red satin lining. I wondered who did her hair.

Once the cameras was rolling, I had to explain all over again how I got this letter from my brother. Then Miss Takahara explained to the camera all about Walter Sutton, as if the whole world hadn't heard about him. Then she turned back to me and said: "What does Walter Sutton want out of all this?" Just as if she didn't know.

"He wants to tell everyone," I said, and then I coughed and started again. I wanted to be a credit to Walter. "My brother is like Paul Revere. He is trying to warn people that they're in terrible danger. Our minds are being poisoned by Killer Enzymes in the food we eat and Radio

Carbons in the air we breathe. The government is putting chemicals everywhere so they can putrefy our brains and we'll obey them and not have a single thought of our own. They're controlling us just like they controlled all those boys who went to Vietnam. They turned those boys into killer dogs and primed their triggers so that when they hear the radio signal the government's going to send out one day, they'll turn and shoot their neighbors and friends."

"Yes, Mrs. Lusky, thank you very much."

"They'll kill anyone who hasn't already been got by the Killer Enzymes and Radio Carbons. We're being sickened and drugged so that the banks and the oil companies and the – "

"This is Tammy Takahara for the News."

The lights went out even though I was still talking and when the lights died, I was invisible. In my own house I was invisible. I was still talking but the camera crew banged and clanked their way out of the trailer and Miss Takahara shook my hand and thanked me like I'd just given her a back rub.

THERE WAS an Esperanza Point before there ever was a town. It's a high cliff overlooking the ocean that slopes back down to the highway. The city has put in a little park up there with privies and picnic tables. There's grass and pine trees and old junipers, but most of the time it's too windy up there for picnics. Even the trees have been bent almost horizontal with the wind that comes up off the ocean. Lots of hang-gliders jump off Esperanza Point and a few suicides too. This was the place where Walter wanted to give himself up at 10 a.m. on the 25th of May.

By the 24th, every motel room in town was three deep with people from the newspapers and TV and law enforcement types and state doctors and nurses. Our town crawled with squad cars and ambulances and camera vans and reporters interviewing everything that walked on two legs. All these visitors wore little badges and tags – law or press or medical – so they'd know who each other was.

By 8 a.m. on the 25th Esperanza Point (the park, not the town) was roped off and all the people with badges was checking out everyone without badges. They probably asked for ID from the gulls overhead. By 9 a.m.

everyone in town was there. Bar none. Except my dad who said he had to work and my two kids. My kids hated me for it, but I made them go to school. I didn't want them to see something so horrible they wouldn't be able to forget because on the morning of the 25th I woke up with worms churning my guts. Fear dried up my tongue and made it thick.

I rode with Ginna and Val and Mom to Esperanza Point about nine. Ray Stoddard strutted around the Point like he owned it, shooing school children and kicking out on-lookers. He tried to shoo me too and I told him to bug off. Ray patted his club. "I can make you move."

"You and who else, turdbrain?" I said. I had the feeling I had maybe said the same thing to him years ago, when we was still kids in high school. But now I hated his everlasting guts and I knew I always would.

Just then Miss Takahara comes up and brushes Ray Stoddard aside like he is bellybutton lint. She nods at my mother and sisters and takes my arm. "We need you," she says and she marches me over to the picnic table where everything's set up and the cameras are in position. Little Tommy was there too. I had a new respect for Tammy Takahara if she could talk Shelly into letting Tommy be there. We all sat down and I put my arm around Tommy's shoulders and we waited.

Miss Takahara looked just lovely. She had nice black patent leather pumps and a gray suit with a short jacket and a lavender blouse. The make-up people fussed over her while we waited. She had a simple enough hair-do, but they fussed just the same and touched up the lilac on her lips and the lilac and gray shadows under her eyebrows. They gave her a nice blush across the cheeks.

Then they came after me with their tubes and pots and brushes. "I am a beautician myself," I said, "and no one puts on my makeup but me. Besides," I turned to Miss Takahara, "I thought we was here for serious business. I didn't think it was the goddamned school play." Miss Takahara's little black eyes squinched up and glared at me.

We waited some more. The camera crews lit up cigarettes and people in the crowd left for the little coffee and coke stands the Chamber of Commerce had set up at the bottom of the hill. The police and law types got restless; you could see them snorting and stamping like horses. The nurses put on pastel sweaters and chatted about the fog coming up off the ocean and the chill it brought with it. We waited.

At 10:40 Miss Takahara says to me, "I'm going to have your ass if he doesn't come, Mrs. Lusky."

"I hope he doesn't!" I said back, "I hope to God he never comes! Walter's so smart he could go on for months – for years! Just stealing cars and bombing out banks. Walter don't have to turn himself in. He's doing this so people will know, but I don't care if they never know! I hope he doesn't show! I hope – "

But even as the words was tumbling off my thick tongue, I could hear it somewhere, far away. I could hear it even if no one else could. Pistons pumping and shafts swirling and gears grunting and gas igniting. Speed and Control. *It's the only control I've ever had in my whole life*

"Go back, Walter! Don't do it! There's no control here, Walter! Go back!" I bolted and ran hollering toward the sound of Walter's car, but a cameraman tackles me and they drag me back to the picnic bench and Miss Takahara gives me a hard shake and a swift kick in the ankle.

"Shut up! Sit down and shut up! You'll ruin everything. Stop blubbering. Get over here and fix this up, will you?" she says to the makeup people who mop me up and give me a Kleenex to hold and make me sit back down by Tommy. I shake and cry and try to hold Tommy's hand, but he won't have none of it. He looks at me like he don't even know me. His eyes are big and clear and eager because by now everyone can hear the car roar (*don't do it Walter, no, no, no*) and the motor snarl and the brakes squeal there at the foot of Esperanza Point. And then Walter kills the engine and gets out.

The crowd makes way for him slowly. Don't no one speak to Walter and he don't speak to them. He comes toward us and the picnic tables. He's carrying his speech in one hand and he's wearing his gas mask. He looks strange to everyone but me. And Tommy. Tommy knows who it is. Tommy springs up from the table, I reach out to catch him, but he's gone, he's past anyone who could stop him and he runs straight into Walter's arms. Walter gets down on his knees and holds Tommy and for one moment, quiet smothers us all. No ocean. No wind. No voices. All you can hear are the ants inching up the trees and the grass straightening itself up and Tommy crying into Walter's shoulder and Walter crying into his gas mask.

"STOP HIM! DO SOMETHING! HE'S CRAZY!" Shelly screams,

ripping through the fog and the quiet. "He's crazy! Stop him!"

And they did. The doctors and the police and the three-piece-suit law types jumped Walter and fell into a pool of bodies and thumps and crunches and strangles and thuds. Someone dug Tommy out of the pile, but Shelly never quits screaming and crying out Tommy's name and I could hear my mother somewhere in the crowd crying out Walter's name. Miss Takahara was up like a shot and threw herself on the lawmen and doctors, but she got a belt in the mouth and fell backward and nobody helped her up because they was all too busy getting Walter Sutton into a strait-jacket and his feet in chains.

When they was done with him, Walter didn't even look human anymore, not between the gas mask, the chains and the strait-jacket. He hadn't a human thing except his voice screaming inside the mask and his kicking twisting and thrashing while they carried him off to the ambulance. The pages of Walter's speech blew away, high over the trees and the heads of the crowd. They flew like tiny tail-less kites out of control.

"You lousy lying shitheads!" Miss Takahara chased after Walter and the lawmen. "Walter Sutton is mine! Mine!" She kicked a cop and started beating on his chest. "I told you you could have him after I got my story! You promised, you shitheads! You promised!"

"He's dangerous, Miss Takahara," the cop said, taking her fists off his chest and handing them back to her. "He might have been armed. We can't take chances with a dangerous lunatic."

They shoved Walter in an ambulance and car doors slammed like a hundred rifles going off at once and sirens screeched and red and blue lights flashed as the ambulances and police cars started their engines roaring, all trying to get off the bluff at the same time. Their exhaust blackened up the fog at Esperanza Point.

Miss Takahara turned around and come back at me. I was still sitting on the picnic bench like I had sprouted roots from my bottom. "You bitch," she barked at me. Her lilac lipstick had smeared across her mouth like an ugly bruise and one of her false eyelashes hung off. "You bitch! You set me up for this."

I opened my mouth and it stayed open, but by now my tongue had got so thick, it filled up my mouth and I couldn't speak. My nose was running and I could not lift my hand to wipe it. I was crying without no sound. I had turned into a tree. I stayed a tree while Miss Takahara yelled and swore at me and even when she quit and went back to the makeup van. I stayed a tree while the sirens wailed and the cars fought to get off the bluff and while the people broke down the ropes and spilled all over the park. I stayed a tree while my sisters carried my mother away because she couldn't walk by herself.

I stayed a tree for a long time, it seemed, until I see Ray Stoddard pushing back the crowds, flinging his club around – not hitting anyone, just using that club to prod and push people into what he wanted them to do, and then I quit being a tree and I become a rocket launched at Ray Stoddard. I hit him so hard he falls over and drops his club and I jump on top of him before he can reach for it. I rip off his sunglasses and gouge at his eyes and bite him on the cheek and kick him in the balls and then people are all over me too, pulling me off Ray, holding my arms and trying to catch my feet while Ray scurries away on all fours.

"Get off her! Leave her alone! Put her down!" someone cries, and people quit pulling at my hair and legs and arms and I fall to the ground.

"She's as crazy as her brother," Ray sputtered through the blood coming out of his nose.

"She's the only sane one here. Come on, Hot Rod. Get up. It's okay now." Jerry Burns picked me up and gave me something to hold against my bloody lips and kept his arm around me all the way back to the mail truck. He wouldn't let no one touch me or come close.

I sat on the floor of the mail truck and bawled. "Go ahead and cry all you want, Hot Rod." Jerry patted my head all the time when he didn't have to shift. "You just cry all you want. Cry all over the mail if you want. Drown it all. It's nothing but a bunch of bills from the banks and oil companies anyway. Drown it."

IT TOOK Esperanza Point about a week to clean up after Veteran's Day and about a month to simmer down. And about a year to forget.

Shelly moved away and took Tommy, but not before she found a judge to certify that Walter was so insane she didn't have to let Tommy visit his father. My mom and dad split up. Never divorced. My mom still goes over there and cooks supper for him now and then and she makes sure he gets his favorite cookies at the DeLite. But Mom lives with me and the kids in the trailer now and she don't cry as much because I won't let her do it in front of the kids and that cuts down on her crying time.

About twice a month Mom and me go to the high-security Loony Bin to visit Walter. This Bin is closer to Esperanza Point so we see more of him than when he was first committed. He still won't eat nothing but eggs and oranges and bananas and melons, that and bread from the De-Lite which we bring him. He's got that baggy look again, like his bones are shrinking inside his skin. His teeth are going bad, but he talks clear as he ever did, and now and then he gives us his old smile. He don't wear the gas mask anymore because he says he don't care if he lives or not. That's what he says, but I know Walter Sutton. I know he's just saying that for their benefit – the meatgrinders at that hospital. Walter's so smart one day he'll turn himself into a kite and fly right out of there, hot-wire a hot car and be gone. He'll outsmart them all. He's not crazy. He never was.

MOM HAS to be to work at five so she goes to bed real early. I sit up by myself and watch the 11 o'clock news. I swear at Tammy Takahara. Sometimes I reach under the couch and I get out the gas mask Walter give me and hold it. I feel better when I hold it, like Walter must of felt when he held that dead man's sandal. I feel like I'm holding onto the promise I made Walter, but I don't exactly remember what it was. Can't imagine what I promised him, but it must of been something important, otherwise why should I hold that gas mask in my arms when I watch the news?

Sometimes I put the gas mask on. Tammy Takahara swims in front of my goggles. It's real quiet inside that gas mask. I can hear myself breathe and I know if I wear it enough, they'll never get me.

Bare Root Season

MARGARET AND FRANKLIN WHITNEY never had a son, but they had two daughters whose names Margaret had chosen. Franklin allowed her to choose them with only a grunt of dissent because he expected he would one day name his son Franklin III, but the son never appeared, and secretly, Margaret was glad. A boy, she felt, would have been a disruptive influence on their family, and the two little girls were such a winsome duo from the beginning. Their charming polka-dotted portraits still hung above the mantel in the Whitneys' neo-Tudor home. Later, Margaret regretted having no son: his disruptions might have been useful; he might have better prepared Franklin and Margaret for the day when their two little girls burst through childhood's frame and stood before their parents as complicated, unhappy women. For years Margaret believed if she could get the girls through adolescence, they would return to being winsome, but she discarded those illusions and took up gardening.

She grew roses and azaleas, camellias and tulips, none native to the region, all requiring soil additives, careful pruning, and regular irrigation. The Whitneys lived in a temperate zone where the last rose of summer was virtually indistinguishable from the first of the new year. Margaret's garden billowed with color continually. The flowers lined up in brigades along the stone paths and waved from shaded recesses like spectators at a parade. She kept notebooks of their ailments, their preferences, plantings and deaths – a flower geneology. They were a family of sorts: after all, Margaret had crossbred an elegant yellow hybrid rose and named it after herself – the Princess Margaret.

She gave her daughters stately names too, the kind that could have been emblazoned on the buildings of the small prestigious women's college she'd attended. She could imagine them: the Elizabeth Olivia Whitney Hall of Letters, the Alice Miranda Whitney Center for the Performing Arts. Both girls attended their mother's alma mater, though Randy (as she insisted on being called) was suspended for a social infraction (a man found in her room) and then dismissed for academic reasons. Not likely that an Alice Miranda Whitney Center would grace that campus. Equally unlikely were the prospects that Elizabeth Olivia would have a decorous building named for her. Liz married her father's junior law partner; they had three lovely and well-behaved children and spent their weekends and money on a series of boats, each one grander than the last. Franklin often went sailing with them. Margaret sent her regrets; she suffered from seasickness and a queasiness she could never quite define or deny when Franklin came home sunburnt and still rolling with the boat and the old-fashioneds he'd consumed.

Franklin was inordinately proud of his late-learned seamanship and of his son-in-law's boats, as if he had chosen and outfitted them himself. Margaret's good manners prevented her from mentioning that the last boat he'd expressed any interest in was the ocean liner on which they'd returned from their honeymoon cruise to Honolulu in the summer of 1941. Her good manners usually prevailed, but more than once she'd pointed out to Franklin that if he could learn seamanship at his age, he could learn tolerance as well.

"Tolerance!" he bellowed over the stone paths and the shiny camellias, "you're not asking me to learn tolerance. You want me to welcome every dope-smoking anarchist, every half-washed, half-educated, would-be philosopher that Randy beds down with under my roof like he's family."

"Some of them have been family," said Margaret before she realized that mention of Randy's three husbands could hardly help her case.

"Yes, and if she's married three men, you can imagine how many men she's slept with," he muttered, easing his bulk into a wrought-iron garden seat.

"That's a very vulgar thought." She packed the fertilizer at the base of the Delta Queen roses with extra firmness; she was resolved that her roses

would not take second place at the Garden Club Show and that her husband would not make her retreat.

"I told her – didn't I – the last time she was here, when she brought that longshoreman – "

"Yes, well that was two years ago. All she wants is to visit. This is Randy's home. She's always welcome."

"Fine! She's welcome! But Christ, Margaret, don't you see, it looks like we approve of her sleeping around. She'll think we approve – "

"She would never think you approve, Franklin. Not in the last fifteen years would she ever think that." Margaret rose from her knees and removed her garden gloves with the same flourish she would have given to suede.

"She's never given me any reason to approve. There's a limit to what I can take. She ought to be growing up and she never does. It's always something with Randy. Three marriages. Five different colleges, rolled her car so many times, she had the only ten thousand dollar VW bug in history. And it's always me that's paid for her foolishness. I paid her fines, her court costs, her tickets. Don't forget I paid for the therapy when she got herself strung-out on drugs, the doctors, the psychiatrists. God, Margaret! I paid her damn rent till she was twenty-five. I always end up paying. I mean, there's a limit and she's reached it. Has she ever given me back a penny of what I've lent her – never mind what I paid out of hand, I mean what I've lent her? Did she ever say, here Dad, here's an installment on that loan – any of them? – and thanks a lot, Dad? I'm about to retire, Margaret, I can't go around handing out money. I'm not a rich man."

"We could afford it."

"We can't."

"We could then."

"That's not the point. Your parents could have afforded plenty, but did they give us money? No, we made our own way in the world. Every generation should – "

"Oh, Franklin, please do save that for the jury." She went to the shed and returned with the pruning shears, their huge well-oiled jaws agape. She clipped a fading Delta Queen. "She only wants to visit and bring a friend. Maybe the friend is a woman."

"Yes and if it is you can bet she's sleeping with her too. When are you

going to grow up, Margaret? You know as well as I why she's coming out here: Dad, can I have five bucks or five hundred or five thousand. That's why."

Margaret touch-tested each rose before she clipped it. If its petals were still moist, she left it for another day, but if it was beginning to go papery, unglued from the center, she clipped it, never waiting for it to brown and disfigure her garden.

"She's thirty-two," Franklin continued; "she's got to accept responsibility. Don't sniffle, Margaret. I love Randy, of course I love her – "

"You only love her when she's doing what you want, what you think she should."

"I know what she shouldn't be doing at thirty-two. She shouldn't be living like a damn gypsy. She's got to cut out the crap and grow up. I may not be around much longer to bail her out. Sometimes you have to be cruel to be kind."

"Oh stop. Please, not that."

Franklin tossed his ice into the camellias and walked to his wife. He lay his graying head against hers and touched her shoulder. "Look at us, Margaret. Look what Randy does to us. Forty years of marriage. Children shouldn't be able to do this to us after forty years of marriage."

"After forty years," she snapped, "children are the only thing that can." She shook herself free and he stalked off, slamming the French doors to the living room. Tearlessly, she proceeded to touch and cut the roses, placing their pale severed heads in her basket.

IN THE BOTTOM drawer of her spindle-legged Louis XV writing table, Margaret kept Randy's letter. It had been mailed in an envelope purchased at the post office, the kind you can buy if you go in with your letter already written and your coin in hand. Randy's flamboyant script covered two pages of wide-line notebook paper and was postmarked from a city in the East where, if the TV dramas were to be believed, one lived in constant peril of one's life.

Hi Mom!

I haven't had time to say thanks for the nice Xmas gifts you sent, the sweater and the gloves and especially the MONEY [this was why Margaret didn't let Franklin read Randy's letter; what he didn't know wouldn't hurt anyone]. *Did that ever come in handy! Now I've paid the last installment on my yoga lessons and once I master the more difficult positions, I'll be able to approach spirituality. Real mastery takes years, but it's worth it. You have to be able to shed the inessentials and look to your spiritual core. Possessions obstruct vision. The spirit is all. The body is nothing. Inner peace.*

Inner peace. Margaret massaged the high bridge of her nose. She could think of no one more in need of inner peace than Randy and no one less likely to find it. With her every new enthusiasm, Margaret hoped Randy would find some direction, something she could cling to and grow with – a trellis, that was the way Margaret envisioned it, to help her stand up-right and bloom. After Randy's third divorce, however, Margaret pri-vately recognized that every new enthusiasm either began with, or was occasioned by, or was intimately, physically connected to a new man; and whoever he was who had inspired Randy to yoga lessons and Zen, he and his beliefs and his friends would go the way of Randy's former husbands, countless lovers, and other passions. She'd been passionately fond of drugs and passionately against the war in Vietnam. She had gone to jail in the service of that passion. She stayed the night in the local jail with the other protestors, refusing to make her one phone call, refusing to call Franklin Whitney, the eminent barrister who could have got her off even if she hadn't been his daughter. She went to jail one other time too; that time she called Franklin. She was caught with her kneesocks full of dope and it was not funny or noble and still she refused to apologize to her parents, though she was abject in front of the judge.

I think what David and I are going to do [the letter continued] *is drive some rich dude's car out there. David has never seen the West Coast and I think it would be good for us to practice meditation in a changing environment. David would like to meet you and Dad. He's an absolute flower freak, Mother. He says we can learn a lot from the lilies of the valley and the poppies of the field. We'll see you in a month or so. At least I think that's when we'll be leaving.* Is this okay?   Love,
                                                                          Randy

P.S. Don't worry. I'm not going to get married again. Marriage is a bourgeois institution that only manacles your body and your spirit. David and I don't need marriage. Our spirits are perfectly tuned. Besides we believe in equality. I told him from the beginning, you do some of the eating, you can do some of the cooking too. You sleep in half the sheets, you can do the laundry half the time. David's very spiritual, but he gets the point. David's different. At least he seems to be.

He seems to be. The seed of doubt: Margaret recognized it, its sadness, its significance. She glanced at the calendar, January 16. She took a silent vow: if in six months David wasn't out of her daughter's life, Margaret would do some sort of penance. That or celebrate.

As she fixed dinner she tried to imagine herself telling Franklin: you do half the eating, you can do half the cooking, or at least half the cleaning-up. The Whitneys had had a maid when the children were little, a maid and a gardener, but when the girls went to college, she found the maid a new position and let her go, doing all the housework herself. At the time Franklin teased her for her budget snipping, but as he approached retirement, he instituted rigorous, selective reforms. He sold the Lincoln and bought a smaller (though equally luxurious) car. He fired the gardener and hired a high school boy to mow and edge the lawn, though the boy was forbidden to touch the garden. He suggested Margaret experiment with margarine in the cooking instead of butter and she said she had been using margarine for years. The sole she fixed that evening was served in a caper and margarine sauce.

Franklin groaned. "Not more fish."

"You know what the doctor said."

He ate his fish in uninspired bites, leaving a third of it on the plate. She knew he consumed a sirloin steak and baked potato with butter and sour cream every day at lunch with his clients and his son-in-law. They lunched at a restaurant they'd patronized for years, where they had the waiters trained to obsequious perfection.

Determined not to be so trained, she folded her napkin in a neat square, placed her wrists on the table and declared she was prepared to welcome Randy and her friend into the house for as long as they cared to stay.

Franklin sipped his wine. "You don't care who she sleeps with?"

"That's right, I don't care." This was not true, but one learns from living with a lawyer that the truth, if it is to have any value at all, must work in the service of desire.

Blood suffused Franklin's face. "Well, I do care. And I care where she does her sleeping. If she wants to visit, you tell her fine. You just tell her no more lovers and no more money." He scrutinized his wife across the table and the everyday pewter candlesticks: there was something of the everyday pewter about Margaret herself: expensive, well-polished, but an ordinary ungleaming gray for all that. "You never give up, do you, Margaret?"

"Never. Not with my children or my flowers. I never give up."

LIZ CALLED the next day and accused Margaret of being unreasonable. How could she expect Father to cast off the values of a lifetime and welcome his daughter's lover under his roof and into her bed? Then she suggested that Randy and her lover come stay with them. Randy could have Jennifer's room and her lover could sleep on the couch. Liz said she didn't care how late he crept down to the couch as long as he was there when the two boys, Jason and Adam, got up at 6:30. Margaret said no.

Even though she was resolute with Liz, Margaret was still unwilling to write to Randy, welcoming her back to the old neo-Tudor homestead. She needed Franklin's tacit — not approval, something less benign than approval — his oblique acquiescence was all she required. He often capitulated gently. He finally paid the medical bills on Randy's last accident after swearing he wouldn't put out another penny on a twenty-nine-year-old woman who was so irresponsible as to drive like a maniac without insurance. Then one afternoon he wandered out into the garden, checkbook in hand, and asked her how much Randy needed. He wrote the check and put it on the glass-topped table, secured by the trowel. He commented on the overbearing red of the camellias that year, and left. After these incidents Margaret could never quite decide if it were she or Randy who had been granted the favor, but hers was a pragmatic nature and these are not questions a busy woman has time for.

For days following the arrival of her letter, any mention of Randy caused Franklin's lips to curl into the peculiar twist of disapproval Margaret imagined he used on juries who returned unfavorable verdicts. Margaret dug through her arsenal, brandishing the weapons that had seen forty years' service in her marriage: tears, silence, a look both hateful and piteous. But this was a different battle, and Franklin's sense of their impending penury made him intransigent. "There's a limit to what I can afford and what I can take. I'm retiring, so I can't afford any more, and I'm not going to take any more crap. She can't have any money and she can't sleep with some man under my roof. If she doesn't want either of those, then fine, she's welcome as any child would be."

But Randy was not any child. She never had been. Even as a little girl, she'd been frail, fretful, with too much imagination and too little restraint. Margaret suffered anxiety over her, but she believed these qualities were part of the bubble that glows inside each child and bursts on the edge of adolescence. Moreover, Margaret saw her own young self in Randy, and she expected that one day social pressures, the pleasures, the responsibilities of adulthood would chisel away at Randy as they had at her. That was the way of the world, after all: one tempered one's laughter, but never quite forgot how to laugh.

Then the late Sixties intervened and whatever else her daughter's life would be like, Margaret was forced to conclude it would be very different from her own. Nothing was tempered. It was all unspeakable, uncouth, ill-bred outbursts masquerading as passion. Randy espoused rebellion and called it revolution. Randy preserved her adolescence inviolate in one university after another. Even marriage didn't bring Randy to her senses. None of her marriages. And if marriage didn't do it, Margaret had reflected sadly, what would?

Motherhood. Motherhood was the reward a woman enjoyed for enduring marriage. Motherhood was the great tenderizer, the feat, the act, the event that changed women from hapless girls into women of stature and passion and wisdom. One loved one's husband, of course, but the attachment to a child was visceral.

Between her second and third marriages, Randy had moved to the Midwest. She called home one day. Collect. "Guess what, Mom!"

"Where are you?"

"In a laundromat. Guess what?"

Margaret stiffened. "What?"

"I'm pregnant. There's going to be a little bambino in about seven months. A little rock-a-bye baby!"

"That's wonderful!" Margaret cried before she remembered that Randy no longer had a husband or any immediate prospects of self-support. "Will you get married?"

"Hell no, I'm having this baby for fun. I wouldn't marry the father even if I could. He's not important. He's smart and pretty good-looking though. Anyway, if the kid gets his brains and my looks – just think!"

Just think. Margaret licked the peppermint-flavored envelope and stamped it. She'd decided to invite Randy and her friend, no matter what Franklin said. In her letter she did not mention his conditions, or even his forthcoming retirement and their reduced circumstances. She decided she would present Franklin with a *fait accompli*: the letter written and mailed. She wrote out Randy's address and took her keys and purse and drove straightway to the post office before she had a chance to regret her haste.

She had regretted her haste then, in the matter of the baby. She'd believed that Franklin should have time to accustom himself to the uncomfortable facts long before Randy came home to have the baby, as she doubtlessly would.

"A bastard," Franklin fumed, "a bastard." And Margaret could not tell from his tone if he were referring to the child or to the man who had pre-sumably seduced their daughter and refused to marry her. Margaret did not tell him that the child's bastardy was their daughter's choice.

Franklin suffered. His fine lawyer's lips, poised, always ready to re-fute or deny, could not refute or deny this, and he suffered. Margaret, by contrast, bloomed like a hybrid rose in springtime. She was careful to speak to Franklin in somber half-tones and contribute to his lugu-brious silences, but the child, the promise and prospect of a child, rose and stirred within her, as if she carried that sweet secret herself, the growing fragment of her own desire. Franklin could go to hell. The Garden Club could go to hell. Margaret would look after Randy and comfort her when she wept that the pregnancy had been a dreadful mistake, that she didn't want the baby after all, that she wanted only to get on with her own young, unencumbered life. Margaret would stroke

Randy's fair head and tell her to take care of her health: Margaret would take care of the child. It would be a boy. A nice, clean-limbed, sturdy little boy with round arms and smooth hands and curly hair. He'd laugh when Margaret wrested a kiss from his warm neck and he'd build sand castles when she took him to the beach and he'd dig contentedly in the section of the garden she reserved for him. Margaret would teach him to clap his hands and wave bye-bye and instruct him in his manners and his ABCs. She'd pack his lunches and drive him to school. The best schools. And she wouldn't care what Franklin or anyone else said or thought, because love is its own reward and requires no other, and her pride could never be impugned because she was — she would be — essential. She would not end up like the women of her aging acquaintance, superfluous, purposeless, empty vessels in a well-upholstered world. Margaret would be useful, contributing, nurturing, and he — the dear boy — would always love his grandma best.

When Randy called again six weeks later, she was not pregnant. It was all quite legal and sanitary and not very painful, but she needed money and she choked and said, "Please Mother, please don't," when Margaret sobbed openly into the phone.

He would have been five this year, Margaret reflected, driving back from the post office. The dear boy had achieved as much flesh and form as imagination can knit around desire. He was dearer to her than Jennifer and Jason and Adam, but then with them she had not performed the miraculous: they did not need to be kept alive and mourned in the same moment.

THE ACCIDENT report stated that the Mercedes had run the red light, but witnesses said that Margaret had not even touched her brakes, simply sailed through the intersection as if there were no other car in the world and certainly no red light. Mrs. Whitney was not available for her version of the accident because she had to be rushed to the hospital immediately and could not sign her copy of the report until the following day. Her daughter and her son-in-law and four members of the Garden Club donated blood for her and Liz came to see her every day, often bringing fresh camellias from the garden. Liz said she should not worry about anything: Liz had already written a quick, reassuring note to Randy, and Father would be eating dinner with them in Margaret's absence.

They wouldn't say how long that absence would be. The doctor said she could go home in a few days, but the bones – all of them with names like Roman matrons – tibia, fibula, ulna – would take a long time to mend. Her right arm and left leg would be bound in casts for a long time, and after that she would be condemned to therapy for months before she could bend and squat, dig and prune, among the azaleas, the camellias, and the roses.

Franklin came during evening visiting hours. He brought Randy's letter, postmarked the day of the accident and mailed in a prestamped envelope. "I would have opened it, but it was only addressed to you," he said, clearly hurt at his exclusion. "Shall I open it anyway? It'll be hard for you."

"No, I must learn to do these things for myself." She held the envelope in her immobilized right hand and slit it with a plastic knife she'd saved from the dinner tray.

"What does she say?"

Margaret read the letter, licked her lips and placed it back in the envelope. She slid it in her book. She was reading *Pride and Prejudice*.

"Well? What does she say?"

"Nothing." Then she remembered that sickbeds are supposed to be places of reconciliation, not further estrangement. "She's not coming out after all," Margaret said; "she can't afford it."

"Let me read the letter." He held out his hand.

"No. It was addressed to me."

"Oh, Margaret, we're too old to have secrets from one another."

"We're too old not to."

After visiting hours ended, the patients had a thirty-minute reprieve before the ingratiating, infuriating, and overly familiar nurses marshaled them into bed. (Just because the nurse had to help one onto the toilet or the bedpan didn't give her privileges beyond those of ordinary social intercourse, after all.)

"Please," Margaret asked the nurse, "would you be good enough to get my checkbook out of my purse and hold it open for me?" The nurse complied, but Margaret found she could not hold a pen with her right hand, so she asked the nurse to write the date and her daughter's name and the sum of Five Hundred Fifty and no/100 dollars. With her left hand and the greatest contortion and concentration, Margaret signed her own name. When she finished, the name she'd borne for forty years looked foreign to her, scrawled, the letters pressing against each other as if they might ignite.

She tucked the check into *Pride and Prejudice*, and once bedtime had been declared like a truce and a hush fell over the hospital, she punched the button that would turn on the light over her head and re-read Randy's letter.

Mom —

Guess I'm not going to come out after all. At least not now. I'll be lucky if I can scrape the coins together to move across town, let alone across country. It's simple — David and I have split. I had the satisfaction of throwing him out, but really, he left me long ago and now I sit here in this apartment I can no longer afford and all I can think of is that I didn't have to wash the sheets half the time after all. Someone else was sleeping in them too, so by rights that cuts it to a third. If only I'd known, I could have saved so much time. Isn't that ridiculous? Isn't that just the absolute limit?

David really is ignorant and not spiritual at all. He was spiritual with me. He was physical with her. It makes me sick. If only I'd known, I wouldn't have wasted my time. I've failed at every relationship. I stink of failure. I'll never be able to wash the stink off me. But what the hell. I've always played the game fairly — struck out every time, but at least I haven't spent my whole life yelling foul. Foul. Foul.

Don't worry about me, Mom. This is a big city. There are lots of jobs. Maybe I'll be a hatcheck girl and be discovered by a big producer and tapdance my way to stardom.

Do not worry. I'll see you sometime soon. Love to Dad.

Love,
Randy

Margaret withdrew the check from *Pride and Prejudice*. The pen still lay on the table, and arching her unwilling left hand around it, she printed carefully, crazily at the bottom of the check: *more to come*. It took her twenty minutes. Then she went to sleep.

BY THE TIME Margaret returned home, January had waned and, with it, the rosy flush of the new year. February gleamed a dull ochre in the garden. Brown camellias rotted unswept from the stone walks, the azaleas drooped and the aphids took their ease on the rose petals. The disheveled garden pained Margaret more than her arm or her leg. Not only could she not work, she could only get around on crutches and with help. Liz came over daily, bringing Jennifer and Jason and Adam after school. Liz was cheery and brisk and insisted her mother get out of the house and sit in the garden. Margaret acquiesced, only because she was tired and could not explain how the ruins disturbed and depressed her. Liz said not to fret, it would grow all by itself. Margaret said nothing. It was a fragile garden after all; it required timing and vigilance and now it would suffer all year from neglect. Now was the busy, the working season – the bulbs had to be exhumed from the refrigerator now and laid out in beds, the ragged fibrous bulbs that otherwise would not sprout, dazzle and bewitch in April. It was now, the bare-root season, when the old roses had to be pruned and the new ones planted, now, now or they would never assemble resplendently like the crowned heads of Europe.

She could not force her bones to knit any faster, and she still forbade Franklin's high school boy to touch her garden, and Franklin was firm on the subject of useless extravagance: he said re-hiring the old gardener was out of the question, especially with her medical expenses and his retirement only months away. Margaret wilted and wept in bed at night, and finally he smoothed her hair and said he would do it himself. He wouldn't go sailing that weekend, he'd stay home and prune the roses. Margaret, swathed in her winter-white cast, said he didn't really mean it. He swore he did.

He swore about a great many other things the following day. A check he wrote bounced, and in an apoplectic froth he called the bank and lectured them about personal service and having been a good customer for forty years. They said they would gladly have paid his check, but it had bounced by three hundred dollars and that was too much even for a customer of forty years' standing.

"More to come?" he snarled. He waved a copy of the check in front of her nose as if it might stink. "What the hell is this? More to come? Where do you expect it to come from? *Do you think I am made of money?*" He kicked her slippers across the bedroom, upsetting the remnants of her lunch tray. "What do you use for brains, Margaret?"

"I'm sorry," she said on cue or reflex. His face reminded her of a salami, coarse, red and white with little blackhead peppercorns. She had not noticed the blackheads before. She smoothed the bedspread over her knees and studied her rings.

"Just what in hell do you think you're doing with my money? Haven't I told you – "

"It's my money too. This state has community property laws." She wished she could cite the proper statute to convince him that he must argue with her as an equal, not as if she were a child to be cowed by mere temper. Besides, she felt shining and inviolate in her white cast, as if she were a mountain peak, enveloped with snow and only her warm face framed by the rock and the clean hard crust of snow.

"Now you're telling me my business. Well just forgive me all to hell, Margaret, but do you mind if I ask how you could write a five-hundred-and-fifty-dollar check and not tell me a thing about it? How could you!" He pushed the seed catalogs off the bed and they landed innocent, open-faced and colorful on the floor. The sight enraged him. "You and your goddamned garden. You care more about your goddamned garden than you do about me. You don't give a damn about me. How could you do this to me?"

"I was afraid to tell you," she said, the hard crust of snow dissolving under the admission. "You were being so nice to me and I was afraid of what you would do."

"Do! You knew what I would do. You made sure I couldn't do a damn thing. What can I do? It's been paid now. But I'll tell you this – this much I can do – there is no 'more to come.'" He mimicked painfully. "This is it. You've pushed me to the limit. I'm taking your name off this account."

"Randy needed the money. Don't you see?" she pleaded. "She needed it. She would have – " Margaret didn't know what she would have done, only that it would have been dire and unpleasant and it was too bad that Randy failed at everything, but it was so and didn't – couldn't – matter.

"She'd have to go out and get a decent job and support herself like everyone else in America, that's what she'd have to do. You've done this. This is all your fault. You've turned her into a parasite and a lousy excuse for an adult. Always handing out little treats behind my back, weren't you? Oh, I know this has been going on for a while. Fifty dollars here, fifty dollars there. You're never going to come to your senses, are you? Well she's thirty-four years old and the Gimme Days are over. She's not getting another penny from me and you're not going to be able to buy her off any more."

"I don't buy her off!"

"You buy her love. She knows it. I know it. You'd know it too if you weren't so damn stupid. Well I don't care if Randy loves me or not, or if you love me or not. I don't want her to love me. I want her to respect me and to respect herself too, and that's more important than love." He jammed the check into his pocket and slammed the door after him so that the beveled glass in the mirror chattered and the perfume bottles rattled in reply.

Margaret sank deeper into her cold cast. Nothing was more important to her than love, nothing was supposed to be. Was it? Wasn't it love that ennobled men and beautified women? Wasn't it love that gave shape and stature to life and wasn't it simple, love? Was she supposed to have shaved and pared love into genus and species, to recognize all the hybrids and varietals? Had her whole life fled and left her ignorant? Wasn't love like the roses and azaleas and camellias that needed only nurture and diligence and protection – what she could have given him – the dear boy – who, never born, comforted his grandmother, appeared to her, bent over her knees and wept. Her cast did not prevent her from stroking his damp cheeks, from stroking his silky curls.

TWENTY MINUTES LATER she heard the new car – a used Lincoln – start up and screech away, and she was glad Franklin had gone. She blew her nose and lay back among the pillows and invited a troubled sleep. When she woke the February twilight had set in and the room was dusted with darkness. Unimpeded, the silence crept around her and she began to hope Franklin would come back. There are ways, after all, not of rectifying the undeniable damage, but of living around it, letting one's differences die a decorous death.

She turned on the lamp, poised her feet on the floor, and dialed Liz's number from the bedside phone. Liz answered, her voice ripe with chagrin. "Let me speak to your father," Margaret said sharply.

"Mother, you really – " Liz began.

"Please let me speak to your father."

He took a long time coming to the phone. "I'm sorry," Franklin said. "Believe me, Margaret, I'm really sorry."

Usually Franklin's sorrow required her supplication. She started to cry again. "I'm sorry too."

"I don't know what came over me, Margaret. I must have been out of my mind."

"I should have told you about the check."

"I just about had a heart attack when I saw that check, but that doesn't excuse me, not at all."

"We all say mean things now and then, don't we?"

"It'll all grow back, Margaret."

"Grow back?" She stopped weeping.

A short, moist pause followed. Franklin said: "Have you been outside?"

"No – should I?" She heard a rattle in the phone and some garbled voices, and then Liz came on the phone and said, "Mother, Mother." But Mother – Margaret – swallowed stones one after another, or so it seemed, because she could not breathe; she left the phone on the nightstand, reached for her crutches, tucked them under her arms, pulled herself from the bed, and made her way out of the bedroom with Liz's far-away voice squawking after her. She thumped carefully down the stairs, then past the kitchen and dining room to the living room where the French doors opened to the garden. She pressed her face to the glass and the darkness and then she switched on the floodlights and stepped outside into the grotesque shadows cast by the half-decapitated branches, the be-headed roses, the slashed azaleas, the mutilated camellias. The pruning shears lay at her feet. She moaned audibly.

Cold invaded Margaret, the cold of the February night, cold she could taste, rage she could fathom, and loathing she could not dispel or resist. She used the crutches to clear herself a path through the severed flower-heads and petals. She took a deep breath of cold. "If I'd known," she said to the dismembered garden, "if only I'd known, I could have saved so much time." The absolute limit. And she wondered if Randy would have stayed with a man who had wounded the one thing she had left to love, or if Randy would have thrown him out long before he discovered what that one thing was.

The Land
of Lucky Strike

IKRAN AGAJANIAN stepped back from the mirror and, with
the pale green tiled splendor of the bathroom for a backdrop, regarded
himself critically. The new shirt collar irritated his freshly shaven neck,
the tie was slightly crooked. He adjusted the tie and smoothed his crisp,
dark hair, freshened his mustache, checking that the ends stood up pert-
ly. Very nice indeed. His face was old enough to have character, young
enough to express enthusiasm. Today, the first day of his new job, both
the character and the enthusiasm were visible. To the figure in the mirror, he said: "Cigarette? Cigar? Chewing gum? Candy bar? Thank you.
You are welcome. Which one? Lucky Strike." Pleased with himself, he
rearranged the towels (borrowed from his brother-in-law) on the rack
and surveyed the gleaming bathroom. The bathroom was his favorite
room in the new house. These Americans, they thought of everything.

He heard a knock at the front door and his wife's heavy step. She moved
slowly these days; she thought the new baby would arrive within the
week. His brother-in-law's voice shook the bathroom door. "Ha! Ha!
Little Armenoui!" (Dikran thought that probably Harry was pinching
his wife's cheek.) "How you doin' today? How's that big baby, Jack?
When's he gonna come out and meet his old Uncle Harry? Huh? Huh?
Hey, Dikran! You ready for the big day?"

"Would you like to drink some coffee, Harry?" Armenoui Agajanian
asked in her still pristine, book-learned English.

"Sure, sure, we got time for some coffee, Dikran, come out here and have some coffee."

When Dikran entered the little dining room, Harry was pinching the fat cheek of the three-year-old, Ahngah.

"Hello, Snooky," he said, blowing his cigar smoke away from the child. "What you want Santa Claus to bring you for Christmas, huh? You want a big doll? You want a model train set? Your Uncle Harry get you anything you want, Snooky." The child screamed with delight and, banging her spoon down on the tin dish in front of her, sent cereal flying around the room. "Hey, Armenoui, come get this kid. She gonna mess up my nice suit. Hey, Snooky, you cut it out." Delighted, Snooky sprayed more cereal. Armenoui lifted the child from the chair, removed her bib, and told her in Armenian to go wash. Then she picked up the cereal dish and took it into the kitchen, re-emerging with two cups of steaming coffee and another tin plate tucked under her arm.

"For your ashes, Harry."

"Sure, sure. We gotta get you some ash trays. Who can work in cigar business with no ash trays in the house, eh Dikran?" Dikran put a small amount of cream and sugar in his coffee and stirred. Harry always made people happy, he thought; Harry made them laugh. Harry paid the first month's rent on the little furnished house for the Agajanians. What a fine man Harry was.

"Well, Dikran, you know all you gotta know today? Let's hear it." Harry struck a match and re-lit his cigar.

"Cigarette? Cigar? Chewing gum? Thank you. You are welcome. Candy bar? Which one? Lucky Strike."

"Very good! You remember that Lucky Strike, don't you?"

"I remember *Lucky*."

Harry heaped sugar and poured so much cream into his coffee that it fell over the cup and splashed into the saucer.

"You right, Dikran! You stick with me, you gonna be lucky all right. We make you rich man in no time. Next year this time, I bet you have a car – what you think? Send word to old country: 'In 1924, Dikran Agajanian Buys Car!'"

Dikran smiled. The thought of owning a car was beyond his imagination – the little house, real, with its cool tiles in the bathroom, its blue hydrangea and stately palm in the front, that was enough for him. The hunger for the car was Harry's and that hunger trebled when Harry's daughter drove off with a young American donkey in the donkey's own car.

"You look real good, Dikran. You handsome man – good thing too: I don't want no ugly babies in this family. That baby, Jack, he better be beautiful before he calls me Uncle Harry, that's all I gotta say. Hey, Armenoui, you hear that? Good thing good-lookin' woman like you don't marry no ugly mug!"

Dikran laughed inwardly. Harry loved American slang; he had probably thought all the way over here how he would use that new one – *ugly mug*.

"I hear you, Harry," called Armenoui from the kitchen. She came into the dining room, since she had been taught at the Red Cross orphanage that only urchins yell. "What if the baby is a girl, Harry?"

"A girl," he blustered. "You ain't gonna have no girl. You already got one girl. What you want another one for? Girls nothin' but trouble. You have a boy, you take my word for it."

Armenoui laughed. She was a handsome woman, Dikran thought, in spite of her swollen body and tired face. She would be handsomer still when the baby came and she did not always look so tired and her face could assume its old, fine planes and contours, the firm mouth, the clear, intelligent eyes, the strong chin. Now her face was puffy; her usually smooth olive skin had a yellow cast to it. He was a lucky man, he thought, and then he laughed out loud: it was the first time he had thought the American word.

"Well, Dikran, we gotta go," said Harry, wiping his mustache with the back of his left hand. With his right hand he dropped some cigar ashes in the plate Armenoui brought him. "You wanna make money in this country, you gotta get out and catch the early worm. You ready?"

"Yes." Dikran rose and walked toward the front door.

"Hey, wait a minute. Ain't you gonna kiss her good-bye?"

"Kiss?"

"Yeah, you know – kisskiss – listen, Dikran, I gotta make an American outta you. When you go to work in the morning in America you kiss the wife good-bye. Everyone does. Me, I kiss Martha every morning. Good for you."

Dikran demurred. He and Armenoui had never kissed in front of anyone in their lives; his wife could not bear for him to kiss her before another person. Armenoui blanched.

"Hey – what's this? You two don't like each other? You have a fight or something? Armenoui, he treatin' you bad? You tell me, you just tell me."

"No, Harry. Dikran is good to me always."

"Then, what – Dikran, go on, kiss your wife," he urged Dikran toward her.

Dikran bent his face down to hers. He did not touch her with his hands. She closed her eyes and raised her lips to meet his; it was a dry, soft kiss.

"Aha! That better. Let's go now."

All the way to the streetcar, Harry sang a song called "Jingle Bell." He explained it was his favorite Christmas song. He sang with such gusto that people would smile at him as they passed on the street. On the main boulevard, the streetcars clanged and thumped, going in all different directions. They all looked alike, however. Dikran dreaded the day he would go to work by himself; imagine catching the wrong one, ending up in some strange place without the language to tell where he wanted to go. Harry sensed his confusion.

"Dikran, you ever get on the wrong car, you just tell them, 'I work at Santa Monica Beach' – you remember that? Say that."

"Santa Monica Beach."

"Right. You never get lost." He went on singing "Jingle Bell" in the streetcar, and the woman behind them said "Merry Christmas" as she rose to leave the car. The December sun was behind them; Dikran could feel it intensified through the windowglass, shining on his shoulder. Everywhere he looked out the window as they rode through the town there were red and green decorations, streamers, banners, figures of angels, and the face of a fat, bearded man. From the streetcar Dikran watched the store owners righting their goods, the clerks bracing themselves behind tills for the onslaught of shoppers, already poised before the glossy windows, clutching bags and the hands of small children. Harry poked him in the ribs. "We get off next."

As the car rounded the corner, beyond the conductor, Dikran craned his neck to see the shining expanse of the bright Pacific. "Pacific," murmured Dikran. *Pacific Ocean* and *Lucky Strike* were Dikran's favorite English words.

"You gotta get off quick. They don't wait for no one. They gotta schedule to keep, you know." The conductor said "Merry Christmas" to Harry as the two men alighted, and Harry tipped his hat.

The beach was bordered by a ragged sidewalk, and it was on this sidewalk, facing the ocean, that Harry's four tobacco and candy concessions stood at quarter-mile intervals. The one where Dikran would work was about as tall as a door frame, as deep as a large pantry, and a little longer than Dikran's armspan. Harry no longer worked in one of the concessions, though he had up until last year. He now had a small office in Santa Monica with an impressive sign over the door, HARKER CONCESSIONS in orange lettering on a red background. Harker Concessions was now so successful that Harry employed three full-time concession salesmen, two part-time, and one secretary (part-time).

"This is my Number One," said Harry, hitting the wooden stand painted to the brilliance of banana yellow. "Number Two, she is blue, Number Three, she is red, Number Four, she is yellow too for the Golden State. Number Five gonna be green. Nice, huh?"

Dikran nodded, but Number One was less impressive than Harry had led Dikran to believe. From his pocket Harry drew an impressive-looking key ring and set about opening the stand's four locks, two holding the wooden shutters closed in front and two locking the Dutch door which allowed access to the inside. An orange and red sign in front said CIGARETTES AND CANDY. Number One itself was decorated with pictures of attractive young women advertising candy and handsome young men advertising cigarettes. When Harry opened the front, Dikran saw a brilliant panoply of colored cellophane on the shelf behind the counter, candy and cigarettes in shiny gold, red, brown, and yellow.

"C'm'ere, I show you all you need to know for the first day." Behind the counter there were a small folding chair and some newspapers. Under the counter were more boxes of goods, some rags and cleaning fluid. The stand was too small for the two men to occupy together comfortably, especially since Harry was chubby. Grunting, Harry pulled forth a small cash register from underneath the counter and set it up. "Now, I show you all this the other night, but here it is again. Easy. The five. The ten. The twenty and so on. You just push the one you want and, bang – there she is. But, in case you need it, I got it all writ down for you." He handed

Dikran a piece of paper with money equivalents and cash register proce-
dures written in a graceful-looking language that was more comfortable
for Dikran than the sharp, bulky English letters.

A customer approached the stand, an older, well-dressed man. He did
not look at Dikran or Harry.

"Cigar," he said.

"Which one?" said Harry.

"Havana."

Harry expertly picked out one for the man and handed it to him. He
tossed a coin on the counter and walked on. Harry said, "Thank you."

"You see," he said to Dikran. "Easy. Now where you gonna put this coin?"

Dikran was stricken with terror. All his life he had worked behind a
counter, measuring out tea, coffee, spices. He had never been afraid.
How could he do it, though, in a language he could barely speak, with
coins that he hardly knew? Harry clapped him on the shoulder.

"Ah, Dikran – you gonna be all right. C'mon – what you do with this
coin?"

Dikran glanced at the paper in his hand and hit the ten-cent indicator
of the cash register. The machine chimed, the figure bounced up in the
window, the drawer flew open, and he placed the dime in with the others.

"Very good. I knew you have no trouble. You just say, 'Which one?' to
them, get them to point, you know. See – all the cigarettes on this shelf;
candy on this shelf; cigars, matches on this shelf. Each thing I marked
yesterday so all you gotta do is look at the thing they want, and there's
the price right underneath it – they hand you the money, you say, 'You're
welcome,' and you are fine. Well, I gotta go now, Dikran. I wish I could
stay here with you and watch the pretty girls, not so many now 'cause
Christmas, but I tell you – in the summer this right here, Number One,
is the best job in the whole world." He laughed. "I come by this afternoon, see how you doin'. Armenoui didn't pack you no lunch, did she?
Well, I'll bring you something today; you gotta tell her you got responsibilities now and you gotta have your lunch. I think when I come back
I bring some Christmas decorations, too. Too early, maybe. Well – I
think about it."

Dikran politely walked out of Number One: his brother-in-law was
too fat to scoot by him.

"Thank you," he said in English.

"Ha! You learn in no time. You speak English good as me real soon now."

The morning passed quickly and without mishap. He found that most people knew exactly what they wanted and pointed to it with no difficulty. He imagined, too, that each time he said *thank you* and *you're welcome* his English improved and the customer could not tell he was foreign. In-between customers he dusted off the stock and leaned over the counter and watched the ocean roll in long, muscular waves. The winter surf gouged the bright sand. He could see the stunted reflections of the walkers in the wet sand. He had been a walker on the rocky Mediterranean shore, and he had been a crosser of the Atlantic, and he had always been a lover of the ocean. The Mediterranean, the Atlantic, what were they compared to the grand Pacific? He wanted to be the acolyte of the Pacific, to serve at Harry's Number One and stand in perpetual awe, facing west.

Harry came back about one with encouragement, some sandwiches and soft drinks. He ate his lunch there at Number One with Dikran. He brought some shiny red and green paper loops, too, and draped them across the front of the stand. At either edge of the counter he placed a picture of the fat, pink-faced gentleman with a full, white beard.

"Who is that?" asked Dikran.

"That? – Whew! Good thing you ask me that question and no one else. They think you crazy and lock you up somewhere. That Santa Claus. Look. For Christmas here in America all kids believe in this Santa Claus – they say, 'Santa Claus, please bring me dolly. Santa Claus, please bring me –' whatever they want, and believe me they always want something you can't afford, especially when they sixteen and stupid." Harry's daughter was sixteen. "Then, their parents go get it for them, and they say, 'Here, Merry Christmas – Santa Claus bring you this.'"

Dikran looked puzzled. Armenoui would probably not like this one bit. She was very straightforward about such things, and he could not envision her telling little Ahngah that this fat man brought her presents when in fact Dikran's hard-earned money had paid for them.

"Armenoui know about Santa Claus?"

"Well, if she don't, she's goin' to, we gonna get you a Christmas tree – have a real American Christmas for you. Martha tells me yesterday she gonna get you some candles for the tree – you light the candles, you sing "Jingle Bell" – what a great Christmas. Dikran, I tellin' you, I'm goin' to get that little Snooky the best present in the world, and if Jack gets himself born before Christmas, him too, him too." Harry popped the last of the sandwich in his mouth and chewed reflectively.

Dikran still had reservations about broaching all this frivolity to Armenoui. He was afraid she would disapprove; she had had so little frivolity in her life, scarcely even a hair ribbon before she was married. Her dark eyes had seen murder, her strong hands had staunched blood, she had bitten through the flesh of her own fingers watching the twentieth century be born, witness to the scientific rather than a random extinction of whole peoples. Armenoui's beauty was dipped in sorrow. She lacked humor, but not courage.

Shortly after Harry left, the trade slowed down in the afternoon. Dikran never tired of looking at the faces of the customers, but most of them ignored the man behind the counter, looking right past him, or perhaps right through him. Then he had a customer who did look at him: she was the prettiest woman he had ever seen. She smiled. She was blonde; her glossy hair, cut short, curled around her face; she reminded him of the attractive young women in the ads who framed Number One. She had china-blue eyes and pink cheeks and a small, red mouth. Probably she wears lip rouge or paint or something, he thought, but she was so pretty, it didn't seem to matter. His eyes drifted from her pert, painted face to her body and the loose dress made of some kind of crushable material, and the brilliant green silk stockings that sheathed her legs. Since he had come to America, he had grown accustomed (or thought he had) to seeing women's legs, but not women's legs in green stockings. She rested her hand on the counter: her fingernails looked like pale little shells against her smooth, unpuckered skin. She took his obvious admiration not as a gift, but as though she were extracting a tax from him for the sheer pleasure of looking at her. He did not even notice: it was a pleasure. She chewed a little gum with which she made rhythmical clicking noises.

"Cigarette? Candy bar? Chewing gum? Lucky Strikes?"

"Chewing gum."

"Which one."

"There," she said, pointing.

"You're welcome," he said.

Taking her gum, she smiled again, and said, "Merry Christmas," as she walked off.

"Merry Christmas," he replied.

Harry had forgotten to show him where the lights were for Number One, but Dikran had found them just before the sun set. By 5:30 the beach was deserted, the tide out, the water barely visible from the concession stand, which glowed like a bright beacon on the dark beach. Just before he found the lights, Dikran had seen a man and a woman walking along the beach, and not too far from Number One, they stopped and kissed. The woman's head tilted back, the man's arms encircled her. Kissing in front of everyone must be American, Dikran concluded. He asked Harry what he thought as they rode the streetcar home. He asked him in Armenian. Harry roared with laughter.

"So, that was it, this morning, huh? I am an American so long now I forget about old-country women. Ha!"

Dikran laughed, too; he thought he would like kissing Armenoui every morning before he went to work.

Armenoui did not like it. Not in front of Harry, she protested to him as they lay in their bed that night. He told her Harry didn't care, and that it was very American. Gradually she adjusted to the kissing each morning when Dikran left for work. Now he carried the keys for Number One himself and got off the streetcar at the beach while Harry rode farther into town. Armenoui packed him a lunch each day. They bought a thermos so he could take coffee with him, because in spite of the warm December afternoons, the evenings were brisk and chilly. He took an extra sweater to work and left it under the counter. His English improved gradually; he became acquainted with the particular brand names of chewing gum and cigarettes. One day he found himself singing "Jingle Bell," as good as Harry sang it, he thought. And every day to his delight the lovely blonde girl came by the stand, bought some chewing gum, smiled at him and said "Merry Christmas" as she was leaving. Every day she looked more beautiful. One day he noted she wore some little bells and a fake spray of dark green leaves and red berries pinned to her lapel. Holly, Harry told him later, for Christmas. Dikran wondered what she would say to him when Christmas was past.

Some days were crisp and sunny, but when it was overcast the sky squatted over the ocean, turning it gray and lavender at the horizon. One day it rained all day. He had hardly any customers, some of the stock got wet, and the girl did not appear. Harry told him when it rained that much, to close up and go home.

If the rain beaded on the shiny cigarette packages, if it chilled Dikran, even if it sobered Harry, it did not alter the tide of shoppers who, unsmiling and intent and clutching their goods, streamed through the frames of Dikran's window as he rode the streetcar to and from Number One.

"Sometimes Christmas is no fun," Harry said one day as they rode home. "No fun. No joy. Only buy buy buy. What's the use, you not going to enjoy it? What's the use you don't enjoy buying the present? They don't enjoy getting the present? Christmas is to make people happy, make them sing – look at them." Harry shook his head, "Look at those faces." Dikran did not reply. There seemed nothing to say. Harry was so seldom serious or sad that Dikran's silence seemed the only appropriate response.

Harry was quite often mad, however, and grew very nearly violent when Armenoui insisted (just as Dikran suspected she would) that Santa Claus was not necessary for Ahngah's Christmas and that a tree of lighted candles would set the house on fire. Harry hopped about the room, sometimes on one foot, extolling the virtue of Santa Claus and Christmas trees until at last Armenoui relented. Then Harry brought the tree in; he had left it by the front door all the time. Martha brought in the candles and some shiny, opaque glass balls, and they decorated it. They lit the candles, turned off the lights in the living room, and watched the tree. The room smelled wonderfully of fresh pine and dripping, sweet wax. It was so quiet that they could hear the candles splutter and hiss.

One afternoon Harry left work early and with Martha and Armenoui took Ahngah down to meet Santa Claus. Santa Claus listened attentively to what the little girl wanted, but she said it in Armenian so Santa could only smile and look at her strangely. He handed her back to her uncle with a pained expression on his face.

"Hmmph. Next year she talk English good as you," said Harry to Santa. It didn't matter to Snooky; she was enthralled. The packages began to pile up under the Agajanian Christmas tree, lots for Snooky and lots for Jack, no matter what he was.

"If the baby comes before Christmas, honey," Martha told her sister, "you can open them then." Armenoui was so moved that she began to cry. They were the first tears she had shed in eight years.

Two days before Christmas, Harry showed up at Number One.

"You gotta present for Armenoui yet? You know Christmas in two days. You better roll it," he said savoring the slang. "I'll stay here and close up. You go get a present for your wife. That boy gonna be here any day."

Dikran stood on the street with the shoppers he had so often watched. He let them jostle and move him as though he stood waist-deep in the Pacific's breaking surf; he savored the electricity generated by their bodies, and the static in their uncrushed bags. As the afternoon waned, the lights everywhere grew more brilliant. The very streetlights seemed to conspire with the season as they blinked red and green. Dark-bonneted women clanged bells on the sidewalks, the wonderful and unrelenting cacophony of Christmas.

Dikran wandered from store to store, looking for something for his wife. Everywhere he looked, the merchandise beckoned, begged to be touched, stroked, bought. He bobbed with the crowd's rhythm as they were forced, like musical notes on a staff, between waist-high wooden counters where soft pairs of gloves lay in repose and new umbrellas stood at attention. There were long aisles of silky slips and stockings and fragile underthings, which embarrassed him, and he found another department of the store in which to browse. Led by his sense of smell, he circled the cosmetic counter where a woman whose face had to be peeled off at night guarded an unctuous galaxy of creams and pots and potions which wafted a cloying fragrance into the stale air. His eyes were drawn to rows of twinkling copper cookware and gleaming china dishes, frail glassware perched in triplicate on mirrored shelves. He passed through stores where substantial-looking furniture and lamp fixtures spread out in a panoramic living room, where rows of pianos stood upright, ornate and respectable. He explored a sporting-goods store with crisp, hard odors of metal and leather and wood, full of items for which he could imagine no earthly use. The odors and the fabrics and the people and the sounds of cash ringing and paper crunching and customers barking at salespeople melded, could no longer be distinguished individually. His senses rebelled, then re-

volted, then ceased to record, and the crowd moved his body like he belonged to them. A woman thumped his back and asked him a question
he did not understand. She asked only once. She was armed with a tin
breadbox; she forged past him and he watched her back retreat as the
packages of others crushed against his shoulders.

A man with a waxed mustache stood guard by a slick icebox in a room
where iceboxes outnumbered the people. Dikran saw a young couple
whose rapt and happy attention was riveted to a vacuum cleaner. Sewing
machines gobbled up material under the expert hands of young women,
and the vast network of pneumatic chutes hissed and spat and sped the
money on its way to distant coffers. His eyes dried out and began to hurt;
he squinted in the artificial indoor light, his lips dessicated and his throat
parched. His brain pulled away from his skull; he lost his balance momentarily and tumbled against an ambulating overcoat which withdrew from
him before he could regain his stance and he fell.

He got to his feet. He could not find the way out of this great commercial bin.

The familiar odor of chocolate accosted him. He bought a nickel's
worth of chocolates and left the store and the downtown district altogether. He walked west. When he came to the Pacific he sat in the cold
sand. He watched the dark water and ate the chocolates. The streetcar he
caught for home was almost empty, and night had cleared the streets and
lit the windows of Los Angeles.

Armenoui was pale with worry when he arrived home. Martha was
with her. When he saw his wife he realized he had no present for her.

"Well," said Harry the next morning, "what you get your wife?"

"Nothing."

"Nothing? What you mean nothing?"

"Nothing."

"What's wrong with you Dikran?" Harry's bushy eyebrows shot up.
"Tomorrow Christmas. What you gonna give your wife?"

He could not articulate his thoughts in adequate English; he could
only paste them together intuitively in Armenian. People on the streetcar stared at him when he spoke Armenian. He knotted his fingers together.

"Too much," he said in English.

"Too much? Too much what? You makin' good money now, you makin' enough for a nice present for your wife."

"Not money. Too much. Too much. Too much. Too much…" Dikran's knuckles went white. He cleared his throat; he clenched his teeth. Harry's shoulders sloped forward; he stared silently at the gum wrappers on the floor of the streetcar. The car made two stops before Harry said, "Dikran. I know. It's hard in a new place." His shoulders straightened and he brought his right hand down into his left with a resounding clap. "You know what I do? When I go to work, I call Martha and I tell her to go downtown and get Armenoui the best Christmas present ever, from Dikran – good idea? Martha, she's got good taste; like they say, she knows things. Armenoui will love it. I promise you. Ha, ha – you gonna be a lot happier man after that baby get born. I'm sure of that!"

Without commenting on Harry's estimation of his domestic life, Dikran thanked him. "Tell Martha I will pay her back tomorrow," he said in his familiar tongue.

"No – not tomorrow. No payin' back on Christmas. Day after."

Dikran nodded. Harry always made people happy.

Late in the morning Dikran rested his arm on the counter and his eyes on the Pacific. Then his eyes ceased to rest, he smoothed his hair: the beautiful blonde was walking toward Number One with several other girls, all pretty, but not as pretty as she. She looked even prettier today, with red stockings and a green dress and the same now-bedraggled sprig of fake holly. She did not look at him today. She was engaged in an animated conversation with her friends. "Well, what did you tell him then, Ethel?"

Ethel laughed. "I told him he must have me confused with someone else. Just because I let him buy me dinner and bring me home, that didn't mean anything."

The young women burst into laughter at this.

"What did he do then?" asked the beautiful blonde.

"He was mad and he said he ought to get a kiss at least and I said if I let you have a kiss, next you'll want to neck and pet." The four arrived at Number One, ignoring Dikran while Ethel finished her story. "I said I'd let him kiss me if he kept his hands in his pockets."

"Did he?"

"What do you think?" replied Ethel, grinning.

Dikran understood the tone and mood and the words and the sound of *kiss* enough to wonder if young American women often related these intimate things in front of strangers. "Cigarettes? Candy? Chewing gum?" he said.

"Gum for me," said the beautiful blonde without looking at him.

He was stunned that she would have bothered to tell him; he knew she wanted gum, he even knew what kind. He had it in his hand before she spoke.

"Get this for me, willya, Ethel? I haven't got a cent," she said.

"Got any Luckies?" asked one of the women.

"Lucky Strike," he said.

"Get me a CocoaNut Bar, willya?" said another.

"Which kind?"

"CocoaNut Bar," she replied, digging in her purse.

"Which one?"

"A CocoaNut Bar, I toldya. Are you deaf?"

Dikran was silent, hoping she would point.

"Are you deaf?" she hollered. Finally, she pointed. "You blind as well?" The girls all laughed again.

He handed her the candy bar.

"Gimme some change for this fiver," said Ethel, pushing a bill toward him.

"Cigarette? Candy? Chewing gum?" he said.

"All I want is some change."

Dikran stepped back so that Ethel could view the whole panorama of candy and cigarette counter to make her choice. He smiled. "Cigarette? Candy? Which one?"

Ethel's lip curled. "Dumb-bell," she said.

"Come on, Ethel," said the beautiful blonde, walking away. "Get it changed somewhere else. Come on, he'll be all day.

Ethel's gaze narrowed to Dikran's smile. "Dumb-bell," she repeated. Then she left.

Dikran stared out to the Pacific for a long time. He tried to think what *dumb-bell* might mean. Perhaps it was some relation to *Jingle Bell*. He would ask Harry. The bead of Ethel's gaze still seared him; a metallic taste formed at the back of his throat. For the first time since he had been in America ambition gripped him, ambition alloyed with bitterness: Dikran had been a foreigner all his life, born to it; he did not want to die a foreigner too. Any Armenian who lived in a Turkish city learned quickly to say little, to tread easy, to fade inconspicuously if he could. He had not been sorry to leave Turkey. Then he had lived in London, one of many particles, one of the foreign fat who floated in the London stew, the first to be skimmed off jobs, out of housing, the dark ones who hovered together and hated each other, the Indians, the Jews, the Armenians, the blacks. He had not lived in London long. Then Athens. Athens was not so bad, but they had buried a child in Athens, and he had not been sorry to leave there either; a grave should not tie one to a city. He faced the Pacific now, and knowledge began to crystallize in his brain; he realized what his life as a perpetual foreigner had deprived him of, and he realized it in an instinctive way that he could not articulate in any language. It defied language. It rose up out of his guts like love. He had lived his whole life without so much as one tendril of a root to bind him, to make him wince when it was pulled up, to make him groan when it was transplanted in yet thinner soil. Not one white root bound him. He would not be one of those who sigh for the old home; there was no old home, there was no old country. There was only the new home and the new country and if he had to divest himself of the old ways in order to have the new home, if he had to strip his old self to wear the new country, so be it. Dikran wanted the rich, rolling tide of life in America to pick him up and take him too. Let it be too much. Let it be anything at all just so he was part of it. He hated the beautiful blonde.

Harry bustled up to Number One around two. "C'mon, close up," he said. "We goin' home. This is Christmas Eve Day; anyone who wants cigarettes have to buy them from a Jew. This is Christian holiday, and by God, we are Christian. Wait!" he said, as Dikran began to lock up. "You and me better take some cigars in case Jack is born in the next day or so — you don't want to come back here for cigars."

"What for?"

"Dikran. In America when you have baby, you pass out cigars to all your friends. You say — Here, have one on me, my wife just have baby."

"No friends," said Dikran in English.

"What you mean, no friends? You got me. You got Martha. You got – " Harry's hands waved through the air. "You gonna have plenty friends, by next year Christmas you have new car and plenty friends. Me, too. Oh, I got plenty friends now, you know, but I have new car then, too. Let's go. What's wrong with you Dikran? You sick?"

"No."

"Well, when that boy born, you give me a cigar and I give you one and we both smoke. How's that?"

"Good."

They walked to the streetcar stop and stood with the sun at their backs and their shadows stretching out into the street. "Harry, what means *dumb-bell*?"

"Dumb-bell?"

"Yes."

"Hey, you learnin' the slang already, I told you so – you pick it up real easy with this job. It mean stupid."

The streetcar came and for the ride home Harry talked about the Christmas dinner, the American Christmas dinner that Martha and Armenoui were cooking for the next day. He promised Dikran he would love turkey.

Christmas Eve Dikran lay in bed next to his wife. "Are you asleep?" he asked in the old familiar language. No matter how well he learned English, he thought he would always use Armenian in bed.

"No."

"When will it be?"

"Soon. Tomorrow, maybe the next day, maybe the day after that. Soon."

"Merry Christmas," he said in English.

"Merry Christmas," she replied.

Leaning over his wife, he kissed her mouth tenderly. He laid his ear on her swollen belly and listened to the heartbeat of the unborn American child.

Habits

Punctual as a matin churchbell by nature, Mary Agnes Knott arrived an hour late, parked her Pinto, locked each door, clutched her purse and made her way through the spring twilight toward International Arrivals. She was a small, trim, visibly anxious woman with fine skin, lank hair, and a pronounced overbite. Being tardy always made her anxious, as if a phantom schoolbell yet tolled and a disapproving gray-winged nun fluttered behind her.

She dodged the traffic carefully, compensating for being slightly light-headed from two glasses of wine. Mary had developed food allergies over the past year and the doctor ordered her to stay clear of alcohol, eat simply, and keep an accurate daily list of her foods, correlating them with her general health and well-being. She kept a small notebook in her purse for that purpose and reminded herself as she rode the escalator toward International Arrivals to add wine, smoked almonds, green olives, and birthday cake to today's list. All of the above were forbidden her and this too contributed to her anxiety.

Her dietary transgressions were the result of an after-hours surprise birthday party organized by her secretary at United Title and Trust. Mary was quite surprised, even touched, since she had never cultivated friends at United Title, kept her co-workers at a discreet distance, privately believing them either too petty or too ambitious. She felt neither the need nor the loss of friendship among her peers: Mary Knott prided herself on her punctuality, thrift, and self-reliance, and if the world had not accommodated itself to her wishes, neither had she accommodated herself to its demands.

However, like anyone who works in an office, she was adept at smalltalk, and at the birthday party she even had a bit of genuine news to impart. "I'm picking up my college roommate at the airport tonight," she told the Escrow and Title Search officers over cake and wine. "She's coming in from London. She's an actress there. Her name is Victoria Jack, but she calls herself Victoria Jacques." Mary spelled the last name carefully and went on to chronicle some of Victoria's appearances on "Masterpiece Theatre" until Title Search drifted away and Trust Deeds joined them. "My best friend is coming in from London tonight," she told Trust Deeds as Escrow excused himself. "We've been friends ever since college. Immaculate Heart College. It's not far from here. Have you ever heard of it?" Trust Deeds nodded intermittently until Mary got as far as their youthful escapade with the toilet seats, and then he asked when the plane was arriving and Mary said six o'clock.

Trust Deeds glanced at his watch. "Shouldn't you be going then?"

"It doesn't matter. Victoria is always late."

The London flight was indeed late and International Arrivals' lounge thronged with families, foreigners, and surly chauffeurs in hotel uniforms. Mary took a seat opposite the doors separating them from Customs and made a mental inventory of her preparations at home: clean towels, fresh tablecloth, California wine, iris sheets on the bed. The single bed. Oh dear. Victoria had a husband now, but her wire said nothing about bringing him. On the other hand, five years ago she had shown up with an utterly unexpected Australian in tow. He was gregarious and tanned from months in the Greek Isles and in no hurry to return to his family's tomato farm. Mary gave them her single bed and slept – poorly – on the couch. Still, she had liked the Australian well enough. He sang a lot. He was the only man who had ever sung in her shower.

Victoria's flight flashed on the overhead TV screen, but it would be a while yet. Mary took out her diet notebook and dutifully confessed her sins. At the top of the page she wrote *feel fine* and *my birthday* beside it. She wondered if Victoria would remember her birthday.

On this birthday Mary Agnes Knott had at last reached her correct age. Everyone has one. Mary had been close-to-forty even as an adolescent and she would go on being close-to-forty for years to come. At close-to-forty one is not expected to indulge in love affairs, or dash about in search of experience and sensation. One is expected to live simply, to dress in the grays and dark blues Mary had always favored anyway, to wear small button earrings rather than gypsy hoops, to clip one's hair severely, to carry an umbrella, to be good at one's job, reliable if not spectacular.

Victoria Jack was also close-to-forty, though this was not her correct age. The girls had been arbitrarily assigned to one another as roommates their freshman year at Immaculate Heart. Mary had been rather shocked by Victoria, who had long, unruly auburn hair and wore low-slung jeans with a cropped T-shirt. Her belly button showed and she cracked her gum in time to the rock music cascading from her radio. Victoria Jack was from San Pasquale, California, a name which to Mary's New Jersey ears sounded very romantic, but Victoria said it ought to be called San Pasqualid. Her father was a judge (both personally and professionally if the unflattering things she said about him were true), but Mary never met the parents who sent Victoria to this small Pennsylvania Catholic women's college to keep her out of trouble. "What they don't understand," said Victoria in between snaps of gum, "is that I like it."

"Immaculate Heart?" inquired Mary.

"No, trouble."

Victoria burst through Customs' doors, laden with luggage, tugging and cursing her suitcases. She wore a plum-colored traveling suit with magenta stockings and short black boots. She had gypsy hoops in her ears. Victoria Jack's correct age was nineteen.

"Oh Mary, Mary, I'm so glad you're here! You can't imagine what I've been through!" She pulled Mary into an embrace redolent of smoke and Victoria's familiar cologne, and Mary hugged her to breathe it in. "Let me look at you!" Victoria's gaze swept swiftly, critically over Mary, who instinctively righted the bow on her blouse. (Victoria was something of a judge herself.) "You look wonderful. I look terrible. I know it."

As ever, Victoria exaggerated. She did not look terrible, though she was pallid as a London dusk and tiny furrows hovered disconsolately about

her eyes and mouth. Her hair was both lighter and brighter, redder than
Mary remembered. "Are you alone?" Mary asked.

"No Australians – alas!"

"Your husband's staying in London then?"

"Oh him," Victoria brushed the air as if to clear it of cobwebs. "I don't
want to talk about him."

So they didn't. They struggled with the luggage on the way to the car
while Victoria rattled on about the dreadful flight and the horrid old
pederast she'd sat next to. "But you don't know that," said Mary, who
seldom speculated on people's sexual tastes.

"Of course I do! He oozed pederasty."

Mary pointed toward the beige Pinto at the end of the lot. "Same old
car. Same old house. Same old me."

Victoria looked relieved.

In fact, for the last ten years Mary had driven this same Pinto, worked
at United Title and Trust, and lived in the same small, sagging bungalow
some 25 miles from the city in the lush Pennsylvania countryside. Her
bungalow (and three others just like it) huddled in a muddy hollow that
flooded every spring, so poorly insulated, badly wired, ill-ventilated, and
wretchedly maintained that Mary had taken to making her own repairs
and deducting them from the paltry rent.

As Mary drove out of the city and beyond the ring of fashionable sub-
urbs, Victoria rolled down the window, and the wind blew her hair and
words around as she chatted briskly about her theatrical career in London, in film and commercials and the BBC, her conversation littered with
names like Nigel and Angela and Reggie. But not Simon. Simon was her
husband.

Mary turned off the main highway and threaded expertly down narrow
lanes where ancient stone farmhouses were occasionally interspersed
with fabulous new dwellings of glass and wood. As twilight thickened,
collected, reflected in the flowering dogwoods clustered near the road,
they sped past a burnt-out farmhouse, engulfed in lilacs, whose pungent
odor assaulted them fleetingly. Mary explained that four years before,
just about this time of year, the farmhouse had burnt to the ground, but
the garden, the lilacs in particular, continued to bloom bountifully, to
prosper independent of any human hand. "That fire burned for hours,

on into the night," said Mary, who had other reasons for remembering the blaze, but she nattered inconsequentially away from the conflagration, steering the conversation toward her friends, Warren and Ceci, who had invited them over the following night. To celebrate Mary's birthday, though she did not say so.

"Warren Robbins?" Victoria asked with alarm. "Who's Ceci?"

"His wife. I wrote you he got married. Four years ago. You'll like Ceci, she's — "

"But you were in love with Warren!"

"No, I wasn't. We dated a few times. That's all. I got them a silver teapot for their wedding. If I'd known Ceci, I would have got them something else. Ceci's not the silver teapot type. But this summer I think I'll polish it up and use it for morning coffee. I'm house-sitting and looking after their dog while they go to Maui. I house-sat for them last year; you remember, I wrote you when they went to Hawaii. I have to leave Cat at my place, though. Cat doesn't get on with their dog. Last year Cat — "

"I never dreamed it was Warren Robbins' house you were in!"

"They're both good friends." Mary guided the Pinto down a rutted muddy road, and the bungalows with their peeling olive-drab paint came into view. Mary's was the only one sprigged with so much as a petunia. "You have to hold on to your friends at our age."

"Our age," Victoria moaned. "Our age. God! It's your birthday very soon, isn't it?"

"Today."

"Today! Of course! I bet you thought I forgot, but I didn't. I brought you a smashing present."

Once inside the bungalow, Victoria threw her suitcase open on the couch and withdrew a long thick shawl whose colors suggested moss and clouds and cold blue lakes. She draped it dramatically around Mary's shoulders. "Happy Birthday! I got it in Scotland. I took one look at it and I thought — that looks just like Mary."

It looked just like Victoria and smelled like her too. Mary hugged it closely. "Thank you, Victoria. It's a lovely present, the nicest one I've gotten." The *only* one, unless you counted the office party and dinner at the Robbins'. "I'll wear it to Warren and Ceci's tomorrow."

"He won't be able to take his eyes off you!"

"He's married," Mary protested, laughing. "I told you, it was nothing."

"It's never nothing. People say that when they don't get what they want," Victoria replied sourly.

"Look, you go take a shower if you want, and I'll fix dinner. I've got a lovely dinner planned. You can have the bedroom. I'll take the couch. How does the old place look to you?"

"The same," Victoria said without inflection, taking her things into the bathroom.

Mary reassessed the bungalow with fresh eyes: her cozy home suddenly struck her as claustrophobic. Victoria always had this effect, as if she consumed more than her share of oxygen, consumed the way fires do, without asking permission or giving thanks. Mary realized she somehow should have concealed the naked dripping plumbing in the kitchen and rearranged the ramshackle dishes on the sagging shelves. New pillows would have perked up the couch; the old ones were faded and threadbare. She should have dusted and done something about the bulging bookshelves, the old magazines and newspapers crammed under the couch, coffee table, bed, dresser, and desk. From the corners, stacked boxes reproached her, boxes full of old class notes, paper keepsakes, private mementos: Victoria's letters and playbills from obscure London productions she'd been in, a menu from a Chinese restaurant in New York, snapshots Mary always meant to put into an album. Mary wished she'd bought the new towels she'd contemplated and chided herself for not getting fresh flowers or new plants to enliven the dun walls and carpet.

She folded the shawl on the bed, on top of a pile of afghans she didn't need this time of year but had no place to store. Cat roused from her customary torpor and regarded Mary curiously. Cat was always sensitive to her moods. Mary picked Cat up and assured her this one would pass when Victoria left. In Victoria's incandescent glow, everything momentarily paled.

BY THANKSGIVING of her freshman year at Immaculate Heart, Mary Agnes Knott had dyed her brown hair blonde. Victoria thought it would look terrific and refused to admit that it did not. Victoria wanted to update Mary in other ways too: she arranged double-dates with a boy who (she assured Mary) would relieve her of her virginity ("a useless encumbrance," Victoria further assured her). Mary liked the boy, but she maintained her virginity past the time she cherished it, until she was twenty-seven and got drunk one night with a visiting auditor. The boy and the blonde hair were Victoria's only notable failures; she shook rather than shattered Mary's habits, changed her clothes and make-up, altered her politics and musical tastes and affected even the way Mary perceived her own family. Victoria came to Mary's home only once, for Thanksgiving, but in those four short days Mary noticed for the first time that her mother whined persistently and her father grunted in reply, that the house was gray and gardenless and smelled of damp and mothballs, and that not a wisp of music or a breath of wind had rattled the Venetian blinds in the immaculate living room for as long as she could remember.

Her parents, of course, loathed Victoria, thought her rude, high-handed, impertinent, and bizarre, and blamed her (correctly) for Mary's newly blonde hair. "You're not Mary Agnes any more," her father said, and jokingly added, "Knott, Mary Agnes." Her parents urged her to get a different roommate for the spring term.

The habitually compliant Mary refused. The girls remained roommates until Victoria was expelled from Immaculate Heart for the ultimate infraction: she was discovered entertaining a man in her room. In her bed. She was caught only that once, but Mary had spent many Saturday nights sleeping in the bathroom across the hall, huddled in the shower stall with her blankets, pillow, and the *Norton Anthology of English Literature*.

If Victoria recognized Mary's sacrifice, she never thanked her, but neither did she blame Mary for her unwilling part in Victoria's expulsion. The dorm matron unexpectedly came into the bathroom and demanded to know why Mary was camped in the shower. Mary lied lamely. The dorm matron marched to their room to look into the matter.

The dorm matron promptly summoned Sister Therese herself, though by the time she got there, the young man was gone. Sister Therese completed a minute inspection while the matron and the two girls stood by. Sister Therese methodically went through Victoria's bureau, pulling out a roach clip and two joints. She inspected them like streptococci.

"Don't forget my douchebag," Victoria quipped.

The matron gasped. Mary reeled and then burst out laughing. Victoria grinned. Sister Therese ordered Mary out of the room, pointed her down the long cool corridors, and marched behind her all the way to the office, where Mary crouched in a chair and Sister Therese glared at her across the desk.

"You're a fool, Mary Knott. She's using you. You're nothing but an audience for Victoria. She doesn't even really like you."

"She does so. We're best friends."

"Friends!" Sister Therese inadvertently broke a pencil in half. "What about the toilet seats? We never thought you were the guilty party in that regrettable incident. It was your so-called friend, but you were punished just the same, weren't you? Victoria has bad instincts. Bad habits. She gets you in trouble."

"Am I in trouble?"

"You're an accessory, aren't you? I'd call that trouble. Sleeping in the shower indeed! How can you allow yourself to be used in such a vulgar manner?"

Victoria Jack, unrepentant to the end, was sent home in disgrace to be further judged by the judge in San Pasqualid. Then one afternoon, about a year later, Sister Therese, her slight mustache quivering with indignation, announced that Mary had a visitor and led her to the huge wainscotted lounge where Immaculate Heart students entertained their beaux. Mary wept with joy to see Victoria, who was wearing purple jeans and a fringed jacket. Sister Therese took a seat on the dais reserved for the nun on duty and eyed them skeptically.

Victoria announced loudly that she had left San Pasqualid for good, that she was on her way to New York to be an actress.

Dazzled by this revelation, Mary could only murmur, "But do you know how to act?"

"I don't know how not to," Victoria retorted.

Sister Therese snorted audibly.

On four daring occasions Mary Knott had signed out to visit her parents, but went instead to New York to visit Victoria Jack in the apartment she shared with a bevy of other aspiring actresses. These trips left Mary with brilliant, indelible memories: for the first time she stayed out all night, ate in a Chinese restaurant, saw a real stage play and her first naked man standing boldly on a fire escape, his arms ouflung, enjoying the admiration or outrage of anyone who happened to look up.

Between visits, Mary relished Victoria's letters, which were full of New York and theatrical life and all its possibilities. "But there's damned little in the way of likelihood," she wrote in one rather despairing note. "Maybe I'm not pretty enough to be an actress."

Mary replied immediately. *All you need is for one person to see you as you truly are*, she chewed her pen, *to notice your remarkable...*, she chewed further and listened to her new roommate turn the pages of "Soap Opera Digest," *...gallantry.* That was the correct word.

Mary imagined that it happened just like that: some one person, a man, perceived the gallant Victoria in a line-up of ordinarily pretty girls and called her to his side. In truth, Victoria had been rather vague about how she happened to hook up with a British producer, or was it a director, someone in British films or television, and went with him to London. Now and then Mary saw Victoria Jacques on "Masterpiece Theatre" when the script called for an American guest at a party. Victoria told Mary to look for her in a film with Alan Bates. Mary went to see it twice without finding her.

Victoria's letters were full of drama – personal and professional – plays, parts, commercials, filming on location in exotic places; she sent gifts and funny postcards and letters with snapshots of herself mugging for the camera. Mary taped the pictures and postcards to her bedroom mirror where they curled with age. Victoria's letters were also full of men, but then there was just one man. Simon. Victoria wrote: *This is the man for me. This is the way it is supposed to be. We have an irrevocable bond.* If irrevocable, their bond seemed to Mary to be at least elastic. (Witness the Australian.) When Simon and Victoria were "off," Mary got despairing letters, and when they were "on," Mary noticed, Victoria wrote less frequently. Then, three years ago, Victoria had called her from London in the middle of the night to say she had married Simon. Mary asked what she wanted for a wedding present. "Nothing," replied Victoria. "It's not that sort of marriage." She never said what sort of marriage it was.

Over the years Mary Agnes Knott had had dramas of her own, though she did not commit them to paper. She stuck to the prosaic: Cat's antics, Pinto's vagaries, repairing her own plumbing, her steady if undramatic rise at United Title and Trust. She did not mention the visiting auditor, or the one or two men after him, and she would not have mentioned Warren Robbins, but Victoria's last visit coincided with the full flush of Mary's love affair.

Mary had met Warren Robbins at a Sunday brunch given by some neighbors who had just moved into their new glass-and-wood home. Warren was a research physicist at one of the universities in the city and he told Mary he was building his own house very near hers. They left the brunch and he drove her over to see the shell of his house. He pointed to the would-be fireplaces, dining room, bedrooms, and deck, and the view each would have of wood, fields, and creek. She fell in love with the vistas he conjured, with the unfinished house, with Warren Robbins. She made love with him under the unfinished eaves. *This is the man for me.* Mary absorbed Warren's weight gratefully. He was a big man with thick black hair on his head and chest and legs. He was cheerful and tender and Mary Knott had never dreamed she could be so happy. *This is the way it is supposed to be.*

It was not the way it was, and their bond was not irrevocable. Their love affair had lasted about a year, while the house was being finished. Warren sometimes mentioned his secretary, Ceci.

Ceci was no longer his secretary, but Mary was still his neighbor, and the only time she lived in the house where she had lain with him was when he and his wife were in Hawaii and she was looking after their dog. And on that occasion, once – only once – did Mary venture up to those eaves to see if the very sap in the boards had curdled, if they yet echoed with ecstasy or testified to her lost dream. But Warren had finished off the attic and it was clotted with great bolts of pinkish insulation the color of flesh.

"WHAT IS IT, Lent?" Victoria, fresh from the shower, pointed to Mary's plate of thin pasta drizzled over with melted margarine. Victoria's plate was heaped with pasta in a cream-and-shrimp sauce.

"I have to eat simply. I've got these food allergies." Mary launched into an account of the allergies and how they manifested themselves, and the foods she reacted to, her notebook, and her doctor's orders; and by the time she was through, Victoria had finished her entire dinner and lit a cigarette.

"Sounds dismal," she said without sympathy.

"Just uncomfortable, really." Mary did not add that the prohibitions appealed to her sense of sin, that she enjoyed the occasional glass of wine all the more for its being forbidden. "Would you like some coffee, Victoria?"

"No, I'm going to crash in about ten minutes. I'm exhausted, but first I want to know what happened with Warren Robbins."

"Nothing. Obviously."

"Five years ago you were madly in love with him. He was good for you."

"What happened with Simon?" Mary parried adroitly. "Have you left him? Will you get a divorce?"

"Divorce! Such a dirty word, Mary. What would Sister Therese say?"

"Sister Therese died last summer. I went to her funeral. Everyone was there, alumni from as far back as – "

"I won't be getting a divorce. I married Simon informally, you might say, in fact rather than in law. Do you understand?"

Mary didn't, and she didn't think Sister Therese would either.

Victoria sighed. "Well I'm glad Sister Therese finally got to heaven. Especially since I'm going to hell. At least I won't have her nagging at me for eternity, will I?" Victoria smiled, a wan, nervous smile, foreign to her face. Her practiced insouciance collapsed by degrees. "I'll go to a special sort of hell reserved for actors. An empty room without any hope for an audience. Ever." She put her cigarette out emphatically. "It's all gone smash, Mary. Simon. Everything. So smashed I can't even look back and tell where I made the crucial mistake, or what I might have done differently. I feel like I've been hit by a truck and whichever way I turn – toward the past or the future – I hurt. I'm all smashed up inside and I'm too old to put myself back together."

"You're not too old," Mary said stoutly.

"Actresses have a finite amount of time. You make it while you're young, or you don't make it. I'm only good at one thing, acting, and I'm not even very good at that."

"You are so. I saw you on 'Masterpiece Theatre.'"

"Yes, I said, 'Lady Ravenswood, how very *charming* to meet you.' I said it well, don't you think? Probably go down in history with Olivier's Hamlet. I should have been a man. I could have rehearsed over the urinal: *to pee or not to pee, that is the question*." She laughed shrilly. "Maybe I should get me to a nunnery. You think they'd have me if I got my virginity surgically reconstructed?"

"You're just depressed, Victoria. A little time away from Simon and – "

"No. It's over. You see, it was like a play. For a brief season we said the same lines and did the same things and then it was done and Simon went on to a new role. My husband was nothing but a stage prop, Mary, but I'm an actress, and actresses need props. I settled for the fake marriage, but I loved the real man. Simon was the only man I ever wanted to marry. I needed him. I had an irrevocable bond with him." Victoria shrugged. "And then he revoked it." She poured some more wine. "At first I thought I would die, and then when I knew I wouldn't, I decided to go back to California. To L.A. I'll put on my British accent and lie about my credits and people will think I'm exotic and desirable. But you can't run away from the sort of person you really are, can you?"

"I don't know. I've never tried."

"You'll never have to. You're not a fake. You're not shallow. You don't tell lies and make stupid gestures. I should have been like you."

"Like me!" The thought struck Mary as preposterous.

"Yes, I should have begged Sister Therese's forgiveness and stayed in school and got my degree and a job somewhere collecting medical benefits and paid vacations and whatever else they give you. At least you've got those."

"But I've never been – " Mary sought the correct word, " – gallant. And even if it's all over with Simon, you can still act."

"Can I? For whom? What's an actress without an audience? A mad woman, that's what, posturing and gesturing in front of mirrors. I've failed. I'll probably end up like you anyway. My whole life stinks like that cat box over there."

Cat, upon hearing her name, rose lazily from the couch, ambled to the cat box, found a niche in the litter, and relieved herself. Mary looked away.

WHILE MARY WAS at United Title the following day, Victoria sunned herself, and by evening her skin was dusted with a light patina of pink and she seemed rested, something of her old balance and aplomb restored. She was beautifully made up and flamboyantly dressed, in an India cotton of bold primary colors, and high-heeled sandals. Mary changed quickly into a sleeveless blue dress and arranged her new shawl around her shoulders, and they drove to Warren's. As they passed the burnt-out farmhouse, Victoria had an inspiration. "Let's go back and pick some lilacs and take them with us. No one will care."

Mary cared, but she backed Pinto up and switched off the motor while Victoria waded through the ankle-deep weeds and tore off branch after heavy-laden branch. The crackling twigs made Mary wince and she wished Victoria had not trespassed on this preserve. When Victoria returned to the car, her arms were full of flowers and their pale, prim color clashed with her dress and her wild red hair.

The lilacs complimented Ceci Robbins' pink sweatsuit and pink running shoes and the permed hair surrounding her face like a halo. She took the flowers from Victoria as if they were an unruly baby. "They're beautiful. From those old ruins? I've often thought of picking lilacs there, but never had the nerve."

"The nerve?" Victoria asked, grimly judgmental.

Unceremoniously Ceci stuffed the lilacs in two huge vases and put one on the table and one on the mantel. Their odor percolated all the way out to the deck, where the four of them sat sipping drinks, listening to the murmur of the nearby creek, while sunset stalked the woods.

Effectively barricaded behind her forbidden gin and tonic, Mary noticed that Victoria was cordial to Ceci, but she lavished herself on Warren. Mary was reminded of the Australian. Victoria spouted uproarious tales of their college days and poor, old, stuffy, incompetent Sister Therese. Occasionally Mary spoke in Sister Therese's defense, but gave it up and allowed herself a second gin and tonic while Victoria bubbled like an Alka Seltzer dropped into the tap water of their lives.

"I never thought you could have so much fun at a Catholic girls' school," said Warren, still laughing at the picture of Mary caught napping in the shower stall.

"When I was in college – " Ceci began.

"Then there was the night we took the toilet seats off." Victoria threw the phrase out effectively on a long ribbon of smoke.

"*You* took the toilet seats off," Mary corrected her. "I only stood guard at the mirror."

Victoria turned to Warren confidentially. "Mary was supposed to be picking her face. It was two in the morning so we thought we were safe, but sure enough, Susan Dennis came in to pee."

"I knew a Susan Dennis in high school," Ceci offered. "She – "

"Not the same one," Victoria assured her. "Anyway, there were three stalls and I'd only got the seat off in one of them when I heard Susan come in. I stood on the rim of the toilet and waited."

"I told Susan that toilet was plugged up," Mary said proudly, "and the next morning Susan Dennis was the first one to scream when she splashed into the toilet! It was worth every bit of punishment."

"It was Mary's fault we were caught at all," Victoria added. "Susan told Sister Therese that Mary had been picking her face and eveyone knew that Mary Knott never had a zit in her life. And then Sister Therese got hold of Mary and put bamboo splinters up her nails and – "

"That's not true. She simply asked me."

"And Mary confessed."

"I couldn't lie."

"Dinner's ready," announced Ceci, and this time she was not ignored.

It was a Chinese meal, sumptuous and sizzling, and against all her doctor's dictates, Mary had some of everything, plus two glasses of wine; and through its pale chablis veil, she watched her best friend wooing her ex-lover, creating an enchantment so compelling that Warren Robbins was nearly drunk on Victoria Jack. Mary knew the next morning it would all vanish, save perhaps for a wistful hangover, but for the moment, Warren Robbins – indeed, Ceci, and Mary herself – was but a vessel that Victoria filled with her fermentation of practiced charm, well-timed laughter, effervescent anecdotes, and perfect mimicry of a dozen different accents. Under the accelerating influence of gin, wine, and the intoxicating odor of lilacs, Mary smiled to watch Victoria fill them all unto brimming. *She's squandering herself on the likes of us*, Mary thought, uncertain if the wine belied or underscored her intuition. *She'd rather have a darkened theater or a rolling camera, but she'll settle for us, perform as long as we give our unleavened attention, our applause. She's transformed us from a dinner party into an audience. We're accomplices in her drama. We're all her accessories, Sister Therese. Is it alchemy? Are we base straw spun into gold? Mere water recast as wine? No, Sister Therese, don't you see? It's like transubstantiation: miraculously we are altered: we become actors and audience in the same moment.* Sister Therese's gray wings fluttered and enfolded Mary and she closed her eyes. *How can you allow yourself to be used in such a vulgar manner? Oh, Sister Therese, I don't know how not to.* Mary opened her eyes and focused slowly on the lilacs and the candlelight which was kind to the concealed shadows on Victoria's face, animated her gallant beauty, dimmed the unhappiness in her eyes. The candlelight lit Ceci's plain face and highlighted the satisfaction evident in Warren's smile. Satisfaction or complacency? Mary noticed for the first time the ring of fleshy contentment around Warren's jowls. Why, he's getting fat, Mary thought. How could I not have noticed before?

"We'll have Mary's birthday cake and coffee in the living room," said Ceci brightly, clearing the plates, "but we can't have a Chinese dinner without fortune cookies, can we?"

"I hate those moralizing fortune cookies," Victoria said, lighting up a cigarette after a studied pause. "I loathe those dull homilies that instruct you to be kind and charitable and thrifty and patient. Why, they're nothing but veiled threats. I don't want to be nagged at by a fortune cookie, I want to be assured I'm about to get good news and money and meet someone handsome and dashing."

"I married someone handsome and dashing," said Ceci with a secret smile. Warren beamed indulgently, but Mary thought her wrong: Warren was handsome, but he wasn't dashing. *Had he ever been?*

They read their fortunes aloud. Warren's and Ceci's were indeed moralizing and Mary's only a little less so. Victoria unraveled hers slowly and frowned.

"Not bad news, is it?" asked Warren.

Mary held her breath: *the wine and now the wafer. The miracle's about to happen again, Sister Therese, the magic: watch, watch, it will be just like fifteen years ago in New York when Victoria said:*

"Expect bad breath and flatulence," Victoria said soberly.

Warren and Ceci convulsed with laughter. The evening was a smashing success.

"THOSE PINK RUNNING shoes! God! Unbelievable!" Victoria cried as they drove home through the inky spring night, through successive aromatic waves of damp grass and turned earth and fresh leaves. "That woman is an unspeakable twit. You should have got him, Mary. How could you let yourself be beat out by a simpering fool?"

Mary steered carefully around a pothole. She should have stuck with rice and tea. Was she drunk or just dyspeptic? She replied carefully. "I told you, I didn't want him."

"Of course you did! Admit it! There's nothing wrong with admitting you want something you didn't get. At least you were alive enough to want him, to love him. Warren's probably the only man you ever wanted, probably the only man you ever slept with. Isn't he? Admit it. You wanted him and you lost him to that pudding-plain twit. You failed."

"Like you failed with Simon?" Mary retorted. "Is that what you want me to admit? Well I haven't failed. I've never failed."

Victoria was silent, and Mary glanced at her face, lit uncertainly by the dashlights: a close-to-forty face anguished with the despair of a nineteen-year-old who has just discovered all things are not possible. "I'm sorry, Victoria. I didn't mean it."

"Oh shut up. I can't abide mealy-mouthed apologies. You're a fine one to talk of failure! Look at the way you live. That miserable office job! This wretched car. Clothes that make you look like a baglady, or worse, a nun," she sneered. "Your idea of a holiday is to visit your parents. And ten years crammed in with all those boxes and papers in that stinking hovel! God! It makes me retch to think of it!"

"I live simply," Mary replied evenly.

"What's the difference between living simply and simply living? You draw breath. That's all you do. You've never lived. You've never loved anyone but Warren Robbins, and now you deny that. Deny. Deny. Don't eat, or risk, or buy, or become anything. Just hoard and deny! God! Why don't you just put on a hair shirt, scratch, and be done with it?"

"I haven't had your luck."

"Luck!" Victoria shrieked. "Luck! Am I beautiful or brilliant or talented or rich? I'm not lucky! I just set myself to it. I wanted to become an actress, and I set myself to it and nothing was going to stand in my way! I made my luck!"

"Such as it was," said Mary drily, as the headlights fell on her petunia-ringed bungalow. She turned off the ignition and got out quickly, feeling rather faint, rather nauseous, her breath coming in short, swift stabs. She hurried to her door, unlocked it, switched on the overhead light, and in its harsh glare the boxes and newspapers and magazines accused her. The kitchen plumbing wept audibly into a bucket, and the shelves creaked and threatened to pull away from the ceiling and smash all over the floor. Ignoring Cat's plaintive mew, Mary went directly to the bathroom, locked the door and sat on the toilet seat, opened her notebook and confessed her sins: *wine and gin and fortune cookies, birthday cake, kung-pao chicken and –* She could not continue. *Feel wretched*, she wrote at the top of the page. *Absolutely wretched*. She stared at the shower stall. How could she have allowed herself to be used in such a vulgar manner? How could she have camped in the shower with her blanket and pillow and *Norton Anthology* while Victoria entertained others?

VICTORIA JACK was not in the habit of saying she was sorry. The next morning, however, she got up first and made the coffee, and brandishing her best cajoling charm, she brought a cup to Mary on the couch. "Why don't you call in sick today, Mary? We'll go out to lunch. My treat. We'll buy you some new clothes. Something to go with your new shawl."

"You bought that shawl for yourself. You forgot my birthday."

"So what? It looks terrific on you. Come on, Mary. Let's do something fun today. I have to leave tomorrow."

"I'm sure you'll be glad to leave this stinking hovel."

"Oh, don't be over-sensitive."

"Over-sensitive!"

"Come on, Mary. Forget your job. Let's have some fun."

"No. My job is important to me. It's all I've got." Mary put on her robe and headed for the shower. "But at least I've got that," she called out before closing the door.

But by mid-morning at United Title and Trust, Mary Agnes Knott did indeed feel sick, weak, and tense. She nearly called her doctor, but he would ask what she'd eaten and she'd have to tell the literal truth. But the intrinsic truth was that Mary's unease was not at all connected to her diet, but connected instead to fear and failure and the fear of failure and loss. Impending loss. Distant smoke, flaming lilacs, and impending, irrevocable loss creeping over her life like the smell of smoke that spring afternoon four years before. Burning lilacs and iris sheets. Mary crumpled an inter-office memo in her fist and saw herself driving home that afternoon, hurrying past the blaze, casting scarcely a thought to the burning house, so eager was she to get home and get dinner ready for Warren and put the new iris sheets on her bed. She'd bought the sheets because the last time Warren spent the night, he had joked about the austerity of her plain white sheets, her narrow twin bed. "Like sleeping with a nun," he added lightly. Mary had known: *whoever else he's sleeping with has floral sheets and a double bed.*

The farmhouse was still blazing, the sky all around lit with a dull ochre glow when Warren had come for dinner. Warren said he was going to ask his secretary to marry him. "I'm sorry, Mary."

"Please don't apologize. I can't bear it if you apologize. Have some more salad."

"Ceci knows I've been seeing someone else, but she doesn't know who, and I won't tell her it's you. I hope you'll be friends. You'll like Ceci, she's – "

"Have some more salad. Smell that smoke. The house is still burning. Terrible, isn't it?" *Isn't it terrible?*

Mary slammed her desk drawer shut and informed her secretary she was sick and had to get home quickly. Quickly. She drove the Pinto toward home as fast as its poor old pistons would pump, though she didn't know what she would say when she got there, or how she would free Victoria from fear, but she must. She must set herself to it and not fail. Fear: with her life and luck smashed, Victoria feared she would duplicate Mary's failures, though Mary did not consider herself a failure and never before realized that Victoria did. She didn't care. She had to hurry. She would not fail this time. She would not lose those funny postcards and chatty letters and silly photos and surprise visits with tanned Australians. She would not risk the loss of gold hoops and gallantry, friendship and all those years of counterfeit enchantment. *You're not Mary Agnes anymore.* Yes, well, Knott, Mary Agnes wanted to go on being an accomplice in the life of a woman she had always fundamentally disapproved of. Her parents were right. Sister Therese was right. Victoria had indeed used her, but Mary had got used to it like the dust and the cramped bungalow and the stacked boxes, and she no longer saw these things as unappealing.

She sped toward home till she came to the burnt-out farmhouse, and then she screeched on the brakes and stopped and dashed out of the car. Crashing through the ruins, through the charred boards and rusted pipes, through the succulent spring undergrowth, Mary tore branch after branch of lilacs. Their tough twigs scraped her hands and arms and ripped her stockings: blossom and color and fragrance pelted her hair and shoulders, blossom and color and fragrance enough to insulate them both from the odor of failure.

The Pinto jounced over the narrow roads; and turning down the rutted embankment toward the hollow, Mary stifled a scream when she saw a thick black plume spiraling skyward. In front of her bungalow burned a bonfire, and Victoria Jack leaned on a rake like an executioner while smoke swirled around her.

"Oh Victoria!" she cried, running from her car, "Stop! No! What are you doing?"

"Burning witches."

"Oh, Victoria, what have you done!"

"I cleaned your house."

Cautiously Mary approached her bungalow and stepped in: the place reeked of smoke and dislodged dust. The carnage was complete: newspapers, magazines, class notes, old letters, and Victoria's postcards and photos ringing the mirror had been marched out and burnt at the stake; boxes, pulled from their secret hiding places, ripped open and dumped and Victoria's own suitcases overturned, their contents spilled, scrabbled through and strewn everywhere. Cat mewed beseechingly from under the bed. Mary comforted her as she walked through the rubble. She turned and went back outside.

Victoria raked the fire. "You had newspapers seven years old stuffed in there," she said without looking up.

"I was saving those newspapers."

"What in hell for?"

Mary could not quite remember. Cat bolted from her arms. "What else have you burned?"

"Papers, postcards, letters. And everything I had from or of Simon. The past."

"It's not your life, Victoria. You had no right. You cannot, you should not, have walked in and smashed up my life."

"I started with my own life, my own things, and then it just seemed like – " Victoria looked at her helplessly. "I started with Simon, if that's any comfort to you."

"How can you talk about comfort after what you've done?"

"Someone had to do it. You'd have died in there, Mary. The wiring is bad, bald and sticking out of the walls, and one night all that infernal junk would have caught fire and you'd have been burned alive. You'd have shriveled up and died like all that rotten old paper, all that moldy junk. You'd have died. I saved you."

The blaze crackled and smoke spewed between them. Finally Mary said, "I saved you too, Victoria. I didn't know it before, never realized that you needed me just as much as I needed you."

"Needed you?" Victoria gave a tinny stage laugh.

"I've always been your best audience. You've always needed me to laugh and applaud and I've never let you down. You came here to get my applause before taking your act to L.A." She was going to say more, but the smoke choked her. She got the hose from under the steps, turned on the faucet, sprayed the fire until damp ashes blew into her hair and eyes. She stared at the dead embers and her unrecoverable loss: *Warren*. He too was an unrecoverable loss and Mary waited for the lamenting refrain she had stifled for four years to swell into an anvil chorus of regret. But it did not. Mary gave in to a reluctant smile. "Come on, Victoria. Help me clean up this mess."

Mary went to Pinto and gathered the lilacs into her arms; their cool lavender blooms lay against the soot and ash on her skin. Sulking, Victoria followed her into the bungalow where the lilacs' lush, promising fragrance mingled with the smell of smoke and regret. Victoria began to right the overturned boxes, but Mary told her to start with her own suitcases.

"You're sure?"

"Yes. You have to leave tomorrow, remember?"

"You want to go out to lunch and go shopping?" Victoria asked tentatively.

"Yes."

Tomorrow, Mary thought as she arranged the lilacs carefully in Mason jars, tomorrow Victoria will go to Los Angeles and fake a British accent and lie about her credits and convince people she is exotic and desirable. She'll make a life for herself as she always has, not by being what she is, but what she believes she could be. That's Victoria's magic, and it's contagious. And tomorrow, Mary decided, she too would set about becoming something of the woman she could be. Divest herself of old habits like the newspapers she'd accumulated for reasons she no longer fathomed. It could be done. You just set yourself to it and refuse to become prisoner not of what you are, but of what you've allowed yourself to become. Habits could be broken, and tomorrow she would certainly set about doing so.

A Time Change

THE HEAT ARRIVED right after Robin Vance returned to St. Elmo County, the very week she rented an apartment in a charmless complex called Shadetree Gardens where there were no gardens and only a few sprigged shade trees, so young they scarcely gave shadow, much less shade. The week she moved in, the sun peaked at its solstice, the torrid days lengthened, and Robin's nerves and skin grew dry and taut. The heat, like a remorseless unwanted guest, arrived in her apartment just after dawn and did not leave until late at night. From her bedroom window she could see the Shadetree's other tenants, many of them women like herself, mothers who had left or been left by men, lounging around the pool. Robin kept her distance from the other tenants and the pool as well; it wasn't crystalline as pools ought to be, but a cloudy blue-green compounded of chlorine and urine and the sweat of too many bodies. In her struggle against the desert summer, Robin armed herself with Diet Coke, ice cubes, a bottle of gin, and two fans that whirred incessantly night and day. The fans annoyed her mother, who came over twice weekly to help Robin clean up, gather the laundry, dust, vacuum, scrape globs of toothpaste off the sink, scour the tub: to set things generally to rights. True, Robin had managed all these tasks when she was married, but when she left her husband, her ability to balance her everyday life deserted her.

She did look after her children, Patrick (five) and Heather (three), but then, like her mother, she was one of those passionately maternal women.

Her mother and father offered to take the children, even overnight, but Robin declined. "We must stay together as a family," she said, "what's left of us." But the unvarnished truth was that Robin needed Patrick and Heather as much as they needed her; their laughter, the reassuring pressure of their small hands, saved her sanity, and caring for them saved her from the abyss of reflection. Patrick and Heather were dark sturdy youngsters, with their father's slender nose and high forehead. They had none of Robin's fair coloring or narrow shoulders, her hair the color of brown sugar. Robin reminded her husband how much the children looked like him whenever she spoke to him on the phone, during conversations that crackled with suppressed anguish and unasked questions and bad long distance connections. She was afraid Jon would forget what his children looked like, afraid he would forget them altogether. He had forgotten everything else.

Robin had not forgotten, but her memories clustered in segregated clumps, like variegated fungi around the stump of her recently severed past. She could not integrate the happy memories – seaside summers, picnics, eight years of Christmases – with the more recent ones of Jon's neglect and casual cruelty. Separation was, for Robin Vance, a last desperate gamble to remind Jon how much his wife and children meant to him. She had not counted on his having no memory whatever.

Robin's parents lived five miles from Shadetree Gardens, and they donated most of the furniture for her apartment and a few pictures, and the television too. Still the place had the air of an encampment. "All you need is some plants," her father said. He was an avid gardener and believed in the universal beatitude of the organic world. One morning he brought over a flat of marigolds and half a dozen geraniums in plastic containers and spent the few cool hours with the children, re-planting the flowers in brick-red pots and grouping them attractively on the porch. "Anyone can grow a geranium," he assured her. Robin agreed, but the geraniums died, casualties of the merciless heat, and in a few weeks the marigolds followed suit; cobwebs laced their brittle stems and spiders moved into the pots. The dead flowers reproached Robin, but she could not bring herself to throw out their skeletal remains. That would have announced defeat. So she learned to pass them without looking and, eventually, without seeing.

Robin's sister Renée lived only two miles away. Younger than Robin by two years, Renée was a manicurist who had already been married and divorced twice, and was currently living with a man named Jim, who seemed a good prospect for husband #3. Renée maintained that all Robin needed was a good man. Her youngest sister, Sally, who lived up north, maintained that all she needed was a good therapist. Her mother did not believe in the efficacy of plants or therapists, or men either. Her mother brought over the family's old typewriter and told Robin to practice an hour a day. "You need a job," her mother said.

"We can live on what Jon sends us."

"That's not the point. You need to get out in the world."

"I don't want to."

"Practice anyway," said her mother; "it will do you good."

Beginning in mid-July Robin cleared the breakfast table of Smurf cereal bowls and milk puddles and the rinds of toast, and while the children were watching the morning edition of "Sesame Street," she practiced her typing. She selected passages at random from the front pages of the newspaper and laboriously re-constructed stories of disaster, earthquake, drought, terrorism, fighting in Central America, and chaos in the Middle East. The machine was rusty and arthritic and, though her typing didn't improve dramatically, the accounts of global destruction gave her a sense of proportion. Now when her gaze drifted out to the pots of dead flowers, they didn't seem so ominous.

After her daily stint at the typewriter, Robin dressed and got the children dressed, and they drove to the refrigerated supermarket and dawdled over their few necessary purchases; or sometimes they went to the cool library and spent hours selecting books; and occasionally they wandered aimlessly in air-conditioned shopping malls. One particularly oppressive afternoon they arrived home to find even the flies paralyzed by the heat. Robin quickly turned on the fans. "If I sprinkled yeast on you," she said to Patrick and Heather, "you'd probably rise in this heat and float to the ceiling."

"What's yeast?"

"It's what they put in bread to make it high and fluffy. Without yeast, bread would be like, well, like cake."

"Hey!" cried Heather. "Let's bake a cake today!"

"Are you out of your mind, sweets? Turn on the oven when we're already living in one! Anyway," Robin smoothed the hair off Heather's perspiring forehead, "when it cools down, we'll bake, cakes and even bread if you like. In the fall when Patrick goes to school, we'll do that."

"I don't want to go to school."

"You'll like school, Patrick. You'll make new friends and every morning Heather and I will walk with you to school and in the afternoons we'll walk to meet you and we'll come home and bake and drink cocoa and we'll have supper early because it will be dark early, dark and cool."

Patrick lay down in front of the fan, rocking one knee over the other. "Tell me some more about the fall, about school."

Robin dredged up memories of her own school days when her mother had met her in the afternoons, trailing little Renée and wheeling baby Sally, and they all came home to a kitchen filled with the smell of baking – bread and cake and cookies, and the cocoa her mother made on cold winter days. Robin did not add that they had waited for her father to come home from work. She picked selectively through her memories, carefully excluding her own father from her account, lest Jon's absence seem too glaring.

"When will it be cool?" asked Heather.

"In the fall."

"When is that?"

Robin wasn't sure, was not at all certain that the grip of the heat would ever ease, unable to imagine that the days would pass and the heat too. She could not – or did not – differentiate weekdays from weekends, July from August. Her calendars were frozen on the June day she left Jon, and she could not bear to hang them up because they reminded her of a past with him and suggested a future without him. Robin Vance lived in a fortified continual present, a bubble, fragile, airless, and protective.

Patrick and Heather had few complaints. With no schedule they watched a lot of TV, went to bed, got up, and got dressed when it suited them to do so. Robin read them as many stories as they wished. She played games and worked puzzles with them in the heat of the day, and at sunset she took them for a walk to get ice cream. Even before supper.

On their way back from the ice cream store, Robin exercised her imagination and consistently pictured Jon waiting at their door when they returned to Shadetree Gardens, smoking cigarettes and putting them out in the pots of dead marigolds. Sometimes she and Jon rushed into each other's arms without a word of reproach. Sometimes he apologized for his cruelty in cutting them from his life and forcing them to leave. Sometimes he said nothing of substance, only commenting on the heat as if they'd never been apart, asking her how she could stand it, and Robin turned the key in the lock and smiled and said she could not stand it, said she thought she would die in the heat.

One evening after particularly rich and sticky Butterscotch Fudge ice cream cones, Robin's stomach cramped into a knot as they rounded the corner, and in the dry twilight she saw two figures at her door. Relieved and disappointed, she recognized Renée and her mother. Robin's mother was a short stout woman who wore flower-printed pantsuits and who had maintained her bright brown hair for twenty-five years with the help of Lady Clairol. Her ill-fitting dentures clicked percussively while she talked. "It's right here," she said, waving a newspaper in front of Robin, "the perfect opportunity." Once inside she handed Robin the Help Wanted column with an ad circled in what looked like lipstick.

TYPISTS WANTED   LIGHT CLERICAL DUTIES   GOOD PAY   FULL BENEFITS

INQUIRE 10 A.M.   MR. BIBSHAW   PERSONNEL

ABC TRUCKING

"Mother and I have decided," Renée declared, "that you can't go on like this. You have to let go of the past and get on with your life."

"My life will get on whether I let go of the past or not," said Robin, handing the newspaper back to her mother.

"That's no way to talk," Renée chided her as she dropped a few old magazines on the table. Renée always brought the magazines when the shop where she worked deemed them hopelessly passé.

"He's not coming back, honey, you have to face it."

"You don't know that. Maybe he just needs time."

"But it's been two months, Robin, and he hasn't made any — he hasn't even suggested — he doesn't — "

"Maybe he needs a little more time."

"Well I don't care what Jon Vance needs," Renée sighed, "it's what you need that's important, and you need to take charge."

Her mother and Renée took admirable charge, fixed supper for everyone, emptied the trash, did the dishes, saw to the children's bath, even destroyed a small battalion of ants trotting about the sink and windowsill. Then the three women sat around the table, her mother fixing the zipper on Patrick's shorts, Renée touching up her nails, and Robin leafing carelessly through the winter and spring issues of *Glamour*, *Cosmopolitan*, and *Vogue*. "Maybe they'll start a new magazine for people like me and call it *Vague*," she said, staring at the predatory models on the covers.

"That's enough of that," her mother announced. "I'm staying here tonight and in the morning, first thing, you're getting dressed up and going to see Mr. Bibshaw at ABC Trucking."

MR. BIBSHAW had thinning drab hair and a scant mustache, and he sparkled with gold: a thick gold wedding band, a class ring, a heavy watch, and, at the edge of his smile, a gold tooth twinkled. He percolated good will as he came out of his office and greeted the thirty or so job aspirants in the waiting room. They were women of all ages, teenage girls, middle-aged matrons, young mothers returning to work. The girl who sat next to Robin wore well-pressed frayed clothes and bit her nails. Robin wore an almond-colored linen suit and Renée had given her a fresh manicure the night before; at her fingertips ten bright little plums bloomed. Renée claimed that hands gave you away, announced the sort of person you were. Renée said she could read a person's character in their hands. Robin wondered what Renée would have made of Mr. Bibshaw's puffy hairless paws. Robin's hands began to perspire and her pantyhose nettled her legs.

Mr. Bibshaw welcomed them to ABC Trucking. He said ABC was an equal opportunity employer and that the average worker there had been with the company for six years. "In these days of high turnover, that says a lot about what a fine place this is to work."

As he droned on about the job, Robin glanced out the window: ABC Trucking did not look like such a fine place. The offices overlooked an asphalt expanse where phosphorescent pools of oil gleamed. The warehouse and garage were big as hangars, tin-roofed and utilitarian. The smell of gasoline and exhaust crept even into this sealed, air-conditioned anteroom with its folding metal chairs and bowling trophies and gum stuck to the all-purpose carpet. What would it be like to work at ABC Trucking? To get up early and get dressed in nice clothes and kiss the children's sticky mouths as they watched "Sesame Street" and say, *goodbye, Mommy loves you, see you tonight*. To have your own desk and smart new typewriter and drink coffee at eleven and eat lunch at one with friends who would talk about bowling in the company league, to go to an occasional party where you'd see people from work, Mr. Bibshaw and his wife and their friends, and have a beer and a laugh. What would it be like to have a life that was all her own, that Jon Vance had no part of?

She was called back to Mr. Bibshaw's speech when he said that unfortunately they had only three jobs at the moment. "You'll all be given a typing test, and those who score highest will be called back tomorrow for interviews. My secretary will pass out the forms and you'll take the test ten at a time. That's all, ladies — good luck to each and every one of you."

The women murmured among themselves as the secretary passed out employment forms and brutally sharp pencils. Robin dutifully filled in her name, address, phone number, and age. She was 29. For marital status she first checked *M* for married and then erased it and checked *S* for separated, but the erasure left a terrible smudge, blighting the appearance of the whole application, and she asked the secretary for a new form. Robin still finished faster than most; she hadn't much experience to account for: a few jobs in college, but she left college when she married Jon and then there was a job or two while he finished his education, but after Patrick was born, she had not returned to work.

Robin was in the first group to be tested. They were shown to a windowless frigid room, with ten old typewriters lined up parade fashion, and each given several sheets of coarse paper and a closed booklet typing test. The secretary told them to take a few minutes to warm up. Immediately the air filled with gnashing, nattering typewriter teeth attacking the pages. The return bells clanged and the carriages slammed back into place, line after line, page after page. Robin's hands poised, perspiring over her machine. She hadn't anything to copy and couldn't think of anything to practice. Haltingly she typed out:

> Fighting intensifies in Lebanon. Terrorists bomb compound. Communists invade Central America. Rebel guerrillas face mounting casualties. Informed sources say the world has collapsed.

The other typewriters clacked and clattered and rang around her, but Robin turned hers off and toyed fretfully with the small heart she always wore around her neck. It was a nervous habit that betrayed her tension or indecision. Jon had given her the locket two years ago on Christmas Eve and kissed her where the clasp lay at the back of her neck. Robin said she would wear it always and she was as good as her word, except that by the following March, the gold chain had dulled to brass and left an unsightly green smudge on her skin. At first she thought perhaps Jon had been cheated, paid for real gold and received cheap brass, but she couldn't quite bring herself to mention it; and in the end she said nothing at all, accepted this small indignity and told herself it was the thought that counted. Quietly she took off the brass chain and threaded the brass heart on one of her old chains of real gold, and Jon was never the wiser.

"All right, ladies," said the secretary, holding up a stopwatch, "practice is over. Put in a clean sheet of paper and type your name in the upper righthand corner. Open your test booklets. Now begin."

The roar of competitive typing deafened Robin momentarily, as if typing were an Olympic event and these women had been in training all their lives. The test booklet contained several letters, the first one from a Mr. McCall, Vice President for marketing at a rubber company some-where in Ohio. Robin got through the formal opening without error and then began the letter.

> Dear Mr. Snow:
>
> Thank you for yours of the 22nd. Our firm, however, will not be held responsible for the damages you cite, and we will not assume the costs.

We must both share the responsibility for what's happened to us, Jon wrote in one of his terse, infrequent notes, *and we must share the costs.* It all sounded very wise and well and good and forbearing, but that was not what Robin wanted to share at all. Robin wanted to share the children and the queen-sized bed and laughter and now and then a glass of wine and a little fun after the kids went to sleep, the days and nights, the months and years.

> Our firm is willing to take whatever steps are necessary to
> come to an equitable agreement that is mutually acceptable.

Equitable agreement? Can we agree on how many small indignities make a big one? How many big ones are permissible before the marriage collapses? How could Jon and Robin ever find anything that was mutually acceptable when they never discussed anything mutually significant? Jon phoned once a week on Saturday afternoons. He asked how they were getting on, but he spurned any details. Beyond their being fine, Jon did not want to discuss, he did not want even to talk: he wanted to chat. Invariably he asked Robin about the weather and Robin inevitably replied that it was hot, that the walls of the apartment must be made of reconstituted egg shell, because they gave no protection from the sun that burned down and beat the world into an earth of brass and a molten sky and a wind that withered everything it rattled. "Yes, yes," said Jon, "it is hot here too." They agreed that it was a hot summer. And then he rang off. Robin had given up calling him back, calling at odd hours, late at night, when she expected he'd be home and he wasn't.

The job contestants tore sheets out of their typewriters and paper spewed everywhere, and the typewriter jaws were fed new sheets as they turned the pages of the test booklet and began fresh letters. Robin returned to Mr. McCall's letter.

> We value your patronage and I am confident we can
> continue to see the fighting intensify and civilians
> tortured by military regime guerrillas shell positions
> hundred seek bodies in rubble in the second straight month
> of casualties.

Robin's hands trembled over the keyboard. Something was terribly wrong. Mr. McCall hadn't written that at all: Robin was the casualty, fighting a war she didn't even know existed until she had lost it.

World collapses.

She tore the paper from the typewriter and stuffed it in her purse and left the room.

"WELL, HOW DID IT GO?" her mother called from the kitchen, where she was smoothing peanut butter on bread for the children.

Robin went into her bedroom and peeled the pantyhose from her legs, took off the linen suit and threw it on the unmade bed, went to the sink and scrubbed the make-up off her face with cold water. She dug in the drawer for a T-shirt and put it on over her slip.

"Well?" Her mother came into the bedroom, still holding the bread-knife.

"I quit."

"Oh, Robin – "

"It wasn't for me."

"Oh, Robin, honey, I know how you must hurt, I hurt for you, but you'll never be able to get on with your life unless you let go of the past; you've got to – "

"Please, Mother, I know what I've got to do. I don't have to do it just now. Thanks for cleaning up. The place looks nice. Thanks, really." She gave her mother a cheerful smile and took the breadknife from her hand.

After her mother left, Robin finished making the sandwiches and called the children from their room. She turned on the TV and found the noon edition of "Sesame Street," and Heather and Patrick sat on the floor, legs crossed, contentedly munching their sandwiches while Maria instructed Big Bird and Grover in the advantages of sharing. Robin brought the children each a glass of orange juice and returned to the kitchen, pouring some for herself, lacing it with ice cubes and a few hits of gin. She slid an ice cube down her shirt and it melted before she sank into the ample lap of the old couch in front of the TV, where a parade of things beginning with the letter *B* flashed across the screen.

"Can I have more juice, Mommy?" Patrick handed her his glass without taking his eyes from the television.

Robin poured him some more and mixed another gin and orange juice for herself. She returned to the living room and arranged the fan so it blew directly on the couch, and curled up and took long gulps, and watched five pink Muppet pigs learning to count. She stretched and wriggled her fingers and toes, but they no longer seemed connected to her body. "This little piggy went to market."

This little piggy stayed home. Maybe the numbness would spread, engulf her body, defoliate her mind, lobotomize her heart. But that didn't happen. The fetters that had held her upright and intact for months snapped open and her vow never to cry in front of the children dissolved; and while the little pigs crooned and danced, Robin wept, her mouth quivered, and the tears rolled uncontrollably down her face. Robin hungered to move to Sesame Street, to have Big Bird and Maria and Grover and Bob for neighbors, to live where everyone treated each other with kindness and dignity and mutual respect and shared responsibilities for what happened to them. She sobbed, and a guttural moan escaped her lips, and Heather and Patrick turned to look at her. Wordlessly they climbed into her lap and put their short arms around her neck, and she wept against their dark, fragrant hair. She wished they could all move to Sesame Street, where it wasn't so hot, and where the fighting did not intensify and the world did not collapse.

HER MOTHER did not suggest looking for a job again, but Renée was undaunted. Renée still believed Robin should find a new man. "Jim says there's a new basketball coach this year," she said casually as she gave Robin a manicure one night. Jim taught print shop at the local high school. "Jim likes him a lot. His name is Ted and he's just your type."

"What type is that?"

"Well, he's pleasant and funny and unattached."

"His being unattached doesn't make him my type."

"No, but we thought maybe the four of us could go out one night. You need to go out."

"Maybe I do."

"That settles it then. I'll fix you up with a date, but – " she dipped her brush carefully in Terra Cotta Rose.

"But what?"

"Well, Robin, you can hardly go on a date still wearing your wedding ring. It's September," she added pointedly, "it's been three months."

"I'll take it off sometime."

"You could put it on your other hand."

"He was my husband and I loved him," said Robin, repeating the phrase inwardly, practicing the past tense.

"Well, whenever you're ready. It's an open offer – unless of course someone else snaps Ted up in the meantime. Jim says the Home Ec teacher already has designs on him and school hasn't even started yet! You know what they say – *a good man is hard to find.*"

"Is that what they say?" Robin held out her other hand and glanced at the brilliantly made-up women adorning the covers of the magazines Renée had brought her.

> SUMMER COLORS – COOL PASTELS ARE HOT
> THE FIVE DAY DIET
> 10 WAYS TO BEAT THE HEAT AND LOOK YOUR BEST
> SUCCESS – HOW TO GET IT HOW TO KEEP IT (AND YOUR MAN)
> HOW TO FLEX YOUR LOVE MUSCLE AND HAVE POWER OVER MEN

"I'll think about it," Robin said vaguely. "I'll let you know."

After Renée left and the children were asleep, Robin leafed through the old magazines, reading sporadically. The "love muscle," it turned out, was the very one she'd been taught to exercise in childbirth classes, but now it was to be strengthened not to push out a baby, but to hold onto a man. Literally and figuratively. The author prescribed certain techniques to be repeated daily, like practicing your typing to get ready for a job interview. The exercises to strengthen your love muscle very much resembled masturbation, though the author hastened to assure her readers that this was masturbation with a purpose – rehearsal, so to speak, for the real thing. Training for guerrilla warfare of the sexes. A good man was hard to find.

Robin threw the magazine on a pile of week-old newspapers and approached the dirty dishes, but spaghetti had already dried on the plates. Discouraged, she simply filled the sink with suds and left the plates to drown. She re-adjusted the fan in the children's room, which sat on a high dresser so their little fingers couldn't find it. She turned off the lights and took the living room fan into her own room and aimed it toward the bed; the sheets fluttered, and through the open window she could hear laughter coming from the Shadetree's pool, water splashing, and the voices of men and women enjoying themselves. Robin reached for the phone and dialed Jon's number, but hung up before the first ring. It was midnight and he wouldn't be home, and even if he were, she decided, she didn't feel like discussing the weather, and that was the only topic Jon would elaborate on. Idly she wondered if Ted liked to talk about the weather. She fell asleep to the muffled rhythms of the Supremes coming from the apartment overhead.

Robin dreamed she was splashing in the Shadetree's pool and woke to hear the people upstairs clumping heavily about, shaking the thin walls – or maybe not. Maybe it wasn't upstairs at all, but farther away and rolling closer. Thunder. Thunder? She sat up and saw rain pelting the window and blowing in, dampening the sheets and dripping from the faulty window frame.

"Mommy!" Heather cried. "What's that sound?"

"Thunder, honey, it's only thunder." Lightning ripped a jagged seam through the clouds as Patrick and Heather came running into her room and climbed into bed.

"It's cold," said Patrick, pulling the damp sheet over his shoulders.

Robin laughed, "It's not really cold, only cool."

"If it's cool, can we bake today?" Heather asked. "Can we bake a cake? Doesn't that sound like a good idea?"

"It does sound like a good idea," said Robin, snuggling close to her children.

When Robin got up, she turned off the fans and the apartment was suddenly quiet, almost serene. She scrambled eggs for the children and made coffee and telephoned the manager and complained about the leaking window and asked, while he was at it, if he couldn't fix the shower head and the drip under the sink.

While the rain slid down the windows and the children watched "Sesame Street," Robin dressed in long pants and a T-shirt, and, carrying an umbrella over her head, she took the stacks of old newspapers and magazines out to the trash. She was about to step back inside when she noticed the dead marigolds and geraniums. Raindrops gleamed in the cobwebs strung among their darkened stems. Heedless of the spiders, she carried the pots to the trash, two at a time, and emptied them into the bin. Today we'll go shopping, she resolved, we'll go to the nursery and get new flowers, and we'll go to the supermarket and buy cake mix and flour and yeast.

At 9:30 Renée called from the shop. "I've only got a minute between customers, but I had a great idea and I've talked to Jim and he agrees."

"That Ted is just my type?"

"You'll have to decide that for yourself. Here's what we're going to do — we'll have a small party, very casual, just some girls from the shop and a few teachers from the high school."

"The Home Ec teacher?"

"Not her, silly, but Ted, we'll certainly invite Ted, and you come too and see if you hit it off. What do you think, Robin?"

"I don't know." Robin reached for her necklace to fidget with the heart, but the chain pulled off in her hand and the heart was gone.

"Listen, you can wear your wedding ring through your nose for all I care. You just come. Okay, Robin? Are you there?"

"Yes, yes I'll come." Robin said goodbye hastily and glanced around the kitchen floor for the heart. She checked the gold chain; the clasp was not broken, it worked perfectly, but somehow it had opened without her knowing it and the heart slid off. It could be anywhere by now, even out with the marigolds in the trash: the brass heart had unaccountably slipped its moorings and slid painlessly from her neck and she hadn't even noticed its loss. *This is the way it will happen. One day he'll slide off my life, slip off my heart, and I won't even notice until he's gone. One day my wedding ring will come off of its own accord. This is the first cool day. The summer has passed and while the heat, even the anguish, might yet mount one final assault, the cool days have returned, though the man has not. The man would not. The man will not be part of our immediate lives ever again.* Robin had endured the summer's crucible. Next week Patrick would start school, and she and Heather would walk him home and bake bread and drink cocoa, and soon they'd be making Halloween costumes and cutting up pumpkins, and the time would change too – back to standard time, to gain the hour they'd lost in the spring. The days would snap shut, no longer the lingering torrid sunsets of summer, but windows closed and lights on early; and Robin and the children would move snugly forward through the holidays and into the winter and the following spring. *This is the way it had to happen: you could not let go of the past – you had to wait for the past to let go of you.*

They went to the supermarket and then to the nursery. Because of the pouring rain, Robin left the children in the car and dashed in and selected small flats of pansies and amber mums. Once back at Shadetree Gardens, she left the flowers on the porch, right beside the empty pots, virtually in the doorway so she would not, could not ignore them. It pleased her to see rain collecting on the pansies' upturned variegated faces.

They started the baking right after lunch, kneading the bread dough and setting it to rise, beating up the cake. The cake – a splendid high chocolate confection frosted in pale vanilla – they left on the table to be admired until after supper. Heather insisted on placing a ring of Life Savers on the top, and in the process she and Patrick snagged several fingers full of icing. When the rain cleared in the late afternoon, Robin put the bread into the oven; and Patrick and Heather joined the other children in Shadetree Gardens, playing in the puddles, dragging out an endless armada of cars and dolls for their imaginary games, and tracking glorious mud through the house.

While the smell of baking bread filled the apartment, Robin put the kettle on to boil and set out a clean cup and saucer by the teapot. Waiting for the water, she read the newspaper, going beyond the dreary headlines to the columns marked Employment Opportunities. ABC Trucking was again advertising for typists. She would not try there again, whatever their inducements. As she read on, she wondered if perhaps she might not go back to school; in a year or two she could graduate and then find a job that offered a future as well as full benefits.

The tea kettle's whistle intensified into a scream and in the distance a siren shrieked, and the two urgent messages briefly, brilliantly harmonized.

"Did you hear it, Mommy!" Patrick burst through the door, clutching his toy ambulance. His overalls were damp to the knees and his face lit with joy. "Did you hear it? Wasn't it wonderful?" He waved the ambulance in front of her face. "The siren – didn't you hear it?"

"Of course."

"I was making a siren for my ambulance," he broke into an imperative wail, "and just then the real ambulance made the sound for me. Just when I did! Just when I needed it! Wasn't that exciting?" He didn't wait for her reply, but tore out the front door, leaving it ajar.

Robin poured water into the teapot and went to close the door, but stood instead, the cool breeze wafting over her, watching Patrick and Heather and the other children, small figures in the damp, gathering twilight. She was filled with an emotion so foreign, so exotic, she was afraid it might pass or perish before she could name it. Caught utterly unprepared, she only knew there are those ineffable moments when the tangible world seems resonant, yeasty with a significance all out of proportion to its mundane, visible merits. Like the real ambulance supplying the siren for the child's game, the imagined world joins the material world; the two come together and fleetingly they dignify and enhance one another. The world of hope and dream collides with the world you can touch and clutch and their union results in something very like happiness itself.

Hunters in the
Fields of August

SHE ALWAYS CLAIMED to have left Italy with only the clothes on her back: a sturdy black dress, a light woolen coat, cotton underwear, cotton stockings, black leather shoes, and a small neat scarf for her head. She had left with more than that; she had a husband and a five-year-old son, but they were – in some ways – less important than the clothes on her back and the babe in her arms, who was no babe at all, only a silk pillow cut down to infant shape and swathed in coarse woolen blankets, with a shawl covering its featureless face. The clothes on her back were not what they appeared to be either. She had carefully sewn little silk bags inside, and in these she placed nothing so flimsy and unreliable as paper money. She sewed every jewel the Zacatos possessed; and what was too big to be carried in a silken bag she broke down or traded for more portable pieces. She was a woman in a black dress, sitting on a ransom, cradling a mythical infant with tangible assets for innards.

She got out smoothly, easily, early, before the boot of Italy was itself booted and spurred, before politics determined one's worth and survival, when she might still rely on the Italians' weakness for *bambini*. This is not to say that she left with honor. She greased every sweating palm she could find. She cherished no misguided affection for the money itself and foresaw the time when the money would not only fail to protect them, but mark them indelibly as undesirables. She always said she could see the writing on the wall.

They were literally merchants of Venice, these rich Jews. Their palazzo had a garden, that most treasured of Venetian luxuries, where wisteria hung down like hothouse grapes. Humble geraniums and basil scented the air, but even so, the smell of the canal sometimes wafted over the wall.

The Zacatos were people of consequence and tradition in Venice. Sylvana's husband, Solomon, scoffed at Il Duce. "My family has been great for four hundred years," Solomon Zacato said. "Mussolini's ancestors were dogs. The Fascists will pass like sewage."

Sylvana said, "In five years we won't be able to cross the canal, let alone the Atlantic. They will kill us. They will kill our son, and then what will become of the great Zacatos? Dogs will live here and pee on your father's portrait."

Solomon cut his father's portrait from the frame and rolled it up to take with him under his coat. He also stashed his family's Menorah and Kiddush cup. Sylvana threw these things to the parquet floor. She told him to take nothing without value. "They have value," Solomon replied. "They are irreplaceable. They have more value than all the – "

"They'll kill your son," she reminded him. "They'll kill us. Hide these things and we'll come back for them after the war."

"What war? There is no war."

THERE WAS A WAR, and later they followed it closely in the American newspapers delivered to their home in Beverly Hills. The garden in Beverly Hills also had a wisteria vine, but the flowers paled and died young. "You see," she reminded him over cups of thin American coffee, "they would have killed us."

"What's the use of living, anyway, when everything you know is gone?" said Solomon.

"Are you crazy? Your son isn't gone, is he? You know him."

But in truth Solomon hardly knew Paolo at all. Not after he became Paul and played baseball; and particularly not after he went to Beverly Hills High School and then USC and dated girls with red fingernails and spoke in a fast, cryptic lingo. Paul grew tall and thin and tanned in Beverly Hills. So did Sylvana – who became Sylvie to her friends. But Solomon's skin blanched and mottled like that of a dappled fish. He hated the ubiquitous sunlight and the sounds of the traffic. He stayed as much as possible with his books in the living room, drapes closed, windows shut. Sounds of wheels – whooshing, grinding, screeching – accosted him continually. Always the brakes and horns, never the sounds of bells and water. No sound of water anywhere in Beverly Hills, except twice yearly when the raingutters gurgled for a week. Then Solomon opened the drapes and watched the rain make tiny canals through the garden. Once Sylvie found him squatting in the rain, fashioning an armada of leaf-boats.

The writing on the wall told Sylvie that Solomon was going soft in the brain like the oranges in their yard that fell from the trees and rotted to a powdery green. The Zacatos' jewelry business fell more and more into Sylvie's hands; it had been hers all along. She had conceived it and brought it forth just as surely as she carried the make-believe bambino third class on the train from Venice to Genoa. They left the city of bells and water and stone and sat on wooden benches in the third-class carriages as the train rattled over dry land. Sylvana soothed and sang to the silk pillow. Opposite her, Paolo sat, frightened into silence, having heard many times how they would kill him – presumably first. Solomon stared at his own reflection in the black windows as the train rumbled westward over the fields of August.

The train made frequent stops. Sometimes soldiers got on; sometimes they got off. They never did anything singly. Just after dawn they stopped at a village where four old women with muscular calves and knotted hands got on. The train started again, but slowly, wheezing as if the old women had infected it.

Dawn deprived Solomon of his own reflection. He looked out across the fields. Poplars stood as sentinels against the morning and sunflowers hung their heads for sadness. In the ochre uncertain light Solomon saw three hunters, men in black shirts with guns and dead rabbits hanging from their shoulders. He shook his son gently. "Come here," Solomon pulled Paolo into his arms. "Wake up. Look." He pointed to the hunters in the fields. "You won't see that again."

"Who knows what they'll hunt next," Sylvana muttered, clutching her silken bambino to her breast.

Sylvana clung to the pillow-baby even as the family stuffed themselves into the narrow, airless, third-class berth of the ship that would take them across the Mediterranean and the Atlantic. She took the baby with her even to the toilet. When she waited in line she overheard women whisper she was the crazy one.

"ME! THE CRAZY ONE!" Sylvie shouted, flushed by the rich dinner and the wine and the Beverly Hills heat. She leaned toward her four-year-old granddaughter and shouted again as if Caraleah were very far away and not at the same table at all. "The ones who stayed behind, they were the crazy ones. Me, I could see the writing on the wall."

"It's almost time for 'Gunsmoke,'" Solomon announced.

"Can't you ever miss 'Gunsmoke'?" Sylvie snapped. "I'm telling a story."

"I've heard it," said Solomon.

Dwarfed by her grandmother's massive table, Cara clutched her doll with the golden hair that resembled her own. She peered at her mother over her plate.

"You must put the doll down at meals," her mother chided her. "You must not hang onto it at meals."

"Let the child alone," Sylvie said to her daughter-in-law, Lorraine. "Believe me, Cara, you would not be sitting here today, not you or your father or your mother or your baby brother Steven, sleeping in the next room, if I hadn't held onto *my* doll. Paul's little brother, we called him." Sylvie's bosom shook with her laughter.

Solomon rose and shut the dining room windows. The breeze and the sounds of the traffic died on the rug. Lorraine turned to Paul. "Tell Cara she must put the doll down. She must do as I tell her."

Paul shrugged.

Lorraine knotted her fingers in her lap and studied her long red nails and the diamond the size of a walnut on her right hand. The ring was a present from her mother-in-law at Caraleah's birth.

"Thirty-five years ago when I married your grandfather, Cara," Sylvie said, addressing them all, "we had to fight his family. His father said, 'Not her, Solomon, she's not good enough for our family.'" Sylvie poured herself another glass of wine. "The Zacatos wouldn't have a family now if it hadn't been for me."

"Time for 'Gunsmoke,'" said Solomon, leaving the room.

Lorraine bit her lip. She said she thought she heard the baby, Steven, crying in the next room, and left.

Cara held onto her doll while Paul lit another cigarette and flipped the match into the ash tray. He missed; the match burned a hole in the lace tablecloth, and he left it where it lay.

FOR THE TWO WEEKS of the Atlantic crossing, Sylvana and Solomon and five-year-old Paolo shared the third-class berth with one another and the third-class toilet with many others. They lived in the serviceable clothes they wore. They did not bathe, and they changed only their underwear. "We stink like peasants," Solomon said. "I have never been a peasant. I have never stunk."

When they arrived in New York, Sylvana's cousin met them at the gate. They told the official they were only there to visit. The official had red hair and blue eyes and a face the color of polenta. Sylvana recognized him for a peasant, and that's when she took the silent swaddled baby who had outlived his usefulness into the bathroom, opened his seams with her hatpin, and left a small perfect emerald in the official's meaty hand on her way out of customs.

Sylvana's cousin and his family lived above their grocery store, and always the smell of brine and vegetables from the store and oil from the street rose up into the room where the Zacatos stayed for a month. "They make me sick, your cousins," Solomon told her. "They live like rabbits."

"They have a radio though," Sylvana offered hopefully.

She refused, however, to help her cousin's wife peel onions. She spent her days "making arrangements," exchanging some of the infant's golden innards for papers with signs and seals, for space at the top of waiting lists and names on documents.

Although Paolo's little brother no longer needed to live, Sylvana said it was better to be the fox than the rabbit. For the next journey she insisted they wear the same serviceable black clothing (after it had been washed; Sylvana attended to that herself, would not allow her cousin's wife to throw their clothes into the wringer washing machine so proudly displayed on the back porch). They might still look like peasants, but the

Zacatos did not travel third class on the train that took them still farther west to Los Angeles and their future – the jewelry store and the house with the pale wisteria. They had only one son, this trip, and the American train took Paolo toward Beverly Hills High and USC and Lorraine and Caraleah and Steven.

When Paul wanted to marry Lorraine, Solomon said she was not good enough for the Zacatos. Her father did not attend synagogue and cared nothing for his religion. Lorraine's father even allowed his children to have a Christmas tree. "What do we care about that?" Sylvie said. "Her father can afford to send her to USC, can't he?"

Paul met Lorraine at USC in a Dante class. He majored in business, but his grades were woeful. He did very well, however, in Dante, and always claimed that his first words to Lorraine were in Italian and that she fell in love with his accent.

She fell in love, that much was true. They were quite beautiful when they married in August, 1952. Paul, slender and graceful, danced the "Anniversary Waltz" with his bride, who had a pixie's face and curling hair of dark gold. Her blue eyes matched her sapphire ring in depth and luster, and her white lace dress cinched in at the waist and flared at the breasts and hips. They looked like the bride and groom on the top of their cake.

Lorraine's parents rented a ballroom at the Ambassador Hotel for the occasion, and the guests danced over the cold tiles. Solomon sat beside Lorraine's mother on the bridal dais while Sylvie danced with Lorraine's father. Solomon sniffed the flower arrangement in front of him. "You chose a good place," he said to Lorraine's mother, "you cannot hear the traffic in here. You cannot hear the fountains either, but at least you cannot hear the traffic."

When the bride and groom were about to leave, Sylvie enveloped Lorraine in her arms and drew from the folds of her voluminous gown a small silken bag. "I've been saving this for seventeen years," she said. The diamond in the pendant was brilliant and cold and perfect and fiery.

"All the way from Venice," Solomon added, "from my family's palazzo. This – " he waved his arm around the Ambassador's gilded ballroom, "this is nothing. Not every American girl can marry into a family that has been great for four hundred years."

"Before the war," Sylvie said to Lorraine's mother, "we left Italy with nothing but the clothes on our backs. I could see the writing on the wall."

SHE COULD SEE the writing on Paul's wall too. He cared nothing for the jewelry business. It was not in him. He cared nothing for Sylvie's sacrifices, nothing for his family; he thought only of himself. "Leave him alone," said Solomon, "he'll find what he wants to do."

He might have left the jewelry business, except that Solomon conveniently died. "It broke your father's heart," Sylvie wept into her handkerchief. "The thought of you leaving the store. It killed him. Think of your father's memory. Think of your children, think of your wife. Who will pay you as well as I do? Think of that." Paul thought. He stayed in the family business – in a manner of speaking. He stayed on the payroll, but he spent much of his time at the track and the library and he often played cards. When he did appear at the jewelry store, he drank coffee and read the newspapers in the back room while Sylvie berated him for his heartlessness: he cared nothing for his mother, who had given him everything and who was getting old and infirm. Then she would blow her nose and go out front to negotiate shrewdly with a diamond broker from South Africa, a goldsmith from Peru, and a movie mogul who wanted something sparkling for a starlet.

Sylvie aged as only successful women can age. Perfectly powdered and coiffed, she wore silk suits in summer and fur coats in winter. Her hair retained its original color against the dictates of time and with the help of a discreet, well-paid beautician. She ate well, drank modestly, swam almost daily in her turquoise blue pool, and laughed off offers of marriage. "What do I want a husband for?" she said, raising both penciled eyebrows. "At my age!"

She paid for her grandchildren's music lessons, their dancing lessons, their tennis lessons, and, with particular relish, paid for their equestrian lessons and the expensive tack and saddles, the trim tailored riding habits they outgrew each year. Cara especially had the athletic grace, the seat and natural command, of a born jumper. Sylvie attended all their equestrian events and put a trophy case in her front hall for their ribbons and medals. She said she was entitled to the medals; she was paying for the lessons.

Steven and Cara brought her unending pleasure. They were lovely. Lithe like their father, blonde and blue-eyed like their mother, they had Lorraine's petite features and Paul's serious charm. They were expensively clothed and well-mannered. "They are very American," she told Mr. Cohen, her accountant. "They go to the beach, they eat hot dogs, they drink Coca Cola, they watch TV, but they are smart, Mr. Cohen. Cara wants to be a doctor. Now, what do you think of that?"

Mr. Cohen thought it was admirable.

STEVEN'S BAR MITZVAH was held in the same Ambassador ballroom of his parents' wedding reception. Paul drank too much and Lorraine said something politically offensive to a diamond broker from South Africa. "I'm the hostess," Lorraine defended herself to Sylvie in the women's lounge. "I'll say whatever I damn want." In the beveled mirrors and softened lighting, Lorraine looked mushy and insubstantial.

"I'm paying for this and you'll say whatever *I* damn want," Sylvie retorted.

Lorraine went into a stall and sagged, weeping, against the toilet paper holder. Sylvie went back to join the guests. She watched Paul lead Cara onto the dance floor. At sixteen Cara had shed her childhood shyness and the odd, silent bookishness that sometimes reminded Sylvie of Solomon. The only thing that stood between Cara and young womanhood was the expensive orthodontic work gleaming across her teeth. She was a straight-A student, accomplished at ballet and piano, and an excellent equestrienne. For her birthday the following month, Sylvie had promised her her heart's desire: a horse, a magnificent jumper of her own.

Sylvie regarded her son, the angular middle-aged Paul. He seemed too dark, too hunched, too coarse to be Cara's father. Cara was spun from the finer cloth of dreams, the dreams Sylvana had cherished as she rode across the fields of August in the third-class carriage, the dreams that sustained her through the ocean crossing when the other black-clad mothers thought the child she cradled was already dead.

When "The Fool on the Hill" ended, Paul kissed his daughter's forehead. He escorted her back to their table and signaled the waitress for another drink. Lorraine returned restored, but still shaken. Cara asked if she could have some champagne.

"Of course," said Sylvie.

"No," said Lorraine.

The band struck up "The Sounds of Silence," and a young man asked Cara to dance. Mr. Cohen came to their table and asked Sylvie for the honor of a dance. Mr. Cohen danced with the decorous tread of the aged while nearby Cara and her partner glided by them. Midway through the song Sylvie and Mr. Cohen returned to the table where Paul leaned protectively over his drink. The martini shone like mercury impacting a jade olive. Without looking up, Paul muttered an unmistakable oath to Lorraine.

"You can shove it, you spineless sonofabitch," Lorraine said. She left without a word to anyone.

The band played "Here Comes the Sun." Mr. Cohen turned to Paul jovially. "Well Paul, when you were a boy leaving Italy in the middle of the night, you probably never thought you'd see this day, did you? What a day! What a fine son and what a lovely daughter. Who could ask for more? Such a lucky man you are, Paul."

"We didn't leave in the middle of the night," Paul said.

"We left with the clothes on our back, Mr. Cohen," said Sylvie, rearranging the orchids at her wrist so they would not conceal her gold bracelets. "That's all."

"Not quite," said Paul. His lips twisted as if speech were painful and difficult. "I had a little brother then. An uncrying, uncomplaining baby brother. Don't you remember, Mother?"

Sylvie flushed an unbecoming rose. She did not usually include the silken bambino in her accounts. It seemed an unappealing appendage to the story, though it was necessary to the truth.

"We crawled out of Italy like lice off a dead dog." Paul finished his drink.

Mr. Cohen offered cigarettes all around. "Those were terrible times for Jews."

"My mother sold everything but the masonry, traded it for jewels that she sewed into her clothes so that when she sat down, she got bit on the ass by a Cardinal's ring, and every time she bent over the baby, she got a Doge's ransom pressed against her heart."

"I didn't know you had another son, Mrs. Zacato," Mr. Cohen said.

"He died young."

"She disemboweled him," Paul said coolly.

"I think I would like to dance, Mr. Cohen."

"She made a baby out of a pillow and stuffed it with the plunder of Venice. She sang to him like he was the new Messiah, isn't that right, Mama mia? You never let him go. Even to go to the toilet, Mr. Cohen, she would not be parted from him. Such devotion. Don't you think that's devotion?"

"Mr. Cohen doesn't want to hear this nonsense, Paul. You're drunk."

Mr. Cohen stubbed out his half-smoked cigarette. "Perhaps we should dance."

But the song had ended, and people stood around the dance floor awaiting new music like it was the last train out.

"He was her *real* son, Mr. Cohen." Paul stood up. "The one with the golden guts. I am the make-believe son. He was the real one." Paul lurched away and pinched the bottom of a young waitress on his way out of the ballroom.

FOR A WEEK after the Bar Mitzvah Sylvie was sick. For the first time since the Hong Kong flu two years before, she was too weak, too dispirited to go to work. She wandered her house like a madwoman, alternately taking draughts to wake up and potions to go to sleep. She had missed the writing on this wall. It had been writ beneath her nose and she had missed it.

She called the jewelry store daily. She did not ask after Paul, but Mr. Cohen always mentioned obliquely that Paul had not come in, nor had he called. He had not been seen. Sylvie summoned all her courage and called her son's house. He was not there, the maid said; neither was Mrs. Zacato, who had taken the children and left for an unexpected holiday.

"Holiday! In the middle of the school year! Is she crazy? Cara is riding this Saturday."

"I'm sure I don't know," said the maid.

The following Monday Sylvie went to the jewelry store. She thought it would take her mind from Paul, and she was right. On Wednesday just before noon she saw him on the other side of the display window staring at the tasteful, extravagant array like any other window-worshipper. He was clean-shaven, sallow, and waxy; his eyes were shrouded behind dark glasses. He waited for Sylvie to notice him, then he walked to the curb but did not cross with the light. Sylvie excused herself to Mr. Cohen; she took her purse and left. This interview – she was certain – was best conducted outside the store. "Shall we get some lunch?" she said to her son.

They sat in the shadows of an umbrella-dappled patio. "I wish you would take those glasses off so I could see your face," she said, nibbling her shrimp salad. "You don't look at all well."

"You don't look so hot yourself."

"How are Cara and Steven?"

"Screwed. Hadn't you heard? Lorraine has left me. She says she won't come back to the house as long as I'm in it, so I'm leaving."

"What is this little trouble between you and Lorraine, Paul? I'm sure it can be patched up."

"With money? Shall we bind up our wounds with greenback salve?"

"Don't be ridiculous. I'm trying to help."

"Forgive me. Another drink here, honey," he called out to a passing waitress.

"You drink too much."

"Forgive me again."

"Sometimes you disgust me."

"Forgive me and thank you. That's all I seem to be able to say to you today, isn't it? All I've ever said to you. All you've ever heard."

"Don't push these things off on me, Paul." Sylvie bit an asparagus spear neatly in half. "If you've made a mess of your life and your marriage, it's your own fault. Not mine. I gave you every opportunity to make good. I gave you everything."

"You did. You gave me everything," he jumped to his feet and bowed from the waist, "and I salute you, Il Duce Mama!"

"Stop it you fool. Sit down."

The waitress handed him a fresh martini as he dropped back into his chair. "You're right. I have made a mess of everything. Of everything you gave me. Forgive me. Thank you. Forgive me."

"Shut up Paul. I'm willing to help."

"Excellent, Il Duce Mama, then you won't mind it when my lawyer calls you. I'm starting divorce proceedings."

"You can't divorce your own mother."

Paul choked on his olive. "Always thinking of others, aren't you? I'm divorcing Lorraine. That's what she wants and that's what she'll get. She'll get everything she wants. I've told the lawyer to give her the house, free and clear. I told him you would make the support payments and the alimony and whatever else Lorraine wants."

"Me! Why should I? They're your children."

"Yes and I hate to lose them." Without lifting his glasses he wiped his eyes. "But you won't mind paying them off. It will give you a stick to beat Lorraine with."

"Lorraine has always hated me."

"Yes."

"She'll never let me see Cara and Steven."

"Probably not."

Sylvie tapped her nails on the table. She studied her rings. "If you leave I won't buy Cara her horse. You stay or no horse for Cara, and I won't pay for any more lessons."

"You wouldn't do that to her. She might have a chance at the Olympics."

"I would."

Paul drank his martini in one gulp. "Well it will be on your head then, won't it? I'm leaving. I have my ticket." He patted his jacket pocket. "Going back to old Italia."

"Italy!"

"Yes, with nothing but the clothes on my back. Going back to see if there are still hunters in the fields and bells ringing and water in the canals."

"Don't be a fool. You can't go back. That's nothing but the past. The past can't be changed or – "

"Bought off?"

"Leave it alone, Paul."

"Ah Mother, you've become so American."

She reached across the table for his hand, but he withdrew it. "Paul," she pleaded, "don't do this. Go back to Lorraine. Take a vacation for a few weeks, a few months if you want. Take Lorraine to Italy with you. Leave the children with me. You and Lorraine take a second honeymoon – my present to you."

"It's over."

"Paul, please. Those children are my life. My breath. You can't do this to me."

"It's up to Lorraine now. I don't care if you never see them again. At least you won't have the chance to buy the world out from under them and give it back on a silver platter. At least they won't spend their lives saying *forgive me* and *thank you*. Forgive me. Thank you, thank you, *grazie mille*, Mama – from the bottom of my heart. And now, you'll forgive me if I leave you with the bill. I have a plane to catch."

Sylvana finished her shrimp salad without unseemly haste. She watched her son's thin figure weave through the Rodeo Drive crowds and vanish into the glare of the traffic and the glittering asphalt. A woman who has crossed the fields of August with nothing but the clothes on her back and a make-believe baby in her arms cannot be expected to go running after a ne'er-do-well, ingrate son or beg the forgiveness of his fur-brained wife.

She called Lorraine and suggested they have lunch one day. Lorraine hung up on her. She called back and said no horse for Cara. Lorraine hung up on her. She instructed her lawyer to call Lorraine and threaten to withhold support payments if Lorraine refused to let her see the children. Lorraine said fine. Sylvie instructed the lawyer to pay the support, but the checks were to be made out to Cara, so that Lorraine would have to ask for the money. The first check came back unendorsed, as did the second, but the third check showed up in Sylvie's bank statement for the month of July. Sylvie smiled.

THE DAY that Caraleah Zacato graduated from high school, her grandmother had a new car delivered to her door. Her mother, who worked at the lingerie counter at Saks, said she could keep the car only because she would be commuting daily to the local state university. Cara called her grandmother and said thank you for the car. She did not say she would rather have had the horse, or that she still rode jumping horses in her dreams. She said thank you for the car and forgive me for not calling sooner.

Cara saw her grandmother frequently after that. They went shopping and out for lunch or sometimes to plays; sometimes they had lunch in Sylvie's patio. Cara noticed that the display case and the medals and trophies were gone. She did not ask after them. She mentioned, instead, that her father invited her to join him in Venice the following summer. Sylvie's face did not register so much as a tremor; she asked after Cara's studies. Cara said she would never be a doctor.

Sylvie called Lorraine and invited her and Steven to come to lunch with Cara. They were punctual and had no sooner sat down in the patio then it started to rain. They waited in the living room, talking above the babbling rain gutters, while the maid cleared the lunch and reset it in the dining room. Sylvie complimented Lorraine on her hairstyle and her clothes and her job and made no reference to her shaking hands or her habit of perpetually rubbing the deepening furrow between her brows. Pixies, as a rule, do not age well.

They had a lovely lunch; Sylvie had broken out the best for them: crystal so thin it looked like threads of carmelized sugar, hand-painted plates, heavy sterling, and pale wisteria drooping in a silver bowl. She had ordered Steven's favorite napoleons for dessert and said she hoped she could come to one of his baseball games one day. Steven said any time. Lorraine dug her fingernail into a tiny brown burn hole in the lace tablecloth.

Cara writhed. She wondered if her grandmother's innards were made out of gold like the now-famous doll she had cradled out of Il Duce's Italy. She wondered if the day would come when Sylvie would demand and exact a measure of Cara's dignity. If perhaps she already had. Could Cara – could any of them – muster enough out of their own innards to resist Sylvie's expensive charm, or her stubborn claims to rightness, or her respect for what money could buy, if not happiness, something perilously close to it, sometimes indistinguishable.

Cara received a strange letter from her father. He said there was still water in the canals. He said he never heard the sound of traffic, only bells and water. He said there were still hunters in the fields of August, and they still shot rabbits.

Youth in Asia

ANDREW BRIGGS and Mrs. McCurty were unevenly matched. The college secretary was stout, resolute, ensconced behind a great wall of Oxford tradition, much as her desk was defensively fortified with African violets. Andrew Briggs, like most scientists, was impatient, even inept, with tradition, and besides, he disliked quarreling. Moreover, he'd arrived in England only three hours before, so he was particularly unsettled and disoriented.

"But you were notified," he protested for the third time. "I wrote Max Waters weeks ago and he informed you I'd only need a single's apartment. I don't want to live in family housing."

"Quite." Mrs. McCurty fondled the furry leaves of her African violets and gave her attention to some birds squabbling in the courtyard outside her window. "I did have a note from Professor Waters to that effect," she said at last, "but these arrangements were made months ago. They can't be altered on whim."

Andrew ran a hand through his shock of thick yellow hair, graying slightly at the temples. He felt suddenly transformed into a turbaned foreigner struggling with the language instead of a tanned American astrophysicist visiting Oxford to research a joint project with Max Waters. "My wife and son," he began less confidently, "aren't, didn't, won't…"

Mrs. McCurty gave him the sort of look the night nurse practices on the enfeebled, and, still stroking her violets, she handed him the key to his flat in family housing. "It's just across the street. You'll be notified when you can move into singles. Make the best of it," she added cheer-fully.

The flat was carved from an Edwardian home which, for all its solidity and austerity, still had the air of an encampment, a place where families hunkered temporarily, engendered domestic squalor, and then departed without a trace. Varicose veins of ivy gnarled around the plumbing and climbed the gray walls; drooping dahlias and hip-high mint plants lined the walk and rustled in the September breeze. Max and Andrew carried his suitcases into the main hall, where Joanna Waters stood in front of her door, babe in arms, her hair pulled under an unflattering kerchief, her soft face sharpened with fatigue. Behind her the shrieks of the Waters' two little girls echoed and the smell of overcooked vegetables seethed like a premonition of disaster. Joanna inquired after Andrew's flight and volunteered to keep some supper warm for him so he could sleep. Andrew nodded, numb with jet lag.

He pushed a pair of skates and a cricket bat off the stairwell and started up, when he felt an insistent tug at his jacket. He looked down into the impudent blue eyes of Amanda Waters. "Where's the boy?" she demanded. "Mum said Tad would be coming with you."

Joanna looked helplessly from Max to Andrew. "I couldn't bring my-self to tell her. Amanda and Tad had such fun together when we visited you in the States last year."

"Where's the boy?" At the age of five, Amanda was sturdy, pert, and freckled, her round face wreathed with red curls.

"The boy didn't come," Andrew replied soberly. "He went with his mother to California."

"Why?"

"Mind your manners, Amanda," her father reproved her. Max Waters might have been a brilliant scientist, but he was unequal to the sassy Amanda, who looked as though she might launch herself at Andrew if she were denied a response.

"Children can't understand these things," said Andrew wearily on his way up the stairs. Could adults? Before reflection could overtake him, he opened the door to his flat and tumbled into the unmade bed. Jumbled dreams snaked through his sleep: the attractive flight attendant, Mrs. McCurty and her violets, stocky Amanda Waters, a girl he'd had an affair with two years before. And flickering among these half-known faces, he caught sight of Linda and four-year-old Tad – so alike with their amber eyes and mahogany hair, Tad's small face stoic and bewildered when he had boarded the flight to Los Angeles, tightly clutching his mother's hand. Linda's eyes, wounded and accusatory, fastening on Andrew un-flinchingly and in his dreams he yet heard her last words to him: *Go to your peace and be damned.*

He woke and groped for his watch. Midnight. Nothing to eat and too late to go downstairs to the Waters'. He got up and poked about the clean spacious flat, uniformly done in serviceable blue and white and still smell-ing of disinfectant. The plumbing was antediluvian, the kitchen tiny; the desk in the living room fronted a window and offered a view of the back garden, a flagstone pathway, a tree laden with apples blushing in the moonlight. In the second bedroom he found a single child's bed, also unmade. Andrew closed that door quickly. He returned to his own room and began unpacking his few clothes, his running shoes, his notes, his figures, the reams of computer paper on which he calculated the cosmic currents of the heavens. A framed photograph of Linda and Tad taken the summer before on their Canadian vacation. Linda, in her blue denim jacket and dark blue skirt, knelt on a rickety bridge beside Tad, who wore a bright red windbreaker. Their arms entwined, they smiled at him, cheek by cheek, balancing their happiness between them like invisible fluid in an unseen cup. Andrew put the photograph back in the suitcase and locked it. He put the suitcase in the closet and closed the door. He made up the bed, undressed, and lay down in the cool sheets. He put his hands under his head and smiled to himself to hear Linda's accusations rattle like shrapnel against the impregnable bulwark of simple distance, six thousand miles of simple distance: *What is it you want?* Andrew heard himself retort, *All I want is some peace.* And now he had it. It pleased him to think how wrong Linda was; he smiled as he drifted into sleep. He had got what he wanted, and he was not at all damned. Quite the con-trary.

The moment his plane had landed and Max met him at Heathrow, a tangible peace engulfed Andrew Briggs – unmistakable, soothing, pre-dictable as a logarithm. The marriage was dead, and Andrew was free of all its ugly encumbrances – screaming scenes with Linda, tears, sneers, nasty reflections on his infidelities, guilt. Free of the burdens of marriage, as well as the burdens of infidelity – those wistful innuendoes of obligation from his latest lover, the willowy computer programmer. Andrew was safe and in England, and before him lay only untarnished vistas: the physical discipline of running, the mental discipline of science. A few beers with Max after work. No shrieking, weeping wife. No hypocritical happy posturing for the sake of the boy who responded like a seismograph to the tremors in his parents' lives. He used to vomit, Tad did; they would go on family picnics where Linda and Andrew did their best to conceal their growing estrangement, and when they returned home, the little boy went into the bathroom, retched and vomited. Linda held his head and then carried him to his room and sat on the bed with him in her arms, crooning endless rounds of his favorite song, "Hush little baby, don't say a word, Mama's gonna buy you a mockingbird. And if that mockingbird don't sing…"

Alone in the living room, Andrew always wrung his hands and longed for Monday and the clean, theoretical, blameless abstractions of astrophysics.

HIS FIRST full day in Oxford, Andrew endured a noisy breakfast downstairs with the Waters family. He sipped his coffee while Max helped Amanda struggle into her rain jacket. "We'll just walk Amanda to school and then go on to the lab," Max said.

Amanda refused to hold hands, except when they crossed busy Banbury Road. She skipped ahead and threw shining chestnuts at imaginary foes as they passed sturdy Victorian structures, whose ivy-bearded façades and upright windows testified to a century's worth of well-conducted lives inside. They turned on Woodstock Road and approached a three-story bricked and turreted monstrosity called Owl School. A stone owl perched over the door, shrewdly assessing all who passed below.

Owl School smelled of spilt milk and rubber boots and freshly sharpened pencils. The walls were dotted with pictures of owls in undusted frames; in varying stages of decay, stuffed owls moulted under glass, one along the stairwell, one above the office door, and one just over the wooden pegs where the children hung up their jackets. Max helped

Amanda off with her coat and hung it up. Amanda kissed him briskly and disappeared into her classroom. "I have to pop into the office and pay the tuition," Max said. "I'll be right back."

Andrew returned to the owls' hooded gaze until he noticed the approach of a woman who could only be described as a mass of affliction: her neck swathed in a high white plastic brace, her left hand dangling out of a taut white sling, her right leg braced with shining chrome that gave her an odd, hobbling gait. A fat hearing aid perched on one ear and she wore thick glasses. Her skin was pink and flawless, but her hair was gray and dry and just brushed the top of her neck brace. She had the air of a sensibly clothed torpedo, and she came toward him, one corner of her mouth twitching in a staccato grin. "I'm Miss Tolle." She held out her good hand and Andrew obligingly shook it. "And what's your name?"

"Andrew Briggs."

"I make it a point to meet all the new parents, but it's early in the term yet, isn't it? You'll find your little girl – boy?"

"Boy, but – "

"Will be very happy here at Owl School. The best education in Oxford. That's our motto. I've run this school for twenty-five years and my dear father did so for thirty years before that. Some of our students have gone on to be leaders, Mr. Andrews, leaders." A little girl burst through the door and ran headlong into Miss Tolle's hardware. Miss Tolle admonished her to walk quietly, to practice grace and civility, but the girl was out of sight, and Max reappeared.

"Good morning, Miss Tolle," Max said dutifully. "Nice day."

"What's that you say? Rain? Not today. Mark my words." She smiled, baring ramshackle teeth, some of which were plaited over one another. "Time for the bell. Promptness is a virtue." And with that she went upstairs, dragging her braced leg behind her.

"Ask not for whom the Tolle bells," Max whispered with a wink, "it bells for thee."

At the last stroke of nine the two men escaped Owl School and hurried toward Clarendon Labs. Miss Tolle's appearance, Max explained, seemed to alarm only adults; children loved her and seemingly took no notice of her oddities. "She lives all alone on the third floor. Can you imagine what that school is like at night?" Max shuddered. "No one but those bloody owls for company?"

ANDREW SPENT that morning happily acquainting himself with Oxford's computer facilities and organizing his work. At eleven he enjoyed a convivial cup of coffee with his colleagues (all male) and at one, several of them walked back to college for a substantial (though hardly inspiring) lunch. "Mind you watch the way we go," Max cautioned him, "you'll have to find your own way back to the flat, because I leave early this afternoon to look after the children."

At four work ceased again for tea and Andrew asked Max how the British accomplished anything at all. Max laughed. "You'll get used to it. We're very civil, but it's not the same thing as being friendly. Americans are friendly."

Andrew thought it an odd distinction to make, but found that civility over tea took so much time, it was past six before he could leave the lab. Vaguely he retraced the path Max had shown him, wandering across University Parks toward the river. Old folks walking terriers and self-absorbed young couples meandered past him; wind tousled the trees and leaves floated languidly earthward, strewing the graveled paths. True to Miss Tolle's prediction, no rain threatened, but a few clouds netted the golden light that mellowed to bronze as it plunged into the inky green water. High-spirited punters vied for space on the river's narrow turns, their shallow boats gliding effortlessly on indistinct currents. A girl in a yellow dress waved to him, and Andrew returned her greeting as he strolled contentedly along the bank. No constraints, no obligations, no one to get home to or get away from: the uncomplicated life. Beautiful bad-tempered swans eyed him and then, disappointed that he had nothing to offer, paddled disdainfully away to ambush an approaching punt and crust of bread. Across the river, light shunted through thick grasses lining a narrow footpath; and trees hung over the water, enchanted with their own reflections: morose willows, stately elms, and a Japanese plum through whose burgundy branches the light turned to blood and stained the water below. A flash of red on the opposite bank caught Andrew's eye – a hard, primary red, the color of a child's beach bucket. Glinting indistinctly through the golden-green grass Andrew thought he saw the back of a small boy in a red jacket who held hands with a dark-haired woman in a nondescript jacket and a navy blue skirt, but they they vanished behind some still-leafy shrubs.

His leisurely enjoyment of the evening seemed to evaporate, and he realized he was quite lost and getting hungry. Hurriedly he found an exit from the park, a small bricked archway that led him to an unfamiliar street. Cyclists fluttered by as he passed solid homes where potted herbs and geraniums lit kitchen windows, and the smell of cooking chops taunted his growling stomach. He headed vaguely north, hoping to meet another pedestrian of whom he could ask directions back to college, but he seemed to be the only person on foot, walking through damp enclaves of new-fallen leaves, pools of hard windfall apples and rotting summer plums that stained the pavement like soft dung. He sidestepped a smear on the sidewalk, and when he looked up, far ahead of him, he saw the backs of the boy in the red jacket and the woman in blue, their figures dappling, dissolving in the restless shadows cast by sycamores. The woman held a furled red umbrella under her arm and walked with a slight, but distinctive, limp. She bent, as if to catch the boy's words, and a shard of childish laughter rippled backward on the breeze. He followed them at some distance, noting that they did not even pause to cross streets, that cars did not pause for them, and when they turned the corner, Andrew quickened his pace slightly, disturbed to find that when he reached the corner, they were gone and he had arrived back at college and his flat. Jet lag, he thought, running a tired hand through his hair. Jet lag.

Within the week Andrew's body began operating in the same time zone as his mind. His work with Max went well. He found he could make small talk at teatime as well as the next man. Over meals in college he struck up a flirtation with a buxom graduate student from Lancashire, named Barbara, who bathed him in uncritical admiration and made him feel young again.

The first few days he breakfasted with the Waterses, but found their familial chaos, the welter of chubby arms and hands and legs, the baby's flying food, the squawk of the TV, increasingly intolerable. He preferred a peaceful cup of coffee and a slice of toast alone in his own flat, though he still walked with Max and Amanda to Owl School. Invariably Miss Tolle greeted him with a sprightly "Hello Mr. Andrews" and a mistaken inquiry after his son. When he protested, she nodded and smiled, her weak blue eyes straining to focus far beyond him. Max advised him to give up trying to correct her.

On Sunday Max and Joanna invited him to join them on a punting picnic, and Andrew eagerly agreed. He leaned back against the cushions and drifted blissfully downriver, nettled only by Amanda's insistent singing to her doll, "Hush little baby, don't say a word…" Amanda got the lyrics and verses all wrong and Andrew longed to correct her, but resisted. Max showed him how to use the punt pole correctly, and Andrew took his turn, inexpertly guiding the boat under narrow bridges and over muddy shoals where water rats scuttled. They had their picnic beside the river in a pasture where cows contentedly ignored them and noisy ducks and swans squabbled over their scraps. The cumulative effects of wine, tranquil autumn sunshine, and the undemanding company of Max and Joanna lulled Andrew into a gentle torpor: the uncomplicated life is best, he thought, flicking a fallen leaf off his nose.

He took his turn with the punt pole once again as they headed back upriver. He was more successful this time, but just as Max commented on his improvement, Andrew lost control: across a distant meadow he very clearly saw the back of the boy in the red jacket and the limping woman in blue, and a spasm of longing seized him like a minor heart attack. Helpless, speechless in its grip, he lost the pole and nearly tumbled into the water with Amanda's delighted laughter grating on his ears. Max caught the pole and Andrew sat down to recover; he gasped and inwardly struggled, but could not resist: Andrew Briggs was about to be ferried, not lazily upriver, but along swifter, more treacherous currents, toward the shores of the past where he heard, as though drowning waters rushed over his head, Linda's cold voice announcing she and Tad would not be going to Oxford with him, that they were returning to her family in California. "It's not a trial separation," she said conclusively: "it's the end."

"Yes," Andrew agreed, "it will be easier that way."

Her aplomb incinerated and she screamed like a peasant. "Easy! Easy! It shouldn't be easy! It's the death of ten years of marriage! The death of this family! Don't you understand?" She took hold of his shoulders and shook him with a strength he would not have guessed in such a small woman.

"Don't." He pulled her hands off. "Don't."

"Don't what? Don't scream? Don't cry? Don't make things difficult? Just let this marriage die peacefully? Is that what you want? Don't want?"

Andrew cleared his throat of debris, broken vows, proved-hollow promises. "Don't go to California. Stay with me and I'll break it off with – "

"Wonderful! I'm touched! I'm moved! I'm impressed! Your computer programmer can join the ranks of all the other sluts!"

"Don't say that."

"Don't say what? Sluts? Or don't remind you how many of these women there have been in the last four years?"

"Christ, don't you ever forget anything?"

"Don't you ever remember?"

He spoke deliberately. "Memory and will. That's all you are, Linda. You never forget anything and you never let anything be."

"I wish I could! I wish I could let it all be and never wonder why it is you have to screw everything that walks and why you have to make sure that I find out about it. I swear, Andrew, that's the pleasure you take in it."

"You don't understand. You don't have any imagination or compassion or understanding."

"What am I supposed to understand? I mean, what have we really got here, Andrew? Great love? Undying passion? Fathomless devotion?" Her voice rasped like a blade on whetstone.

"Cut it out, Linda."

"You don't feel any of that, Andrew." She grabbed his hands again and held onto him pleadingly. "You don't even love these women. I could understand it if you actually fell in love, but you don't. Do you? Do you love all these women you go to bed with?"

He didn't love them. He hated her. He could not say so because he was not an emotionally articulate man; he only now vaguely, abstractly, saw that his chronic infidelity was a way of saying he hated her. He pulled his hands away from hers and turned his back to her probing amber eyes.

"Well, are you in love with that simpering twit who punches your buttons? Your computer buttons, of course," she added disdainfully. He felt rather than heard her sink to the couch. "You don't love anyone, Andrew. Maybe yourself, but I'm not even sure of that."

Andrew snorted. "Hard to believe there's something you're not sure of." He turned to see her defeated, her arms folded over her narrow chest.

"I'm sure this marriage is over, Andrew," she said softly, "and if that's the case, then so be it. I'll let it be, but don't ask me to make it easy on you. I won't do that. I'd go to hell first."

"What is this if not hell?"

"Death, Andrew." Her voice began to crack and quaver. "This is death. Don't you see it? Don't you recognize it? How can you let love die without trying to save it? Ten years together! Oh, Andrew, what is it you want?" she implored.

"All I want is some peace."

She rose off the couch with the alacrity of a cadet. "Peace at any price," she scoffed, "the last bastion of cowards."

"You go to hell, Linda! Hell or California or anywhere else as long as you take your sharp tongue with you."

"Is that what you hate about me? Is it?" She drew nearer, as if she might once again physically seize him. "There must be something you hate about me so much. What? What is it?"

How could he tell her what he hated? Her certainty. Her energy. Her high spirits. Her having supported him through graduate school while she worked as a librarian. Her having insisted on the baby to complicate their lives. He hated her unerring sense of direction through life. Sure of herself. Sure of what she wanted. He hated the strength of her assumptions. He hated her very loyalty. He was not an emotionally articulate man. He said again, "All I want is some peace."

"No," she contradicted him coolly, all passion drained from her voice. "What you want is mercy killing. You want to slide out of this marriage peacefully and unconsciously and passively and without pain. You want someone to pull the plug. Well, I won't do it. I'm sure you're accustomed to women who will, but I'm not one of them. No," she pushed her dark hair away from her face, a gesture of futility since it fell right back. "If this marriage is dead, at least give it the dignity of pain and don't ask for euthanasia."

"I'm asking for peace. Is that so much?"

"Peace is for the grave."

"Then leave me to it. Leave me alone."

TWO DAYS AFTER the punting picnic with Max and Joanna, two envelopes from the States greeted Dr. Briggs at Clarendon Labs: a wistful note from the computer programmer, which he read and tossed in the trash, and a large envelope from Linda, enclosing a picture Tad had drawn and a crisp typewritten note informing him of her job possibility in the UCLA library and their new address. As nearly as he could remember the vacuous geography of Los Angeles, he judged Tad and Linda to be living about five miles from her parents, brothers, and sisters. "The whole damn Kandinsky clan," he muttered. "Her old man is probably telling her how lucky she is to be rid of me. The old lady too." He was about to shove her letter in his bottom desk drawer when a smaller envelope fell out, an envelope with a single iris on it and his name written in Linda's precise hand. He put this in his pocket, and not until his workday ended and he had fortified himself with a solitary pint in a dingy pub fronting St. Giles did he read:

Have you found any peace, my lost love? Any fine and private place? Has the death of our love and our marriage been as easy as you'd hoped? Even mercy killing still entails death, you know. Or do you?

We are both diminished by this death and always will be. Or perhaps I shouldn't speak for you. Perhaps I shouldn't be so certain that I know you well enough to do that. Perhaps I don't understand you and haven't any imagination or compassion, but I put up a good fight, didn't I? Wouldn't you give me credit for that? I willed our love to live, and I lost. Now I have to use my will and strength to make sure I don't die too. I will go on. That's my nature. Tad too. Oh, we'll hobble a bit at first, but what do you expect after an amputation? They say that after amputation you continue to feel pain in the missing limb. I continue to feel pain. I loved you so. But all that's over, and now I have to learn not to love you and to go on with Tad, and I am learning. I am even learning to forget. It will take all the strength I have, but I will do it.

And you, Andrew? What of you? Do you weep on women's naked shoulders and tell them how your nasty, willful wife left you? Do they cluck

consolingly and smooth your graying temples and kiss the mole on your
chest? Have you found your peace, and at what price?
Tell me, how have you found the youth in Asia?

The youth in Asia. Very funny. Never forget, Linda, a weakness or an in-
discretion or a perfectly understandable mistake. Never leave a wisp of
pain moribund, Linda. Andrew finished his second pint, left the smoky
din of the pub, and caught a nearly empty bus lurching up Banbury
Road. At the next stop Miss Tolle got on and he hunched down so she
wouldn't see him. He kicked the seat in front of him. Very funny, Linda.
The youth in Asia.

ANDREW BRIGGS first met Linda Kandinsky in composition class his
freshman year of college. He'd instinctively chosen a seat beside her,
drawn to her air of completeness: fresh paper, fresh pencils, fresh blouse,
and the uncluttered amber of her eyes. One day the young teacher asked
them to go home and write a five-page essay on the morality of
euthanasia. Andrew remarked to Linda on their way out of class that it
was a big topic to cover in five pages and so short a time. He declined
her suggestion of coffee, saying he had to go to the library for research.

The following day he listened with mounting horror as the teacher discussed their essays on death. When she came to Andrew's carefully re-
searched paper documenting the morality of youth in Asia, she began to
guffaw. In Andrew's account, youth in Asia lined up, acres of them with
uniform haircuts and Mao jackets; their arms linked, they chanted slogans eschewing sex in favor of Revolution. In his paper Andrew declared
that youth in Asia were extremely moral.

"You misunderstood me, Andrew," the teacher said, suppressing a last
chuckle. "The assignment had nothing to do with the Chinese." She
laughed again. "We were talking about death, about mercy killing. Is it
morally defensible?"

Andrew did not reply. He simply gathered up his things amid the
giggles of his classmates and walked out of the room. He did not return
for a week.

Later that night Linda Kandinsky found him sulking in a corner of the library. She murmured something about his perfectly understandable mistake.

"Don't mention it," he snapped. "Don't ever mention it again."

"Don't bark at me," she retorted. "It wasn't my mistake."

She turned to leave, but he grasped her hand. "Don't," he said. "Don't go."

Andrew made love with Linda Kandinsky for the first time that night. Andrew was not one of the youth in Asia. He did not eschew sex in favor of anything else, but he slept with Linda not so much out of desire, but because he wanted to imbibe, to ingest something of her strength: for all her seeming fraility, he recognized that she had strength, had it to give. Beneath her fresh blouses and narrow shoulders, the core of cast iron in Linda Kandinsky tolled like a bell when struck. He admired her for it. He envied her for it. And ultimately he came to despise her for it.

THAT TUESDAY evening, returning to college for dinner. Andrew sought out Barbara, the graduate student from Lancashire, and she made him forget all about Linda's note and youth in Asia. They went out for a drink after dinner and returned to his flat and made love with the unslaked enthusiasm of all first times. They slept together, haunch by haunch, but Andrew's dreams were troubled; he rolled over, away from Barbara, trying to escape the sound of retching that echoed in the corridors of his mind. He woke to find it echoing in the corridor of the flat as well. Barbara lay peacefully beside him, arm outflung, mouth slightly open. Andrew got out of bed and followed the awful retching down the hall. As he approached the bathroom, it faded. He got a drink of water and stared at himself in the mirror.

On his way back to bed, he passed the empty second bedroom. Cautiously he opened the door and beheld the single child's bed, the blankets still primly folded at the foot, the bleached walls damp with disuse; peeling off them like diaphanous banners of paint came shards of song: ...*don't say a word. Mama's gonna buy you a*.... He closed the door abruptly, and the pale melody ceased.

Barbara left before Andrew woke the next morning, propping a cheerful note against the electric kettle for him to find. Later, when Andrew went downstairs to go to work with Max, he found Max at the breakfast table in his robe, wanly sipping weak tea, his face drained and feverish. "I'm bloody sick," said Max.

"It must have been you I heard vomiting in the night."

"It wasn't me."

"Dad's got the diarrhea," Amanda announced. "Will you take me to school, Andrew?"

"Do you mind?" Joanna asked, as she swept up the remains of baby's breakfast. "It would be such a help to me, Andrew."

Amanda refused to hold Andrew's hand even crossing Banbury Road, but she walked beside him, chatting about Owl School and their forthcoming Sports Day. Andrew replied elliptically and only when necessary. Without Max he felt awkward escorting the self-sufficient Amanda, who waved and nodded to other children, in groups of two and three, hastening with parents toward Owl School. Amanda picked up a stick and thwacked it rhythmically along an iron fence as she sang, "…and if that mocking bird don't fly…."

"*Sing!*" Andrew cried. He coughed. "If that mockingbird don't sing…." Ahead of them and in the crush of parents and children going toward Owl School, he could see the back of the boy's red jacket and the woman in blue holding his hand; her limp was less pronounced than before, but he was sure they were the same ones. "You see that boy in the red jacket up there?" he interrupted Amanda's ruination of the song. "Is he in your school? The one in the red jacket?"

But Amanda had paused in front of a rickety garden gate, pointing to a note pinned to a milk carrier. "'No Milk Today,'" she read proudly. She remained rooted there until Andrew commented approvingly on her accomplishment, and when he looked back up, the woman and her son were gone.

He looked for them inside Owl School, but they were nowhere to be seen. Amanda lifted her chin and indicated that Andrew should unfasten her rain jacket. Miss Tolle clanked into the hall. "Good morning, Amanda. Will you be coming to Sports Day, Mr. Andrews? I always urge the parents to come. It means so much to the children."

"My dad and mum are both coming," Amanda declared, "and Sybil and the baby too. I'm going to win a red ribbon." She took the hand of

Miss Tolle's good arm. "A red ribbon means you've come in first. You've won." They smiled confidently before they left him among the jackets, the furled umbrellas, the all-seeing, unseeing stuffed owls.

That evening, walking back from dinner with Barbara, Andrew knocked at the Waters' flat. He could hear Amanda bullying Sybil in the background. Joanna opened the door; Andrew inquired after Max's health and added that he couldn't possibly walk Amanda to school the next day: he was leaving for the lab very early. Joanna kept nodding, covertly eying Barbara. That would be fine, she agreed; tomorrow was Owl School's Sports Day anyway.

Barbara left his flat before dawn again. Andrew got up and made himself a cup of instant coffee, which he drank at the desk overlooking the small shared garden. Frost limned the grass and a thick, chill mist jelled the air.

Andrew only half-finished his coffee, then buttoned his jacket and left the building, walking the deserted streets, passing drawn-curtained unlit windows. Cats in doorways eyed him furtively and continued licking their paws as, cold and vulnerable, he hurried through the enveloping murk. Occasional footfalls dogged his steps, but proved to be only the sad *plops* of windfall apples. Granular and oppressive, the mist magnified the crunch of his shoes as he ducked under the now familiar archway and crossed the graveled paths of University Parks. Fog shrouded each tree, lay like a quilt of foreboding over fallen leaves and frosted grass, so heavy he could not even see the massive buildings of the lab, but near the distant deserted tennis courts – a flash of red – shot through the impacting dampness. A flash of red. A swirl of blue. The woman and her son. Their backs to him, they walked hand in hand, her limp still perceptible. He could not take his eyes from them, but he assured himself that the laws of physics would not tolerate such ambiguity: Linda and Tad were living in Los Angeles near the whole damn Kandinsky clan. He knew that to be true, and the truth comforted him, but when the woman stopped and knelt before the boy, he unwillingly hurried his pace: a glimpse of their surely foreign, unknown faces would comfort him even more than the unambiguous laws of physics. The woman's blue skirt brushed the ground as she pulled the boy's hood over his head and kissed his chin, but her face blurred like watercolor as the mist thickened into rain; her face was blocked from his view altogether as she opened her umbrella and put it over her shoulder.

Andrew Briggs began to sprint, running after the whirling brightness, the vortex of red umbrella that sucked him into their wake, knowing that the laws of acceleration were surely on his side and that he would, he must catch up to them, but their figures diminished, though their voices seemed to remain constant. Hovering high-pitched voices in unison, aimless musical notes, firm and rotund as windfall apples, coalescing into translucent lyrics: *...Mama's gonna to buy you a diamond ring....* "Linda!" he shouted, hating himself, speeding up. "Tad!" He broke into an ungraceful gallop, his fists clenched, "Linda! Tad!" smashing through the fog.

...And if that diamond ring don't....

"Linda, Tad! Wait for me! Please!"

But the laws of physics, the equations known to govern mass and acceleration, failed Andrew Briggs. He found himself, hot and breathless, face to face with the unmistakable solidarity of Clarendon Labs, where a charwoman greeted him cheerfully and commented on the early hour.

DR. ANDREW BRIGGS told himself that Oxford was a small town, really, and that if one kept to the same routes, one was bound continually to see people whose lives and schedules coincided with one's own. He quit walking with Max and Amanda in the mornings and consciously, carefully chose roundabout routes to and from work, but still he saw them: their dark heads, their clasped hands, their brave metronomic stride. When he went running, he took off in different directions, getting hopelessly lost more than once, not caring, concentrating solely on the demands of his own body, but he saw them just the same: the woman, unlike every other female in Oxford, carried no bag at all, only the red umbrella, her limp now gone and their pace correspondingly quickened. He ran once all the way to an abandoned nunnery far out of town, so exhausting himself that he had to take a bus back into Oxford; and as he collapsed, panting in his seat, he saw their backs among the ruins. They never spoke to anyone else; they remained complete unto themselves, always beyond him, on the opposite side of the river, down alleys where the boy's red jacket clashed with rusting ivy climbing up sooty walls; they vanished into bricked courtyards and thread-like lanes that dead-ended at the river. The same wind that ripped leaves from the trees blew the boy and the woman across Andrew's path and blew them away again. He and Barbara bundled up one day, borrowed bicycles, and went for a ride on Port Meadow, and he saw them again – within calling distance and utterly out of reach. Andrew hastened his bicycle onward, and Barbara pedaled hard to keep up with him as he turned an unexpected corner and rode on and on, past a sleepy churchyard, so old that the dead lay forgotten, their graves unembellished with flowers; there, defying the laws of mass and acceleration, he saw them again fleetingly framed by mossy headstones, their small figures bobbing, their direction unwavering, their destination assured.

Andrew dreaded leaving his flat, or, once he got to work, he dreaded leaving the sanctified halls of Clarendon Labs because the woman and her son flickered across his vision over distant bridges and in grassy quadrangles; on rainy evenings he caught them moving briskly under heavy arches, so close he could hear the smart tap of the woman's boots on uneven stones. He lost them among lunchtime crowds of students, released like tiny molecules into the city's stone capillaries. He lost them under the vaulted ceilings of the market, where they dissolved among the Saturday shoppers, the beefy vendors, the smells of roasting coffee and decaying organic matter. He lost them in the fog and the rain and the traffic. He lost them again and again.

MAX WATERS got well, and Amanda won her red ribbon on Sports Day in the skipping race. She pinned it to her lapel for two straight weeks and brought it to the attention of anyone who might be so callous as to ignore her victory. She so annoyed Andrew that he could not tolerate her mere presence, and his association with the Waters family dwindled into civilities exchanged on the stairwell. Andrew still saw Max at the lab, but their working relationship grew so brittle as to undermine their collaboration. Once, as they were charting a computer print-out, Andrew tried to tell Max why he so detested Amanda, admitting that it was foolish and horrible to feel that way about a little girl, but – and – and – Max regarded him askance. "And?" Max asked. Andrew floundered impotently, became grossly inarticulate as he tried to explain how it was that he blamed Amanda for the shards of lullaby that punctuated his dreams and the nocturnal pitiful retching resounding down his long hall.

Barbara too ceased to please him when their relationship reached that inevitable point where she began making assumptions rather than requests. He broke it off tactfully with her, using the line he'd rehearsed for four years: "I'm a married man," he said, "and I feel guilty." He expected that like all the others, Barbara would agree tearfully that they couldn't go on hurting people, much as they might love each other.

But Barbara greeted his announcement casually, adding, "You haven't the air of a guilty man, Andrew, not that odor of domesticity that doesn't quite come off with the clothes." She shrugged, "It's all the same to me. I don't take these things seriously."

Neither did Andrew, but with Barbara and the Waters family effectively out of his life, an awful isolation set in; he found himself without family, friends, or cohorts, stranded and alone in a foreign country. His colleagues at the lab, civil over tea, did not include him beyond that congenial hour, and the pleasures of the uncomplicated life paled for him. Evenings were worst. Returning to his spacious empty flat after dinner in college, he tried to work and couldn't. He tried to read and couldn't. He tried to sleep, only to stare at the high-ceilinged darkness of his room. He took to going out drinking at night, frequenting a few favored pubs and striking up conversations. He learned to play darts with unemployed pink-haired youths and participated in intense political discussions with well-coiffed undergraduates. He found if he drank enough, sleep came to him and he did not have to search for it.

At Cornmarket Street one night, Andrew and a group of drunken, roistering students boarded a bus and called cheerful obscenities back and forth to one another as one by one the students alighted. By the time the bus reached North Oxford, Andrew was the sole remaining member of his company and rather embarrassed to have been so loud and noisy and drunk in front of the bus driver, who regarded him critically in the mirror. He burped and cursed again as the bus went up Woodstock Road instead of Banbury, realizing that he'd have to walk those extra blocks and even the liquor couldn't protect him from the November cold that cut like a scalpel through his clothes, slicing his flesh to the bone. The bus halted, the driver said something unflattering, the doors opened with a hiss, and Andrew stepped out. The bus pulled away, and through the grainy veil of exhaust and alcohol, he saw he was opposite Owl School; to his horror, he beheld Miss Tolle hobbling along the sidewalk. In the light that fell through naked branches, her white brace and white sling shone irridescently. She called out to him. He ignored her. But she clanked quickly, and against all the laws of physics, she caught up with him.

"Good evening, Mr. Andrews. We were quite disappointed you didn't come to Sports Day. Quite the most successful one we've ever had. You would have been proud of your little boy, Mr. Andrews. Proud indeed. Oh yes, that reminds me – it wouldn't do for me to forget anything about Sports Day, would it?"

"Look, Miss Tolle, you don't understand. My boy is in Los Angeles. He was never here. My boy is six thousand miles…" He shouted at her impassive, indulgent smile. "Oh, never mind. Look, it's late and I'm drunk and I'm tired and all I want is some peace and I'm going home."

"No, Mr. Andrews. You must come with me. I have something for you." She took his arm and escorted him through the school's gate, nattering about Sports Day in the odd, unconnected quack of the near-deaf. He stood beside her, shivering under the stone owl as she opened the door with a heavy key. She switched on the overhead light. "Just have a wait here, Mr. Andrews. Shan't be a moment."

"Miss Tolle, you've got it all wrong, I – "

She smiled at him, her broad face perched on the pedestal of her neck brace. "Now now, you wait here." She thumped up the stairs, her un-natural tread disappearing into the dark upper reaches of the old house.

Andrew lowered himself into a diminutive chair. He could not bear to return the punitive gaze of the stuffed owls, so he kept his eyes riveted on the few leftover jackets hanging from low pegs. Among them was a red windbreaker.

Miss Tolle descended noisily. "Here we are, Mr. Andrews. Now, that didn't take a minute, did it?" She held out her good hand, her puffy white fingers curled up. Andrew stared, not quite knowing what she expected. "Take it, Mr. Andrews. It's yours. It's your son's." Into his hand she

dropped a bright red ribbon, like a soldier's decoration. "Your boy won
it on Sports Day. He won the jumping race! Pity you didn't come. So
proud, he was. His little face just lit up. That's why he forgot his ribbon,
I expect. Too excited. And Mrs. Andrews was just thrilled! She picked
him up and kissed him and whirled him into the air!" Miss Tolle clucked
approvingly, "Americans are so demonstrative and friendly."

"My son – " his tongue swelled up, ballooned in his mouth, "is not – "

"What's that?" She pointed to her hearing aid; behind her glasses her
pupils spun, contracting in pools of opaque blue. "What, Mr. Andrews?"

Stupidly Andrew pointed to the red windbreaker. "Is that my son's
jacket?" he asked thickly.

"Is it?" She looked surprised. "You should know better than I."

Andrew stumbled out of Owl School clutching the bit of ribbon. Once
past the stone owl, once past the gate, once the cold air struck and refreshed him, he broke into his old athletic run: fists doubled, eyes straight
ahead, concentrating on the distance, drinking in gulps of air to thin the
alcohol in his blood, his heart racing to keep pace with his flying feet.
He ran forward, but tripped on a sidewalk tile, fell, and when he came
up on all fours, headlights careened wildly into the street, illuminating
in the distance the figure of a woman in blue kneeling before a boy in a
red jacket. For the first time they turned their faces to him, the boy's stoic
and bewildered, the woman's wounded, accusatory and tearful; cheek by
cheek, the ghosts met his eyes, balancing their disappointment between
them like invisible fluid in an unseen cup; and then the headlights passed
and they all drowned in darkness.

MRS. MCCURTY left a summons in Andrew's mailbox, and he found
her reigning over her immaculate desk and still fondling her violets. "Ah,
Professor Briggs. I have good news for you. Would you like to take a seat?
You don't look well."

"I'm hung-over."

"Are you growing a beard?"

"None of your damn business."

She bristled at this and tossed a paper in front of him whose contents
he could not quite make out. It read in part like the Magna Charta.

"What's this?" he grunted.

"Your transfer, Professor Briggs! Your flat in singles' housing. You can move tonight if you'd like. It's all ready for you. Did you hear me? You should be pleased. You're getting what you wanted."

Andrew crumpled the paper and gazed out the window. "All I wanted was a little peace," he said finally. "It didn't seem so much to ask. Just peace at any price. No more struggle and no more pain. I guess you can't have death without struggle or pain. Maybe you can't have life, or anything else worth having, without struggle or pain, but I couldn't...I just wanted it over with."

"What are you talking about, Professor Briggs?"

Andrew rose to his feet. "I'm talking about youth in Asia, Mrs. McCurty. Can't you see them, lined up out there?" He pointed to the window, the stone courtyard, the river beyond. "Acres of them, Mrs. McCurty!" he shouted. "Shoulder to shoulder in their Mao jackets! Chanting slogans! I'm talking about the morality of youth in Asia!"

"Have they any particular morality?" she inquired, as if they were about to embark on an academic discussion.

THAT EVENING Andrew Briggs ate a solitary meal in a local Chinese restaurant and walked back to his flat. He thought about stopping at the Waters' flat to tell them he was moving; he had his hand poised to knock, but thought better of it and went upstairs to pack.

The flat was dank and cold, but he didn't bother to turn on the heat. He withdrew his suitcases from the closet and opened them on the bed, confronting the framed photograph of Tad in his red windbreaker and Linda in her blue skirt. He buried the picture under his sweaty running clothes. He hadn't much else to pack; his books and computer print-outs were at the lab, so he threw in some shoes and shirts and dirty socks. He went to the dresser to get his underwear out of the drawer, and there, on the top of the dresser, lay the red ribbon. He was not an emotionally articulate man, and for lack of any better response, he once again cursed Amanda Waters. He walked down the long hall to retrieve his toothbrush and razor from the bathroom, turned on the light, and beheld himself in the mirror: a pale, unshaven man whose sunless roots dangled almost visibly from his body. It was too late to retreat from that death he had selected, too late to regain that mortal coil of family without which we are amputated from fleshly connection, from strife perhaps, but from growth as well. The past could not be altered, and so, neither could the future. Diminished by the death of their love, he and Linda would nonetheless go on. Certainly Linda would go on. The core of cast iron in her would not permit her to do otherwise. Linda Kandinsky Briggs would go forward, unhurried, assured, accompanied by her unerring sense of direction through life and by her son. And Tad? Tad would grow up. All boys do. He would grow up and out of his bright red jacket.

Andrew grabbed his toothbrush and razor and walked slowly back to his room, where he flung them and his underwear – and the red ribbon – into his suitcase and snapped it shut. He left the flat, door ajar, half-hoping that the shards of shattered lullaby would yet follow him to singles' housing. He no longer feared meeting the ghosts he had created. He feared not meeting them. Because when they ceased to haunt him, he would be truly alone, and the peace he so assiduously sought would close over him forever.

The Last Page

R EBECCA JENNER retained her second husband's name, though she had only been married to him four months and four days. At least Jenner had a clean, harmonic ring to it which her first husband's name, Bukowski, did not. Her marriage to Bukowski took place the day after Becca's high school graduation, lasted eight years, and brought her a daughter, Sasha, and a son, Jason. Sasha – upon reaching the volatile stages of puberty – suspected an enemy in her mother and chose to live with her father and his second wife. Jason, at eleven, regarded his mother with a mixture of curiosity and chagrin, which is the way most men regard most women anyway. Becca and Jason lived in a rented clapboard house with poor drains and rickety rain gutters, across the street from the county hospital where sirens blared day and night. After six years, Becca hardly even heard the sirens; they no longer woke her at night, and she had ceased speculating on the sorts of human dramas the ambulances might be coming from or going to.

Becca's own thirst for drama was slaked by reading. An inveterate, voracious, democratic reader, she no sooner closed one book than she opened another. Becca took most of her reading from the Book Bin in the ladies' lounge of the insurance company where she worked as secretary to two junior executives. (She had moved up from the typing pool in a mere eighteen months.) In fact, Becca had founded the Book Bin after the break-up of her second marriage, when she went on a cleaning rampage and brought boxes of once-read books to the ladies' lounge. Now all the women (from the typing pool girls to the President's secretary) contributed to and borrowed from the Book Bin: dog-eared romances, well-thumbed best sellers, books with tattered pages and broken spines and coffee stains on their soft covers, if indeed they still had covers. An informal reviewing system developed among the borrowers. Scrawled on the inside front covers you could often find pithy comments like: "Don't bother," or "Chapter 39, yum, yum," or "Forbidden love, my ass."

On her lunch hour on Monday Becca took from the Book Bin *Salome*, *The Tollbooth Mystery*, and *The Unwilling Heart*. Before she left the office she returned *The Tollbooth Mystery* because a previous reader wrote, "Hubert did it" on the title page. On Tuesday she returned *Salome*, concurring with the reader who had commented on the last page, "John the Baptist probably had it coming."

On Wednesday after supper Becca told Jason if he wanted to use the bathroom, do it now. Then she locked the door, filled the deep, old-fashioned tub, added a few drops of lavender bath oil, pinned up her hair, and got in with *The Unwilling Heart*. She studied the cover picture of a young woman looking perplexed and elated. Becca could tell she was elated from the little stars in her green eyes; and the perplexity went without saying, since in the background a casually elegant man lounged against a rose arbor. The roses were a vivid crimson.

Steam wafted around her, wilting the pages of *The Unwilling Heart* as Becca began to read. *Heathurst Hall stood just as Angela imagined it might, grand, glorious, venerable, its outbuildings sprawling into the vast garden, and soaked in the golden light of sunset. I hope I shall be in time for tea, Angela thought, for she had had nothing to eat all day and her journey was a long one. Angela thought Heathurst Hall far too big for just one old woman – and then corrected herself. As Lady Stemhope's companion, it would not to do think of her as an old woman.* However, Lady Stemhope was indeed an old woman, crotchety, difficult, of very great means and uncertain health. Her nephew, Trevor (her only direct heir and the only child of her dear, dead brother) came frequently to visit. Trevor was sullen and unapproachable and Angela at first suspected him of base intentions: keeping tabs on his Aunty's health so that he might swoop down on her fortune when the old woman croaked.

"Trevor": Becca fondled the name as she added more hot water and sank deeper into the tub. Angela was clearly the girl on the front cover. Becca read on. *Against the very fiber of common sense and her unwilling heart, Angela anticipated Trevor's visits far more than she should. They seldom spoke, but Angela's nerves quivered at a glance from Trevor's flashing eyes.* Angela longed to believe that she had misjudged Trevor; perhaps he was only cranky and overworked, to say nothing of being tall, dark, handsome, and single. But he would not be single for long, Lady Stemhope proudly informed Angela as they had their tea in the library: Trevor had a lovely fiancée named Miss St. John.

On a rainy day in June, Trevor found Angela in the library, where she was cataloging Lady Stemhope's botanical books. Trevor offered her his hand to help her dismount the library ladder, and Angela hurriedly removed her spectacles and then reproved herself for this vanity. He glanced furtively around to make certain they were alone, then pulled Angela into the velvet green drapes and whispered fiercely, "I have reason to believe a man will be coming to see my Aunt who must not be allowed an audience. If you have any regard for my Aunt's health, you'll heed me and insure that Mr. Duckworth does not get past the French doors." Trevor released her roughly at the first sound of Lady Stemhope's tapping cane, leaving Angela flushed and breathless.

Becca grimaced when the phone rang. "It's Grandma, Mom," her son called.

"Tell her to call back."

"She says you never have time for her and she won't bother you anymore." Jason recited his lines like a veteran actor and Becca responded on cue. She marked her place in *The Unwilling Heart* and got out of the tub, put on her robe and woolly slippers. The drain protested noisily as she shuffled out of the bathroom.

"Your father is a heartless slob," her mother snuffled into the phone. "I'm the one with arthritis and he still expects me to pick up after him. I wish I could retire! Can I? There's no rest for me. What about me? Do you think he cares?" Her mother blew her nose. "You're lucky, Rebecca. You're lucky you don't have to pick up after a man."

This was not a new conversation, and privately Becca agreed; but instead she said, "Really, Ma, I'd give anything to have a marriage like you and Dad. I have to go now, Ma. I have to check Jason's homework."

She checked his homework and told him to go to bed. From the living room she could hear the distant whimper of the TV in Jason's room, but decided to be deaf. She poured herself a glass of wine and snuggled into the overstuffed chair with *The Unwilling Heart.*

Lady Stemhope fluttered, "Miss St. John, I'm so tremendously glad you like Heathurst Hall, since it will one day be your home." Angela poured the tea and handed a cup to Miss St. John, who accepted it with cold disdain in her Wedgewood-blue eyes. Trevor thanked Angela for his cup, but clearly he had eyes only for Miss St. John, who had crimson painted nails and a huge engagement ring. Angela stared miserably at her own unembellished hands.

Becca got up and refreshed her wine glass, wondering if Miss St. John would die a violent death or commit suicide, though *The Unwilling Heart* did not seem that sort of book. She never permitted herself to read ahead, but Becca reasoned that she might sleep better if she were assured of a happy ending, despite these unpromising beginnings. She returned to her chair and flipped forward, but on the last page her eyes were riveted not to the novel's conclusion but to a note scrawled in handwriting ironed to a vicious slant and tiny enough to fit on the last page.

He hit me like I knew he would and then he left. That's 5 days ago now and he ain't back. What do I care? Oh, I care. Plenty. I always cared and loved and worked, but I'm done with it. I'm done with everything. Sick of it. Finished. I cant go on living with my husband no more and I cant live without him. Not with 5 kids. How am I sposed to manige? But I've loved that man and that's why I've took it all these years. Loved him from the beginning. And now this is the end. 17 years. And not a day without diapers, or a penny to spare, or a beer can that wasn't rung dry, or a bed that wasn't wet, or a time I didn't have to go to work and come home to it too. He's hit me before. He's left before. But he always come back. He never stayed away five days. It's different this time. I know. I cant take it. I cant take watching them boys grow up just like their old man. That Davy especially. I can see it in my oldest boy especially. There's no excape for Davy. No excape for me even if the old man does come home. I'll die if he dont. I'll probably die if he does. I should of told him I don't care who yr. screwing anymore, just come home and bring yr. paycheck. I cant make any money and I cant face raising them 5 kids on my own. I cant face living. Dying's easier. I've worked my whole life and never had enuff of nothing. I earned my day of rest even if I have to die to get it.

Becca read this, the last page, a half dozen times before its full significance assaulted her, then she reached for the phone, regardless of the late hour. She rang up Netta Ernst, who had been in the typing pool for three years, longer than anyone. Becca kept moistening her lips and stumbling over the words as she read Netta the last page. "Who is it? There's no name in the book. Who left it in the Book Bin? Who read it last?"

Netta didn't know, but she said to bring *The Unwilling Heart* to work the next day and maybe she could recognize the handwriting.

But she couldn't. No one recognized the cramped, fierce scrawl or knew where *The Unwilling Heart* came from, and no one else had read it. The typing pool buzzed with questions and the women regarded one another with renewed affection, sympathy and camaraderie in the face of this anonymous suffering. They concluded that the author of this terrible note was a woman who had already left the insurance company; girls did it all the time, some without notice and without having made any friends. Maybe the author was Mary Sparetto, who sometimes came to work with bruises before she was fired for being late all the time. No, said Becca, Mary's oldest child was a girl. Someone suggested Ruby Washington, who left a few weeks ago, sullen and unhappy as when she came, but Ruby had only three children. Netta thought maybe it was Ethel Frank, who was some years older than the others, brassy and efficient, and had five children. But Ethel's husband had left years ago and someone else had seen her at a weekend garage sale and said she looked fine.

On Friday morning Becca went to Mr. Ingalls, the Personnel Director, a carefully coiffed young man who wore pale suits and loud shirts. Like all the men in the insurance company, he had pictures of his wife and children dotting his desk (but Netta swore he kept more than typing scores).

Mr. Ingalls greeted Becca cordially and asked how he could help her. She said she'd like to have a look at the files of recent typing pool employees to see who might have five children and an oldest boy named Davy. Mr. Ingalls said it was impossible and a strange request indeed.

Becca handed him *The Unwilling Heart*. "Read the last page," she commanded, though she had not meant to take that tone.

Mr. Ingalls blanched. "To the best of my knowledge, none of our former employees has died recently."

"She may not be dead yet. Maybe this was a warning. Maybe she wanted someone to read this note and save her."

"And how would you do that?" inquired Mr. Ingalls, raising his eyebrows.

Becca had not considered this. "We have to save her," she said stubbornly.

Mr. Ingalls said he would be happy to save her, but it was against company policy. "Besides," he added, "there's no date. That note might have been written years ago. Look how old the book is." He laid *The Unwilling Heart* on his desk and they gazed at the blonde Angela, the crimson roses, and the water ring defacing Trevor. "People who write about suicide," he assured her as he showed her to the door, "seldom commit it."

When she left work on Friday, Becca locked *The Unwilling Heart* in her desk drawer, to protect it, though from what, she could not say. She took nothing home to read because lately the sirens screaming past her house broke her thoughts by day and punctuated her dreams at night, leaving her sleepless and listless. She returned to work on Monday certain that the author of the last page would secretly reveal herself. Maybe standing at the ladies' lounge sink, Becca would stare into the mirror and see the woman at the next basin staring back, a tired-looking woman with puffy eyes and sad, pinched lips. The woman would glance along the floor to make sure the stalls were empty and then she would surely whisper, *It's all right now.* Her face would soften and suffuse with light. *My husband's come home and he promises to be faithful and even Davy's not the trouble he once was.* Becca would embrace her and promise to keep her secret.

But the week passed without incident. Two girls quit the typing pool and two more were hired. The new ones were told the story of the last page, but it ceased to have the currency of newly minted news. Though several girls asked to borrow *The Unwilling Heart* when Becca finished, she could neither part with the book, nor bring herself to finish it, though she knew she inevitably must and would. On Friday she took the book home, hoping that something in the novel itself might offer a further clue to Davy's mother's identity.

Becca watched TV with Jason until his bedtime and then, when the house was silent, except for an occasional groaning pipe or screaming siren, she returned to the novel. *Angela was in the library when the butler announced a Mr. Duckworth and ushered him in. The butler then withdrew to tell Lady Stemhope she had a visitor. Angela rose, surprised to find that she towered over Mr. Duckworth, who was plump as a pudding, with eyes hard as currants, skin lumpy as porridge, and a mouth that reminded Angela of a string bag. Fearfully, she remembered Trevor's warning. Coldly she inquired, "May I ask the nature of your business?" Mr. Duckworth regarded her scornfully. "I am Lady Stemhope's long-time friend and family solicitor." He took a seat by the fire and would say no more. When Lady Stemhope hobbled in, they greeted one another warmly. Lady Stemhope ordered Angela from the library. She left as she was bidden, but against every rule of good breeding and ladylike conduct, Angela found herself listening at the keyhole.* Becca fell asleep there at ten-thirty.

On Saturday morning Becca put a snake down the kitchen drain to clear it and used the plunger on the sluggish bathtub. She picked up the dry cleaning and did the grocery shopping and got gas for the car, thought about washing it, but decided not to. She told Jason if he didn't clear up his room to her satisfaction, he couldn't go to the movies that evening. He did clean it up, not to her satisfaction, but she took him and his friend to the movies just the same, so she could finish *The Unwilling Heart* in solitude. The friend's mother agreed to pick the boys up and take them out for ice cream afterward.

Becca got into her red flannel nightie, poured herself a glass of wine, and climbed into bed with *The Unwilling Heart*, reading the heartbreaking last page once again before returning to the novel. *From her post at the keyhole, Angela heard words that burnt her ears and heart. The pleasantries past, Mr. Duckworth began, "Lady Stemhope, would that I could spare you this revelation, but it is my grim duty to tell you that your nephew, Trevor, is not your nephew at all, but the bastard brat of a cheap shop girl.* Duckworth elaborated: Lady Stemhope's feckless brother had bought the young slut off with a few shekels and raised the boy as his own, using him to secure a place in Lady Stemhope's affections and thus gain access to her money and Heathurst Hall. The brother's childless wife not only went along with this plan, but (Duckworth intimated), it may all have been her idea in the first place. Alas, both the ingrate brother and his grasping wife died in a motoring accident, leaving young Trevor as his Aunty's sole heir. Mr. Duckworth had proof of his allegations. The shopgirl, he said, now penniless, aging, and more tawdry than ever, had turned up at his chambers with her story and her hand out for money.

The watercress sorbet lay untouched on Angela's plate at dinner that night. She could not eat, and watched amazed as Lady Stemhope plowed through her food with unusual greed and gusto. Lady Stemhope wiped her lips with a flourish. "Angela," she said sharply, "if Trevor calls or comes to Heathurst Hall, you must tell him that I am indisposed. I never wish to see him again." In the following chapter (and after a sleepless night) Angela went into the village to post Lady Stemhope's letters as was her custom. Trevor was waiting for her, his handsome features eroded with pain – which only made him more attractive to Angela.

Suffering men. Becca's lip curled as she got out of bed and poured herself another glass of wine in the kitchen. What woman can resist a suffering man? What man can abide a suffering woman? She glanced at the wine and decided to take the whole bottle back to the bedroom with her. She put it on the bedside table next to Sasha's photograph.

Trevor and Angela lunched in the darkened corner of a noisy pub. Angela longed to touch his hand, smooth his brow, ease his sorrow. (Did Trevor ever give a thought to Angela's sorrow? Becca wondered. What about Angela?) *Painfully Trevor confessed, "I am indeed the offspring of that shopgirl, but I am also my father's only son, born out of wedlock, it's true, but conceived in love. That scheme was the only way my father could think of to bring me into his home, to raise me as his son, to get me past that childless shrew I had to call 'Mother.'"* Further, Trevor assured Angela, Mr. Duckworth knew the truth and feared it: if he could convince Lady Stemhope of her nephew's bastardy, Mr. Duckworth stood to inherit Heathurst Hall. Trevor concluded that he loved his low-class mother and would never disavow her: better to live without his aunt's money than to stoop to the dishonorable. *Lowering her eyes so that Trevor should not see the love shining out of them, Angela replied, "Virtue knows no price, and love, however humble, should always be rewarded."* For one electric moment Angela thrilled to his touch as Trevor pressed her hand with his own, murmuring, *"I knew I could trust you, Angela. You have an understanding heart."* (What heroine doesn't? Becca scornfully fluttered the remaining pages. Understanding hearts were required of fictional heroines; when they were required of real women, the toll was altogether different.)

Predictably *The Unwilling Heart* finished in a satisfactory manner. Miss St. John – upon being told that Trevor would not inherit Heathurst Hall – dumped him. Lady Stemhope was apprised of the truth by the shop-worn natural mother herself, who cared nothing for the money, but could not bear that Lady Stemhope should think ill of Trevor or his sainted father. Mr. Duckworth was banished. Trevor cornered Angela in the rose arbor and planted passionate kisses on her lips. Her heart now willing, Angela gave her hand in marriage to Trevor, and they had a grand wedding at Heathurst Hall, where they lived happily ever after.

Becca closed the book. So – Angela's virtue was rewarded by love. Or maybe her love was rewarded by Trevor's virtue. When heroines like Angela staked their passion on men like Trevor, those men rewarded them, recognized their virtue, valued their love. The passion of heroines was always indemnified, as the insurance adjustors might say, against loss, defeat, tarnish, and corruption. Becca sipped her wine and re-read the last page. What about the passion of women like Davy's mother – or of Rebecca Jenner?

Becca scrutinized the front cover: the rose arbor, the ancestral hall, the hero who would be redeemed by love, however unpromising he might appear in the beginning. The last page testified in dismal, harrowing contrast to everything that preceded it. Becca (and no doubt Davy's mother) had been a heroine addict since girlhood, had devoured, imbibed, ingested hundreds of books just like this one, savored them not so much for escape, but for the comfort they offered: they assured women that – all experience to the contrary – the false lover could yet prove true; love would be rewarded, virtue recognized. *The Unwilling Heart* was the sort of book you read in an empty bed, when you had no lover, when your husband had left you five days before. Davy's mother was right. There was no escape for her. Whether she killed herself or not, that woman was doomed: she had read *The Unwilling Heart* and rejected its comforts – and when you repudiated romance, what choice had you but to hate the man you loved? The man who cheated on you and left you with children and without resources? What hope had you but of peace, relief, rest? What was the alternative? Unremitting struggle. Sometimes women, unlike heroines, were not equal to the struggle. Sometimes Becca was not.

She finished the wine and flung the empty bottle to the floor. Pressing her face into the pillow and with an unwilling heart, Becca remembered her handsome first husband, the man on whom she'd staked her passion and her love and who was forever fixed in her mind with the love lyrics of her youth and the romantic notions she had culled from books. Romance and rampant hormones resulted in the backseat conception of Sasha. Jason was not an accident. Becca had wanted one more child, though she knew her marriage was doomed, that her husband was incorrigibly faithless, and that all her tears and threats, her alternate spasms of loathing and longing, were to no avail. He remarried within a year of the divorce and Becca had heard around town that he was equally unfaithful to his second wife as well.

Heartbroken after the defeat of divorce, Becca Bukowski nonetheless clung to romantic notions of finding a man worthy of her love. She balanced these dreams against her daily responsibilities: the job, the children, keeping the house in order and the creditors at bay. But the men who frequented her life and her bed – however unpromising they might appear in the beginning – remained unpromising, and Becca remained lonely. She mistook in her second husband a salve for that loneliness. He was a good man, a nice man, but she didn't love him with that urgent combination of glandular excitement and enhanced awareness that passes for love in all but the lobotomized. On the morning of her second wedding, Becca Bukowski locked herself in the bathroom of her mother's house with a bottle of Scotch. She poured the Scotch into a cup that had a garland of toothpaste at its rim, and with the woman in the mirror, she drank to mature love.

Mature, maybe, but a mistake all the same. Becca Jenner found to her dismay that you could not get out of any marriage, however shortlived, gracefully. She apologized to her second husband, assured him the mistake had been due to her own faulty judgment and did not reflect poorly on him.

In the years since her second divorce, the balance of dreams and daily life tilted in favor of the latter. Becca typed insurance forms, snaked out the drains, cared for her son, and consoled herself with reading in bed, books about heroines like Angela whose struggles were finite, whose difficulties ended on the last page. But neither dreams nor novels ever quite rendered Becca immune to heartache: her still-handsome first husband could always inflict a pang or two – like last weekend, when he had dropped Sasha off for her visit, laughed good-naturedly, and said that Sasha was the walking image of Becca all those years ago when she was young and fresh and eager.

Becca pulled Sasha's picture into bed with her and studied the lovely young face. Did Sasha suffer from romantic notions and rampant hormones? Was Sasha a heroine addict? Might Sasha be doomed as well? Surely there was a way a woman could proceed through life without incurring despair, without exchanging heartbreak for loneliness and then inuring herself to that loneliness the way one might come to ignore a persistently rattling rain gutter, a consistently bad drain. Maybe Becca had done Sasha a disservice simply in telling her about Kotex and tampons and contraception. Perhaps she should have told her to prize her passion, to find a man who could touch the precious fruit of her body without bruising it.

A siren ripped through the night, and fleetingly Becca wondered what human drama, what compelling need it answered. She turned up the electric blanket, rolled on her side, still clutching Sasha's picture and *The Unwilling Heart*.

Jason found her like that when he came home. Gently, he pried the book and picture from her hands and set them on the bedside table. He put the empty wine bottle in the trash, turned off the light, and closed the door.

On Sunday morning Jason hollered for her from the kitchen. The pipes had backed up again and the sink had overflowed. Becca hitched up her flannel nightie, waded into the kitchen, got out the plunger, and applied it again and again to the drain. The sink coughed and vomited up sodden bits of everyday life, coffee grounds, tattered egg shells. Jason mopped the floor while Becca dumped chemical drain cleaner into the sink. She threw a load of laundry into the washing machine and ironed a fresh blouse for work. When the drain was clear she cleaned the sink and scoured a pot that had spaghetti sauce burned on the bottom. Then she called Sasha and asked her to come to dinner on Monday night.

"I'm not supposed to see you till next weekend," Sasha reminded her.

"I know. I'd just like to see you sooner. Talk to you. We'll go out if you like. To that Chinese restaurant where they only have good fortunes in the cookies."

"That would be nice," the girl agreed; "I'd like that."

Then Becca took a businesslike shower instead of a leisurely bath and had just finished wrapping her hair in a towel when the phone rang.

"It's Grandma," Jason yelled from the living room. "She says if you're too busy to talk to her, she'll understand."

Becca marched out of the bathroom, tightening the belt of her robe. She snatched the phone from his hand. "What is it now, Ma?"

"What do you mean, 'what is it now'? I know you don't care that I'm suffering. No one does. Your father has never cared. He'd only know I was dead if his socks didn't get picked up."

"That's not true, Ma."

"It is so!" she wailed. "None of you care a thing for me or my arthritis. Even God got a day of rest. I deserve my day of rest, don't I?"

"Yes, Ma," Becca replied more gently, "but you might have to die to get it."

That night Rebecca Jenner made lunches for herself and her son and set them on the counter. She laid the checkbook beside the lunches so she would not forget to go to the bank. Then she took *The Unwilling Heart* and carefully sliced out the last page. She felt no remorse in depriving future readers of the end of Angela's and Trevor's romance. Their end was assured from the beginning. From before the beginning. That was the comfort of romance; the deceit was part of the undoing. Becca folded the last page and put it in her jewelry box alongside her two wedding rings and her children's baby teeth. She returned *The Unwilling Heart* to the ladies' lounge Book Bin, and it was gone the following day.

Hairline Fractures

EVERYONE IN their crowd drove foreign cars. So it was no surprise to see Scott Robinson's dilapidated, bent-fendered, octogenarian MG parked in his driveway behind Dana's car. He almost pulled in behind it, but realized briefly that then Scott wouldn't be able to get out. It may have been that thought alone that urged his foot back to the gas pedal and made him drive on past his wife's car, past his friend's car, past his own house. Alex did not know why he couldn't bring himself to go home; he didn't want to know why. He felt wretched and conspiratorial and lacking in all the basic decencies and casual good manners men of his age and upbringing were supposed to have.

It was afternoon still, but too late to go back to work; and besides, he'd headed home early in the first place because he'd had a rotten day at the lab. He felt foolish driving around town; and at the same time he didn't want to talk himself into going home, pulling in boldly behind Scott's car, walking into the house and saying something obvious and ill-timed like: "I'm home!"

He drove instead to the Doritzers' house; he liked Barbara and Stan. There was something steady and reassuring about them. They would be happy to see him and not ask any personal questions aside from: How are you? How is work? How is Dana? And he would smile and say that he and work and Dana were fine and they would smile and say something about how nice that was. They could be counted on to be polite. The same could not be said of Alex's wife; while Dana was not outright rude to the Doritzers, she was only barely cordial. Hers was that fine oil of social intercourse that floats atop colder waters.

Barbara greeted him at the door wearing a loose Mexican blouse and clutching an organic gardening manual with tomatoes the size of cantaloupes on the cover. "Alex! What a nice surprise. I was just going to insist that Stanny take a break and have a cup of tea with me. You're just in time."

"I just dropped by."

"You know we're always happy to see you. How's Dana?"

Alex said that Dana was fine, reflecting that maybe she was. He, Alex, was not fine, but he lied and said he was. Barbara and Stanny were certainly fine.

Stan brought the rough draft of an article he was writing into the kitchen with him and asked Alex's opinion of the opening paragraph. Barbara put on the water for tea and laid out three china cups and saucers. It was herbal tea – Barbara and Stan were strictly organic – an unappetizing greenish color and faintly bitter on the tongue. Alex basked in their collective warmth and conversation as he slowly sipped his tea. The tea seemed to drain away, and the cup dripped when he lifted it.

"Alex got the cup with the hairline crack," said Stan.

Barbara whisked it away from him, though Alex protested that he didn't mind. "No, no," she insisted, "you get a fresh cup."

"You ought to throw that cup away, Barby," said Stan.

"I know, but I can't bring myself to do it. Besides, the crack is so tiny you can't even see it."

"Barby's very sentimental," Stan explained.

She brought Alex another cup and saucer and poured him more tea. "I'm not sentimental at all, Stanny. One little crack doesn't mean it's ruined, does it Alex?"

"I guess not."

They went through another pot of herbal brew, and in the course of an hour, Alex all but forgot why he'd come to their house in the first place. Stan asked him to stay for dinner and Alex said no, he had to be getting home; then he remembered he'd already been home. "Dana will be expecting me," he said, and that much was true; she would be expecting him now. Scott Robinson would even be expecting him now, if the blue MG were still there.

The Doritzers walked Alex out to his car, still maintaining that he should stay. Stan draped his arm around Barbara's shoulders; she rubbed his tummy. Stan nibbled her ear and then said, "Alex, why don't you call Dana and you can both come for dinner?"

"Yes," said Barbara, "we haven't seen Dana in a long while."

Alex declined gracefully and Stan said, "Some other time." Alex smiled rather sadly because the Doritzers knew that Dana did not like them, though they were too polite to say so.

Scott Robinson's ancient MG was not in the driveway when Alex drove up this time. He was both relieved and annoyed, and before he could explore either sensation, he went in. Dana, fresh from the shower, stood in the slightly steamy bathroom, her hair dark and damp against her sprigged print blouse. Alex lounged in the bathroom door, watching her put in her earrings, singing some aimless ditty about rain and pain and *I'll be your baby, baby*, working over a wad of gum with unusual energy. Even though she was a tall woman, she always wore high-heeled shoes, and she reminded him of a swaying sunflower, with her dark blonde hair and brown eyes. She smiled at him in the mirror – and the gold cap over her eye tooth sparkled. She looked especially pretty, Alex thought; her mobile, mirthful face would probably age well if she were spared great sorrow.

"Why are you so late?" she asked between neat rhythmic snaps.

Fresh chewing gum. He could smell it from where he stood. Gingery. "I stopped by the Doritzers."

"Oh. How are they?"

"Fine."

"That's nice." She turned and gave him a peck on the cheek. "Let me by and I'll fix supper."

"I was going to come home early," he said quickly, still filling the doorway with his body. He wanted to suspend her there in front of him, freshly lipsticked and perfumed and spicy with chewing gum, bending toward him like a sunflower in the wind. "But I decided to stop at Barbara and Stan's before I came home."

"Oh."

Did she make the tiniest little grimace? "And I stayed for a cup of tea."

"Oh." She smiled, giving him the full benefit of her gold cap, and without waiting for him to move, she brushed past, leaving her scent behind like a green silk scarf.

He hated the way he felt, somewhere between apologetic and apoplectic. He wanted, given the latter emotion, to goad her into a fight where the truth would come hurling out like grapeshot – and on the other hand, he didn't even know why he'd driven past. Scott's visit might have been perfectly legit. He might just have dropped by to return a salad bowl or serving spoon, the things good friends always borrow from one another and share. Scott might even have had his wife with him. Scott and Julie might both have been here. Alex might be a first-rate fool for thinking anything else, and what did he have to base it on? A reflexive recoil of the guts. Some long-standing miscalculation of the sunflower smiles Dana bestowed on Scott? Some low-voltage current that ran between Dana and Scott when their whole crowd assembled and foreign cars crowded the driveway?

The evidence was inconclusive, limp and scarcely even circumstantial. Alex had all but convinced himself to laugh it off when he realized that, if Scott's visit had been legitimate (so to speak), Dana would have, certainly *could* have said: *Oh, Scott stopped by this afternoon and I told him you'd be home and he should wait*. Alex ran through the possibilities as he dried his hands on her still-damp towel. She hadn't said anything of the sort. Of course, it wasn't all Dana's fault; he hadn't given her the opportunity.

He followed her into their kitchen, which was shadowed by a huge trumpet vine whose vanilla blossoms drooped against the kitchen window like eavesdroppers.

"Want a gin and tonic, Alex?" she said.

"No thanks."

"Too much tea is bad for you, especially that ghastly herbal stuff." She whipped out a cutting board and began pulling off the skins of avocados.

"Where is our old teapot," he asked, "the one that was my grandmother's?"

"On the shelf where it usually is." She gave him a quizzical look over her shoulder and withdrew the shiny seed from the pulp. "Really, Alex. What's with you today? Why do you ask about the teapot?"

"When I was at Barbara and Stan's, the tea kept leaking out of my cup and Barbara said it had a hairline crack, and it made me wonder, is that the reason we don't use my grandmother's old pot? Doesn't it have a hairline crack in it? Isn't it pretty worthless?"

"Alex." She rinsed off the seed and dried her hands, walking toward him. "Let me get you a gin and tonic. You must have had a terrible day. Is something wrong? Did you have a bad day, honey?"

Alex searched her eyes looking for flecks of discomfort or guilt. "I guess I will have a G&T. I did have a rotten day."

When she went to the cupboard for the glass, she brought out the old teapot and put it on the table in front of him. "There, have a look if you want. The crack runs right down the spout, but I certainly don't think a little crack makes it worthless. Toss me a lime out of that bowl, will you?"

"If it's cracked, what good is it?"

"Don't be silly, Alex. Of course it's still good – it still works, more or less, and even if it doesn't, who cares? It still looks good. It's useful. There, try that and quit worrying about your grandmother's teapot. More lime?"

"That's fine."

"Good."

She kissed him briefly right at the edge of the eye where the creases were beginning to form on his thirty-two-year-old face. The cold, mercurial-looking drink made him feel better; he relaxed and expanded, listened to her sing some doo-wah-doo nonsense in rhythmic contractions with her gum. "That's what Barbara said," he added.

"What?"

"That even though she knew the cup was cracked, she couldn't bear to throw it out."

"Very sensible of her." Dana threw the avocados into a bowl and beat them with a silver fork, generously squeezing lemon over them.

"Stan and Barbara said we ought to get together sometime."

"Sure."

"Maybe you and me and Barbara and Stan and Scott and Julie and a

few others, just the usuals." Stupid, to have phrased it like that. He
should have said something stronger, more incriminating, and walked
over to the counter so he could see if she flinched when he said Scott.
Scott Robinson. Our old friend Scott Robinson. *What was Scott Robinson's old car doing in the driveway? How long had it been there and how often?
How long has this been going on and why? Why?* "Why don't we ask them
over?" he asked.

"Sure," she licked the avocado off the fork.

"Barbara and Stan asked after you," he blundered on. "They asked why
they never see you."

"What did you tell them?"

"I told them you were busy."

"So I am. I have thirty third-graders to worry about. Barbara only has
to think about the white flies on her Swiss chard."

"That isn't nice, Dana, and it isn't fair."

"Yes, I know. Barbara is the salt of the earth and I am as flighty as a
moth."

"You used to like them."

Dana took a red onion in one hand and a paring knife in the other. "I
like them, all right, but — "

"But?" He took a healthy swig of his drink, hoping the liquor would
race to his brain and loosen his tongue.

"Alex. Are we going to go through this again? Please. Why do you insist that I love them? If you like them, that's fine with me."

"But you don't."

"They bore me, Alex. They. Bore. Me."

"They didn't use to."

"They've always bored me. I'm less polite about it now, that's all. Really, Alex — do I say to you, 'Don't go see Barbara and Stan'? No. Do what
you want! But I expect the same of you."

"To let you do what you want?"

"To let me have my own friends that are not necessarily *our* friends."

(Like Scott? It teetered on the edge of his tongue. *Like Scott Robinson
whose battered blue MG was in the driveway? He is not necessarily my friend.
Not if he's your lover. My wife's lover. You fool, Alex. You stupid, antediluvian
fool. People don't say that anymore; it sets you back a hundred years.)*

Dana turned toward him with the knife poised over the onion. "Would you like to know honestly – "

(Tell me honestly: *Is Scott Robinson your lover, Dana?*)

" – Why I can't bear Barbara and Stan Doritzer, aside from the fact that they bore me to tears, which ought to be reason enough?"

"Boredom's not a cardinal sin."

"It's not a capital virtue, either, but if that were all, I could stand that. What I can't stand is the tight little two-by-two world they live in where no one has his own name. I'm not Dana. I'm Dana-and-Alex. She isn't Barbara, she's Barbara-and-Stan. It's all sickening and sing-song and repetitive and claustrophobic. Dana-and-Alex-and-Barbara-and-Stan-and – "

"Julie-and-Scott?"

If she blanched it was quickly and she recovered herself with: "It can be Jack-and-Jill, Hansel-and-Gretel, Cinderella-and-the-Prince, for all I care. It's oppressive and stifling, this couples business. People like Barbara and Stan make me feel as if I can't or ought not to make a move without my husband. Husband and wife. Two-by-two. Always two-by-two. I hate it." She turned her back to him and he could hear her peeling the crackling jacket off the onion.

"Are you tired of going two-by-two?"

"What's that supposed to mean?" The uncloaked onion fumed upward. Dana rinsed her eyes in the sink and turned toward him with the water still beading on her face. She reached for a dishtowel. "I'm tired of being forced to go through the world as though you and I are piggy-backed," she declared, "appendaged to one another as though our being married makes us Siamese twins. That's why I can't abide the Doritzers. If they want to live like that, then fine, but don't ask that I do it."

"No one has asked you to do that, Dana."

"No one has to *ask*, Alex – it's implied, implicit, part of the bargain, accepted behavior. *Comprende?* They make me feel like we all have to be neutered so we can ride around maritally piggyback and safe." She started to laugh, the old Dana laugh, and tossed the towel to him. "Just imagine, everyone piggyback!"

"And you're tired of being safe too, is that it? Isn't it better safe than sorry?"

The smile drained from her face. "What do you want me to say, Alex? Better wed than dead?"

"Maybe you're tired of being married."

He thought he saw her eyebrow arch momentarily upward before she burst out: "What is with you, Alex? What did they put in your tea? Vinegar? What did you do, sit at their table and admire their neat little life and come home looking for a fight? I've told you the truth."

(Not the real truth: what about Scott Robinson's MG in the driveway this afternoon? Tell me the truth about that. Tell me the answer to the question I haven't even asked.)

"Listen, Alex, I can't stand Stan's bedside manner, so calm, so solicitous, so ingratiating, so thoughful – he drives me up the wall! And I can't stand hearing about Barbara's organic garden with her white flies or the books she writes for children where all the baddies use processed sugar. How can you stand them? So sanctimonious!"

"You're wrong, Dana. They're not like that."

"All right – if that's not enough – what I really can't stand is the way they want to kill me with kindness. If I don't sit there and be quietly victimized by their suffocating kindness, I've been naughty and I won't be asked back. They want me – damnit, Alex, they want us – to sit there, slack-jawed and green with envy, coveting their connubial happiness. Alex – don't you see? – we're *supposed* to think, what a lovely marriage Barbara and Stan have, and isn't it too bad that ours is so lousy. Don't we wish we had a USDA choice marriage like theirs? We're *supposed* to feel that. We're *supposed* to envy them and want to be like them and I *absolutely* refuse."

"You think you know everything. You'd rather – "

"Oh shut up!" She flung the knife down and hurled the naked onion across the room. "Everything was fine until you came home. Everything. Till you came home from sitting around with those two – those squash blossoms. Let me tell you this, Alex – they're not so perfect. Anyone who takes such pains to let you think that everything is peachy-creamy cannot be that perfect. But you go on believing whatever you want – I'm going out for a walk."

Stalking across the kitchen, she slammed the door behind her and glass rattled in the frame. Beyond the trumpet vine he could see the shine of her retreating hair, and then she vanished.

Alex finished off his diluted drink quickly and pulled the old teapot toward him, fingering its faded pattern. It was once, no doubt, in his grandmother's day, a burnished amber color with bright blue trim; but that had all paled now, and the paint itself had peeled due to the injudicious use of some cleaning fluid or other. There was a hairline fracture at the lip and a long brown stain all down the spout where the tea leaked out continually.

He rose to his feet and made his way to the bedroom. The sight of the unmade bed did nothing for his qualms, but still he accused himself of being ungenerous and incorrect to have thought anything amiss in the first place; he should never have picked the quarrel with her. He was wrong. Besides (he sat down and removed his shoes), the bed was always unmade.

He picked a penny up off the rug. That penny hadn't been there this morning. Of course, this morning he hadn't looked for it. This morning he hadn't known Scott Robinson's stinking heap of an MG would be in his driveway this afternoon, and that Scott Robinson would be in here, in this – with –

Well, the penny could have dropped out of his own pants. Still, the room had a peculiar scent to it, stuffy and shady, and that was unusual. Dana always insisted on open windows and fresh air and breezes whenever the weather permitted. He raised the shade and the protesting window. The curtains billowed back, bringing a whiff of spring jasmine.

He would not apologize. Dana ought to apologize. Well, maybe no one needed to come out and actually apologize. He'd say something casually and Dana would laugh at him for being so paranoid as to think anything of Scott Robinson's car being there in the afternoon. Alex would approach it in a mature fashion. No screaming. No recrimination. No below-the-belts. He'd just say....

He could not say that instinct told him to drive on when he saw that rusting MG. He could not say he'd gone to the Doritzers' because his involuntary nervous system pulled him away from his own house. The Doritzers were very nice to him. He could say that, and to show Dana he wasn't rigid, he could admit that maybe Stan Dortizer was a trifle bedside-mannery and that honestly, there were times when he too wondered about their untrammeled domestic bliss. But maybe he should be

direct. Simply inquire: *Are you having an affair with Scott Robinson, Dana?*
Is that why his car was in the driveway when no one would have expected me
home? I just hope that you and Scott aren't so tawdry as to indulge yourselves
in "nooners," as the men at the lab say, "quickies." I hope you have the good
taste not to do that, Dana.

He would just ask her and be done with it; none of this hedging and
sniping. Best to have it out in the open. If she told too big a lie, it would
show on her face. Wouldn't it? What if the thing with Scott Robinson
had been going on so long *(how long, and how often?)* that she had learned
to lie reflexively?

Alex regarded the tousled pillows as if they were co-conspirators in this
affair. *Affair.* He wanted to lie down and beg sleep to take him, but the
bed, the very sheets, revolted him. He put his head in his hands, wishing
he were back in the Doritzers' sunny kitchen drinking from their frac-
tured teacups, listening to Barbara champion ladybugs as the best defense
against white flies. He pictured Barby and Stanny now, having a quiet
dinner and enjoying themselves.

He envied them.

When he looked up she was leaning in the doorway as if only lathe and
plaster could support her. She was not even looking at him; she stared at
the curtains blowing in like bridal veils. "I didn't hear you come in," he
said.

"I didn't want you to." The gum was gone and the sunflower Dana had
wilted. She crossed the room and closed the stiff window. The curtains
died.

"I drove by earlier," he said obliquely. Not at all the rash, nasty statement he'd meant it to be.

"I thought I heard your car."

"I drove on."

"I thought it was you. I wasn't sure."

"Scott Robinson was here, wasn't he?"

"Yes."

"He was alone?"

"I was here."

"I mean, Julie wasn't with him."

"Yes. I mean no. Julie wasn't with him."

"Were you – are you – did he – have you – " The words shriveled on Alex's tongue and silence engulfed them. In six years of marriage one substitutes for the verbs and vowels of spoken English a more telegraphic, telepathic language whose grammar escapes all but the husband and wife. Lovers have no comprehension of this language; it takes time to master, bleary mornings and banal afternoons. Expiring time and enforced intimacy this language requires. No lovers – however ardent, however passionate – can speak this tongue. Dana sat at the opposite end of the bed. Her foot twitched erratically and she fidgeted with her wedding band. Alex played with the penny. "I know," he said.

"Know what?"

"I know about Scott."

"What about him?"

"Can't you make this easier for me, Dana? Please?"

"Why should I?" she snapped. "Do you think it's been easy for me?"

"I can't believe you love him, not like you love me. Loved me."

"Oh Alex, please don't. You sound so Victorian. Of course I love you." She pulled a lank strand of hair over her shoulder and began braiding it furiously.

"Do you love Scott Robinson?"

"Scott is married."

"You're married."

"Yes. I'm married. You're married. We're all married. We're all so married we can't possibly be anything else. Piggybacked for life. Marriage doesn't mean you put your gonads in cold storage, you know."

"What are you saying? Is this some kind of glandular passion you have with Scott?"

"I never said that. You did. I said nothing of the sort. You think I'm having an affair with Scott."

"It certainly looks that way. It looked that way this afternoon. What am I supposed to think when I drive by and see – "

"What are you supposed to think!" she nearly shrieked. "What do I care what you're *supposed* to think? I don't give a damn what you're *supposed* to think! What if I were having an affair? What of it?" She bit her lip and wrung her hands till the nails went white. "Would that be the worst of it?"

Would it? Perhaps Scott Robinson was only the hairline fracture in their marriage. Perhaps the worst of it lay elsewhere. "What *is* the worst of it?" Alex took a deep breath: adultery, divorce, letting lawyers untangle the mess you made of your life: these things happened to other people, people who were neurotic or immature or couldn't control themselves, people who looked for trouble. Alex had never looked for trouble, but as he sat in the blue, gathering dusk, he knew he had never looked *at it*, either. He had ignored the fissures in his marriage until they cracked open like wounds.

"The worst of it," Dana said more calmly – she had anticipated the question – "is that we'll never be like Stan and Barbara Doritzer. That's what you want. I don't want that, Alex. I've never wanted it. I never will."

He wished she would look up so he could see her eyes, see contrition, though perhaps her pain was undiluted with remorse. He couldn't see, and he couldn't bear to say more, not any more, not right now. Silence as palpable as darkness hovered over them, and when Alex spoke, he felt himself strangling. "Will you do me a favor?" He coughed and began again. "Will you do me a favor? Will you change the sheets?"

"Alex, it's not what you think, Alex, I'm only trying to – "

"You don't have to explain now."

"I don't want to explain! I want to talk."

"We'll talk later. I can't talk until you change the sheets."

"I'll change them." She sank back into the rumpled sheets and flung her arm over her face.

Leave, he told himself. If he didn't leave he would lie down beside her. Sheets and all. He would have to. He would put his arm over her, his hand under her shirt, feel her heart beat under the ribs and the flesh softly mounded into breast. *Leave*. The bed creaked, protesting his departure.

Alex closed the bedroom door behind him. He walked through the darkening house to the kitchen and turned on the light. He made himself another drink, but the ice cube tray stuck and a cube shot out, careening across the floor. Methodically he took a paper towel and went in search of it. It lay beside the red onion Dana had flung. He brought them both to the sink, rinsed the onion off, and peered at the kitchen window. His reflection was mottled by the pendulous creamy blossoms of the trumpet vine.

I am a sensible, educated man, he told himself, not some half-barbaric Goth who caught my wife in another man's tent. Besides, he hadn't caught her at all: his guts told him to drive on and he did. He'd driven to the Doritzers, who percolated domestic peace. His own domestic peace was shattered, but surely, surely it could be mended. He loved Dana; Dana loved him. That ought to be enough, and if it were not enough, at least it was a beginning. They had love; they had time, six years, in fact; they only lacked – what? "Understanding." He supplied the word himself. "But it will be all right," he reassured the troubled man in the kitchen window. A little more love, a little more time, a little more talk – and understanding would follow. Then it would be all right. *But it will never be the same,* said his reflection.

His heart felt like old earthenware, the thick, heavy, old-fashioned plates that endure forever because they do not break; they chip and crack and split around the edges, but the centers stay intact and they go on being useful even when they are no longer pretty. Alex picked up the paring knife, slit the onion open, and quartered it quickly. The fumey, redolent, red-and-white onion stung his eyes to tears, but he chopped that onion, hacked it into little pieces, and wiped his running eyes and nose with the back of his reeking hand.

Sonata in G Minor

HIS FACE WAS changing almost daily from the unsharpened features of childhood to the more pronounced flesh and bone structure of an adult. At fifteen Gideon Douglass shaved once a week, though his beard only sprouted in unconnected patches across his jaw. His nose was disproportionately large for his face and his legs too long for his narrow shoulders. Dimly and against his will, Gideon began to perceive that the world itself was a place of uneven proportions, full of dilemmas so foreign and confusing he sometimes could not name them, or say why he was stirred, disturbed, or sleepless.

He was a student at St. Elmo High School in 1906 when he first went to work for Dr. Lucius Tipton – who had been a family friend, a family fixture, for years. Every morning before school Gideon walked to the Doctor's combined home and office. He let himself into the downstairs office, fired up the stove, boiled the day's water and sealed it in sterile jars, cleaned, swept, disinfected, and arranged the day's linens in a neat stack beside the examining table.

After he performed these tasks (and while he waited for Doctor to return from breakfast, which he habitually took at the Pilgrim Cafe) Gideon was free to retire to the study and read until school started. Gideon liked the study. A young man with five women in his family, after all, isn't likely to mistake a male domain. Lucius Tipton was fanatical and immaculate about the office, but the study was strewn with cigar butts, cups and glasses, some virtually carmelized with old coffee and brandy;

books and professional journals lined the walls, and week-old newspapers from distant cities rustled whenever the wind blew through. The
study smelled of the Doctor's own aroma, cigar smoke, and soap. There
wasn't a frill or a crimp in sight, none of the starched textures and laun-
dered odors that characterized Gideon's own home. Lucius Tipton had
never married; the only woman in his house was Blanche, a skeleton who
hung contentedly in the study behind the desk chair, as if she were continually reading over Doctor's shoulder. Lucius said you could tell Blanche
was a woman because of her pelvis.

The Doctor's study was exotic to Gideon, but in fact there was not
another room like it in all of St. Elmo. St. Elmo was a desert town laid
out some fifty years before by the Mormons, who, in their typically un-
imaginative and efficient fashion, gridded the streets "A" through "K" and
1 through 11. By 1906 the town had grown so that Gideon and his family – his mother, four sisters, and one little brother – rented a house at
the intersection of "Q" and 25th in the unpaved, nether reaches of this
nether town, which had been rescued from oblivion and the desert wind
not by the Mormons (despite their sobriety and efficiency they had not
quite managed to dent the landscape) but by the Railroad. The Railroad
laid claim and track to St. Elmo in the 1880s and established it as their
southern terminus, the link between the southwest and the sea.

Lying in bed at night at the intersection of "Q" and 25th, Gideon could
hear the trains shriek and rumble through Jesuit Pass on their way east,
to places that were exotic simply by virtue of being east of St. Elmo. Gideon enjoyed the trains' rhythm and rattle, though he was not afflicted
with restlessness. He was a good student, diligent and methodical, but
lacked the imagination that restlessness requires.

To Gideon the Doctor's study was itself a foreign country populated
with hundreds of books of varying hues and shades of opinion as well.
Since his mind had been trained and directed by the Mormon Church,
Gideon was terribly confused by the possibilities these books implied;
indeed, they testified to multiple convictions of correctness. On those
occasions when he did glance through the volumes, Gideon always re-
placed them carefully so they would not betray his curiosity. He didn't
want anyone to know that he'd been tempted, much less that he'd succumbed.

One day, however, he was thumbing through one of the Doctor's big anatomy books when the Doctor walked in and caught him. Lucius laughed and tossed his hat on Blanche's head. "Here, Gideon, let me help you." Lucius turned right to it: men on one page, women on the other. There they were, not only with no clothes, but with no skin either.

"That's it?" said Gideon. "That's all there is to it?"

"That's all," said the Doctor, patting Blanche's hip bone affectionately. "We're all universally the same."

In the anatomy book the male and female organs did not look sacred or holy, contrary to everything Gideon had learned from the Latter-day Saints. It was very confusing. But then the Saints had also taught him that an atheist and a cigar smoker was not only doomed in the afterlife, but could have few claims to goodness in this life as well. This was particularly disturbing because Lucius Tipton was certainly the best friend Gideon's family had. Since their arrival in St. Elmo six years before, Lucius Tipton had come to every Sunday supper, carrying a small bunch of half-wilted wildflowers which he presented to Gideon's mother, Ruth, with the aplomb of a dancing master. Gideon's mother (who was otherwise a paragon of Sainthood) tolerated the Doctor's cigar smoke and atheism. She even kept a bit of coffee in the house for his visits. When well-meaning Saints occasionally suggested to the Widow Douglass that Lucius Tipton might be a baleful influence on her family, Ruth simply glared at them and they shut up fast.

Gideon was only fifteen and hadn't had time to practice his glare. His friends at church and school made snide remarks about the atheist Doctor, and Gideon cringed, retreating into the ample arms of the Constitution, which guarantees the right of religious freedom to all. The Constitution notwithstanding, St. Elmo was dominated by the Mormons. For the sake of appearances they suffered the sprinkling of Catholics, Methodists, Baptists, heathen Chinese, and even a group of Spiritualists who met weekly at Sister Whitworth's Boarding House down by the depot. Sister Whitworth herself was a practicing Mormon who did not hold with Spiritualism, but she couldn't refuse them the parlor because they paid their rent on time.

Amid his confusions, Gideon consoled himself with the thought that at least atheism, scoffery, and cigar-smoking were not infectious, and he could sit in the Doctor's study and still keep his faith intact despite the overwhelming presence of so many books. Lucius urged him to read, but Gideon blushed and cleared his throat and said that truly, he could not waste his time; the works of Voltaire, Rousseau, and Robert Ingersoll were merely dread afflictions upon the mind. "They are anathema to me," Gideon concluded.

"'Anathema'!" cried the Doctor. "Where did you ever find such a word?"

"It was Arlene's first Word-of-the-Week. Miss Arlene McClure."

"And who might she be?"

Gideon flushed to a vivid peach. "She is my classmate at St. Elmo High. She has a new word every week. Alphabetically. She finds a new word and uses it over and over."

"Commendable," said the Doctor, lighting his match on Blanche's sternum and wreathing them in smoke. "What's her word this week?"

"'Fructify,'" Gideon replied, unable to decide why the word so disturbed him.

By the time Doctor met Miss Arlene McClure she was on the letter "H" and her Word-of-the-Week was "hirsute," an unfortunate choice, perhaps, because there seemed no delicate way to welcome it into Sunday supper conversation in the Douglass dining room. Ruth and Lucius sat at either end of the table with the three young women – Eden, Afton, and Lil – lined up on one side and the two children, Cissa and Mason, on the other side with Arlene and Gideon, who were so close that occasionally their elbows touched; they jumped as if they'd been electrified with current and apologized without looking at each other.

Like Gideon, Arlene already wore glasses; she was plump, rosy, with a face as round and friendly as a fry-pan – a marked contrast to Gideon's sisters, Eden, Afton, and Lil who were tall, a little taciturn, and rather on the sallow side, like their mother.

"Miss McClure," said the Doctor, passing her the potatoes, "how did you happen on anything so novel as the Word-of-the-Week?"

"The Church of Jesus Christ of Latter-day Saints believes in Knowledge," she began didactically. "It's every mortal's duty to learn as much as you can while on this earth so you can take your knowledge with you into the Celestial Kingdom. The Doctrine and Covenants tells us the more knowledge we have in this world, the more our advantages will be in the world to come."

"You mean to say that when we die, the knowledge we've accumulated doesn't die with us?"

"That is correct, Doctor. We take it with us to the Celestial Kingdom."

"So – pass me that cucumber relish there, will you Afton? Thank you – so, if I know how to cure a colt of bots on this earth, I'll know how to cure colts in heaven?"

"There aren't any colts in heaven," said Afton.

"How do you know that?" asked Doctor.

"Everyone knows that."

"Now, if Afton is right, Miss McClure, what shall I do with my knowledge in heaven?"

"It isn't likely you'll be going to heaven to find out, Doctor," said seventeen-year-old Eden. Ruth admonished her and Afton laughed and Gideon strangled on a wayward pea.

"Well," Doctor wiped his ample mustache. "Do you reckon there are colts in hell?"

"Oh Doctor," Gideon pleaded, mortified that Arlene should witness the scoffery and atheism, "what kind of talk is that?"

"What indeed?" Ruth snapped. "Why can't you just talk about the weather and gossip like everyone else, Lucius?"

"Well, I've been known to indulge in a little gossip," Lucius leaned toward Arlene confidentially. "But I don't suppose it's gossip when everyone in this town already knows what happened over at Sister Whitworth's Boarding House this week. I don't suppose there's a Mormon or a Methodist or a Chinee, for that matter, who don't know about the Professor Rabinowitz who got off the train."

"Who got thrown off the train," Eden corrected him.

"Who had a fit at Sister Whitworth's and she had to call you because his eyes went clean out of his skull and he frothered," Afton offered.

"They say he is a hirsute foreigner and an unconverted Jew," Arlene volunteered.

"And they're right," the Doctor agreed, "but Professor Rabinowitz is also a musician, a violinist, an artist, if you will. He's played with the great orchestras of Europe. He's got more talent and education than every man in St. Elmo all put together. Bar none," Lucius added, as if to implicate the Mormon patriarchs unmistakably in ignorance and inferiority.

"Well, he hasn't got a speck of money," Afton announced. "And Sister Whitworth's plenty mad. He won't lift a hand to work off his bill."

"He shouldn't have to," said Lucius. "Professor Rabinowitz's hands are artist's hands and he shouldn't have to sink them in gummy dishwater. Pass me some more of that pork and onions, Lil, if you please."

"And what should he do, Lucius?" Ruth said. "I can tell you're coming to something."

"Well, I am at that. I was thinking of Gideon here. I was thinking that Gideon might just like to learn to play the violin."

"We don't have no violin."

"Well, Ruth, it just so happens that I do. I got it in payment once from a patient and I almost didn't take it, but he was moving on and said he didn't have no use for it. I didn't have no use for it either, but I surely would love to hear Gideon play. Yes I would."

"We can't afford music lessons."

"Well Ruth, I have discussed this with the Professor and I think I may, without breaking any confidences, say that Professor Rabinowitz has an ongoing medical problem which I am willing to treat, but instead of paying my fee, we thought he could give Gideon lessons." Doctor unbuttoned his vest, leaned back, and lit up a cigar, to the unmasked horror of Arlene McClure. "Ruth," he said, blowing a smoke ring for Cissa, "that's the finest meal to date and I salute you. All Hail to the Conquering Cook!"

"Codswallop."

PROFESSOR RABINOWITZ had skin like slick wet stones and smelled of garlic and unwash. He claimed to have been born a genius, educated as a man of the world and committed to the overthrow of the bourgeoisie. He said he dedicated his life and soul to his art and dedicated his art to his politics, which were radical in the extreme. He advocated revolution the way some people advocated chloride of lime to get rid of mildew. Professor Rabinowitz punctuated his sentences with vivid, erratic gestures.

No one in St. Elmo had ever heard talk like this. His violin students and their parents, the Mormons, Methodists, Catholics, and Baptists, to say nothing of the Spiritualists at Sister Whitworth's Boarding House, were spellbound by Professor Rabinowitz. He was more foreign than the Chinese. He was small and shabby and dapper, with a pince-nez and a weak chin under the only goatee in town.

He came to the Douglass home on Tuesday afternoons for Gideon's lesson. "Muzeek, Gideon!" the Professor screamed. "Muzeek! Zis is ze violin, not ze broom! Make ze muzeek! Caress ze strings! Ze strings are ze flesh of a beautiful woman, Gideon! Make love to zem!"

Gideon grew red of face and moist of palm and could not concentrate on the violin at all when the Professor used these unfortunate metaphors, and he used them so often that Gideon was horrified when one Sunday Dr. Tipton asked if he might bring Professor Rabinowitz to Sunday supper the following week. Ruth agreed.

Gideon felt it his duty to warn Doctor that Professor Rabinowitz was not fit company for women and children.

Lucius laughed. "Unfit company is the best kind. If you surround yourself with people who think just like you do, why, you'll give up thinking at all."

"He'll say something awful to my mother and sisters," Gideon maintained.

"Like what?"

Gideon could not bring himself to repeat that the violin strings were the flesh of a beautiful woman. "You'll be embarrassed you ever asked him," was all Gideon said, "you wait and see."

Gideon was both gratified and chagrined the following Sunday when his judgment was borne out. It was a hot afternoon, all the windows were open, and the dry wind animated the lace curtains. Professor Rabinowitz did not seem to know or notice that sweat dripped off the end of his chin; he held his knife and fork funny and stoked his mouth with food. Gideon was glad Arlene was not here to witness this spectacle.

When he was done eating, Professor Rabinowitz launched into praises of Ruth's cooking. He seemed to be handing her bouquets full of foreign exclamations. "Splendide! Manifique! And the custard, my dear Madame!" He kissed his fingers, "Ze most superior of anything I taste in ze Second Empire. Royalty do not dine as we have zis day!"

The Professor accepted one of Doctor's cigars, smoked, sweated copiously, and talked incessantly of the violin and radical politics. He spat (almost literally) upon the bourgeoisie (a depraved group of whom Gideon had never heard), and he reveled in the upcoming Armegeddon. No one could divert the conversation, though Afton several times mentioned the weather and Lil agreed it was very warm for May. Gideon himself interrupted the Professor and asked if he would play the violin for them.

"Later – " the Professor rubbed his stomach. "Let us allow ze body its delights before we commence ze muzeek of ze soul!"

Gideon nearly slid under the table. No one of his acquaintance ever rubbed his stomach or used the word *"body,"* and certainly not in connection with anything so questionable as delight. Gideon looked at his mother, whose high collar surrounded the long stem of her pale throat and whose face betrayed nothing, except a tiny shred of smile twitching at her lips, which Gideon figured was indigestion. And Doctor, well, he was clearly enjoying himself and you just had to wonder about a man who could actually *like* a foreigner and an unconverted Jew.

The Professor's gestures grew more exaggerated as he waxed on about Armegeddon and the Blood of the Oppressors. His terms were not familiar to Gideon, but Gideon recognized the general scenario – The Last Days, The Last Judgment – which were immediately impending, just like they said at church, though the church and the Professor seemed to have in mind the blood of different oppressors. The Professor wept as he described the gallant Paris Commune where he said he'd eaten rats and suffered terrible wounds and slept in the Arms of Morphia.

When the Professor's weeping did not of its own accord cease, Ruth suggested Gideon get his violin. "Yes," Lucius agreed, "play us something, Professor."

The Professor blew his nose on a soiled handkerchief. "An honor, Doctor. But after such a meal!" Again, he kissed his hands, "Only a sonata will do. A sonata, then!" He stood, executed a brief, percussive bow with clicking heels.

"Think of it," said the Doctor, thoughtfully puffing on his cigar, "we'll be listening to the only sonata in a thousand-mile radius."

Professor Rabinowitz allowed Gideon to remove the violin from its wooden case and blue velvet lining. He tuned it and waited till Gideon had taken his seat and all noise and snuffling in the dining room had ceased. He held the violin patiently until the distant train whistle dwindled into oblivion. He even waited until the wind diminished and the billowing curtains died. Then he drew the bow across the strings, caressed them like they were the flesh of a beautiful woman, made love to the violin. Foreign, exotic, benign as angels' voices, the only sonata in a thousand miles rippled out the windows and lilted among the sunflowers.

NOT UNTIL many years later did Gideon Douglass discover that the Paris Commune was not an unorthodox arrangement of freethinkers and freelovers who ate rats. But a mere four weeks passed between the Professor's sonata and the night Gideon accidentally stumbled on him in the Arms of Morphia.

Gideon went to the Doctor's one night with a geometry problem he could not solve. Gideon had never knocked at the study door and he did not knock now, but when he walked in, he knew what Sister Whitworth had seen when the Professor first arrived, and he knew why she had called Lucius Tipton. The Professor's eyes glowed like the end of a cigar. His white lips were sucked in with suffering. His head was thrown back, his goatee stuck up in the air, his sleeve was rolled up, and Lucius Tipton stood over him with something shiny in his hand.

"Get out!" Lucius yelled. "Get out now!"

Gideon got. He did not mention what he'd seen to anyone. He did not sleep well. And the next morning when he arrived to clean up the office he found Lucius Tipton still sitting at his desk, dark triangular patches under his eyes and a shadow of beard across his jaw. Blanche hung behind him, eyeless and protective, and the study stank of cigar. Doctor managed a wan smile and mumbled an apology for having yelled at Gideon the night before.

"I should have expected it," said Gideon. "I should have known that no good can be connected with a depraved foreigner and an unconverted Jew. I am going to quit taking violin lessons. I can't associate with people like that."

"Don't be a fool, Gideon."

"I'm not a fool. I am a Latter-day Saint and I know corruption when I see it."

"You're young, Gideon, that's all. Don't be so hard on Professor Rabinowitz." Lucius rose and started toward the stairs. "You know some folks want lots out of life and get it, and some want lots and don't get it. Some want a little and don't even get that. And some start out wanting a lot and end up wanting nothing, only peace and oblivion – and if that's what they've done to their lives, they're more to be pitied than castigated."

Gideon looked up "castigate" after Doctor left the room and later he told Arlene, thinking it was a good Word-of-the-Week. But she was on "T" that week, and her word was "turpitude" – which she could say with such relish and refinement, it was a pleasure to hear her, no matter what it meant. By the time she got back around to "C" she had forgotten all about "castigate," but Gideon hadn't. Gideon didn't forget for a long time.

The very next morning, however, Gideon arrived at the Doctor's office to find the window broken and the floor strewn with overturned basins, linens, instruments and bottles – broken and whole. The office reeked of medicinal stench. Gideon's feet crunched over broken glass from the bottles, the window, and the pharmacopia cabinet; the cabinet doors had been nearly pulled off and the lock broken. Gideon cleaned up and waited for Doctor to return from breakfast.

Lucius said: "Well, that's the end of Professor Rabinowitz."

"The Professor did this! How do you know?"

"I know from what's missing."

"What did he steal? Why did he do it? When?"

"I can't answer all that, Gideon. I had a late-night call up in Jesuit Pass. I didn't even look in the office when I got back. So I reckon he did it last night."

"Well, let's call the Sheriff! The Sheriff will catch him! He can't be that far away."

"Oh," said the Doctor, fingering the broken lock, "he's far away all right. He's just about as far away as he can be this side of death and heaven, and besides, even if the Sheriff caught him, Gideon, can you imagine Professor Rabinowitz in jail? He'd die like a rat in a trap."

Gideon stared at the broken cabinet and thought about the rats the Professor had eaten in the Paris Commune and his sleeping in the Arms of Morphia.

"No, Gideon." Doctor slid the lock into his pocket. "You go to school and don't say a word about this. If Professor Rabinowitz wanted it bad enough to steal, and if what he stole was enough to give him peace or illusion or let him escape his tattered hide, then let him be."

"But stealing is illegal! It's immoral!"

"Well Gideon, they're not necessarily the same thing. You have to learn to distinguish between the illegal and the immoral. Making distinctions is the hardest thing you'll learn in life, because you have to make them carefully and one at a time. But if you don't make distinctions, if you let your church, or family, or simple custom divide up right from wrong for you, then your brains get rusty and something in you dies."

Gideon regarded the pharmacopia cabinet, amazed that such a lesson could be extracted from simple theft.

"Well, well, too much metaphysics in the morning. Bad for the constitution. You better go to school, but don't say anything about this."

Gideon didn't have to. By suppertime everyone in St. Elmo knew that the Professor had absconded owing Sister Whitworth three months' back rent and that he had left like a thief in the night, though only Gideon and Lucius knew that he had been a thief in the night.

For a few months after the Professor's hasty depature, Gideon continued to play the violin, but he never again attempted anything new or difficult. He stuck to hymns that were popular in church and came easily to him. The violin that once played the only sonata in a thousand miles seemed to grow rusty, just as Gideon's fingers seemed to stiffen when he held the instrument. The violin lay in its wooden casket with the blue velvet lining, untouched for so long that Gideon could not lift the creaking lid and look at it without twinges of conscience. He could not hold it under his chin without smelling, somehow, garlic and remorse.

And Departing
Leave Behind Us

WHEN MY BROTHER Gideon graduated (Valedictorian, St. Elmo High, Class of '09) he give his speech three times, not to mention all his practice. I begged him, "Gideon, please go outside or somewheres I don't have to hear 'Lives of Great Men/All Remind Us/We Can Make Our Lives Sublime/And Departing Leave Behind Us/Footprints in the Sands of Time.'"

And Gideon says to me, "Afton, you are just jealous."

"I may not be smart as Eden or as pretty as Lil, but God give me a few gifts too, Gideon Douglass, and don't you forget it." Then I wished I hadn't been so sharp. Gideon's eyes got big behind his glasses and I knew he hadn't meant no harm. "Anyway, Gideon, if you was suddenly struck dumb, I could give that speech and not miss one tiny word. I'll be glad when all this graduation business is over and Mr. Henry Wordsworth Longfellow don't live in the same house with us night and day."

But Gideon was real impressive on graduation day and a few days later at church. No applause is allowed in church, but Gideon knew the Latter-day Saints was just as proud of him as we could be. We hadn't had a valedictorian in seven years. Always the Methodists. The damn Methodists, as Doctor would say, but then he damned everything, and though Mother didn't approve, she didn't correct him either. Doctor was the only one she spared. Eden always said when Mother got to heaven, she'd fault St. Peter on his manners. Mother sees a lot of bad manners at the Pilgrim, even if it is the best restaurant in this town, maybe in California.

Mother says St. Elmo's mayor, for instance, don't eat no better than a railroad man. Mother says the mayor is vulgar and that's the worst Mother can say about anyone.

I don't know why Mother don't think Doctor's vulgar. He's an atheist after all. Him and Mother's partners, owners of the Pilgrim; and before the Pilgrim got so successful, every Saint in this town was telling Mother that a decent Mormon widow shouldn't be such good friends with an atheist unmarried Doctor and letting him influence the tender minds of her six children when he came to supper every Sunday for eight years. Once I heard Mother tell Bishop Myles that she was only friends with Doctor in hopes of converting him to our faith. That seemed to cork the Bishop, but I knew it was a pile of peach pits. Mother and Doctor never talked religion in their lives. That was left to Gideon. They're both bookish. Gideon and Doctor talked religion and history all the time. Doctor says religion's always been bad for history, but they are tethered to each other all the same.

Gideon insisted Doctor and Bishop both come to his graduation party. He claimed they'd been the guiding lights of his life and he wouldn't slight one for the other. Mother just shrugged. Besides Doctor and Bishop and Mrs. Myles and their son Lloyd (who was Gideon's best friend), Gideon invited his sweetheart, Arlene McClure (who could have been valedictorian herself if they'd let girls do it). Doctor's coming upset Arlene. She'd long ago sworn she'd never again break bread with that atheist Lucius Tipton. I reminded her we wasn't breaking bread, but eating cake. Arlene said she wasn't speaking literally, only fig-ur-at-ively. And then her pie-plain face lights up and she smirks like she always does when she knows she's sent you to the dictionary to find out what she meant.

It was then I asked Mother if Tom Lance could come to the party too, even though it wasn't my graduation. Mother's brows knit and purled into grimness and she said, "Afton, you are just sixteen and I hope you're not thinking of anything so foolish as marriage."

"I swear by all the Doctrine and Covenants, I will graduate from high school before I marry Tom Lance."

"High school!" Mother sniffs. "You'd better do better than that. You better do as well as Eden. Eden's got a good job at the bank. She is her own woman with her own money and no man's ward."

And no man's wife, I wanted to say, but I held my tongue. Eden's getting on, nineteen now and still not married. The church tells us marriage don't make a girl the ward of a man, but his wife and helpmeet. Besides no unmarried girls – or women – get into the Celestial Kingdom. You got to be married. I'm going to the Celestial Kingdom as Mrs. Tom Lance. I knew that the minute I saw him, even if he ain't beautiful, what with that scar alongside his nose down to his chin. That scar come from a railroad accident. It can't be inherited and I think we'd have real handsome children. Besides, I know it ain't the scar that bothers my family, nor Tom's being twenty and so much older than me, no not even his working for the railroad. It's that he don't talk. Mother asked me how I could want to marry a man who never had a word to say. "Tom's a good listener," I said, "and I'm a good talker, and the Lord likes things that work in pairs."

Is Tom supposed to recite Mr. Henry Wordsworth Longfellow, I'd like to know? The Doctrine and Covenants? The begets and begats? And what does it matter if my family don't love him? They're not marrying him. I am. Or I will one day. And when Mother said Tom could come to Gideon's party, I knew she knew I'd marry him and she'd all but give up talking me out of it.

Gideon got a new wool suit for his graduation. He had his picture took – his first one alone. He wore his suit and held his diploma and some day lilies and didn't smile because he was a man now and had to look grave and like he was ready to put away childish things.

Gideon will die in that suit, I thought. It was just dawn on graduation day, the last star still hanging in the sky like a hanky someone forgot on the clothesline. When I looked out my window, I could see the mountains was already sharp against the hard eastern sky. I could smell the dairy half a mile distant and the tomatoes and geraniums toasting in the garden below. I got up quiet so as not to wake Lil and Little Cissa and put on my coolest wrapper and stole downstairs to bake Gideon's cake. I had tried my best to interest Gideon in a nice Orange Sponge for his graduation. Orange Sponge I could have baked the night before, but he insists it's my Chocolate Marbled Supreme he must have. In this heat that cake can't last a minute, much less overnight.

So, I'm up at dawn, blanching almonds, chopping citron, shaving some chocolate and setting it on ice and swirling the rest with butter-cream. The batter beat up, I poured it into three shallow dripping pans. Downright sinful to fire up an oven on a day like this, but I done it. You don't graduate but once after all and Mother says graduation's the most important day of your life. "What about your wedding day?" I asked her. Mother said graduation was all your very own and your wedding you had to share with someone else.

The cakes was in the oven and my hands dusted off when Doctor Tipton come to the back door. "Your mother's closed up the Pilgrim for the day, and if I am to sit through all that mush and humbug of graduation, I have to have some breakfast."

"It's too early for breakfast."

"Not for me. I've been up all night with old man Hutchings."

"He die yet?"

"Not yet." Doctor mopped his brow with a big cotton handkerchief. He was gray-faced and dark-jowled and his eyes was rimmed with red and whatever suffering he'd beheld all night. He took off his coat and hung it over the chair. "The wind's coming off the desert. It's going to be a flint and tinder day. What's that I smell, Afton? Cake? Ah, my dear, the gods have gifted you. No one can bake a cake like Afton Douglass."

"There ain't but one God, Doctor," I remind him as I get breakfast together. I put on some hash and eggs and toast Frenched the way Mother does it. I even boiled him up some coffee (which we keep just for Doctor as Saints don't touch the vile stuff) and he ate and stretched his legs out and grinned.

"Doctor you look to have something up your sleeve today."

As if to prove he don't, he takes off his cuffs, rolls up his sleeves and sets about washing his own dishes.

"Neither of my brothers would put his little finger in dishwater."

"Well, Mason's only eleven, so you got time to train him. And Gideon — "

"I what?" says Gideon, looking waxy and pale as he stands in the doorway carrying his *Delsarte Elocution Book* with his fingers stuck in all the parts where it tells which gestures go with which words. " 'Lives of great men/All remind us,' " says Gideon.

"You all ready?" says Doctor.

Gideon licks his lips and looks at the table piled high with all the party fixings, the blue vase washed and waiting for the day's best roses, the lemons squeezed for lemonade, the ham all scored and poked with cloves, and the orange sauce all ready to be basted on the ham. (If Gideon had settled for an Orange Sponge, I could have used the peel from the sauce in the cake.) "I can't do it," says Gideon.

Doctor smiles as he snaps his cuffs back on and puts his arm around Gideon's shoulders. "Gideon, my boy, today you're the spokesman, not just for your class, but for your whole generation. They're going to believe your every word when you tell them they will meet with destiny, when you assure them all their battles will be glorious. You're going to fill the young with courage and the old with tears, Gideon, because the old know that all battles are finally only against time and time can never be bested."

Gideon must have understood all that because he took heart and went on, " 'We can make our lives sublime/And departing…'." And Doctor took his coat and left and I washed out the coffeepot and hid it.

THEY SHOULD HAVE had the ceremonies right then, just after dawn, because by noon the grass was dry as kindling and the speaker's platform near wavered in the heat. Everyone in the audience was sitting on hard benches, fanning themselves with their programs. All them waving white programs looked like tiny sails on a bay of faces. I looked for Tom, but couldn't find him, so I took my place with my family and Dr. Tipton. Cissa was whining and Mother told her to hush and then she told Mason to put his licorice bits away because the smell was making her sick. For this day Mother'd softened her widow's black and she was wearing gray gloves and a soft gray silk bodice with a white silk rose at her throat. All four of us girls was in white and though we all had hats, they didn't do us no good. Sweat prickled all along my scalp and my bodice was sticking to me even before the Principal got up to speak. Gideon sat between him and the vulgar mayor. The Methodist minister and Bishop Myles was up there too, them and half a dozen others, all looking hot and important.

They all had their say. Every one of them. All saying the same thing, if you ask me. Then Gideon got up. He had all his Delsarte gestures just right and his voice was clear and strong and manly and you could hear him just fine, talking about how the Class of '09 was saying hail and farewell to the past and going forth to meet its destiny. Mother wept and even Doctor daubed his tired eyes.

Us four girls left right after Gideon's speech because we had to get the party ready and besides, we was all glad to go home and strip off our clothes for a time and work in our drawers. And work it was. Me and Eden decided we'd all perish if we didn't have some shade so we took two clean white sheets and tied them across the tops of the trellises that face one another and hold up our grapevines. The vines was thick and leafy and dusty and the grapes was a hard coppery green. The desert wind kept snapping the sheets away from us, but finally we got them fixed to the trellises, one side at a time. Then the four of us moved the kitchen table out underneath the sheets, though Cissa is so little – and so lazy – she wasn't any help at all. She kept moaning about the heat until Eden told her to go soak her head and Lil had to stop her from doing just that.

Me, I stood there for a minute. I love the smell of bleach in the noonday sun. My nose tingles and I always think something nice will happen on a day you smell bleach in the sunlight.

We spread the table with our very best starched cloth. From the front of the house Eden clipped an armful of red climbing roses that smelled thick, like overripe fruit. She filled the blue vase and put it in the center of the table. I got the Chocolate Marbled Supreme frosted, all three layers, and sprinkled with shaved chocolate and put in the pie cooler with some ice on the shelf just below. We got the ham quick-baked and basted with orange sauce and the vegetables all creamed and ice chipped for lemonade and when everything was done, we went upstairs and bathed our faces and got dressed again except for our hats and gloves. Cissa swore she was going bare-legged and Eden swore she was done with corsets forever. But I put on lots of talc and Orange Water and all my clothes. I told Lil, Tom Lance is coming to this party and I'm looking my best even if I faint from the heat.

It was a fine jollification, that party. The sheets billowed overhead and the girls and women billowed with eau de cologne. The men took off their coats and took their ease in shirtsleeves. The lemonade glasses went slick and frosty in our hands and the orange sauce lay bright and sticky on our plates. My cake hadn't fell at all and when I brought it out, they all clapped. We lingered over cake and lemonade, everyone laughing and talking, everyone except Tom, and he was listening to Lloyd Myles. Doctor was being extra nice to Arlene, who was pink as a baby's bottom, downright dewy with sweat. Cissa and Mason was minding their manners and Lil and Eden was listening to the Bishop tell about a Chinee who wanted to convert to our religion. Only Mother still looked cool, nodding and bending with the wind toward the voice of Mrs. Myles, whose collar had wilted about her neck.

Then Doctor says Gideon should give his speech one last time. I groaned and Doctor says, "Now Afton, Gideon won't ever get to give that speech again and we ought to listen one last time."

Bishop Myles pats his fair slick hair. He just keeps at it like he's commending himself on a job well done and finally he coughs and says Gideon would give his speech again. In church on Sunday. And maybe Doctor would like to come hear him then.

"No, no," says Doctor, pulling out his cigar to Mother's horror and delight, "I want to hear Gideon's speech here, enjoy it here with this cigar and the faces of lovely young women around me and that su-perb dinner stirring up my pancreatic juices."

Well who knew what juices they was and didn't no one ask. Gideon (who was at the head of the table) pushed his chair back and stood and placing his fingers on the cloth (just as the Delsarte advised for Beginnings) he leaned slightly forward. " 'Lives of great men/All remind us/ We can make our lives sublime/And departing leave behind us/Footprints in the sands of time.' Friends, families and fellow graduates, these are words which we, the class of '09, must ponder as we say hail and farewell to St. Elmo High and go forth into the world to meet our destinies. Today marks the end of one era in our lives: we bid goodbye to the past we have in common. But today we also mark a new beginning: we greet the future as individual adults. Each one has a destiny and each one will make a separate pilgrimage. What will we need for this journey? Courage and strength, yes, surely those, but they are not enough, not if we are to make our lives sublime. For that we must always carry with us the past, the knowledge we have learned at St. Elmo High, the love of our families and friends, and last, but not least, our faith in God. These are the requirements of the future."

Gideon stretched his right arm out toward the future and Arlene. She was in a swoon. You'd think it was the *Gettysburg Address*. I knew what come next, all that grandness about going into a world which will test us daily and make us stronger and better and wiser for our efforts. Oh I knew it all by heart, I could have said it, but somehow I couldn't hear it anymore. Gideon's voice got far away, elocutionary and foreign, like he was calling, calling to me and I couldn't make him out. It must have been the heat. The heat and the wind that blew the words around with the sheets and shadows, ruffled the vines and lifted the hair from Gideon's brow and dusted the hems of our white dresses with gravel. All his words and all they meant and all who was listening to them – my nearest and dearest – was blowing away from me, like we wasn't flesh at all, like we wasn't even gathered for a party under this bleach-bright sheet.

Then suddenly they was all clapping and congratulating Gideon on a fine speech, and the sound of all that crackling flesh on flesh stirred me and I dipped my napkin in my lemonade and daubed my neck and temples. Then Tom Lance give me that smile of his where one side of his mouth is nailed shut by the scar and I felt better.

Gideon got some fine presents. Binoculars from Eden and an *Illustrated History of the World* from Mother and a leather-bound Doctrine and Covenants from Bishop and Mrs. Myles. Me and Lil and Cissa went together on some fine lawn handkerchiefs with a "G" on each one and Arlene give him a fountain pen with a tag that said "For all your great thoughts." Mason give him a spinning top Mason's been wanting for months.

Gideon give his thanks to one and all and another speech about how much we have all meant to him. Oh, Gideon was just full of words that day and him and Arlene was smiling at each other like two cherubs on a Christmas card. Suddenly Doctor pulls a little leather book from his pocket and starts to fan himself with it. "I just about forgot," he says, "you got one more present." He hands Gideon the book entitled *St. Elmo First National Bank and Trust* and then he puts his cigar back in his mouth and laces his fingers over his waistcoat.

Gideon's eyes bug out and his mouth falls open. I thought maybe he was speechless, but that was too much to hope.

"That money's for college," says Doctor, not taking his cigar out. "If you don't want to go to college, I'll get you a watch so you can tick off your life and squandered opportunities." He laughs, but you can tell he don't think it's funny.

Mother gets a pruney look and Arlene goes green as fresh alfalfa. Mason quits licking his fingers and picking up cake crumbs and Cissa gnaws the air. Eden and Lil look like twin Indianhead nickels and I look at Doctor. He's real pleased with what he's wrought.

"I haven't applied to any college."

"I've taken care of that. You'll be admitted to Piedmont Men's College about forty miles north of here. If you want to go."

Gideon gasps and falls back on the Delsarte Elocution Method, palms out for surprise. "I am the oldest living man in a family of women and children and I was going to get a job here in St. Elmo." Arlene's head is bobbing up and down. I know she's wanting him to get a job so's he can support one woman and any children she and Gideon might muster up. "I'd have to talk it over with – " Gideon looks at Arlene, " – Mother."

Mother looks at Lucius Tipton the way the hawk looks at the field mouse, amused and anxious at the same time. She pulls herself up straighter than ever and though she don't take her eyes off Doctor, she says to Gideon, "The Pilgrim's doing just fine for this family, Gideon. If you want to go to college, you go."

Well, it might just as well have rained for all the flurry. Everyone asking Doctor about Piedmont Men's College and what it was like and what Gideon would study and passing around the savings book and when it came to Mother, she says, "Lucius, you have been at this a long time and you should have told me."

Doctor says nothing. Just lets that smile flit over his face which I notice for the first time was ugly. Not ugly like Tom's, no scars or nothing, but I wonder that I never saw before that his skin was pocky and loose and his nose was too big and the mouth too big too, even if it was hid under that droopy mustache. But the eyes was just fine. The eyes saved him from ugliness, though they didn't make him no beauty either.

I urge another piece of cake on the Bishop, but he declines. I ask if a fly's got into his lemonade because he don't look well. He don't say nothing to me. He asks Doctor if there are fraternities at Piedmont Men's College and Doctor says he thinks so and then Bishop tells us how fraternities was based on pagan practices and un-Christian rites and that no young man needed to belong to anything but the church. The wind snapped the pages of the bank book like tiny rifle reports as the Bishop goes on. And on and on about how Saints had to beware of snares everywhere around them and how a Gentile school would test Gideon daily, just like Gideon said in his speech, but it didn't sound glorious coming from Bishop, but dark and terrible. Bishop said Piedmont Men's College would try to shake Gideon from the tree of faith, to cast him down like unwise, unripe fruit. He said Gideon would meet unconverted teachers, unenlightened men who mistakenly believed in knowledge without faith. "Knowledge without faith is useless. Faith alone makes you free."

"Gallstones," says Doctor through his smoke. "This is Gideon's chance — his one chance — to unshackle himself, to learn to think, to learn to question."

"Some things are beyond question."

"Nothing is beyond question. Without questions there's no science, no progress. If men didn't question, we'd still be wearing animal skins and eating roots and berries."

"Lucius," says Mother.

Doctor ignores Mother. "If you don't question and weigh and criticize and imagine, what's the use of being human? Why not just go join the cattle in the field?"

"Or the lilies of the field," says Bishop, "who neither toil nor spin, but are sustained by God's all-merciful love."

"And who die in a day without knowing they were ever alive! Men can't live like that. Not now. Great galloping entrails, man! This is the Twentieth Century! We are coming into a world none of us will recognize in the next ten years, we're coming into a world we're not prepared for!"

"We must always be prepared," says Bishop. "We are coming into the fullness of time, to the end of the latter days when the wheat shall be separated from the chaff and not even the prayers and supplications of the Chosen will save the chaff," he stares hard at Doctor, "from the Last Harvest."

"The Last Harvest," Doctor scoffs, puffing himself into a furious cloud. "There's only last year. And the one before that and this year and the one after that. History goes on. Only life ends."

"Life is everlasting."

"Tell that to Old Man Hutchings."

"The End of the World is nigh," Bishop insists.

"There isn't any end," Doctor snorts. "There isn't any beginning."

"The Beginning is revealed in the Book of Genesis and The End – "

"The end and the beginning are so raveled they can never be picked apart. No one in the present sees anything but the end of the world around him and no one in the future, looking back, sees anything but the beginning of the world he knows. Gideon's got the chance to be part of the future. If he doesn't learn to think and question and criticize and imagine, he'll be mulched back into the past like every yahoo in St. Elmo."

"Lucius," says Mother.

Bishop puts on his coat and motions to Lloyd to do the same. "A young man can learn anything he needs to know from the Bible, the Book of Mormon and the Doctrine and Covenants. He needs faith and a good, upright life, and that's all he needs." Bishop puts his hand on Gideon's shoulder and congratulates him on a fine valedictorian speech and thanks Mother for a lovely party and says he has things to attend to. Then he left with Lloyd and Mrs. Myles right behind him. They was all coupled together like the east-bound freight.

Doctor just sat smoking and scowling and didn't even get up when the Myleses departed. That was bad manners, vulgar, if you ask me. I couldn't tell if Mother thought so or not. Her face is blank as the sheet overhead.

But Gideon's ain't. Gideon is a mass of sorrow and uncertainty. He folds and refolds his hands into boneless-looking lumps. I say, "Have some cake, Gideon, please. It's your favorite and it don't keep well in this heat. Have some cake."

But he don't. And neither does Arlene. She thanks Mother and says she must be leaving and that she can get her own hat and Gideon don't need to walk her home as he'll be too busy getting ready to go to Piedmont Men's College. Gideon scrambles to his feet and opens the screen door for her and still Doctor don't budge. Then Tom too says he must be going. I pressed some cake and lemonade on him, but he says, "Thank you all the same Afton. I'll see you in church on Sunday."

I want to hold Tom's arm and say, *Tom, Tom, please don't be revolted by Doctor's goings on, please Tom stay, I forgot to warn you, Tom, that Doctor is an atheist, but he don't mean it, Tom, he don't mean half of it.* But he did mean it and for the first time ever I was ashamed of Dr. Tipton and wished we didn't know him.

So, they was all gone, our guests and friends, and though the wind blew wrapping paper around the yard, didn't no one run after it to collect it. We just sat, not looking at each other, like strangers at the station. Finally Doctor puts out his cigar and says, "It's too damn hot to sit in this valley. Let's all go up to Urquita Springs in the Flyer. It'll be cool in the hills. Heat like this bakes your brains and makes you – "

"Act like a fool," says Mother. "Look what you've done, Lucius."

"What I've done! You don't believe that old humbug, do you? You don't get *born* into being one of the Chosen, you got to choose it yourself – I'm offering Gideon that choice, that chance he'll be one of the few who can greet what's ahead with a little wisdom, a little knowledge. If he goes to Piedmont College he can – " Doctor stops and looks at Gideon, who's slumped forward in his chair staring at the screen door. "You'll go, won't you Gideon?"

"Sure, I like Urquita Springs."

"No, no," Doctor's voice near trembles, "to Piedmont College. You're not going to be talked out of it, are you? You're not going to let that – I mean, it's a marvelous opportunity, my boy; you're so bright and I've been hoping for years – I so want you to go."

Gideon looks at his big twisting hands and then he wipes his glasses on his wool pants. "I guess I'll have to go, won't I?" he says finally. "If I believed my own speech, I'll have to go. I must have courage and go forth and meet my destiny and make my life sublime."

I thought Gideon was going to cry, or maybe break into Henry Wordsworth Longfellow and all the rest of it, but he don't. He says he'll go inside and change to go up to the Springs.

Slowly the family gets ready and they pile into Doctor's Flyer, but not me. I didn't want to be around Doctor Tipton and if the rest of them did, well fine. I said I'd tidy up a bit and though Doctor pressed me, I was firm. I'm good at being firm. It's one of my gifts.

After they leave I take off my good white dress and put on a plain, work-a-day cotton. I pick up the wrapping paper blowing around the yard and clear off the table and fill up the sink and set to work on them dishes till the suds flew and water sloshed over the floor. So naturally after I got the dishes done and the roaster and dripping pans scoured, I had to mop the floor. I found some grit and a spider behind the stove so I had to clean behind the icebox as well. My fingers wizened up and whitened with the bleach in the mop water and sweat run down my neck and bubbled along my brow and trickled down my ribs. I did everything I could think of in that kitchen, even rubbing down the cabinets with linseed oil, but it didn't none of it banish my anger. If that's what it was. So I decided to take a bath and cool off.

I turned on the cold water in the tub and started looking for my *Girls' Own Journal* to read in the bath when suddenly it come on me that I have never been alone in this house. Maybe I should have gone to the Springs. Least I wouldn't be alone in this house that has never been empty so far as I can remember, not with all of us – Mother and Gideon and Eden and me and Lil and Mason and Little Cissa – living here, our voices on the porch, footsteps on the stairs, the doors squealing on dry hinges, plates and pans banging in the kitchen, and laughter from somewheres, even if you didn't know quite where or whose laughter it was. I go back to the bathroom and turn off the tap, but it drips. I can hear it drip all over the house as I go from room to room. I can hear it drip and I can hear the clock in the parlor tick and even the window sashes rattling with the wind that wanted in, like a guest who come too late for the party.

I set little things to rights, things I never would notice if my family'd all been there. I listen to the emptiness as I smooth Mother's bureau scarf and set Cissa's doll up straight in her corner. I arrange Eden's brushes and put Lil's hat back in the cupboard. I straighten the books on Gideon's shelf and pick up bits of lint from the rug. And I wipe dust from all the windowsills while I look out to a street so empty and dusty and dry, not even the dogs is out.

I never did find the *Girls' Own Journal*. I couldn't have read it anyway, not with that silence pressing all around me. I got in the tub and washed off quickly and then stuck my head under the tap and washed my hair too, though it didn't need it. I put a towel around my head and my wrapper on and go outside because I couldn't stand that awful silence one minute longer.

I sit on the back steps and brush out my hair. It was getting on toward sunset and the sky's colors was running, like indigo in the washwater, like vermillion in the rinse. The whole yard was afloat in a queer yellow light. Graduation day had only just passed, but it looked like our party wasn't just a few hours gone. It looked to have long since hailed and fare-welled. The tablecloth was all stained and rumpled and held on only by the blue vase which had fell over and spilled out the roses, and they lay gasping. One of the sheets come down and lay, dragging in the dirt, like a shroud over the grapevines. But the other sheet still snapped in the wind and the shadows stretched far, far beyond the vines and it was still hot.

The Last Dream
Before Waking

THE ROAD TO APPIN village hugged the coast of Loch Linnhe; and it was a short drive from Vivie Henderson's bungalow to the B and B she had recommended, the Twin Sisters. She had said they couldn't miss the Twin Sisters, and she was right; but Liza Derwent's recognition was far more acute than simple apprehension of the high white gabled house with its steep roof, manicured garden, and smart sign out front with B AND B and VACANCY carefully lettered in black. Liza stepped out of the family car, her feet crunching on the freshly raked gravel, and she squinted against the sunlight reveling, beveling from bright windows. Liza's breath came sharply and she longed to seize her sister's arm, to validate her own vision: didn't Susan, too, instantly and instinctively perceive that this was the home Liza had longed for all her life? But she resisted: the illusion was too precious and too fragile to share. Liza Derwent, quite simply, confronted the place she had created out of longing and imagination; she had never expected to encounter it at all, much less in this remote corner of western Scotland. That the house was hers only temporarily and belonged to others made no difference. All her homes were temporary and belonged to others.

Liza was the eldest child of a minor American diplomat, and in all her fourteen years, she had never lived more than two consecutively in any one place. Liza could endure this nomadic life by keeping framed, fresh, and inviolate the vision of her home. Her real home. The one before her now, which she would inhabit for this night and no longer. Liza's father was posted in London and they were vacationing in Scotland, which could hardly be considered exotic by a girl who had grown up in Singapore, Kingston, Melbourne, Kuala Lumpur, places that only dot the imaginations of less fortunate children. Liza did not think of herself as fortunate.

The Twin Sisters had been built in the early part of this century, brought stick-by-stick, stone-by-stone, tile-by-tile, beam-by-beam, by boat from Glasgow to satisfy two prosperous widows who wanted to live out their remaining lives side-by-side in Appin. Their names were lost and they long dead, but the houses retained the relationship, though one sister had turned slatternly, her decay all the more marked by the smart sister's garden of stately delphiniums patroling the painted porch where Liza's father now stood, inquiring after a place for the night – maybe longer, he told their hostess, Mrs. Moffett – for himself, his wife and two daughters.

Mrs. Moffett was taciturn but benign, with hair of gun-metal gray and wearing an unsullied apron. She had the air of curator rather than resident and greeted the Derwents individually as though she were casting players for bit parts. She told them to mind their steps as they followed her up the polished staircase. Liza lingered behind the family, resting her hand reverentially on the rail. Mrs. Moffett gave George and Caroline a spacious room with a view of the back garden. Liza and Susan each had smaller rooms with bay windows looking out to the road, a field, the loch, a small rocky island, and the mountains, glowering and resplendent in the distance. From this window Liza watched as Mrs. Moffett hung a shingle inscribed NO in front of the VACANCY sign out front.

"Well, let's all go for a walk," said her father, marching into her room, zipping up his jacket. He wore stout Wellies and looked fit and exuberant for all his middle-aged girth.

Susan came in behind him. "It's going to rain again, Dad."

"You can't let the weather deter you! Come on girls, let's go."

Liza scrutinized her father carefully, regarding him not as integral to her life, but as though he had just impinged on it. Trespassed. She cocked her upper lip in the adolescent sneer she had perfected and announced that she would not go for a walk with them. "I'm going to vomit," she concluded decisively.

"Ever the charming one, aren't you Liza?" he returned.

"What's wrong, honey?" asked her mother, a tall thin woman with neat, graying hair and exquisite hands. "Did something disagree with you at the picnic?"

Something had, but Liza did not say so. Caroline too declined the walk with George and Susan and said she preferred to take *Jane Eyre* into the Twin Sisters' enormous tub and read there. George grumbled and muttered, asked if she ever read anything that wasn't a hundred years old. On her way out the door, Caroline retorted that Henry James was as close to the present as she cared to come.

So Liza was left in sole possession of her room, which was immaculate, anonymous, and high-ceilinged; cornflower-sprigged wallpaper surrounded her, and tiles the color of fresh lettuce framed the fireplace and sink. The bedspread was hard and white, and when Liza put her head on the pillow, it crackled with starch. She was glad there were no family photographs or intimate bric-à-brac she might have to account for imaginatively; she was free to possess and imbue this room with her own best self, cobbled and mortared with wish, dream, and longing, all momentarily fulfilled. She lay perfectly still, floating on that fulfillment and hating her father more than she would have thought possible. She ought to be able to delight in this home, her real home, wholeheartedly and without distraction, and her father had made that both possible and impossible. Possible because they were only in Scotland at his insistence. Impossible because he had betrayed them all. Betrayed their past and imperiled their future. *They're lovers — don't you understand anything? Don't you know?* Liza covered herself and curled into a small knot, fighting an interior chill and insidious nausea. She had not lied on that score. She covered her face with both hands. Weren't a wife and two daughters enough for any man to love? How could he be so gross?

THE DERWENTS had been comfortably settled and midway through their vacation in the Lake District, when George suggested a short jaunt to Appin on the west coast of Scotland. A day or two, that's all. Caroline replied that it was a day or two just to get up there, but George shrugged off the objections of distance. Caroline then pointed out that it was wasteful to leave this cottage when they were paying rent, but he brushed aside considerations of money and said the girls should see Scotland. Caroline raised her eyebrows in an arch way Liza was certain she had learned from 19th-century novels – the only expression of visible disgust permitted those pallid heroines.

Despite her mother's protests and within the week they had packed, locked the cottage, and were on their way north, the girls alternately lolling and squirming in the back seat of their new Alpha Sud. "You girls will love Appin," George said over his shoulder. "There are ghosts everywhere. Appin figured in Robert Louis Stevenson's *Kidnapped*, you know."

"The Lake District hasn't exactly been neglected in literature," Caroline retorted.

"Vivie and her family have gone to Appin for their holidays for years," George continued. (Liza knew he was unwilling to enter a literary dispute he would surely lose.) "They wouldn't think of going anywhere else. And I can see why just from the pictures Vivie's brought to the office."

He launched into a description of the photographs of Appin that Vivie Henderson had brought to the office where she was secretary to George Derwent and two other minor Dips. Liza liked to refer to her father and his colleagues as "Dips," but her mother said this irreverence for the Foreign Service was unseemly and advised her darkly to stop it at once. Naturally, Liza said she would and didn't. Particularly at school she affected a way of saying that her father was a Dip that gave her a reputation for being flip and jaded, which was exactly the way Liza liked to think of herself. She had begun to think of Mrs. Henderson as the Dip Sec, but when the term slipped out one day, her father turned red in the face and told her she was never to say that again. "Why not?" she inquired coolly. "You've done nothing but bitch about her for three months."

Liza was grounded for saying "bitch," but it was true. Mrs. Henderson had originally annoyed George Derwent to no end and he brought his irritated tales home to the dinner table. She was an American married to a British businessman, and George thought her cheeky and impulsive and inefficient. She was very popular at the office, however, and eventually George's anecdotes lost their tarnish of ill-will and he remarked on her cleverness and spirit.

Caroline had met Mrs. Henderson at the Legation Christmas party the year before. "She's quite nice," Caroline reported to Liza and Susan, "but I spoke with her only briefly. She said how nice it was to meet me and I said the pleasure was mine."

"Is she attractive?" Liza asked.

"In a manner of speaking."

"Really, Mom, you are maddening! Can't you be more specific?"

"She has the jaw of a horse," said Caroline specifically.

Even the horse's jaw must be in keeping with her personality, Liza reflected in the back seat of the Alpha. Dad was saying she was an expert horsewoman and loved Appin for the splendid riding. A cool breeze blew through the car and intermittent showers followed them as they drove northward, slowly through straggling villages and speeding up along the coastal hills, beside lonely fields that swept down to lonely lochs where small, weathered boats were moored.

George pulled the car over to the side of the road and let the motor idle. "This is Loch Linnhe," he said, pulling from his pocket Vivie Henderson's much folded, hand-drawn map. He followed it with his finger. "She says their cottage is up the road that lies directly in front of Castle Staulker."

"What's Castle Staulker?" asked Susan.

George started the car again. "Vivie says we'll know it when we see it."

And indeed they did. The Alpha slowed as they pulled by and gazed mutely. Turreted with tiny windows, proud, high, grim, Castle Staulker rose out of the water, a stone tower founded on a rock not far from the shore. "The home of fifteenth-century kings," George announced, as if he'd just bought it.

Sunlight escaped a net of clouds and spilled buckets of brightness over the water as three horses and riders galloped in the shadow of Castle Staulker, splashing through the mud flats, small perfect prisms of light spraying behind their flying hooves. Liza was transfixed, beholding in them colorful fifteenth-century couriers hastening with news of battles and the fate of hundreds inside their leather pouches.

"It's her!" George shouted. "It's them!"

Foliage cut them off from a view of the loch for a quarter mile, but he put the Alpha in high gear and sped to the next low field, honking all the while. One of the riders glanced shoreward, brought her horse up, and raised her arm in a broad, beckoning gesture of recognition. The others, who had gone on, turned back and followed her reluctantly as George brought the car to a halt and turned the motor off.

Hooves beat a dull crescendo over the earth as Vivie Henderson's figure galloped toward them. She wore American jeans, expensive boots, and a red sweater that cast her face in a geranium glow. The Derwents were out of their car before she dismounted and stood, flushed and eager, before them. Liza had imagined Mrs. Henderson much younger than her own parents, but she wasn't; her light brown hair was attractively frosted with gray (whether by nature or design, Liza couldn't tell) and she was lithe and tanned, but not lovely. She had a heavy jaw and, consequently, an unlovely mouth and she greeted them in a voice that had resolutely clung to its flat American accent. "George! What a surprise! Your note said Wednesday; I'm sure you said Wednesday!" Her horse pawed the ground, anxious to be off again, but Vivie Henderson held the bridle firmly. "Didn't you tell me you were coming up on Wednesday?"

"No, Tuesday, I think, I said Tuesday," George stammered. "I must have."

"Well, maybe you did. What does it matter? You're here, that's all that counts." She shook hands all around and said how good it was to see Caroline again and chided George for never mentioning that his daughters were great beauties.

Mrs. Henderson's sons were not great beauties. Richard was a bit older than Liza, James a bit younger than Susan, and they both had their mother's jaw. Richard had bad skin, while James's teeth were clotted with orthodontic work. Both boys seemed surly and ill at ease, rather like their horses.

"I'm so delighted you're here," Vivie beamed after the introductions were complete. "And Edward was so disappointed that he had to leave and miss your visit. My husband," she explained to Caroline and the girls, "was called back to London unexpectedly."

"That's a shame," said George.

"Yes, well, it's his tough luck, isn't it? I was just saying to the boys last night how we'd probably bore each other silly with Edward gone. And now here you are. To rescue us," she added with a smile. She turned to her boys. "Aren't you the lucky ones – rescued by two fair maidens!"

"Mum's so dramatic," murmured James.

"Well I wish I could think of something dramatic for lunch. Honestly, I thought you were coming on Wednesday and so I didn't – well, we'll just have to wing it, won't we? The boys and I will take our horses back and meet you at the house in about an hour. All right? Oh! That house. Have you seen it?"

"Not yet."

"Well, you drive about half a mile up that road – " she motioned to a gravelly thread that wound to the east of them, "and watch out for the hedges – they grow so close to the road, they'll scrape your new car – and take the right fork and you'll come to it. You've never seen anything so grungy in all your life! Make yourselves comfortable – if you can." She began to hand the key to George, but thought better of it; she gave it to Caroline.

She mounted her horse and rode off, and the Derwents – all of them stunned and a little breathless – got back into their car. Vivie's very language fell on Liza's ears like music; no one at the Legation used all that wonderful American slang. The Dips tended to be a dry lot (which was perhaps the reason they were Dips), bland and colorless in order to absorb new cultures and discharge their duties. But Vivie Henderson seemed determinedly and dramatically American – and not at all ashamed of it. Perhaps, thought Liza, that's her charm.

Liza tucked "wing it" and "grungy" away for use later at school, but she was a little dismayed to find that the latter phrase seemed altogether appropriate for the bungalow which stood in a clearing without any garden or other amenities to soften its awful utilitarianism. Inside, the squalor surprised her; it suggested somehow a want of balance and dignity that Liza had been taught to prize, values she ostensibly rejected (since they came from her mother), but to which she clung secretly. Sagging chairs clustered around a scarred coffee table like beggars around a street fire. Clothes, shoes, and boots lay where they had fallen; and a half dozen unemptied buckets were strategically placed to catch water from the leaking roof. The breakfast dishes had been abandoned; grease congealed on the plates, and the smell of bacon still hung heavy in the air.

"Maybe we ought to wash up," said Susan, eyeing the stagnant coffee and old crusts.

"No," Caroline said emphatically, "these people are strangers and it would look – well, presumptuous."

"Oh, Caroline," George scoffed, "presumptuous isn't a word people use anymore."

"Maybe they should."

The girls had the kitchen tidy by the time Vivie Henderson burst in, laden with bounty, banishing the squalor and infusing the bungalow with her tonic presence and the aromas of sausage and cakes and fresh bread and fine mustard, the fruit and cheese she carried. Richard's arms were full of bottled beer, and as he set it on the table, Vivie winked at Caroline. "I know how fond George is of beer – and of course, it shows on him." Belatedly George pulled in his stomach and Vivie laughed. "Who cleaned up?" Liza and Susan smiled and stared at the floor. "How nice of you girls! I always wished I had daughters. Men are such pigs, aren't they? Boys too," she added blithely.

Liza was shocked that neither James nor Richard seemed to take offense at being called pigs. She could not imagine her own mother referring to her own father – or indeed, to anyone – as a pig, even in such a lighthearted fashion.

"If I'd known you were coming today," Vivie continued, digging in her bag, "I'd have done something about this awful sty. Really, have you ever seen such a hovel? Look at that leaking roof! The landlord acted like I wanted him to gild the bathtub when I said I wanted it fixed. And now I have to lose a whole morning of my holiday tomorrow waiting for the man to come fix the roof. A whole morning lost! It isn't fair, is it?" Her face clouded with the injustice of it all and then she told Richard to get the backpacks for their picnic. He sulked out of the room. "The boys are so English," she told Liza confidentially, "they like their picnics in baskets, but I've got these wonderful American backpacks, and they're perfect, because I never travel light and I never leave anything to chance." She raised her eyebrows as if to underscore the intimacy of this admission.

"Mum would pack the loo if she could fit it in."

"Now, James, these girls are going to think you're very vulgar." She turned her attention back to Liza. "An Englishman's idea of a picnic is a woman in a flowering print dress with a straw hat floating over the fields while she lugs a damn, three-ton basket. I say – let the men carry backpacks! What do you say?"

Liza laughed because she didn't quite know what to say, and James chuckled in spite of himself. Vivie Henderson dealt with her sons in the way that supremely confident women deal with men: she always got her own way by deferring to them, by making men believe that whatever she might have suggested, they had surely inspired her. Vivie's femininity and all its illusions had been preserved inside the family; she was flirtatious and bantering and skilled as the mother of sons is likely to be. A woman with daughters has no such practice. Daughters, however unwillingly or unknowingly, eventually betray their mothers: much as flowers taking substance from the same stalk, one fades, wilts, crumbles as the other insists on its own beauty. Mothers and daughters are shell and shadow to one another, while mothers and sons relentlessly rehearse the drama that will be central to their lives.

In two cars they drove to a field of Vivie's choice and walked to a meadow she suggested and spread the blanket where they had a grandiose view of the loch and the beautiful, grim Castle Staulker. The smell of crushed grass, water, and wildflower mingled pleasantly with the odor of dung. The loch rippled nervously with a threatening wind and clouds jostled overhead. Vivie began pulling out the contents of the backpacks while Caroline held her palms up. "It doesn't look very promising for a picnic," she observed.

"Yes," said Vivie, "won't it be awful if it rains? Think what will happen to the bread. Still, I never let the weather deter me." She passed around the beers, even giving one to Richard and – much to Liza's surprise – asking her if she wanted one. Liza declined as if beer did not agree with her, while she envied James and Richard. How fortunate they were to have a mother who took their dawning adulthood for granted, who said "damn" casually, who left nothing to chance and would not allow the weather to deter her.

The breadknife had apparently been left to chance and left behind, but Vivie made do with Richard's pocketknife and said she hoped Caroline wouldn't object to such scraggly slices. "You have to understand this is an impromptu picnic and you can't insist on what's proper."

"I wouldn't insist," Caroline replied, rather insistently.

"Well, personally, I think it's just as well Edward went to London. My husband doesn't like anything the least unplanned. Can you imagine – after all these years of living with me! Isn't that right, Richard?" She inquired pointedly of her eldest son, but he only sourly responded that he was going for a walk. "That's great, Richard! We'll sit here and have a drink and you four go for a walk."

"I want to go alone."

"Nonsense. You and James take Liza and Susan and show them that wonderful path we found through the woods."

"What if it rains?" asked Caroline.

"Oh, they'll manage. Children are endlessly inventive, aren't they? Go on, now, we'll see you in half an hour."

"It's at least half an hour each way," Richard said savagely.

"Is it? All right. We'll eat first and then you can take them. You girls will absolutely love this path. I'm convinced that the ghosts of people tortured at Castle Staulker still roam these woods looking for revenge."

"Were people tortured there?" asked Liza, uncertain if this enhanced or diminished the castle's romance.

"Look at it," Vivie commanded, and Liza obliged. "Treachery cries out from every stone. Appin is famous for treachery and murder and betrayal. It's haunted. That's why it's still so wild here: nothing plain and domestic can quite uproot the ghosts. I hope you believe in ghosts," Vivie added, as if the ghosts might be eavesdropping. Liza said she did, and as they ate Vivie told them centuries-old gossip of Appin, legends of loyalty and revenge, murder and madness. Everything tasted better than anyone expected – the sausages and chunks of cheese sawed off with the pocket-knife, two kinds of cake, three kinds of fruit – expensive, thick-skinned oranges, frail peaches, and berries which burst and stained their fingers like blood.

After lunch the adults lay back amid the heather, Vivie and George lighting up cigarettes. Vivie urged them off, and obediently the girls and James followed Richard. He led them, with the brusque detachment of a bus driver on his regular route, along a crescent shore festooned with a necklace of moss and stones. When the path turned and disappeared into the woods, Richard quickened his pace and left them behind. Susan took Liza's arm. "Ask him to slow down, Liza, please. I don't want to get lost. I'm afraid of ghosts."

"Richard!" James called out. "You're going too fast for us. Wait up a bit!"

When they caught up with him, Richard regarded them all with cold contempt. "You show them the bloody path," he said to James. "I'm going on alone."

James and Susan cringed before his unvarnished wrath, but Liza refused to be daunted. She kept close behind him, matching his pace with long strides. The path narrowed and made several turns before she announced in her flip, jaded way, "I've lived all over the world."

"The bloody hell you have."

Stung, Liza retorted, "Even if we interrupted your holiday, you don't have to be rude, you know."

"The bloody hell I don't."

"Anyway, you shouldn't be angry with me and Susan. It wasn't our idea to come up." He leapt over a crumbling log and Liza nimbly jumped over it too. "But I'm glad we did. There's something very strange here. I think it's the first really haunted place I've ever been, and I've never seen anything like that castle just stuck in the lake and the mountains – "

Richard broke into a braying laugh. "Do you really think you're up here for the bloody scenery? You little twit. Don't you know *anything*?" He stopped and brought his pimpled face close to hers. His voice was coarse and hoarse. "Don't you know what adultery is?"

"Of course I do. Who doesn't?"

"Why do you think my father left Appin? He wasn't called back to London. He left when we got your bloody father's bloody note. Your father and my mother, they're *lovers*." He spat the term like a king condemning traitors. "He's screwing her arse off. Don't you understand anything? Don't you *know*?"

"Liar."

"Oh, yeah?" he hissed. "Every chance they get they're screwing, and everybody knows it. Everyone except twits like you and your little twit sister."

"Liar." Liza froze to the moist, musky leaves beneath her feet. "Liar."

"Ask your bloody father. Ask your bloody mother."

"Leave my mother out of this!"

"She's been left out! My father's been left out! Everyone knows your bloody father is screwing the – "

Liza cracked his jaw with the flat of her hand. Her palm stung and a large welt arose on his cheek amid the angry sores.

"Bloody – little – twits." His words came in short, hot gusts. He turned from her and ran.

BY THE TIME they returned to the picnic, the threatened rain had made good its promise, and only the impression of the blanket in the grass testified to their earlier presence. The adults were waiting for them in the Alpha as the bedraggled threesome, their shoes squealing in the mud, made their way back.

Vivie opened the car's back door and called out, "Where's Richard?""

"Didn't he come back here?" asked Susan. "We thought he – "

"Why didn't you stay together?" Caroline demanded. "What's wrong with Liza? What's wrong with you, Liza? You look like you hurt, honey."

"I fell." Liza slipped into the Alpha as Vivie stepped out. She did not look at Vivie; she scooted to the opposite corner and slumped there, her arms clamped over her narrow chest.

Vivie laughed. "Well, don't anyone worry about Richard. He knows his way home. He's not a very sociable creature, I'm afraid. He takes after his father." She pulled her hood up and brightened visibly. "Well let's go back to the bungalow and have a cup of tea."

"We ought to be looking for a place to stay, George," said Caroline. "It's getting late."

"Why don't you stay with us? Edward's gone, so you two can have my bed and the rest of us can wing it."

"We wouldn't think of imposing. We'll find a place."

"Oh, let's go back to Vivie's now," said George, putting the key in the ignition. "There's always a B and B somewhere."

"Not in July," Caroline reminded him.

"There's a place in the village I've heard about," Vivie offered. "The Twin Sisters. Why not go there and get rooms and then come back and have dinner with us?"

"No." Caroline gave a brief, sallow laugh and added that she was exhausted. "I've got to have a bath and rest. We've driven a long way today. And – "

"Well, let's go to Vivie's anyway," George interrupted her. "Let's have a cup of tea."

"Yes," Vivie chimed in, "the English think that's the answer for everything. Who knows, they might be right!"

Vivie and James tramped back to their car. Caroline turned to George. "We're *not* spending the night there."

"Of course not."

"And we're *not* going back for dinner."

"But – "

"We're going to find a B and B and have dinner and sleep there and leave in the morning."

"We just got here!"

"Oh, Mom – " Susan protested.

"You hush." Caroline faced George, her lips trembling. "A day's jaunt, that's what you said."

George turned the key; the motor hummed; the wipers swept over the window in their dull, predestined course.

LIZA DERWENT woke in the high-ceilinged bedroom; she stared at the blue-and-white wallpaper, the green tiles, without surprise. She knew exactly where she was. She lay there for a moment to further absorb the room, which was preternaturally quiet, like an empty stage set where everything of substance strains for ineffable effect. She unwound, stretched, and got up, walked to the window, and pulled the lace curtain aside. Cows stood belly-deep in meadow grass in the field across the road; and above them, chalk-colored gulls called raucously as they circled the waters of the loch. The spate of rain had come and gone, but the weather was changing yet again; new clouds massed overhead, draping the loch in dappled violet; and in the distance, the mountains undressed before Liza's eyes, exchanging their bright blue frocks for costumes of amethyst and umber. On the island across the loch, a stone shed blurred in the fine-grained rain.

Liza started when her mother touched her shoulder. Caroline smelled of lavender water, and her hands were powdered, and the ends of her hair curled damply and stuck to her neck. She put her arm around her daughter. The two might have been twin images, sisters, save that one was crisp and angular and the other dulled by time and talc.

"It's a lovely place, isn't it, Liza?"

Liza nodded, not trusting herself to speak.

"You know, I'd rather look at something from a window than stand on a hill and see everything for miles and miles around me. It's too breathtaking that way, but when things are framed," Caroline indicated the window's pattern with her hand, "you can absorb them and understand them better. It gives you perspective. When your dad and I were first married, I used to take pictures from all the windows – homes and hotels – we ever stayed in. George always teased me and said I should put him in the picture, but I said no. All I wanted was the window and the view. That way, I could look at those pictures and stand in those windows again – any time I wanted." She added as an afterthought, "If you put people in your pictures, all you notice is how they've changed."

Liza put her head against the lavender scent of her mother's neck. She wondered – fiercely, tenderly, protectively – about the home and hotel windows her parents had shared in their years of knocking about with the Dip Corps. And what else had they shared, unknown to their children or anyone else? Unknown to Vivie Henderson. And what had Vivie Henderson and Liza's father shared unknown to anyone? *Everybody knows it. Everyone except twits like you and....*

"I wish I'd brought the camera with us and then you could take a picture from this window, Liza."

"I don't need a picture." *I remembered this room and this house and this window before I ever saw them.*

"Are you feeling better, dear?" Caroline smoothed her hair affectionately. "Less sick to your stomach? Did you hurt yourself when you fell?"

Liza lied and said she was fine.

"I worry about you, honey. You're so secretive sometimes."

"Maybe I take after Dad," Liza replied harshly.

Caroline drew her robe more tightly around her and clutched *Jane Eyre* to her breast. On the way out the door she said she was going to read until dinner and that Liza could have the bath.

Liza stood at the window, not quite disconsolate, not quite desperate, but not quite the flip, jaded girl she'd been the day before, either. *Liar. Liar.* It was revolting, but not impossible, to picture her father and Vivie Henderson together. It was impossible to picture her mother alone. Caroline without George. And her fledgling intuition told Liza that Caroline could not picture herself alone either. "But how can she stand it?" Liza whispered. Did her mother simply tell herself that adultery was nothing, really, an unsightly thing that came to you at a certain time of life, like gray hair or pimples? Liza fingered her own chin. A simply physical act? Something that did not touch or tell on the rest of your life? Or was it more complicated? Was it, in fact, akin to the treachery that cried out from the stones of Castle Staulker, treachery that required compound lies, performances commanded by the need to maintain one sort of life while you pursued another? "How can she bear it?" *How can I bear it?* Liza was not given to tears, and she did not cry now. She stood and watched the clouds retreat northward, brooding on the mountain like troops defeated in battle, leaving the loch basking in the long, gilded embrace of sunset.

DINNER WAS plain and plentiful, served by the ghostly Mrs. Moffett in a dining room made cheerful by an electric fire and the smell of cooking potatoes. George and Susan were full of their walk; they'd been caught in the brief downpour, but the soaking was well worth it. Appin was astonishing in its beauty, and Susan couldn't wait to read *Kidnapped.* Liza dawdled over her soup and envied Susan her appetite, her ignorance and high spirits. Her father's hazel eyes were flecked with gold and animation. From an afternoon in Vivie's company, he had sucked some consummate pleasure, and he was returning it to them now: donating to his wife and daughters some of Vivie's own charm – her ability to convince people they were worthy of the confidences she would never betray to anyone else.

"I'll tell you what sort of name 'Vivie' is," George said in response to Susan's question, "but you mustn't let on that you know." He pressed a napkin to his lips, smothering a smile. "Her real name is Veronica Victoria. Imagine, sticking a little girl with a name like that! She said she nearly died of shame in school, and that's when she shortened it to V. V., and then just became Vivie. She hides anything that has her real name on it, and no one at the Legation knows.

"You know," said Liza.

George poured himself some more wine and filled Caroline's glass. On impulse he gave Liza half a glass and topped it off with water. "You're young women now," he said, "almost grown up."

"No, they're not," said Caroline.

"They soon will be, and besides," he added expansively, "we're on vacation, and if you're going to do the ordinary on vacation, why go?"

Mrs. Moffett brought their coffee (three cups) into the sitting room and then vanished silently as a moth drawn to other flames. This room, like the ones upstairs, was as clean and free from human debris as if it had never been used before Liza Derwent arrived, waiting for her alone to galvanize and adopt it. No photographs clustered on the walls or mantel, no radio or television or telephone, no newspapers, or footsteps in the flat above, no traffic in the street below. The northern dusk lingered at the tall windows; and swaddled in this envelope of light, the Derwents floated out of the ordinary and into the extraordinary.

They assumed their places. Sitting on the low sofa, Caroline poured their coffee, expertly, her skirt trailing to the floor and the aroma of fresh coffee mixing with the scent of lavender water. George accepted his cup and Liza hers. George retreated to the fireplace to warm himself, and Liza sat beside her sister. Their cups poised, the Derwents appeared to be awaiting cues, but cues were not forthcoming, so their dialogue proceeded unrehearsed, accumulating conviction and velocity as they went along. The prim, theatrical aura of the Twin Sisters enhanced, ennobled them and their unspoken suffering; haltingly they extended to one another the courtesies they might otherwise have squandered on strangers. The girls neither giggled nor bickered. They neither slouched nor sprawled; they adopted the posture required of ingenues. George was gallant and Caroline charming, and their pleasant words hung suspended like heat near the ceiling. George lit a cigarette and Caroline asked if he had another. He crossed the room and lit it for her and she tilted her head back and blew the smoke self-consciously upward. Liza knew her mother was unaccustomed to smoking, doing it for effect and doing it well, as Caroline commented casually that this was (she thought) the nineteenth time she'd read *Jane Eyre* and tenderly George added that she probably didn't have to read it at all; she could probably recite it by heart. She said, in fact, she could. "'Reader, I loved him,'" she said.

Liza asked for another biscuit and Caroline passed the tray to her. The biscuit was dry and sweet and crumbled awkwardly at her lips. Susan handed her a napkin and Liza thanked her and passed the tray on to Susan, who started to mention some anecdote from her school, but it died on her lips, as if she too knew that any reference outside this family was inappropriate at this moment. But before the hesitation could become a void, Liza mentioned a letter from their cousin Julia in California, and George asked what cousin Julia had said, and Liza told them, and then Caroline related a funny story of the time cousin Julia and Aunt Helen had come to visit them in Jamaica. They'd all heard the story before and pretended they hadn't, pretended their lines were new and fresh, as actors must, night after night: actors in a drawing-room drama that had no name, a play they nonetheless knew: the story of their family and of what that family might have been had someone fashioned for them a footlit world where nothing happens randomly, where, in three acts, chaos coheres into resolution, where heartbreak may be foreshortened to end in a round of applause.

No one mentioned Vivie Henderson.

And later, much later, months later, in the chill, bare environs of February when the Derwents had been disbanded like actors in a failed play, Liza found she could still remember her own lines and everybody else's, recall that sitting-room scene, return to the Twin Sisters' curtained windows, to the Highland loch, the castle and the mountains. And she found, moreover, that all of these retained for her the unleavened clarity of the last dream before waking, the one we cling to even as we know we're being rowed toward morning.

THE NEXT MORNING George Derwent flung their suitcases in the trunk and slammed it shut. He got in the car and waited for the rest of them to say goodbye to Mrs. Moffett and take their accustomed places for the long ride south. He started the car and sped away from the delphinium drive and Liza's home. The acting was finished; now they must be themselves.

As they skirted Loch Linnhe, clouds hovered about the mountaintops like dirty farthingales. Caroline ventured a comment on the weather. George did not reply. Liza rolled down her window and let the mist spray in and dampen her face and blow her hair into her eyes. Her father told her to close the window and she told him, flatly, no.

"Your father has asked you to do something, Liza," her mother cautioned, her voice ripe with warning.

"Why should she?" George grunted. "Why bother? No one else in this family does anything I ask. No one cares that I'm the one who works. I'm the one who needs the vacation. No one else cares what I want to do, why should Liza?"

"You're being unreasonable, George. You said a day's jaunt and that's what we – "

"Me, unreasonable! Ask the girls if they want to leave, ask them!"

"I want to leave," said Liza without being asked.

"I don't want to leave," Susan volunteered. "I love it here and I want to go riding and sail out to some of those little islands and go for a hike."

"Do you really think you're up here for the bloody scenery?" Liza asked in her jaded, flip fashion.

"Liza!" Caroline's grim face turned to the back seat. "You apologize immediately!"

"I'm not the one who needs to say I'm sorry," Liza retorted fiercely.

Silence, palpable as rain or smoke, filled the car as George thrust the Alpha around curves and thumped over potholes. Liza kept the window down, grateful for the damp wind that whipped hair into her face. She leaned slightly out the window and listened to the audible, uneasy ghost who panted after them, his footless slippers running alongside, never letting them escape his sightless gaze.

"What's that sound?" George demanded.

Caroline tensed. "What sound?"

"Listen." George slowed the car, and the ghost who had been following them slowed too. George stopped, and the ghost halted in its unseen tracks. George stepped out and checked the back tire on Liza's side. "Bloody, buggering, goddamn hell!"

"George! What is it? What's happened?"

"The goddamn back tire is flat. Flat! How can this happen? This is a new car! Goddamnit!" They all got out and huddled around the crippled wheel, shivering in the warm rain. "Get back in the car," he ordered. "I'll fix it."

They listened while he unloaded the luggage from the trunk and flung it to the side of the road, while he freed the spare tire and the jack from their compartment. He cursed, setting the jack beneath the car, and puffed as he pumped it up, and it clicked rhythmically with his exertion. Metal rang on metal as time after time he applied the tire iron to the lug nuts. Liza watched the rain drip off his hair, soak and discolor the shoulders of his shirt as he struggled with the tire iron, twisting it, grunting, panting, swearing. "Caroline!" he barked. "Hand me that instruction booklet that came with the car." She passed it out the window and he read it in the rain. "Goddamn! Goddamn!" He threw the book into the mud and ground it with his heel. "I knew I should have bought an English car! The bloody instructions are in bloody Italian!" He kicked the door.

"Really, George," Caroline remonstrated, "it's not as bad as all that. Someone will come along and help, I'm sure."

"Some Italian?" he sneered.

"Well, let me help. Maybe it just takes two."

"No." He tossed the tire iron back in the trunk and pulled out his rain jacket, slid into it and brought up the hood. "I'll walk to Vivie's and call from there."

"Call who, George?"

"Call Rome for all I know. Call someone who can fix this bloody wop car."

"No!" cried Liza. "Don't go there. Just walk back to the Twin Sisters. That's much closer. Don't go all the way back to – "

"Hand me my wallet, Caroline."

"Does Vivie speak Italian?" asked Caroline, the words crackling like ice chips and mercury.

"Look, Dad – she's probably not even home." Liza scrambled furiously through her arguments. "They're off riding or – something. You will have walked all that way for – "

"She's home. She had to wait for the man to fix the roof this morning, remember?"

"Oh, Dad," Liza pleaded, "please go to the Twin Sisters. *Please.*"

"Stay out of this." He wiped the rain and perspiration from his face. "Caroline, the longer I stand here, the longer you'll have to wait in the car. Hand me my wallet please."

Liza watched: her mother's face, her father's outstretched hand. She watched, she even saw, but she never could remember the wallet changing hands; her mother's actions escaped through memory's net and were caught, hopelessly entangled in the net of dreams: because for many months, for years thereafter Liza dreamed that Caroline had placed in his hand a flower, a baby chick, or more homely objects, a book or button or bit of cheese. Never a wallet. And Liza's dreams were always eloquently silent; in the dreams he never said, "I'll be back as soon as I can."

"Dad!" Liza called after him, "Dad!"

Susan's voice was small and pinched with fear. "Why don't you want him to go, Liza?"

"Don't be a twit." She grabbed and rattled her mother's shoulder. "Mom, don't let him. Please. You've got to stop him, Mom! Go after him. Please. You go after him. Stop him!"

"No."

"Then I'll go!" Again, in her dreams, Liza saw herself flinging open the car door and bolting, running down the sodden road that twisted and diminished, swallowed her into undergrowth, meshed her in a net of heather and longing where she heard her mother's voice: *Reader, I loved him.*

But that was not what her mother said. Her mother peeled Liza's fingers from her shoulder and rolled them, gently, into a small clenched fist while Liza sobbed and begged her to go after him. Caroline said: "It's too late for that." And then, as wind plowed the waters of Loch Linnhe and planted rain in the furrows, they watched while George's figure retreated, rounded a slow bend in the road, and vanished from their sight. Caroline picked up *Jane Eyre* and carefully opened to the place she had marked. She said: "There's nothing to do now but wait."

Fair Augusto

IN THAT SUNNY afternoon hour when the restaurants are empty and expectant, the cafés are noisy and full. At a table in a steamy Venetian square, two Americans sit, looking uncomfortable and conspicuous while heat ripples around them, hovering under their umbrella, refracting upward from the golden, well-worn stones. In a sea of voluble Italians, they are mute. They drink silently, furtively regarding the life at other tables as they watch their ten-year-old daughter feed the pigeons.

The man is big, broad of girth and shoulder; he dwarfs his rickety chair and the tiny table before him. He has a round face and a halo of wild hair that was once red, but appears now dull with gray and middle age. His wife is pale and restless, her jaw long and her forehead narrow, her striking angularity accentuated by a short, severe haircut. The daughter looks like her mother, though she has her father's curling red hair.

"Don't get too near the pigeons, Sally," the wife cautions her.

"Oh let her alone," the husband says, "pigeons can't hurt her."

"What do you know about it?"

He knows nothing about it, so he lapses back into indifferent silence, attuning his ears to the feminine, foreign voices behind him. He drops his napkin; as he bends to pick it up he peers at the women in the way Americans have of looking and not looking, an inherited, innocent shiftiness of the eyes. Three tawny-skinned young women, he notes, cool in their pale dresses despite the unendurable heat of mid-August. Their dark heads close together, they bend over tall glasses of rosy, translucent liquid decorated with floating scraps of lemon. He wonders absently what they are drinking. (Gil's Italian is so feeble, he can only order beer or wine.) The women laugh and seem to lean back in their chairs. He leans back in his. He wishes he could change tables, join the foreign cascade of their language and laughter rather than sit with Judy, absorbing her perennial ill will.

"Have you told them at the hotel that we're leaving tomorrow?" Judy demands.

"Yes."

"Good. I'll be glad to get out of here. I hate Venice. Too hot and damp. Too much sewage. Everything here is old and rotten and stinks. Have you noticed how it stinks?"

"Yes," he repeats, keeping his eyes on his wife, but straining his ears toward the women behind him. A husky voice. A peculiar cadence. A lilt recognizable even in Italian? But not good Italian. She speaks slowly and with too much prompting from the others. Still, the voice tugs at Gil, stirs him familiarly; his memory and imagination ignite simultaneously. Too many years, surely he's wrong, but he turns around just the same; and yes, the broad mouth and dark eyes, and yes, the mahogany hair — shoulder-length now — shorter than he remembers. It's been so many years he's not even sure he remembers at all, much less correctly, but still he says, "Jessie? Jessie George?"

The woman in the middle looks up from her drink, her dark eyes focussing on him with effort. Her face lights with disbelief, then dismay. But she meets him midway between their tables and embraces him quickly, as if she is afraid she's mistaken and perhaps he's not Gilbert Sherman after all.

"Gil! I can't believe it! After all these years! Yes of course it's you. I'd know you anywhere. What are you doing in Venice?"

He finds himself answering by rote, devouring her eyes, her smile, her clothes, the unfamiliar scar disfiguring her left hand. "We've been traveling this summer. We're going to Rome to fly back to Baltimore tomorrow, Jessie, but you're not Jessie George anymore, are you?"

She laughs, and on the tide of that laugh Gil rows momentarily backward to the safety of the past and the Park Place Bar where he sat with Gene and Lyle and Michael Devereaux and Cindy Dalton and they were all half-drunk and Gene said Ellen Campbell told him Jessie George had married a scientist in California. A man named – named what?

"I'm Jessie McCarren now."

McCarren. And Gil took his arm off Cindy Dalton's shoulders and drooped inwardly to think that Jessie had married. *Well, I guess she's gone forever now,* Gil said. *Hasn't she been gone forever anyway?* Michael asked. *No,* Gil said, *it hasn't even been a year since she left.* Then Lyle said (Lyle? Yes, Lyle sighed and said) *All the girls marry dull husbands who take them to suburbia, which is all they ever wanted anyway. Not Jessie,* Gil said: *Jessie George is, well, she's extraordinary somehow, you just felt it;* then he added qualifyingly – *I just felt it.* Michael said Jessie was too flat-chested to be extraordinary and Cindy (who was not flat-chested) blushed and everyone chuckled. Gil remembers thinking: *What do they know?*

"What's your wife's name again, Gil?" Jessie asks.

"Judy," he says, but he does not dare look back at his wife.

"Oh yes. And is that your little girl? She's so big. She was so little."

"Seven years," says Gil. "It's been seven years." He wonders if it's possible Jessie can look better after seven years. He searches for the little furrows and puckers unhappiness leaves on women's faces, but he finds none. She is tanned and exuberant and well-dressed, and "You're taller somehow."

She winks at him confidentially. "Success does that for you, Gil."

Jessie McCarren: how could he forget? "Oh, Jessie – I've read all your books, all six or seven – "

"Eight."

"Of them. They're terrific. You're right there with P. D. James – much better than Agatha Christie by a long shot. That one about the body they find in the desert, *The Dead – The Dead – "

"The Dead Giveaway."

"That one especially. That was, well, extraordinary." He wants to say he recognized her talent from the beginning, but doesn't; he didn't recognize talent – what he recognized was something more elusive than talent, something for which he has no words.

She is obviously pleased, but she shrugs. "They're just murder mysteries. I don't ask that they be extraordinary, only that they sell well. And they do!" She grins self-consciously and adds, "Isn't there some old

Beatles song about the paperback writer?" She peers at him in her old intense way; he tells himself she hasn't changed. "That's my song."

Jessie's friends seem to have abandoned her, gone on with their conversation, evidently much accustomed to Americans' reunions in Venetian cafés. Gil sneaks a backward glance to Judy, who fixes her proprietorial eye on him nonchalantly, an expression she's perfected with practice.

How long would they be in Venice, Jessie inquires politely, and Gil says again that they're leaving in the morning, and Jessie says oh yes. Gil asks how long she'll be in Venice, and she smiles and says she has lived here for the past six months and will for yet another four. Her husband's work brought them – a very special kind of geology concerned with keeping the city afloat. Venice In Peril. All that.

"Your husband's here too?" Gil says, scouting the café tables.

"Not right now. We've been staying at a friend's country villa this week and Neal's still there. He's on vacation, like everyone else in Italy. You know today is Ferragusto." She says it with a cultivated Italian lilt, fluttering the *r*s, "The only Italians working this weekend are the waiters. Even the wheels of State and Science grind to a halt for Ferragusto!"

"Say it again," Gil asks, partly for the pleasure of her voice.

"Think of – Fair Augusto – like Caesar Augustus and the Roman emperors. You know, coming not to praise Caesar but to bury him. All that? Ferragusto's been going on since the days of the Empire."

"August 15, isn't it? Feast of the Assumption too. The Virgin ascends into heaven." Unaccountably, he blushes. "And all that."

"I didn't know you were a Catholic, Gil."

"A lapsed one. There's lots you don't know about me. You never did." He takes her scarred hand in his; the skin is puckered and brown, as if she is wearing a badly patched, threadbare glove. But Jessie seems radiant. "Italy agrees with you. I can see that."

"I love living in Venice. I forget sometimes that the twentieth century is going on out there – somewhere." She withdraws her hand and motions vaguely to the right.

"You haven't changed."

"Oh, I probably have."

"You still smell the same though – expensive cologne and cheap suntan lotion." Jessie bristles and Gil suspects that was too intimate a recollection to have mentioned so soon and in such a public place, but he doesn't really care. He casts about for some further paste to bind her experience to his, to obscure Judy, Jessie's geologist husband, to obliviate the seven years. "Have you heard about Michael?" he says.

Her buoyancy subsides and her dark eyes cloud. "Yes. I'm sorry for you. For all of you."

"I've changed, Jessie. When Michael died – "

"Oh, you look fine, Gil," she says; her voice is bright, but she bites her lip. "You don't look one bit different."

He ignores her observation. "It's been so many years since you left Maryland that I thought maybe no one told you about Michael. I would have written you myself, but I didn't know where you were. I guess I could have asked your old roommate, Ellen, but I wasn't thinking straight. God! I wasn't thinking at all. It was as if my whole life – "

"Ellen Campbell wrote me about Michael Devereaux." She says it formally, as if introducing a foreigner, a stranger to them both and oddly conjured in this Venetian square, Michael Devereaux's name floats over their shoulders like smoke, lingers, dissolves, lost among the clinking glasses, trilling Italian voices, and rustling lire. "Ellen told me how he died," she adds, indicating that further discussion is unnecessary.

"Michael was real proud of you, Jessie."

She brightened as the conversation returned to her success. "Oh Michael looked down his Roman nose at murder mysteries and you know it!"

"That's not true. He read every one of your books and he thought they were great."

"Did he?"

No, he didn't, but Gil doesn't say that. Doesn't say that Michael thought mysteries weren't worth the paper they were printed on, or bound in, to say nothing of the paper money, the tons of paper money they doubtless made. Michael thought mysteries in general – and Jessie's in particular – were nothing but trash. Escapist tripe. Disposable artifacts of American culture. That's what Michael said when they were talking about one of Jessie's books as they sat at their favorite table at the Park Place Bar, the table that was more or less reserved for them and whomever they cared to include in their golden circle at any given golden moment.

Michael said standards were important. Standards had to be maintained. He said he wouldn't write trash, not even for money. Gene put his cigarette out on the floor and said, *Michael, you're an artist; you couldn't write trash if you wanted to.* And Michael said: *I wouldn't want to.*

"I wouldn't want to interrupt you," Gil gestures toward Jessie's friends.

"Oh, don't worry about that," says Jessie, glancing anxiously behind him and catching Judy's baleful stare. "Do you think Judy will remember me?"

Judy swears she does not recall Jessie in any way, though she gives her a languid hand, flexing memory enough to mention a party many years ago, at Gene's, or was it Lyle's? She thought Jessie might have come with Michael, but they all agree it is hard to remember one party from another in Bremerton back in the good old days. Her interest flickers briefly when Gil mentions that Jessie is living in Venice. "How can you stand it?" asks Judy. "It stinks."

"I love it. It's like living in the past."

"But not your own past," Gil contributes.

"No one can live in his own past, can he?" Jessie replies.

Gil isn't sure of that, but it's too theoretical and uncomfortable to pursue. Gil is uncomfortable enough: he can see that Jessie is taking them in, assessing them, and he knows that after fifteen married years, he and Judy wear their aging antagonisms like old clothing.

"It's the water I love here," Jessie explains cheerfully. "I grew up in the desert, so the constant sound of water is exotic. Disturbing, really. Neal and I have a flat between two sleepy canals, and for the first few months I'd lie in bed at night and wonder if the water might come all the way up to the third floor and under the bedroom door!"

Gil pictures her lying in bed with Neal McCarren, though he cannot picture Neal McCarren.

"We traded places with a scientist who's gone to UCLA for the year," Jessie continues. "Our house in L.A. is nice, but this place is four hundred years old – all beautifully restored, of course, but I can never quite believe the marble floors, the eight-foot-high windows, and the balconies! And the place is absolutely stuffed with antiques. Some of this stuff was probably carted off at Lepanto!"

Gil cannot remember what or who Lepanto is, so he introduces his daughter to Jessie. She makes all the same comments about how big and how little and then she says again how nice it is to see them, urges them to have a good trip home, bids them an unselfconscious *ciao* and returns to her friends.

Gil sits back down with Judy, who does not deign to comment. Behind him, he can hear Jessie telling her friends about him in her unmusical Italian. He recognizes all the proper nouns, and he can fill in the rest: Bremerton College, Bremerton, Maryland. Jessie was a scholarship student at this small private school, and Gil was a professor of English. He and Michael had both been hired the same year, fresh out of (different) graduate schools, and they had been there three years when Gil met Jessie. She had been there three years too. Gil found her arresting from the first: a quick, intense, intuitive, serious girl. The woman he's just met is more confident and relaxed. But perhaps that was to be expected of Jessie McCarren. He strains to catch the drift of her conversation behind him, but Jessie's Italian (patched as it is) eludes him and he gives up, remembering instead how he had introduced her, drawn her into their charmed and lively circle at the Park Place Bar: the four men and any number of pretty girls. And like any number of pretty girls, Jessie had been – in quick succession – Gil's student, then his friend, then fleetingly his lover, and then she was gone. Like any number of pretty girls.

"*Troppo freddo*," says Jessie to her friends. "Maryland was *troppo freddo* for me!"

Too cold? Was that it? Her last winter in Maryland Gil had gone with her to buy some new boots; he knelt at her feet and zipped them up for her. Jessie took a few tentative steps and looked down at her feet. *Fetters*, she said, *damned fetters*. He'd taken her out to dinner in the new boots, and afterward, back at her apartment, she'd unzipped them: there never was a woman who could peel off a pair of boots like Jessie George. Or a pair of stockings, for that matter.

"What are you smiling at?" Judy says in a tone both inquisitive and offended.

"Nothing. You want another beer?"

"It was a long time ago," he hears Jessie say in carefully enunciated English. "I was only twenty-two." He wonders if her Italian friends know that she left Bremerton without graduating, left the East Coast altogether and went home to some awful burg deep in the desert, some place with a ridiculous name. Chagrin. That was it. Chagrin, California. Who could go back to a town with a name like that? Momentarily, Gil can feel the eyes of Jessie's companions piercing his back, but then they go on to discuss where they'll have dinner.

Gil keeps his gaze on Sally and the pigeons. He cannot look at Judy; she knows him too well. She will recognize his perplexity and hunger and guess that it's libidinal at bottom. Gil sips his tepid beer in silence: personally, he never bothers with these distinctions; perplexity and hunger are all the same to him, whether he experiences them in his heart, or mind, or groin.

Despite the warning tugging grimly at Judy's lips, Gil rises and takes a few hasty steps back toward Jessie. "Listen," he says a little breathlessly, "why don't you meet me – meet us – for a drink tonight?"

Jessie regards Judy warily. "I don't think I can. My brother and sister-in-law are coming in tonight from L.A." Her friends snap their purses open, place their lire on the table, nod to Jessie, and leave.

"Meet me in St. Mark's Square, Jessie, at Florian's. Just a quick drink. Say 9:30 or so?"

"All right," she says reluctantly. "I'll try and be there, but don't count on me." She smiles hastily and adds her money to her friends'. "It's not real, is it? Italian money? It never seems quite legal tender." Jessie skirts the islands of tables, moving through the fluid shadows cast by café umbrellas, and without looking back she vanishes behind a wall of crumbling stucco and unrestored brick.

2

JESSIE MCCARREN would not have been in Venice on Ferragusto at all, but for her brother and sister-in-law, whose ill-timed arrival conflicted with the McCarrens' vacation. Jessie had ridden the train into Venice by herself just that morning because Neal flatly refused to cut his holiday short. "They're your family," Neal had said.

"Yes, but that doesn't mean I have to like them," Jessie had responded. And in truth, she did not much like her brothers (who were ten and twelve years her senior) or their wives. She had never been close to them as a child, and as an adult she was repelled by their gridded, predictable lives, their uniformly dull marriages; they lived a dead-end domesticity that Jessie always feared might be catching. Until she met Neal McCarren, in fact, Jessie took a dim view of domesticity: marriage seemed a kind of martyrdom whereby you not only tied yourself up, but lit your own faggots as well.

Jessie was cordial to her brother and his wife, who were fuzzy and disoriented and full of awful tales of their plane trip. She nodded, now and then, restless, eager to be off; she offered them a glass of wine and smiled inside when they declined. She showed them to her own bedroom and assured them she would sleep just fine in the study. "We can talk in the morning and you can tell me all about Chagrin," she said as she closed the bedroom door. Relief overwhelmed her as she flew down the stairs and reached the tiny courtyard path, lined with six-foot dahlias, that led to the gate. It snapped shut behind her and she was free to meet Gilbert Sherman at Florian's. Just Gil. Judy would not be with him. Jessie was quite certain of that.

She wore a tailored white skirt and a crisp aqua-blue blouse with matching combs to hold her hair back from her face. She wanted to look especially pretty, because of course Gil would tell her she was beautiful. More beautiful, probably. Mentally she composed dialogue with Gil as she threaded through the streets, crossed wide *campos* and narrow bridges, winding through alleys darkened by arches and flanked by water. Venice at night was safer than any American city for a woman alone, but she always kept a purposeful expression on her face and walked very fast, because as long as she looked like she knew where she was going and kept her mouth shut, she could not be readily distinguished from other Venetian women – proud, insouciant, and inaccessible.

She returned to her confectionary vision: Gil would say he'd never forgotten her. He would make her smile. He had such a way with anecdotes. No one could tell a story like Gil. Michael always said, *Gil, you should write them all down,* and Gil said, *No, Michael, you're the writer and poet, you write them down,* and Michael said one day he would: write all about Gil, the raconteur and wit, Gene the radical and Lyle the critic, the four young professors who exuded energy, who enlivened the staid Maryland town and lit up the otherwise drab Park Place Bar with its flickering beer

signs, broken linoleum, and Christmas tinsel that no one bothered ever
to take down. Collectively the four men created a flame that drew moths,
primarily female moths, young women who could, every year, be dazzled
and flattered and seduced by Gene and Gil and Lyle and Michael. Michael
the Fair. Michael the Beautiful. Michael the Dead at the age of thirty-six.
So said the obituary Ellen sent. The clipping did not say what Ellen explained: dead by his own hand. Blew his brains out in the merry month
of May. Blew his beautiful golden head off.

On impulse Jessie stopped at the Café Teatro and bought some cigarettes. She did not habitually smoke anymore, but the thought of Michael
made her uneasy: she might need to smoke. What if Gil wanted to talk
about Michael? "Let's hope not," she said aloud. The cashier regarded
her quizzically; she paid for her cigarettes and left, telling herself that the
night of Ferragusto was better spent with Gilbert Sherman in St. Mark's
Square than with her brother and his wife, listening to dreary tales of
Chagrin, of desert wind, date growers, truck stops, and tumbleweeds.

At least Gil would be amusing. He was always amusing. Michael was
beautiful. Gene was flushed and fleshy, with a paintbrush mustache and
a chin dimpled to the point of cleft. Lyle, by contrast, was hollow-cheeked
and somber, as if he were balancing some secret sadness he had long since
learned appealed to girls. Lyle's unhealthy pallor always reminded Jessie
of Gorganzola cheese. She liked Gene better than Lyle, but she liked Gil
best of all. Gil: his wild hair flying, his coat unbuttoned, toothbrush
sticking out of his breast pocket, and sweat gleaming on his brow as he
hurried off to some assignation or another, some alternate form of in-
duced excitement. Gil cartwheeled through life, and Jessie had never
known him to be cheap or mean-spirited, except perhaps with his wife.
Gil and his wife lived in the strangest, most affectionless marriage Jessie
had ever witnessed, and she could never understand why they didn't just
admit their folly and divorce.

Catholicism – however lapsed – would explain it. But she also knew,
now that she was older, that in marriages one man's folly is another man's
fixture. Look at Neal McCarren. He was undemonstrative and a trifle
dry, but at least Neal never counterfeited, not his affections or his beliefs.
He was serious and reliable, and Jessie loved him. But she didn't want to
think about her husband just now, not when she was nearly at the Piazza

San Marco to meet a man who had been doggedly in love with her for years.

She arrived at the lip of the arcade and gazed out over the turbulent, crowded Piazza San Marco. On rainy days and damp nights like this one, the Piazza seemed to bob and sink, a stone wafer in the lagoon. She always paused at the arcade, like a swimmer at the Pacific shore, paused before plunging into the Piazza, paused, half succumbing to the sheer power of the Basilica (that monument to the glory of Venice and God – in that order), which stood at one end of the huge Piazza and towered over the throng. The sight of the glowering Basilica and the scurrying crowds made her slightly dizzy and uncertain, like a swimmer caught in a riptide, wave-washed, watching the shore recede: she felt helpless before the Basilica's Byzantine majesty, humbled by its scorn for mere flesh – poor, puny, minute mortals, mere guests of God, heirs of death.

Jessie took a deep breath and dove into the Piazza, pushing her way through energetic elbows and foreign laughter. This year's gimmick – electric yo-yos – sparkled around her like captive, engorged fireflies. Random flashbulbs made her blink as she swam toward the heart of the crowd, where the strains of three different café orchestras competed. They played the geriatric standards full of sentimental violins and sad flutes, old American tunes guaranteed to pluck some chord in everyone.

"Jessie!"

Gil sat in the outer crescent of tables assembled around Florian's. He was the only person in that crowd who sat alone. Several beer bottles lined up before him, although a small carafe of wine and a glass awaited Jessie. So, he had known she would come. Still, his eyes did not light with quite the vivacity she expected, and he did not tell her she was more beautiful than ever. He said he was glad she came; he said it in such a way that she felt compelled to ask after his wife.

Gil laughed. "The tides, the seasons, the planets in their heavenly orbits will change, my dear, before Judy and I do."

Jessie mumbled something flip in reply, to distract him from the topic of marital woes. She had come to be amused and admired on this deep, hot August night while lithe waiters in mummified white jackets skirted the tables and flicked off bottle caps with the finesse of dancers. She made random cheerful remarks about the orchestras, the sparkling yo-yos, and the number of Germans this year, while she regarded Gil more closely than she had this afternoon. He was right; he had changed. He was still big and ruddy and unkempt, but he no longer emanated that roughshod urbanity which allowed him to walk through the world unharmed and enthusiastic as a cherub. He responded to her bright, brittle comments in kind, but Jessie only began to relax when he started on a funny anecdote of his travels, an account of a bout of "Lafayette's Revenge" in Paris and the trouble he'd had communicating his needs to a French pharmacist.

He told the story with his old aplomb, but lapsed afterward, sank – or was it merely slouched – before Jessie's eyes. "Tell me about your work, Gil," she said. Work was *terra firma* for Jessie. Work would eventually bring them around to the new mystery she was writing with its Venetian setting. But work, in this instance, failed her.

Gil said he hadn't been able to work since Michael's death in May. Since Michael's death, he could not do anything at all. "Nothing is the same without Michael, not like the good old days at the Park with the boys." He laughed without conviction and nursed his beer without relish. He suppressed a belch and pointed to her hand. "How did you do that?"

"I burned it accidentally."

"You didn't have that scar the last time I saw you. Do you remember the last time I saw you?"

"Should I?" she said coolly, but she lit a cigarette just the same.

"Michael and I and Cindy came by your house one night. We were on our way to Annapolis and we wanted you to come with us, but…"

"It's not important now."

"Of course it's important! Michael said you – "

"Have you and Judy been traveling in Europe long?" she said, with all the inflection of a court reporter.

"I never saw you again after that night. Why didn't you tell anyone you were leaving?"

"I'm not obligated to tell anyone anything."

"I mean – I gave you the money and I didn't ask why, but I never thought you'd take it and leave. I thought maybe you needed it for – "

"Please." Jessie reached out and touched his arm beseechingly. "Don't. I can't bear it. I paid you back. Why do you even bring it up?"

"I just couldn't believe you'd leave without saying goodbye to anyone. Michael said, 'oh, Jessie'll be back.' But I knew you wouldn't. I knew it. Michael always knew I was crazy about you. I always lusted after you and you always lusted after him. You used to call him the Golden Boy."

The wine in Jessie's throat turned hard and she swallowed with difficulty. "Golden Boy" had been a private joke between Ellen and Jessie, but if Gil knew she called him Golden Boy, Michael must have known it too. She blushed for her old, inadequate self.

But he was a Golden Boy. Michael Devereaux's fair hair curled around his face, and he was a bit jaundiced in coloring, except in the summer, when he tanned. His blue eyes were made bluer yet by tinted contacts, so they seemed preternaturally blue, forever twinkling. His nose was straight, high-bridged, downright Roman; and beneath that, his fleshy mouth lounged. On a woman (or a statue) that mouth might have been attractive, but on a man it came perilously close to decadence.

For Jessie (a refugee from Chagrin, where everyone was transient, transferred, or stuck; where everything not visibly nailed down blew away with the dry wind), Michael Devereaux represented an enviable rootedness she thought unique to Easterners. He was exotic. He wore impeccably ironed, monogrammed shirts and talked with a broad Massachusetts accent, and had a way of referring to his "auwnt" that Jessie took for Family. He had the Eastern education (Harvard *and* Yale), which implied all sorts of Well-Bred Connections, and had too a certain lack of evident vulgarity, which suggested to her that there was Money in his Well-Connected Family. Besides all this, he was a writer. His stories and poems appeared in thin, rag-content quarterlies. She read them in the library where she worked part-time. They were sad, static little pieces about people with Family and Connections and Money.

Jessie had always wanted to like Michael's stories and poems better than she did. After her inclusion in their circle at the Park, she always longed to say to him casually, "I've read your work and I like it very much" – and have his eye light on her like she was a spring twig and he was the bluebird of happiness. But she could never bring herself to say it. Not even when she knew him very well. Especially when she knew him very well.

"All that Golden Boy business was just a joke," said Jessie, sipping her wine and staring at Florian's flamboyant orchestra conductor. "I mean, really, Michael Devereaux was too good to be true."

"He was too good to live," moaned Gil.

"And anyway, I didn't lust after him," she continued, as if such a thing were beneath contempt. "I never even cared for him very much. I certainly had more sense than to get involved with a man who had hordes of adoring women – most of them with big boobs and all of them stupid."

"Did you ever meet his wife, Diana?"

"No, but Ellen wrote me that he got married a couple of years ago."

"Diana's very bright. Not stupid at all."

"But," Jessie added shrewdly, "I'll bet she has big boobs and is many years younger than he."

Gil nodded. "About twelve I think. She was just finishing up her first year of law school last May. Some people think she drove him to it. She was about to leave him."

"Men don't kill themselves over women." Jessie spoke with an air of unquenchable rightness.

Gil began on another beer without seeming to hear her. "But most people think it was his work. Michael couldn't write anymore. He hadn't been able to for a long time. He was trying to write a novel and got very depressed. He took a semester off and he and Diana went to England so he could work where there was more inspiration and less distraction. But he couldn't even write in England."

"You can't write novels if you're only interested in yourself." Then she added tartly, "No matter where you live."

"Michael always said the creative process was painful."

Jessie snorted. "How creative do you have to be to write a suicide note?"

"He didn't leave a note. But he planned everything out to the last detail. He left a final for his students and he told them he wouldn't be in the following week. He said he was going away." Gil mopped his face with a soiled handkerchief. "Michael took care of everything. Where he wanted to be buried. Who he wanted for pallbearers. What he wanted for the funeral service. He wanted me to give the eulogy, but I was too broken up."

"The next best thing to attending his own funeral, wasn't it?"

"Everyone came to Michael's funeral," Gil carried on obliviously. "It was packed."

"It must have been a real orgy."

He searched her face. "Don't you have any reverence for anything?"

"Reverence! You expect me to get weepy about a staged, theatrical funeral? Michael must have relished that sight for months before he did himself in."

"Not everyone is as hard-hearted as you are. Cindy Dalton came down all the way from New York. You remember Cindy Dalton, don't you?"

"Yes," Jessie said curtly. "Of course I remember that button-eyed buxom bitch. I'm not surprised she came down for the funeral; she went down for everyone."

He sighed and smiled. "It's true that if Cindy's brains and her boobs could change places, she'd be Einstein." He winked and Jessie laughed. He caught the waiter's attention and ordered another small bottle of wine for her and five more beers for himself.

"Do you plan on getting drunk, Gil?"

"No, I plan on staying drunk. I haven't been sober since May 18th."

The clouds were tumescent with rain, the air palpably moist. Electric yo-yos swirled in tiny constellations, and Florian's orchestra began (and ended) the "Beguine." Jessie blew exasperated smoke rings and listened while Gil rehearsed every incident, however trivial, that led up to, or pointed toward Michael's death.

"One night we were all at the Park, at our table with a couple of girls. This was about three months before it happened."

"It didn't *happen*. Michael *did* it."

"Lyle says to me, 'Gil, you want to hear something really morbid? Michael's writing a story about suicide.' Then we got to talking about it, you know, how people do it, pills or pistols or whatever and what happens with a shotgun, and how Hemingway did it. God! If I'd thought ─ "

"He wasn't Hemingway," Jessie said coldly. "Michael Devereaux may have had money and family and connections and some abilities, but he wasn't Hemingway."

"Some abilities? He was terrific. He was a poet!"

"He was mediocre."

Gil gurgled down half a beer and wiped his mouth with the back of his hand. "Michael had standards. He didn't write trite, trashy mysteries."

Jessie leaned forward so he would not miss or mistake her words. "I'm good at what I do. I work hard at it, and I'm good. I'm successful too. I make more money than Michael ever dreamed of making."

"Michael didn't care about money."

"Oh, I know, Michael had money. And family. And connections. But there was one thing he didn't have."

Gil's dour expression perked with curiosity. "What?"

Jessie had stumbled unintentionally over a shallow grave. She lit yet another cigarette. Her hands trembled, but her voice did not. She evaded the question. "Michael was a failure, Gil. He must have known it at the end. He must have guessed he'd never get any better, just older." She shrugged as though nettles prickled her shoulders. "Still, that's no reason to kill yourself."

"Was he any good as a lover?" Gil whispered. "Was he a failure as a lover?"

Despite the orchestras and the crowds, silence fell between them, tangible and translucent as dead Michael Devereaux, who, pared from his flesh, palpitated in memory. Jessie met Gil's eyes without flinching. She kept her voice calm and cruel, and her words spun out in a caul of smoke. "What do you want to know? If he was better than you?"

Gil flushed visibly, and he lifted his beer and spilled some. "How can you hate him so much when you used to love him?"

"I never loved him." The cigarette disagreed with her; she stomped the life out of it. "I slept with him occasionally, that's all. I never loved him." Her muscles grew taut and quivery with tension, and an internal roar filled her ears, clouded her eyes, veiled everything except the face of Michael Devereaux, static as George Washington's on a quarter, floating up to her out of the August night as she slipped downward, away from Ferragusto and San Marco and into the damp earth of Maryland under another sky gravid with rain and the end of a different summer.

She could hear them – the dozen others who'd reconvened at the creek after the Park closed. Their voices drowned in the water's silky roar, but their laughter carried into the distant woods, rattled in the trees above Michael Devereaux, who lay above Jessie George. Twigs cracked and leaves split underneath her; perspiration and expiration of the earthly underbrush dampened her clothes and ran in rivulets from her creases. Michael's tongue was in her mouth and slid, wet, down her throat, and his hands covered her small breasts and held them till they seemed to swell. "Do you want me, Jessie?"

"Yes."

"Do you want me to make love to you?"

She wrapped her arms around his back and put her lips to the warm, dry shell of his ear. "Love me. I want you to love me. I've always wanted you to love me."

3

MICHAEL'S HANDS were cold, but brisk and knowing; the buttons on Jessie's shirt cracked open easily, the zipper on her jeans fell, and she closed her eyes, stroking his golden hair.

"You smell like expensive cologne," he murmured into her navel, "and cheap suntan lotion."

"Well," she whispered, "you just have to take what you can get."

"No, you only ever get what you take."

She wanted to ask him what he meant, but his mouth covered hers, so she slid her hands under his shirt instead. His skin was smooth and slick and sweaty and his mouth every bit as decadent as it looked and his kiss was more practiced than she could have imagined. Words were lost and questions moot: taking or getting, what did it matter?

"Excuse me!" exclaimed Cindy Dalton. "I was looking for a place to pee!"

Jessie scrambled to her feet, clutching her blouse together. She leaned weakly against a tree and met Cindy's black-button eyes and impish smirk. Michael sat up slowly, stood, pressed hip and thigh to Jessie, his lips at the corner of her eye, his warm breath cascading down her cheek as he held her against the tree.

Cindy crashed through the underbrush and then there was silence.

"All done!" she cried cheerfully. "Don't worry, next time I'll pee somewhere else."

They heard her footsteps retreat toward the creek, and Michael pried Jessie's blouse from her fingers and peeled it off her shoulders. "I can't, Michael. Not now. It's too humiliating."

He picked the leaves from her hair, kissed, caressed her bare shoulders. "How can it be humiliating? I've wanted you, wanted to make love to you since I met you, Jessie. I've wanted to touch you." His hands encircled her hips and urged her jeans downward. "Here."

THE NEXT DAY Jessie was covered with poison ivy. Mercifully her roommate Ellen did not compound the torment by asking indelicate questions, but then Ellen had been at the creek with the others and might have guessed how and with whom Jessie had incurred the poison ivy. Jessie spent the whole day in the bathtub soaking in bicarbonate of soda, hoping Cindy Dalton was equally miserable.

Michael called. He too had poison ivy, but not badly. "You want me to come over and rub calamine lotion all over you?"

"No thanks."

"Why not?"

"Well, for one thing, Ellen's here."

"So?"

"So I believe in discretion, Michael."

She had many occasions in the course of their affair to regret having said that: almost instantly it became untrue. Jessie let go of discretion and succumbed to hunger and impulse and Michael Michael Michael. They made love often, often indiscreetly. They experimented until they found postures suitable for the floor of Michael's tiny office. Once they locked the bathroom door and made love in the bathtub during a party at Gene's house, while other guests hammered on the door. More than once – often, in fact – they began by agreeing to have lunch together and finished breathless and satiated in Michael's bed before he had to dash back to teach a one-o'clock class. They committed the impossible in the front seat of Michael's VW bug when it was parked on a staid residential street just before they went into the Chairman of the English Department's Christmas party. Jessie was a willing and eager partner in these indiscretions. She could even laugh when the Chairman's wife remarked – casually – that Jessie's blouse was buttoned wrong. Her notions of discretion had dissolved as if they were just so much base metal in the alchemist's fire.

Some nights they went out and Jessie went home with Michael, and some nights they did not go out and she went home with him just the same. He phoned her at midnight from the Park; she could hear Gene's ragged laughter in the background and bits of broken conversation. "Jessie," said Michael, his voice husky with liquor, gilded with desire. "I want you, Rosebud. I'll be by in twenty minutes. We'll go to my place. Can you be ready?"

Jessie was ready. She was seemingly always ready. Nothing in her limited experience (with men with limited experience) prepared her for a man who made love with his whole body, who could be tender and ruthless in the same moment. Jessie responded in kind. She was surprised, sometimes afraid, at what she could and would commit. Frequently. So frequently that a day seldom passed when she did not carry the fluid fragments of Michael Devereaux inside her: even when she was not with him, he was always with her.

Questions of discretion ceased to trouble her, but her initial question – the one about taking or getting, the one she did not ask that first night at the creek – continued to rankle. Michael took without malice aforethought and gave without intending to, while Jessie gave without malice or forethought and took without intending to, absorbing him through her pores; he clung to her like a fragrance, the way that mint or musk or lemon cling relentlessly to your hands.

She fell in love the way some people commit suicide: filled her pockets with stones and waded in, not quite knowing what to expect, fearful and welcoming. Sometimes the fear got the better of her and she vowed to break it off, but these vows were fragile and private, rather like Jessie herself. She grew more fragile, more vulnerable, as she grew less private, as she gave up her past, her present, her friends, her time, her innermost self. She was intense and monogamous by nature, though Michael was not. He was a man of persuasive, almost schooled charm and convivial habits, and he surrounded himself with convivial admirers. They all did – Gene and Michael and Gil and Lyle; they held what amounted to a continual court at the Park. They were witty and uproarious and endlessly appreciative of everyone who joined them, everyone they allowed into their golden, congenial circle. As her affair, her attachment to Michael, deepened, Jessie gradually dissociated herself from the crowd at the Park Place Bar; she wanted her love kept fresh and inviolate and sensed that the boys at the bar had no such reverence – in fact, that love was a foreign word to them; only lust was worthy of comment. Eventually Jessie affected a public nonchalance, a casual disdain, an exercised indifference toward Michael when she happened to meet him socially. If Jessie and Ellen did go into the Park Place, they always took a table some distance from the ebullient foursome and their followers.

Jessie could feel him unbuttoning her clothes with his eyes. Across the steam and stink and cigarette murk of the Park, Michael's gaze traveled over her breasts and rested on her thighs until she thought the seams on her jeans would pop. He was amused, and – she could tell – so were Gene and Gil and Lyle. Jessie felt like public currency, fingered by many hands, soiled at the edges. She asked him not to do it.

"Do what?"

"Look at me like that in front of people." She pulled the covers up to her chin as if she could shield herself from that look.

"Like what?"

"You know what I mean."

"Sometimes I like to imagine you with your clothes off." Michael threw his leg over her and laughed.

"Just don't do it in public."

"When we're not in public, Rosebud, I don't have to imagine."

Jessie woke at five and dressed quickly in the cold. "Michael," she shook him gently. "I want you to take me home."

"Not now. It's been snowing all night."

"Now."

"I'll take you in the morning."

"It is morning."

"It's dark. I'll take you on my way into work."

"Now."

"Why won't you ever just spend the night? Just spend one whole god-damned night with me when I don't have to get up and drive you back to your goddamned apartment?"

"We've been through this before." Jessie pulled on her socks. "It's too easy."

"Easy?" He groaned and rubbed his eyes and tried to focus on the clock.

"I've told you I don't want to fall into anything easy or domestic."

"Spending the night isn't exactly marriage."

"I didn't say it was. I just don't want to end up fixing your tie before you go to work."

"I don't wear a tie."

"Or fixing your breakfast, or washing your back, or bringing you cof-fee." This affair, she feared, was not a rehearsal for the happily-ever-hereafter; her insistence on going home before dawn was a kind of calis-thenic exercise, the only way she knew to snip hope – or, rather, delu-sion – at its roots. "I don't want to end up like someone's boring wife."

Michael put his hands beneath his head. "What makes you think I want a wife? Boring or otherwise?"

"I don't know what you want. I don't care." Jessie put her coat on and stood over the bed. "I only know it could get domestic fast."

"Why can't you ever let anything be easy, Rosebud? Why do you always have to work at things and make a struggle out of nothing?"

Although it was freezing, Jessie waited for him in the car, hugging her-self protectively against the cold and Michael Devereaux. She smiled to watch him cross the frozen lawn, blowing on his hands, cursing under his steamy breath.

Jessie had recurrent dreams in which she lay in a cool, dark room. Dressed in white, freshly groomed and feeling rather like a cut, refrig-erated rose, she waited for Michael Devereaux. Unmoved and unmoving, she waited for Michael to come and touch and animate her. She waited and wilted despite the preserving cold, but Michael did not appear, and instead, the cold penetrated Jessie, and frost limned her petals, and ice formed on the innermost core of the cut rose who is already doomed – graced with the appearance of life, but dead already. One night she fought her way out of the dream and opened her eyes. Her room was cold and dark, and distantly she heard a knock. Not in the dream. At the door.

She threw a shawl over her nightgown and went to the door, where she found Michael Devereaux. Though he never appeared in the dream, he often arrived (in the middle of the night) in the flesh. "It's two in the morning, Michael. What do you want?"

"A match." An unlit joint and a smile dangled from his lips. "That's all."

"You're already lit." She rubbed her bare feet against one another. "You've been drinking. I can smell it."

"A little." He stepped into the dark apartment closing the door after him.

"And you stink of perfume."

"A little."

Jessie's nose wrinkled with recognition. "You smell like Cindy Dalton. You must really be desperate."

"You're too hard on Cindy, Rosebud. She's really very sweet."

"Well, you're not getting into my bed stinking of Cindy Dalton."

He took the joint from his lips and grinned at her. "There's always the shower."

"You really are a heartless bastard, Michael. Go to one of the other women – one of the gaggle of girls the four of you always have in tow. Don't come to me."

She started away from him, but he caught her and wrapped his arms around her. "It's you I want, Jessie. It's always you. It will always be you."

"Don't give me that tripe." She freed herself vehemently. "Not at two in the morning. You make me sick."

"You're too hard on me, Rosebud."

"Don't call me that. I hate it. You ought to be hard on yourself now and then."

Snow fell from his jacket as he threw it on the couch. "I'm tired."

"What? Did Cindy wear you out?"

"No. She bored me. They all bore me except you, Rosebud. You always surprise me. You always make me uncomfortable, but I always come back." He lifted her nightgown. "You've got great hips."

"Your hands are like ice."

"I know. I'm sorry they're always cold."

"How can you do this to me?"

"You need me, Rosebud, and no one else does." He put his cold fingers over her lips, sank into the overstuffed chair, and pulled her into his lap. He reasserted the old wordless tyranny and pulled the flannel nightgown over her head as she lifted her arms slowly in a gesture of resignation, if not defeat. He knew all the places Jessie could be plucked like a chord and tuned like a string.

"Don't count on me, Michael. One night you'll come here and I'll be in bed with someone else. What will you do then?"

"It will depend on who it is." He pushed the hair from the back of her neck and reflexively Jessie bent her head. "Go ahead and sleep with some-one else if you want to." Michael's lips moved against her spine. "I know you will. It's not a question of when, just who."

"And who do you think it will be?"

"It doesn't matter to me."

"I see." She reached for the shawl and wrapped it around her shoulders. "You don't give a damn about me."

"That's not true. I love you in my own way, but not like you love me. It's not in me to love like that. It's like committing an act of faith for you every time, Jessie. Maybe you commit it every day, but it's always fresh and you always close your eyes and hold your breath before I even touch you. Do you know that, Rosebud?" he murmured against her throat. "You believe in me and you trust me and you give on faith."

"And what do you do?" she said drily. "Take on credit?"

"I don't think I can live up to all that faith, if that's what you mean." He unwrapped the shawl from her shoulders. "But maybe it doesn't matter. Lift your arms, Jessie, high above your head." He smiled to watch her, smiled as she lowered her arms over his shoulders and touched his golden hair with her cheek. "You'll always be faithful to me no matter who I sleep with, Rosebud. No matter who you sleep with. None of that matters. You'll only commit one act of faith, and only with one man. And I'm that man, Jessie." He kissed her with ineffable tenderness. "And I know it."

Jessie did not know it until she had gone to bed with Gilbert Sherman, who, unlike Michael, was not beautiful or corrupt or dangerous, and who, unwittingly, convinced her that she had indeed committed an act of faith, committed it once, or once too often to be able to renege.

Gil came out in his underwear and peered across the patch of moonlight staining the living room floor. "Jessie?" He fidgeted with his glasses. "Jessie, where are you?"

"Here. In the chair."

He crossed the room, knelt beside the chair and nibbled her knees. "God, I love the way you take your boots off! Put them back on and take them off for – "

She rose abruptly. "You better go home, Gil."

"Why? Ellen's not here and – "

"I don't want it to get domestic."

"What! What the hell? Come back to bed, Jessie. It's freezing out here."

She shook her head. "No. Thank you, but – "

" 'Thank you!' Did I just hand you a dozen roses or something? What's happened!"

"Nothing. You're married, Gil."

Gil got to his feet slowly. "You could have thought of that before."

"I'm thinking of it now."

"It's Michael, isn't it?" Gil said before he went back into the bedroom. Jessie stood at the window listening to the ice-crusted branches knocking together in the wind outside and the change in Gil's pockets clinking as he drew on his pants. When he came out he was fully dressed, coat on, toothbrush sticking out of his breast pocket. "You're throwing me out because of Michael."

"Please, Gil. Don't think I'm awful, just leave. Please."

"Why should you be faithful to him? He's not faithful to you. You know that. Michael has lots of women. He needs lots of women."

"It's got nothing to do with Michael."

"You think you're so damn superior, Jessie. Michael doesn't think so. You're no different than – "

"That's not so! I am different! Michael loves me!"

"You don't really believe that."

The windows rattled for hours after Gil slammed the door. Or maybe it wasn't the windows at all: maybe it was the ice and wind outside that Jessie only imagined were inside.

She had to avoid Gil for about a month after that. She missed him more than she would have thought, missed his lively company, his fund of anecdotes and rambunctious wit. He was certainly livelier company than Michael. With the publication of a slender poem in the February issue of a lightweight review, Michael grew increasingly impressed with his poetic powers. His very voice exalted, his tone hallowed, when he held forth on Art, and he would hold forth for anyone who would listen, and at the Park they listened reverentially.

These were, to Jessie's mind, his most unattractive moments; they betrayed a lack of modesty that was itself indicative of a want of character; she liked to think she loved him for his character and not for his golden hair. The mere mention of the Creative Process made her surly and snarly. Finally, when Michael once suggested that Creative Process might be organically connected to his person, Jessie could no longer restrain herself. "You mean something like your bowels?" She snickered into her coffee.

Michael's eyes glinted like coins. "I don't expect you to understand. How could you? You're not an artist."

"I'm not a fool either," Jessie retorted. But by that time she knew better. Jessie was a fool. Michael was a fool's Golden Boy.

"Golden Boy" was a jibe Ellen had invented. It would not have occurred to Jessie to make fun of his chiseled beauty, his monogrammed shirts, or his 14-carat accent. But, she reflected, if he could call her by the detestable name of Rosebud, she could call him Golden Boy, and by the winter's end, between Ellen and Jessie, Golden Boy was virtually the only name they ever called him.

By the winter's end Jessie was in need of an occasional joke. Though she had endured other Eastern winters, this one seemed particularly unrelenting. A woman whose sense of season relied on desert winds and sturdy cactus flowers could not be expected to notice frail signs of spring sprouting in the mud. She felt helpless in winter's grip, even if Michael Devereaux plowed her every night like a spring field. Unaccountably fatigued and depressed, she wept easily, even as she pushed the cart around the library stacks, putting the books back in their proper places.

A hand grabbed her bottom and Jessie would have shrieked out loud, but Michael put his other hand gently over her mouth and muttered something pleasantly obscene in her ear.

"Stop it, Michael. Not here. Someone will come by."

"Let's see." He slid his cold hands inside her jeans and peered over her shoulder at the shelves. "No, we're in the TXs, no one will come by."

"You've been drinking."

"So what?"

"So go crawl on top of Cindy or one of the others. Leave me alone. I'm working."

"I just thought the library floor might provide us with a new thrill, Rosebud. Or what about the service elevator? You want to get in the service elevator and punch the UP buttons?"

"Cut it out. And take your hands out of my pants!" She freed herself and began re-shelving the TXs.

"Look at it this way. You could be doing Art a great service."

"Screw art."

"That's what I had in mind."

"Go away, Michael. I'm not in the mood."

"You don't mean that, Jessie." He wrapped one arm tightly over her breasts, lifted her hair and kissed her neck.

"I do mean it."

"You can't lie to me." He lifted her shirt and his touch was cold and tender like the inside of a mushroom. Involuntarily she shivered. "What are you afraid of, Rosebudd?"

"Someone's going to come by."

"Besides that." He kissed the slopes of her nose. "You haven't been yourself lately."

"I'm afraid," she said, afraid of saying she was afraid of anything, "of what's going to happen to us."

"If someone comes by?"

"Of what's going to happen to *me* when all this is over."

"All what?"

"Us."

"Why should we be over? I'm not riding off into the sunset tomorrow; are you?"

"I don't see us living happily ever after, either."

"Oh Jessie, I don't want to get serious now. I'm not in the mood. Let's have a little fun."

"I just want to know how it's going to end," she persisted; having come this far she might as well go on: it was not a question you could ask twice.

"How will it end? Let me count the ways. Well," he said brightly, "I could die and bequeath you to Gil. He'd like that."

She twisted out of his embrace. "I'm not property you can hand around. Who do you think you are?"

Michael grinned. "That's the old Rosebud. You're off at eleven tonight, aren't you? I'll be waiting outside when you get off."

"You go to hell! I'll never go anywhere with you – not even to bed."

Michael shrugged. "You've said that before." He walked down the long library aisle. "See you at eleven."

"Cram it, Devereaux!" she called after him. On the other side of the high shelves, someone dropped a book.

Jessie left the TXs unshelved, took the service elevator to avoid Michael (and whoever had overheard their conversation), begged off work early and walked home seething. In fact she avoided him for nearly ten days, though she thought of a hundred different pretexts to call him or see him, but she dismissed them all. Almost all.

Ellen and Jessie went into the Park one night and glanced over toward Michael and his friends and the half dozen young women who surrounded them. They seemed to be in particularly high spirits, which Jessie took as a personal affront, but she ignored them just the same. She and Ellen made their way to the bar and took the last two stools. The bartender ran a soiled rag over the chipped formica. "What'll it be, girls?"

"Two beers."

He drew two beers and brought them cold popcorn in a plastic bowl. The jukebox wailed nearby and Gene loosened a volley of oaths when beer spilled all over him. Ellen turned to have a look, but Jessie kept her eyes steadfastly on the rows of expensive unopened liquor bottles lining the shelves and the short-circuiting beer signs flashing on the walls.

When did Michael come up behind her? She didn't know for certain, because he did not touch her at all. He crystallized along her spine as if he could move by reconstituting his molecules and materialize at will; as if, without sound or warning, he could percolate fragrance and stir desire. Ellen excused herself to go to the bathroom. Jessie did not move.

"I'll take three more beers, Charlie."

"Sure enough, Michael."

As he put the money on the bar, Michael pressed against Jessie's back. "Would you like it better," he said in a low, urgent voice, "if I promise never to die and bequeath you to anyone? Would you come back to me if I promise never to let you go?"

4

HE DIDN'T let her go. She left him after telling him an explosive lie, but not before he had exploded her faith and stripped her of pretense and dignity, which in Jessie's case were the same thing. She left him and everything attached to and surrounding him, up to and including the entire East Coast, which was the only way she could have left him at all. She packed hastily and without sentiment. Sentiment is useless when you already know there is one lover you will carry with you always, indelible as a stamped medallion around your neck to clank and chafe with every subsequent lover. She knew all this and she knew it had nothing to do with genuine commitment or love's longevity. On the contrary, the counterfeit lover, like the counterfeit coin, only victimizes the individual who tries to redeem it for legal tender.

Jessie borrowed a lot of money from Gilbert Sherman. She called him because he was the only person who could and would lend it without demanding answers in return. She waited in the car while Ellen went into his office to pick up the check. They cashed it and then Ellen drove her to Baltimore to catch the night flight to Los Angeles.

She stayed in Los Angeles nearly two weeks before taking the bus back out to the desert to her parents' house in Chagrin. She offered no explanation regarding her flight and would answer no questions. She let her parents think she'd only just arrived in California. She did not mention her two-week stay in L.A. with a friend from high school who was an aspiring actress by day and worked in a donut shop by night. Neither did she mention her visit to the friend's doctor.

"I'll want an abortion," she had said evenly as she stared into the cold fluorescent lights overhead.

"You get dressed and we'll discuss it in my office." The doctor stripped off his gloves.

"There's no need for that."

"You're quite sure, then, you know what you want."

"I know what I don't want."

She had the abortion the next day. She paid in cash. It was legal and painful and quick and left no visible scars. The doctor told her she would experience some further pain and bleeding, but he did not tell her – perhaps he did not know – that she could bleed figuratively as well as physically, that she could ache and twinge and writhe in places the doctor's instruments never touched.

He gave her a refillable prescription for pills to kill the pain, and her friend had bottles of similar drugs in the bathroom. The more pills she took, the less she felt. The pills killed the pain, silenced the anguish: stilled everything, in fact, except her heartbeat and respiration rate. She stayed virtually comatose for days and in fact never quite knew, could not remember, how she happened to be in the kitchen at all, much less what was in the frying pan or how high the flame had been. But certainly there was a fire. Flames shot out of the pan and scorched the ceiling. She must have reached for the pan and lifted it, not guessing how heavy it would be, or how hot. The only clear picture she retained of the accident was of the flaming grease spilling – the fire frozen in mid-air – just before it splashed all over her other hand; and the dishtowel she was apparently holding caught fire too. Then someone must have come in, because when the smoke and dust from flour and baking soda cleared, Jessie was on the floor weeping. She could smell her burned hand as she wept into it. She could smell it – but she couldn't feel it.

Later she felt it. She took a great many more pills and they numbed the pain in her hand as well. If they had not, Jessie's left hand might not have been permanently scarred. She adamantly refused to see another doctor in L.A. She kept it wrapped in strips of clean sheeting until she returned to Chagrin; when the doctor there peeled off the sheeting, her skin came off too.

Despite the medical bills for her hand, Jessie paid Gilbert Sherman back within six months of her return, which had fortuitously coincided with an opening for a reporter on the local paper. The *Chagrin Chronicle-*

Observer (affectionately known as the *Chronic Observer*) appeared only three times a week. The front-page stories were usually of Eagle Scouts, or couples celebrating their fiftieth anniversaries, or date growers with bumper crops, or watermelon farmers posing with melons the size of small camels. Fire or flood might push these stories off the front page, and sometimes the Sheriff found an unidentified dessicating body in the desert foothills.

Jessie rented a cheap studio apartment with a view of dry, distant foothills and a nearby truck stop. For months she wrote copy for the *Chronic Observer* by day and letters to Michael Devereaux at night. The *Chronic Observer* printed her stories, but Jessie herself burned the letters to Michael, burned them carefully and over the toilet. She might have mailed them if Michael had written to her, but the only letters from Maryland were from Ellen, who missed Jessie and wrote that life in Bremerton went on as it ever had; the boys at the bar did not change. Nothing changed.

A few months later Jessie interviewed Neal McCarren, who was part of a team of geologists from Los Angeles investigating earthquake phenomena in the desert. She liked him immediately; their attraction, their affection, was mutual, though their affair was discreet and rather domestic from the beginning. They spent their nights together, and when the geological team returned to Los Angeles, Jessie and Neal ran up large phone bills and commuted on weekends. Jessie was comfortable with Neal McCarren; he did not lie or pry or demand from her acts of faith. He asked only once after her left hand and how she had happened to ignore such a burn.

When Neal and Jessie got married in February of the following year, they stood before a dry, droning judge in the St. Elmo Courthouse annex, a flimsy building little better than a tent pitched in Chagrin. Dust drifted in through the cracks and left a powdery grit on their lips as they said their vows. Wind rattled the windows like an angry, unremembered guest – the reaction Jessie expected of her family when they discovered she had not included them in her wedding.

After the marriage, Jessie McCarren moved to Los Angeles with Neal, but she found that her experience on the *Chronic Observer* didn't exactly awe the Los Angeles *Times*. Newspaper writing was the only kind of work she wanted to do, but the job-hunting was fruitless and dispiriting. In between rounds of rejection Jessie devoured paperback mysteries. She stayed up late reading them, and then she began to stay up late writing one. She found an impecunious L.A. agent who sold her book to the first paperback house she approached. Jessie quit looking for work; she had found it.

Jessie's books were all slick, stylish mysteries. The first one, *The Dead Giveaway*, was based roughly on her experience at the *Chronic Observer* when someone had found a nameless, decomposing body dumped in the desert and called the Sheriff and the editor at the *Chronic Observer*. The editor sent Jessie out to cover the story, but she arrived at the scene before the Coroner's boys had the corpse in the body bag. Jessie's pencil froze in her hand and she retched audibly as she tried to ask the proper, professional questions of the Coroner and the Sheriff's deputies – who milled around the body, smoking, chatting, searching the surrounding brush, filling out official forms in triplicate. *Caucasian male. Age: mid-thirties. Date of death: unknown. Dead approx. ten days. Cause of death: single gunshot wound through the head. Autopsy pending.*

"If you're going to throw up, miss," one of the deputies instructed her, "go over there and do it. Don't do it here. We got enough trouble."

"I'm not going to throw up."

She threw up in the sagebrush, and the deputy dumped his canteen over a red handkerchief, wrung it out and handed it to her. "Maybe you better wait here in my car until we get the body out of here," he said over the squawk of the police radio.

"Yes, I think I'll do that. Thank you."

"Never seen anyone dead, have you?"

"No. Never." Never seen what death – unpumped blood, unchurned guts, sensationless nerves, unwarmed flesh – could do to the body. No wonder people believed in souls. How could you live – how could you die – knowing only ten days separated you from utter putrefaction?

Jessie utilized the dead man in the desert, two grains of imagination, and a grammar manual to write *The Dead Giveaway*. In this and her subsequent books, the murders were sanitized: the dead rotted off-stage. She wrote in the staccato style of the *Chronic Observer*: no paragraph longer than half a dozen sentences, no word longer than three syllables. The books had lurid, embossed covers and lined up at the supermarket check-out line, right beside the candy, gum, and disposable lighters, just like all the other consumable, combustible throw-away items. Jessie smiled to see them. Once she actually bought one, and the checker assured her it was a terrific read; he said he'd read all the McCarren mysteries and couldn't wait for the next one.

JESSIE'S SUCCESS brought her new friends (or at least new acquaintances); it brought her the opportunity to create more than paperback books – paper money. She had the will, and now she had the means: she systematically created herself anew. Jessie George had committed acts of faith, committed adultery, abortion, countless indiscretions, hungered, lusted, loved, slept with and wept for Michael Devereaux, and done all this in the murky name of passion. But not the disciplined mystery writer, the newly minted Jessie McCarren: she was someone else altogether. Jessie McCarren was happily married, and if the connubial bed lacked passion, it also lacked anguish. The Jessie McCarren that Jessie George created in her own best image was a woman of uncomplicated indomitability. This Jessie could deny any affliction and casually circumvent complexity. This Jessie espoused athletic affirmation – the kind that's only possible for people who have never suffered anything more than a hangnail. And if, occasionally, her scarred left hand reminded her that she had suffered more than that, then she redoubled her calisthenics.

Jessie pulled herself visibly up in the world, not by her bootstraps, but by her sweatsocks. She did it without Family or Money or Connections, but she possessed the one thing Michael Devereaux did not have – and moreover, did not value. Golden Boy would never have recognized Jessie's dry, unvarnished toughness of spirit. Had she not left him, Jessie herself would not have known that she was indurate, obdurate, and grainy – that she could be splintered, perhaps, but not squashed. She would never again perceive herself as a doomed refrigerated rosebud. She could bloom in the desert.

IT WAS THIS woman – the relentlessly cheerful, insufferably successful, happily married Jessie McCarren – who walked down the marble stairs of her Venice apartment building and into the foyer to get the mail one day in May. There was a letter from her agent and one from her eldest brother saying he and his wife would like to come visit in August. There was a letter from Ellen, too. Jessie saved that for last, to enjoy with a cup of espresso in the sunny kitchen. As she opened Ellen's letter, a clipping fell out: and Michael's name lay on the marble floor, his name and "died" and "in this city on May 18."

Dear Jessie –

I have some sad news. Michael Devereaux is dead. I've enclosed the obituary though it doesn't say the cause of death which was suicide. I went into the Park (though I haven't been in there since I started to teach) and the bartender told me Michael shot himself in the head, but he didn't know why. He said I should ask them – he pointed over to Gene and Gil and Lyle.

They were sitting in their old place with a few girls and dozens of bottles. One chair was empty like they expected Michael to come fill it. Anyway, it looked to me to be reserved for him. I couldn't bring myself to go up to them and ask why Michael killed himself. I couldn't even go up and offer them my condolences. The girls were comforting them as best they could and nothing I could have said would have made any difference. So I left.

Nothing I can say to you can make any difference either, but I know what Michael meant to you. Maybe I'm the only one who knows what he meant to you. I am sorry, Jessie…

Caucasian male: mid-thirties. Cause of death: single gunshot wound to the head. Autopsy pending. Date of death: May 18. What was today? May. May what? May 28. Ten days. *Dead ten days.* Jessie struggled for breath, choked and wheezed like a drowning swimmer. Could Michael look like that putrefying dead man in the desert? Fair Michael? Michael's golden head blown off? Corruption mottling Michael's beautiful body? No. Never Michael. Michael promised: *I'll never die and I'll never let you go.*

Jessie threw up in the marble splendor of her Venetian bathroom. She started to wash her face, but stripped off all her clothes and got in the shower, as if the news could be washed off, but it clung – like mint or musk or lemon. And when she stepped out of the shower, she faced herself dripping in the mirror, the woman who could circumvent complexity. She said: "Face it. He looks like the dead man in the desert. If he were mortal, that's what he looks like; and if he's dead, then he must have been mortal."

When Neal came home, he found her in a rumpled heap in the antique bed among the soggy pillows – eyes swollen, face flushed. Neal held her shoulders and stroked her hair while she tried to tell him how a friend of hers, a man she'd once known, had shot himself in the head. Was dead. Had been for ten days.

"Why?" said Neal. "Why did he do it?"

"I don't know. Ellen didn't know."

"Can I see the letter?"

"It's around here somewhere. On the floor I think."

Neal picked it up and read it twice. He took his wife's scarred hand in his. "What was he to you, Michael Devereaux?"

"Nothing."

"I don't think I believe that, Jessie. He must have meant something to you, something more than…"

"Nothing." She pulled her hand back and slid it under the pillow.

"Did he have something to do with your leaving the East?"

Jessie sat up, wiped her eyes, blew her nose. "No." She mustered athletic affirmation – "Not at all" – those sterling powers of uncomplicated indomitability she had spent seven years cultivating – "I left the East because I could not bear the cold. I could not take the cold and damp any longer."

"Yes," said Neal, "but you left in the spring."

5

APRIL, TO BE PRECISE. After the forsythia had waned and as the narcissi were beginning their golden graceful profusion down the walkway in front of the library. Jessie picked a few as she left work in the spring dusk.

She had called Michael at the office that morning and asked for a ride home, so he would be expecting her, yes, but not expecting what she had to tell him. Jessie had not expected it, would not have believed it, but the testimony of her own body was undeniable and she didn't need the doctor or a dead rabbit to tell her what she already knew, though she had not framed the irrevocable words, or rehearsed the speech, or gone through the catalogue of Michael's possible responses. She had denied until she could not deny any longer. Whatever else she did, she couldn't go on denying.

The halls were deserted and all the office doors closed, even Michael's. Her hand was poised to knock when she heard a cough and Lyle's voice. "That's great, Michael. Congratulations!"

"I don't think it's so great." Gil's voice. "I think it's pretty cruel, Michael. Jessie is going to be – "

"What makes you think it's about Jessie?"

"Who cares who it's about?" Gene's voice. "It's published in the *Chesapeake Review*! It's a damn good poem!"

"It's a good poem." Gil's voice, conceding, but not defeated. "But it's not fair to Jessie."

"You've always had a thing for Jessie, haven't you, Gil?" Jessie could imagine the glint in Michael's contact lenses. "You've always lusted after her yourself."

Gil took a long breath, audible even through the door. "It's obscene, Michael."

"Good God!" Gene cried. "You're not talking censorship, are you?"

"I'm telling the truth. Jessie will read this as obscene and she'll be right to do so."

Lyle's drawl: "A work of art stands as a text. You can't impugn it with vulgar historicity. Art is a reification process and can't yield to paraphrastic analysis."

"Oh Christ," said Gil, "you know what I mean, Michael."

Michael laughed, a hard laugh like splashing quarters. "If Jessie leaves me, do you want her?"

"Don't you?"

Gene's voice. "I have to take a leak. Come on, let's go to the Park and have a beer and celebrate for Michael."

The men agreed they needed a beer, and a billow of cigarette smoke preceded Gene out of the office. He looked startled, then gray and queasy as he stared at Jessie George. The three men scooted past her as quickly as they could, and Jessie stepped into the office and walked to the desk where Michael stood before his open briefcase. She clutched the narcissi so tightly their heads drooped and their thick, sick-sweetness overwhelmed her.

"I thought you were off at seven," he said.

"Six."

"Oh."

"Let me see it."

He handed her the *Chesapeake Review* and sat down, casually lighting a cigarette and holding it between his thumb and forefinger in his inimitable way.

"What page?"

"Forty-six."

The poem itself was probably mediocre, of the rump, raunch, hump and haunch, expletive and explicative variety. A dark-haired woman in an unglamorous position eagerly (though submissively) awaits what the poet has to bestow. "I didn't know you could hold a pen with your prick," she said tartly, handing the volume back to him.

"You should have knocked when you got here and not waited outside." He dropped the slender magazine in his briefcase.

"And miss the great Socratic Dialogue?"

"Now, Rosebud."

"Is that how you see me, Michael? What you wrote? Is that all you feel for me? Is that really me?"

"It doesn't have to be you," he said philosophically. "It could be anyone."

Retrospective clairvoyance is the worst kind. The deeds are done, the acts committed, and the mitigating circumstances – lust or hunger or love itself – shrivel into tiny husks when clairvoyance strikes you retrospectively. The only possible recourses (barring retreat, which is out of the question, and drunkenness, which is too temporary to be useful) are revenge or atonement. Neither is truly satisfying because they both imply measure of guilt. "I've never been anything special to you at all, have I? I've never meant anything to you," said Jessie. "I've never been anything but an assured lay, a sexual promissory note you could redeem any place, any time, any way, and as often as you liked."

"That's not true, Rosebud. You're being too hard on yourself."

"Don't call me Rosebud." She tossed the narcissi in the trash can, but their scent wafted up, unbidden, indelible as melancholy.

"Come on, Jessie. Let's forget it. I'll take you out to dinner and we'll go home and I'll even drive you back at five a.m. without complaining. I promise. Cheer up." He buttoned his briefcase shut and put his coat on. He touched her shoulder, but she recoiled.

"It's all come so easy and effortless for you, hasn't it, Michael?"

"You come easy, Jessie." His mouth curved into a voluptuous smile. "You always have. You always will."

Jessie didn't know if his last statement were true or not, but she couldn't risk it: her strength, like her clairvoyance, was undeveloped and would require repeated exercise before she could rely on it. She turned and left the office, and he neither came after her nor called her name.

By the time she had walked back to her apartment, it was full dark with only the bloated edge of the moon just visible at the horizon. Jessie found a note from Ellen, who had gone to Baltimore for the night to see her family; and momentarily, Jessie thought she might call Ellen, tell Ellen what she had not told Michael. She picked up the phone and just as quickly put it back down. Is it a chemical, physical, or organic process that turns resolve into resolution? Jessie didn't know. She only knew for certain that she could not, would not, must not stay pregnant, or in Bremerton, Maryland, one minute longer than necessary.

Jessie put on her nightgown, wrapped herself in a shawl, and sat in the darkness, knees drawn up, watching the moonlight waver uncertainly around the room. She waited — rather like the refrigerated rosebud in her dream, certain that Michael Devereaux would come, not to touch and animate, but because he would need to reassert his old sovereignty: the tyrant's right to be welcomed into vanquished territory.

It was almost one when she heard his car pull up. Doors opened and drunken voices hushed each other. As Jessie started for the door, she stumbled; her feet had gone to sleep and would not support her. "Just a minute," she called; she waited for the blood to flow again, otherwise she would have been on her hands and knees. "Hello, Michael," she said coldly. "Gil. Who's that with you?"

"It's me!" Cindy Dalton stepped out from Gil's shadow, and he draped his arm over her shoulders as if he were the walking wounded.

"We're on a little expedition, Rosebud," said Michael, leering at her pleasantly. "We're going up to Annapolis and watch the sun come up over the Chesapeake and then we're going to have breakfast at this terrific little place Gil knows up there."

"Best ham and eggs in the state," Gil said. "Best grits too. You grab my grits, honey!" he snorted into Cindy's neck, and she collapsed into helpless laughter.

"Gene and Lyle and a couple of others have gone up in Lyle's car, but I said, 'We have to get Jessie. I'm not going without Jessie.' That's what I said."

"Well, you can just go to hell. Without me. I wouldn't go anywhere with you."

"You've said that before," Michael reminded her.

"This time I mean it."

"You've said that before too."

"I wouldn't walk across the street with you and a bunch of aging, drunken boys."

"Hey, what about me?" cried Cindy. "I'm not a drunken boy."

"No, you're a twit, Cindy. You're an ass. A piece of ass."

"Now, Jessie." Gil stepped forward as if he could protect Cindy with his sheer girth. "That's not fair."

"But it's accurate and as for the rest of you – all of you – "

"Jessie." Michael wrapped her in his arms and she could smell the piquant aftershave at his collar and the beer on his breath; she wanted to press her face against his familiar shoulder and brace her breasts against him, just once more, and if he kept his arms around her, she would do exactly what she wanted – which was exactly what he wanted.

"Take your cold hands off me," she demanded. "I'm tired of warming you up."

Gil tugged at Cindy's hand. "Let's go back to the car. We'll wait in the car."

"Why should we?" Cindy looked from Jessie to Michael to Gil. "What happened to the party? What happened to the expedition?" She followed Gil reluctantly, back to the car.

Michael drew Jessie into the dark apartment. He kissed her throat at all her pulse points. "Can't we forget what happened this afternoon, Rosebud? I'm sorry, okay? Let's make this as easy as we can. Okay, Rosebud?"

"I'll make it easy for you," Jessie said in an astringent voice. "I had an abortion last week. Is that easy for you?" *Next week this will be the truth. Resolve into resolution. Lies into truth. Base brass into shining gold.*

"A what?"

"You heard me."

He dropped his hand from her shoulders. "You're not serious, are you?"

"Would you like the gory details? Would you like to know how I had some six-celled effigy of you scraped out of me? Sucked out through a little tube? Destroyed. Would you like to know all about it?"

"I don't believe you."

"Why would I lie?"

"Was it mine? I guess you're telling me it was mine."

"It was mine. To do whatever I chose with it and I chose to get rid of it, just like I choose to get rid of you. I don't want anything from, of or about you, ever again."

"Well, Jessie, you should have told me. I mean, why didn't you tell me before you had the –, before you did it?"

"Why? What do you care?"

"Well, it's –. It's just that I should have been told."

"What would you have done? Married me and lived happily ever after?"

"I don't know. I guess it doesn't matter now that you've already – " his voice trailed off. "I don't know what I would have done."

"Would you have paid for it?"

"Well, I – "

"Or held my hand?"

"I don't know, but – "

"Would you have begged me not to? Would you have loved me more? Loved me less? Hated me? Would you have felt responsibility or rage? Would you have put it – the bloody little it – in the *Chesapeake Review*?

Would you have called it 'Knocked-up Woman and Fetus'? Called it art? What would you have done, Michael?" She was shrieking; she could not stop. "Answer me, what would you have done if you'd known I was pregnant?"

"I don't know."

"You mean at last there's something that troubles you? Something that's not easy and effortless? What a shock. Pass me the smelling salts."

"Jessie, I'm sorry. It must have been terrible. If only you'd told me."

"Could you have made it less terrible, Michael? Could you have made it pleasant?" Her voice was spiraling up again, out of control; forcibly she lowered her words to a harsh whisper. "It was the worst thing that ever happened to me, and I hated myself and I hated you and I hated whatever it was they took out of me. But I said to myself – if this is what it takes to get rid of Michael Devereaux, then it's worth it. The whole time my innards were being sucked out, I thought: I'm getting rid of Michael, tearing him out, tearing him up, and I don't mind the pain. I don't! Because when it quits hurting, it will all be over and you'll be out of my body and out of my life. For good. Forever."

Michael ran his hands over his face and then stared at them as if he expected to see flecks of paint. "I never meant to hurt you, Jessie. I didn't hurt you intentionally. I couldn't help myself. I never asked you to love me the way you do."

"Did."

"I never asked that or wanted it even; you just gave – and so, I just took."

"What you could get?"

"What you *gave* me, Jessie; I didn't bargain or barter with you. You were always there: Jessie the tender, Jessie the faithful, Jessie the – "

"Fool."

"I don't think you're a fool. I think you're – "

"What do I care what you think?"

"It's not my fault, that's all I'm trying to say."

"Of course not. You're as blameless as a plaster lamb, aren't you?"

"What should I have done? Seven or eight months ago, said to you, 'Jessie, don't do this. I can't love you the way you love me.' Would that have stopped you?"

Jessie caught her breath and walked to the window. She was running out of lies and resolve – which were, at that moment, the same thing. "It wouldn't have stopped me." The truth was acrid and she licked it off her lips. "You're cold at the core, Michael. Where most people have something warm and beating, you have something cold and metallic. You're like a statue that only needs to be admired, that can't return love even if it's offered."

"I recognize love. Give me credit for recognizing it."

"But you don't respect it. You used me like you use everyone else – for a mirror. You can only love your own image, your golden – " She turned to face him, but the contrite, confused man of moments before had vanished, transubstantiated into Golden Boy. Michael's blue eyes lit with affable curiosity and his elegant body assumed its easy posture.

"My golden what?"

Jessie tightened the shawl around her shoulders as though it were her sole protection against unraveling. "I'm finished. I'm not giving you anything more. Not even the privilege of knowing what I really think of you."

"The privilege!" He laughed, the Michael-icon laugh, head thrown back, his profile pallid in the moonlight. "Jessie George isn't granting any more privileges. Well, I'm just sorry all to hell to hear that, Jessie. Let me know when you change your mind. I'll be around, but you'll have to come to me."

"That will never happen, Michael. It's over. I'm leaving."

"Oh? Me too. I'm going up to Annapolis, and I guess I'll just have to find someone else to go with me, since it's pretty obvious that you don't want to come."

"You're a perfect shit, Michael."

"At least I'm perfect, Rosebud." He started toward the car. "I'll see you later. When you change your mind."

"You'll never see me again! I hate your everlasting guts!"

"Isn't Jessie coming?" Gil called.

"No, I don't think so." Michael stood by the car and hollered back to her, "Little Jessie is having a tantrum. Isn't that right, Jessie? *Isn't that a fair assumption?*"

ISN'T THIS *Ferragusto?* Isn't Jessie McCarren sitting in the Piazza San Marco showered with laughter dubbed from a million foreign movies, punctuated with the violinic fripperies of three café orchestras and surrounded by swirling points of light flickering from electric yo-yos? *Yes.* And isn't she *alive? Yes.* Doesn't the August heat soften the very stones beneath her feet, liquefy the very bones beneath her flesh? *Yes. Yes.* And isn't she suffocating, swathed, and stifled in the shroud Gilbert Sherman has spun from memorescent thread? *Yes.*

And isn't she *alive? Yes.* Doesn't the August heat soften the very stones beneath her feet, liquefy the very bones beneath her flesh? *Yes. Yes.* And isn't she suffocating, swathed, and stifled in the shroud Gilbert Sherman has spun from memorescent thread? *Yes.*

"Michael and I went up to Jersey about two weeks before it happened," Gil mumbled into his empty glass. "He gave a reading up there, but they didn't like his stuff very much. I overheard people talking. They thought it was shit. Can you believe that? Couldn't they tell he just wasn't a very good reader? I made a tape of it. Thank God I did. I gave it to the Bremerton Library, though it isn't the memorial he deserves."

"He doesn't deserve a memorial," Jessie snapped. She lit another cigarette and passed the match to a French girl who leaned over from the next table and asked for fire.

"I guess you think I'm pretty morbid. It's just that Michael and I were so close. Closer than anyone. I haven't been the same since he died." He hunched over his glass as if he expected it to speak to him. "I've been so haunted."

"Well, you mustn't be." Jessie lifted her chin affirmatively. "It's just giving in."

"You think he was a coward, don't you? Lots of people thought so."

"I don't think he was a coward." Jessie exhaled a long blue banner of smoke. "I think he was a perfect shit."

"You're awfully hard on him, Jessie."

"I believe in being hard on yourself, and Michael never did – which is why he was such a self-indulgent shit as to kill himself and bring down untold suffering on people who loved him. People like you, Gil. Like his wife. Michael never loved anyone. If anyone else had ever been important to him, he never would have blown his brains out."

Gil insisted that Michael was a loving husband, a reliable friend, caring, committed, and genuine. Gil plowed over the fields of the past, the good old days, the boys at the bar. Jessie could picture them, the whole antique cast, sloshing toward the grave as the girls got younger, the nights got shorter, their hopes waned, and their energies dwindled, proportionate to the growth of their delusions. If Michael Devereaux hadn't shot himself, one of the others eventually would have had to; otherwise, how could they justify their wasted talents and sanctify their loveless lives?

She lit another cigarette from the stub of the first and kept it between her lips, puffing furiously so she wouldn't scream while Gil drew bucket after bucket up from the well of memory: the day they all went up to New York to see Michael and Diana off for England; the wonderful letters Michael wrote even though he couldn't write a novel; the party they threw when Michael and Diana came back and the Park Place was draped with *Welcome home Michael* banners; and the last glowing evening they'd all spent together in the Park, just three nights before — .

Jessie couldn't bear the incantation, but Gil achieved a liturgical rhythm that could not be altered or halted: Michael's artistry and benevolence, his charm and intelligence, his unflagging good taste, his golden good looks. Jessie concentrated on the crazy yo-yos gyrating about the Piazza. She grew dizzy watching them whirl and unfurl, rather like her own life spinning out in lighted arcs. Centrifugally pulled on a slender waxen cord, Jessie had spun away from Michael and the boys at the bar, who shielded one another from the ravages of women and ambition, protected one another from failure and from love. Michael taught them they couldn't protect each other from death. In future they would have to buy Death a few beers at the altar-bar; and then they could (Death and all) genuflect to St. Michael of Devereaux, who had ascended into heaven, whose every mortal word was sacred now, and whose presence at the smallest episode bathed it with significance: Saint Michael of Devereaux who was too good for this world and who died because he couldn't work and his young wife was about to leave him. Enshrined in their flushed memories, he would always be the Golden Boy, the Fair Fallen Hero, the Emperor of Might-Have-Been, shining curls round his temples, crowned with the laurels of Money and Family and Connections. The Fair Emperor was dead; long live Fair Augusto. They would mint sad coins with

his profile, pass them around until they grew positively dim with fingering. They would share those sweet medallions with anyone, buxom or
not, who also believed in the romantic currency of suicide and unfilled
dreams. *Fair Augusto*. Fair, fair Augusto.

6

GIL CALLS her name twice, but Jessie just keeps walking across San
Marco Square. He pulls out his wallet and fumbles with the tissuey blue-
bearded faces on Italian currency and drops them on the table. "Jessie!
Wait!" He catches up with her at the edge of the arcade. "Why did you
leave?" But she keeps walking, right past, or right through, him and he
runs after her again. "Jessie, I'm sorry if – wait, please." He grasps her
wrist.

"Did any of the boys at the bar ever think about the living?" Her voice
rings up and down the colonnade, and people turn and stare. "What
about his young widow? What about her? What's she going to do on May
18 for the rest of her life while all of you weep in your beer, 'Poor, poor
Michael'? Shit on Michael! Did you ever think of the living? Oh no, ven-
erate the dead! That's all you know. Shit on all of you. Shit on Hemingway too," she adds, wrenching her wrist from his hand.

"I'm sorry, I really am. I thought you'd want to talk about Michael.
Want to hear about him. I thought you loved him."

"Loved him!" Jessie cries and it echoes *loved him*, amplified *loved him* by
the marble columns *loved him*. "Of course I loved him! Is that all you've
wanted to hear all night? I loved him, but I'm free now, don't you see?
And I'm not going to love him again just because he's dead."

"No one's asking you to."

"You are! You're not going to let me go until you sink me into his – his
stinking, rotting death! Well I mourned him too long when he was alive
to give a damn now that he's dead. But you – you do what you want,"
she adds as she pushes past him.

"I always knew you loved him," Gil calls out, as if across a great chasm.
"You still love him."

Gil can see her shoulders heave and shake; and then Jessie turns and
comes back to him, comes very close to him. Her teeth are clenched. "I

took him on faith. It was an act of faith every time I made love with him, and as long as I had that faith and went on believing, then I would have done – I did – anything he asked of me. Now he's dead and I am alive, but I was never more alive than when I was with him. Michael made me ring – body, soul, all of it. He was the root and stem and branch of me, and I loved it, and I loved him." She licks her lips and grimaces, as if what she tastes is sour. "But there came a moment when I no longer believed, or had faith – and what else could I do after that? Could I breathe the same air, walk the same streets as Michael Devereaux without believing in him? Knowing – knowing!" she shouts, – "that anytime he chose, whenever he wished, he had the power to make me believe again, make me give on faith, if only for a night, or for an hour. Could I live like that? No. No! I had to get rid of it. Of him, I mean. I had to be irrevocably done with him. He had to be," she whispers, enunciating harshly, "as good as dead. I mourned him then." Jessie's hands clench prayerfully over her lips and then burst apart, as if a wish or a winged creature has escaped. "Michael didn't want to be loved. He wanted to be adored. He had magic and people adored him. Men, women, everyone, didn't they? He was so beautiful." Unheeded tears spill down her face. "Everyone adored him, and what did it matter that he was absolutely shallow and self-serving and faithless and cold at his core? What did it matter?"

"He's dead, Jessie," Gil stammers. "Even if everything you said about him were true, wouldn't he still deserve your pity?"

"Just for being dead?" She encapsulates the question in a laugh and wipes her cheeks clean. "You go ahead and worship his bloody, bullet-blasted memory if you want, but I won't. I'm free. I'm sure he'd be very happy with your worship, with being idolized, even if he had to blow his brains out to get it."

"If you hadn't loved him, if he'd been a stranger, you'd have some pity."

Jessie's lips stick together, mortared; she speaks dryly and with difficulty. "You mean, if I came upon a dead man in the desert, would I pity him? Would I offer that much to a stranger?"

"Isn't everyone who kills himself finally a stranger to us all?"

Gil thinks Jessie will cry again, but she doesn't; she remains clear-eyed and calm now. She actually takes his arm and they walk up shallow steps and under an ill-lit arch where the briny smell of water rot is particularly pungent and reflections from the canal wash over the stone. Gil retreats into the trivial, and as they walk he remarks on the rocking gondolas tied for the night, and he comments on the heat and asks how she can bear the peculiar omnipresent stench of Venice.

At a narrow bridge she stops and says in a cool, inflectionless voice, "Do you want to walk home with me or go straight to your hotel? Either way is fine with me."

If he hoped for more, a mumbled apology for her outburst, a disavowal of her unkindness, she does not reward him.

"What do you want to do, Gil? I turn here."

"I'll come with you."

A steamy, unrefreshing drizzle dampens their faces as Jessie points out landmarks so Gil can find his bearings to get back to his hotel. Lovers sit on backwater bridges, and nearby a motorboat rips through the waters and sends them sloshing. They turn two more oblique corners and walk beside a small canal. An unlit boat slides by; the oars creak, dip rhythmically, and foreign voices melt into the darkness under the bridge. Jessie stops at a high, lacy wrought-iron gate and gets her key out.

"This is quite a place," he says, looking into a tidy garden lit with ambered lanterns and lined with towering yellow dahlias. "Which windows are yours?"

"It doesn't matter."

He folds her in his arms and kisses her; it's not the kiss he remembers, but then, she's not the woman he remembers either. "Let me come upstairs with you, Jessie. Let's make love."

"I have company. Oh Lord, I forgot all about them," she says irritably.

He pulls her close again so he can smell the cologne and suntan lotion. "Then don't go in. Let's go to the Lido. Let's make love on the beach. Let's make love once more before we die."

"I'm not going to die for a long, long time, and neither are you."

"I liked you better the other way, the way you used to be."

She frees herself without seeming to and turns the key in the gate. "Everyone changes. Unless you die. If you die you can stay the same. Like Michael. He'll always be the same. For you," she adds, as if disentangling herself from any complicity in his memory. "And you might as well admit it — you only want to make love to me because of Michael."

"It's got nothing to do with Michael. I want to make love with – "

"People who don't exist anymore: Jessie George and Michael Devereaux. I loved him and you loved him, and in our separate ways we were both loyal to him. You still are."

"I loved you too, Jessie. I've always been loyal to you."

She pushes the gate open with her scarred hand. "I know that," Jessie McCarren says, tenderly as the old Jessie George might have. "You are loyal. It's your great virtue." She kisses him, tenderly as the old Jessie George might have kissed him. "Goodbye, Gil."

"Goodnight, Jessie."

"Goodnight, then, if you like that better."

The gate squeals forlornly and closes of its own volition behind her. As she walks up the cobbled path, the dahlias nod and droop under the weight of the rain and heat of mid-August. She turns and waves to him once before the darkness and the cool marble halls swallow her up.